"IS THAT A *PERSON*

I didn't answer at fi...

I considered calling Black.

The thing was reaching the wave break. I watched as it went from swimming, if you could call it that, to curling into itself, reorienting its body.

Then it was on its feet, walking towards us.

The waves buffeted his chest and belly at first, but the man never slowed.

It *was* a man, I realized.

It was definitely a man.

He wore all black, what looked like a wetsuit.

He continued to slog through waves and current, walking forward, seemingly straight for where Keon and I stood. The water wasn't up to his chest anymore; it was up to his waist and upper thighs.

Now it was splashing primarily against his calves and knees.

Black, I sent, alarm in my mind, bleeding sharply into my thoughts. *Black... you need to get down here. Bring Marshall. Something is going on.*

I felt Black's presence flare up in mine.

It filled me so swiftly and completely I sucked in a breath.

Black didn't bother to ask me anything. He just began looking through my eyes. As he did, I could feel everything around him so clearly, it felt like being inside his skin.

I could see Fournier, standing next to him.

I could hear Narcisse talking, his mouth curled in an annoyed frown as he addressed something Black had just said—

Then I felt a sharp spasm of reaction go through Black.

My attention flickered back to me, to where I was.

Seeing the man coming towards me on the beach, I felt a second stab of feeling go through Black.

MIRI. His mind exploded in mine. *RUN!*

But it was already too late.

BLACK HAWAII

Quentin Black Mystery #13

JC ANDRIJESKI

BLACK HAWAII: A Quentin Black Paranormal
Mystery Romance (Book #13)

Copyright 2020 by JC Andrijeski

Published by White Sun Press

First Edition

ISBN: 9798615847608

Cover Art & Design by Damonza http://damonza.com

2020

Link with me at: jcandrijeski.com

Or at: www.facebook.com/JCAndrijeski/

Mailing List: http://hyperurl.co/JCA-Newsletter

White Sun Press

For more information

about any book published by White Sun Press, please go to www.whitesunpress.com

Printed in the United States of America 2018

To W., friend to dragons and non-dragons alike,
and king of the mountain under the sea

COUP

"Is it verified?" the seer snapped, his voice hard as he spoke into the comm. "They definitely have both of them? Lucky *and* his lead infiltrator, Jalisa?"

"Confirmed," the voice said. "Both of them. One after the other."

There was a silence.

In it, Tahi stared down at the monitor, his jaw hard.

The voice of the seer on the other end of the line grew more subdued.

"The construct is failing, sir—"

"I can feel that," Tahi growled, cutting him off. "Tell me something I don't know. Something that will help me to stop this... at least long enough for us to find Charles."

Another silence.

That one was briefer.

"They have no idea how it happened, sir," the infiltrator said, now sounding apologetic. "All report visuals of the wife appearing just prior to our people being taken. She appears next to a predetermined target... then both of them just *vanish*. Of course, for all we know, the visuals themselves are some trick, akin to the dragon seen in California—"

"And you're positive *more* of our people have been disappeared in this way?"

There was a silence.

In it, Tahi gazed over the West Wing bullpen he could see just outside his office door. He watched it via the Barrier, the nonphysical space utilized by seers, using that space to track the work of his underlings. Those underlings had been assigned to him nominally by the human president, but Tahi knew it had really been Charles.

Tahi watched seers and humans rush around as they shared drone and satellite footage, fighting to get around the encryption to Black's systems, both satellite feeds and his networks back in California.

So far, they hadn't had much luck.

Even working late into the night, like now—like they had been for days, weeks—it wasn't enough.

Black must have better-than-decent tech expertise among his seers, possibly even among his humans. He'd managed to thwart every attempt at hacking, often using Tahi's team's probes as a means of going after their own systems, here in the West Wing.

More critically, Black's team had gone after theirs in the Pentagon, where the bulk of these operations occurred. The group Tahi oversaw more triaged and supported the *real* infiltration work conducted out of human military and intelligence.

It would take decades to update these clunky government computer systems well enough to operate at even a fraction of what Tahi deemed "acceptable" compared to what he'd known on Old Earth. Everything here was medieval in comparison, despite the dates lining up almost exactly to the corresponding dates on Old Earth.

The difference was seers.

Vampires hadn't contributed much to technological advancement on this version of Earth, from what Tahi could tell.

On Old Earth, the one where Tahi was born, seers advanced tech so rapidly, human governments grew alarmed. Starting in the mid-Twentieth Century of that world, the human oversight authorities actually *banned* many of the tech gadgets and practical applications of organic tech designed by seer scientists. They followed that by restricting and regulating the research and design facilities that created them—not to mention the seer scientists themselves.

Seer scientists were no longer allowed to work alone.

They could work only under special licenses, directly overseen by humans.

They became the property of the human labs that employed them—not exactly an incentive to work harder, smarter, or faster, particularly when humans seemed to primarily want seer tech as a means of non-human oppression and control.

The seer on the other end of the line sighed, pulling Tahi's attention back to them.

"Confidence is high, sir. Very high," he said, grim. "...On the number of disappearances. They're still occurring, sir. We have eye-witness reports on three more in the last half-hour: Mulki, Dresden, and Shana. A growing number of others are missing or nonresponsive. All reports come from verified sources. All of those targeted are highly-ranked operatives. We only have video documentation for a handful of those, including Mulki, but I've seen the footage, sir. It's definitely the same phenomenon—"

"You're *certain* as to the person abducting them? You're certain it was—"

"No," the other seer said at once, making a slashing motion in the air with one hand, one visible through the VR interface. "We are not certain, sir. We have been unable to track this phenomenon in the Barrier with any amount of accuracy. After the debacle at the border, none are willing to take the visuals at face value—"

"But based on the visuals, they all definitely indicate this person, correct?"

The seer hesitated.

Then, seeming to think about the question, he nodded, his

dark red and green-flecked eyes shining in a light on the other side of the line.

"Yes. The individual who *appears* to be behind it remains absolutely consistent, sir. Obviously, at the very least, the usurper and his people would like us to *believe* this person is responsible... but that does not make it so, as we have learned."

There was another pause.

"...And yet," the seer admitted with a seer's Old World shrug. "We can think of no obvious motive for them pushing this narrative. Up until now, he's been extremely protective of his wife. He's downplayed her abilities, rather than the reverse."

"Do we have visual confirmation, at least?" Tahi said, frowning. "Of *her,* I mean. Is that all from on-hand testimony? Or is her actual *face* caught in those instances where there is recorded surveillance?"

The other seer gestured another "yes" in seer, if more reluctantly.

"Yes, sir. Facial-rec and my own eyes confirmed that much... it was definitely Dr. Fox. In all cases, including those critical first two, Dr. Fox appeared, naked, in close physical proximity to her target. On the drone footage, she appeared less than two feet from Mulki while he was directing operations by the border wall. From the footage, she appeared to touch him. In less than a second, both she and Mulki disappeared... leaving his clothes behind."

"How many are missing in total?" Tahi frowned. "I know you cannot confirm all of them, brother, but what is the number? How many, including those unconfirmed?"

"Somewhere in the neighborhood of three dozen now, sir."

There was a silence.

"All seers?" Tahi said next.

"All seers, sir."

"Who's left?" Tahi's voice grew harder. "What is the chain of command now?"

There was a silence.

"I'm sorry, sir?"

"Who's in charge?" Tahi snapped. "Who is running operations, with Charles gone?"

"Sir... *you* are, sir." The male infiltrator sounded confused. "I'm sorry. I thought you knew. We were directed to you as the new head of overall operations—"

"Me?" Tahi frowned. "How is that possible? What about Var? Emmerich?"

"We haven't been able to get ahold of either of them, sir."

Tahi stared into the row of virtual screens in front of him without seeing any of them.

Via the Barrier, he watched the seers working at virtual and hardware stations on the other side of his office door. He could see the inward focus of their eyes, the barely-perceptible movements of their lips as they spoke to those in cubicles next to them, even as they used sub-vocals to speak with team members not currently on site.

He felt them trying to use the construct to coordinate.

But something was off.

The well-oiled machine jumped and started, stopped and jerked.

Tahi felt the instability there... a kind of virus running through its veins.

The network seemed to shudder, even as he thought it.

Tahi understood. He knew the fundamentals of construct creation. All nonphysical networks needed more than simply a firm grounding in the physical world. Constructs needed a "head," that person who made up the apex of the Pyramid.

With Charles gone, they'd lost their head.

They'd lost their apex—the guiding principle behind the network.

That loss threw the entire network into a state of confusion.

Consciously or not, it threw them all sideways, off-balance.

Tahi fought to think, even as he felt another shudder in the nonphysical structure. For the first time, he noticed the construct trying to reconfigure itself around him, with Tahi himself as "head," the one sitting in that apex chair.

Realizing the male infiltrator was right, that he was in command now, he immediately began downloading the information coming to him from other areas of the construct.

It was sheer chaos.

His living light, or *aleimi,* fought to adjust.

He fought to hold up the pyramid-like structure.

But Tahi wasn't Charles.

He didn't have Charles' structure, his know-how, his vision.

He didn't have his raw ability, either in working rank... or even in potential.

The construct shuddered again as he thought it.

The maze of threads and connecting points, what they'd used to control everything and everyone since Charles seized control of the human government—it all seemed to be in freefall. From his new vantage point, Tahi could feel individual network seers, even those at the higher levels of the structure, reacting to that loss of control.

Some of them, even seers of whom Tahi never would have suspected such a thing, were already succumbing to full-blown panic.

They didn't have a contingency plan for this.

No contingency existed for any of this.

Refocusing out the window of his West Wing office, Tahi fought with what to do.

Black was gone.

They had no idea where.

He could not be used as leverage against his wife, not any longer.

They'd tried to capture him, alive, during that final fight down at the border, the one Mulki had been leading, but Black escaped, just before this nightmare began.

The usurper slipped free... likely also due to his wife.

Charles had warned them.

He'd warned them what a grave danger his niece posed.

Now, it appeared, that danger had come to pass.

The rumors about Black's wife, Dr. Miriam Fox, proved to be true.

Tahi finally understood—now, when it was too late—why Charles had been so adamant about capturing Miriam first, why he'd so badly wanted her husband alive, when capturing Miri herself proved impossible. Tahi understood why Charles remained fixated on his niece, even proposing that they torture her husband to get her to turn herself in.

In this, as in so many things, Charles' vision bordered on prescient.

Charles saw the risk, just as he foresaw so many things.

He warned them.

And now it was too late.

Tahi fought to think, staring out at the midnight view of the White House lawn and gardens. He glimpsed a Secret Service agent as they walked past, making the rounds of the outside of the building.

Checking his watch, Tahi frowned again.

The President would be asleep by now.

There was *some* chance he'd be up, watching the feeds of the ongoing conflict at the border as vampires continued to flee into the United States... but Tahi had his doubts.

In any case, he wouldn't inform him.

Not until morning.

It wasn't likely human President Bradford Regent would understand these new developments anyway, even if Tahi did tell him, even if he explained them in detail... which Tahi definitely would not.

Regent was human, and therefore wholly incapable of helping Tahi with this disaster. Not only that, Regent happened to be a particularly stupid human.

That particular trait of Regent's had been useful in some ways, of course.

Manipulating Regent had been painfully easy, making him the perfect front for their operation. For a seer at Charles' level, Regent himself barely merited consideration as a sentient being; rather, he functioned more as one piece on a complex chessboard.

Charles confided to Tahi that he'd barely had to push Regent directly at all to get him to play his part... which Tahi believed, since he guessed a Sark child could likely push Regent into compliance without breaking a sweat.

As one who worked alongside him in the White House, Tahi found Regent's stupidity annoying as hell at times.

Like now. Regent was more or less useless in a crisis.

He was useless, even a liability, in any situation where having a human leader who could actually *think* might have been a real asset.

Tahi checked his watch again, frowning.

He was running out of time.

He could feel it. He could feel the spotlight on him, the target aligning on his chest, in his new position as head of the construct. He could feel how visible he was.

After the barest pause, still staring out the window at the dark grounds of the most famous residence in the world, he picked up the phone.

He hit through a key sequence for one of the most secure lines in the Pentagon.

"Simon Chu here," a calm voice said.

Tahi didn't bother with a greeting.

"Are any of them working yet?" he said. "I need to know. Now."

There was a silence.

"How do you have access to this—"

"I'm in charge now," Tahi said.

His voice cut a hard path through the other's. He noted his accent resurfaced as well, coloring his words in a way that would have been difficult to identify for most of the denizens of this world, yet would have outed him as a seer in most parts of Old Earth.

"Lucky's out," Tahi added. "Jalisa is out. We've lost Mulki, Dresden, Shana. There's a good chance we've lost Var and Emmerich."

The calm in the other's voice tremored.

It was enough that Tahi heard it.

"The female? Black's wife?"

"Yes."

"How verified is that?"

"It is verified enough," Tahi said.

"Who is left? If we've lost all of our senior—"

"Me," Tahi interrupted. "You've got me." Pausing, he felt his jaw harden as his own words sank in. "...although I don't know for how much longer. I'm assuming the construct around the White House is buying those of us here some time."

Letting that sink in, he hardened his voice.

"...Do you have any working yet? Or not? I must know now."

The silence stretched longer.

Tahi could almost hear the other seer thinking, even with the intense shields around the bunker-like labs where Chu worked.

It struck Tahi that his changed status within the construct gave him more access to everything. That didn't just mean the secondary, security constructs of the labs and other restricted, need-to-know areas—but the actual minds of his fellow seers with whom he shared the Barrier network.

He was still thinking about that, noticing he could feel the presences and minds of other seers working in Chu's lab, when Chu's voice returned, eerily calm.

"We have three dozen of the latest iteration. Possibly four... if you include those in various stages of the testing phase. Maybe two of those three dozen who are more or less stable. The newest phase isn't ready yet. We had our timetables moved up, but we're still struggling with elements of the interface. Many of the subjects still die before—"

"Could they be activated? Now, I mean. Those of the proto-types that more or less work. If you had to do it quickly—"

"Activated?"

In his mind, Tahi saw the seer's eyebrows rise to the middle of his forehead.

"Activated how?" Chu said. "With what target?"

"What target?" Gordon let out a disbelieving sound. "Are you fucking serious right now, brother?"

The other grew flustered.

"I just mean... we have no location track. We have nothing. We can't even track her through the Barrier, even using Charles' markers. She completely disappears, every time she conducts one of those—"

"She has to stop sometime," Tahi cut in.

Feeling the other's doubt through the construct, he made his voice cold, uncompromising. "We're at war, brother. A war we're losing, by the way... as of about three hours ago. They are overthrowing us as we speak. They took our damned *leader* right out from under us."

"I understand—"

"Do you?" Tahi snapped. "Then answer the damned question."

There was a longer silence.

"Are you authorizing me to—"

"Authorizing?" Tahi cut in. "I'm *ordering* you to activate the assets, to operationalize them for defense. Consider this me giving you the green light for a full-blow field test, as of now. Run the voice code on me, if you need to... the construct should have changed my security access by now, even down to the organic machines where you are."

There was another silence.

In it, Tahi realized Chu had already run his light credentials.

Chu wouldn't be talking to him at all, if Tahi's claims hadn't been verified already by the security construct in the lab where he worked.

In fact, the more he thought about it, the more Tahi realized Chu probably ran his creds before he picked up the phone.

Chu took his job seriously.

He was by the book, all the way. It was a good trait to have, given his position. It was also a large part of why Charles entrusted Chu with running those labs, in addition to the older seer's extraordinary light-structure and brain.

If Tahi hadn't checked out, he'd likely be under his own desk by now, bleeding through the eyes, nose, and ears from a heavy dose of electrified Barrier venom dumped from the construct inside the White House. The combined load likely would have broken half the structures in Tahi's *aleimi*... assuming it didn't kill him outright.

Tahi knew every bit of that was protocol, that Chu would have been *right* to do it, but his jaw clenched at the thought, anyway.

Charles could be a cold-hearted son of a bitch.

He also ruled with an iron fist.

Now, with Charles gone, Tahi could feel Chu doubting, hesitating.

He could feel confusion, misgiving on the other seer.

He could even empathize.

"It might be our last chance," Tahi spoke into that quiet. "I know it's risky, Chu, but it's our last line of defense. It might be the only way left to save our people..."

Trailing, thinking about this, Tahi gave a seer's shrug.

"Well, that's assuming she and Black have them locked up somewhere, and Dr. Fox didn't just rematerialize with them in space, or toss them out of this dimension totally—"

"They're unstable," Chu broke in, his voice actively tense. "Even the best-working ones aren't reliable yet. We can't predict with absolute certainty what they'll do, particularly without direction. If faced with circumstances we can in no way control—"

"I understand."

Realizing he did understand, Tahi frowned, his lips pressed together.

"...If you have another scenario, a better one, I'm all ears, Chu," he added.

A warning went off in his headset.

Tahi had left the organic machine on in the background while using his Chief of Staff's secure office phone.

In a corner section of his virtual monitor, a secondary screen rose up.

On it, text scrolled, along with headshots of three seers Tahi recognized.

Three more of theirs down.

Mauria, Robin and Nurai could no longer be located.

That new seer, Elan Raven, had also disappeared.

"We're out of time," Tahi said, his voice sharpening as he focused back on the seer on the phone. "She's still taking people, Chu. Can you activate them? Or not?"

"I can," Chu said.

"Then do it. Tell only who you have to."

"Understood, sir."

"Good. And Chu... you might need to have a failsafe on the oversight controls."

"Sir?"

"Just rig something up, would you? If they take you and the rest of the lab..."

His voice faltered as he felt something shift in the room.

The hairs on his arms and the back of his neck stood up.

Tahi rose with them, regaining his feet even as he hit an emergency pulse on his headset. His eyes darted to the window, then back to the door of the office.

He stopped breathing, listening with every molecule of his being.

When he couldn't hear anything, couldn't feel or see anything at all with his *aleimi*, or with his physical eyes, he swallowed.

The sound of that swallow was deafening to his ears.

He was being ridiculous.

He still had time.

He had to still have some time... she'd only just taken those last three targets.

There was nothing there.

The few staffers he could feel twanging the edges of the construct on the other side of the door were mostly human. He could feel the seer techs working from a quieter, more still space, lost inside their virtual headsets. He felt Secret Service agents patrolling, the cleaners making their way from the main residence into this part of the building. The normal, late-night sounds he heard most nights might have been more amplified than usual, more frenetic... but they fell within what he would consider "normal," at least under the circumstances.

All this talk of Miriam Fox and her quasi-mystical powers had the whole network in a state of irrational panic.

There was a rational explanation.

There had to be a rational explanation.

Staring fixedly at the door, Tahi tried to shake it off.

He walked slowly around his desk, fighting to move purposefully, to force his body to act normally. He continued listening with his light, stretching deeper into the construct that covered this whole side of the West Wing.

Chu, clearly not feeling the shift Tahi reacted to, continued to talk.

"...I guess I'm not entirely sure what you mean by failsafe, sir. Are you concerned about one of our prototypes being recovered? Or is your concern more about having a backup means of controlling them, in the event—"

But Tahi heard him that time.

"What is my concern about?" he broke in, incredulous. "What is my *concern?* Are you serious right now, brother Chu?"

The other fell silent.

Tahi snapped, "My *concern* is having someone or something to protect us, brother, in the event we can't recover Charles. My *concern* is having some final line of defense, in the event our *entire fucking leadership team* is wiped out. What about that is confusing to you, brother? It's not like you don't have adequate security clearance to know we're up against—"

Just then, she was there.

His words cut off, unconscious... abrupt.

He stared at her.

Long, nearly-black hair.

Pale hazel eyes. They glowed at him, whispering... flickering around the rings of her irises like a sparking, golden-green flame.

Like in the drone footage Gordon saw, she was stark naked.

She stood in front of him, panting lightly, a faint sheen of sweat on her face. The expression etched into her features struck him as dangerous, holding an intensity that made him flinch back, even before she reached for him...

Her fingers circled his wrist.

A hard pressure hit at his chest.

That pressure suffocated him.

It crushed his lungs, his belly, his chest.

It pulled at his face, at his limbs.

He couldn't breathe.

His sense of up and down reversed.

Everything around him seemed to flip upside down in a dizzying wave, one that turned rapidly into a spinning, twisting vortex.

That spinning ripped apart everything around him.

It ripped apart the fabric of his Oval Office-adjacent office.

Tahi watched it all get blown away, like soft rock in a sandstorm: bookshelves, books, papers on his desk, the antique landline phone, his night view of the White House gardens, the antique oak desk, the gold carpet, dark blue curtains, antique lamp.

He watched it rip apart the glass case he had on his desk—the only thing of genuine sentimental value to him in the entire building.

It was a piece of a volcanic cave.

It was a piece of the same volcanic cave where he'd been led to a portal to get to this world. Tahi, who'd been known as Gordan Kent to the humans here, brought the dark volcanic rock with him when he passed through that portal.

He'd recently paid to have it handsomely encased in glass—a last token from Old Earth, the place he still thought of as his true home.

The rock was gone now.

Tahi screamed into that vortex.

He saw stars.

Blue and green nebulae, shocking pink and purple starlight clouds.

Then, just as abruptly, he snapped back into one piece.

He stood, panting, entirely naked.

His bare feet kissed concrete.

He was covered in sweat, trembling, making a faint whimpering sound. Urine ran silently down one leg and puddled on the concrete floor as his bladder unexpectedly voided, spraying some of it up to hit out in front of him, since he wasn't exactly holding his dick in his hand, trying to aim it—

A voice rose.

He peed again.

He hadn't realized he wasn't alone.

"You got him?" she said.

The voice was cold, clinical, unnervingly calm.

It also sounded just the slightest bit impatient.

Tahi's eyes shifted instinctively to the face that came with that voice.

He knew who he would see, even before he turned. By then, he remembered. Not all of it, but he remembered enough to be terrified out of his mind—

But those glowing, gold-green eyes weren't looking at him anymore.

They focused somewhere else.

"You got him?" she said again, the impatience more discernible. "Any day now, sister... I'm only in a cage with him. Naked. Unarmed."

Tahi turned, following her gaze.

He saw another female, standing on the other side of iron bars.

Most assuredly a seer, from her nearly white eyes with the dark-blue rings, she raised a tranquilizer rifle to her shoulder as Tahi watched.

His eyes tracked every increment of the motion, as if it happened at one-fourth of the regular speed.

Even so, he was still slow to react.

He lifted a hand, whimpering.

He sounded like a trapped rabbit, even to himself.

He whimpered, gasping, fighting to catch his breath—

—when a dart hit him, a perfect bullseye in the middle of his naked chest.

2

LOOSE ENDS

I mentally checked my watch.

I was trying to listen to the man standing in front of me.

I was really trying to listen, to absorb his words.

It was hard.

It was really hard to give a shit about anything he was saying.

I wanted to get back to Black. Every part of my mind, light and body screamed it was time to get back to Black, that I wanted Black, that Black needed me. Everything else my mind muttered was just some variation of the same tune.

This was taking too long.

I should be done with this by now.

What did this person want from me?

Why were they expecting me to spell everything out to them?

Couldn't the rest of the team step the fuck up? Take some damned ownership? I'd passed them the baton. Why wouldn't they take the damned thing and run with it? Why were they asking me all these damned questions, instead of figuring out the answers on their own?

And finally...

Why was everyone acting so damned confused about *why* I'd done this?

Why was everyone acting like I'd done this on my own?

Me and Black's reasons seemed pretty damned self-evident to me.

Hell, I'd just won the war for them... hadn't I?

I'd more or less single-handedly stopped my uncle's insane plan to take over the world. Black and I did it alone, without getting any of our people killed... and they were all looking at me like I'd lost my damned mind.

Like what I'd done was somehow shitty, cheating, or out of bounds, or too weird to be some sort of military strategy... or like they were sure it would bite us in the ass.

Telling them that Black was one hundred percent on board with me taking this drastic step didn't seem to do anything to ease their minds.

For all of these reasons—most of all, me wanting to get back to my *husband,* who I'd still barely talked to after weeks and months of us being apart—it took everything in my power to keep from tapping my foot, rolling my eyes, scowling, staring pointedly at the clock, or just being a full-fledged bitch to get them to leave me alone.

I forced my expression still, my eyes on the tall, ex-Marine while he spoke.

Well, I did for a while.

In the end, I couldn't take it anymore.

Standing there—stark fucking naked, by the way—listening to Dex detail all of his questions, confusions, and *what nexts* concerning the large group of detainees I'd brought him to deal with, was finally enough to make my patience snap.

Holding up a hand, I cut him off, even as I stepped out of the cell, wincing as my bare feet landed on the freezing cold concrete on the other side. Exiting the rest of the way through the opening, I shut the transparent door behind me.

"I don't understand what's so complicated about this," I said, keeping my voice level with an effort. "What's confusing about this, Dexter? Seriously? What don't you understand?"

Dex blinked.

Still fighting to keep my voice polite, I added,

"Charles is dealt with. Okay? He was the complicated one, and he's not a risk to us anymore. Taking out all of Charles' top lieutenants should dismantle enough of their construct that our infiltrators can pummel that thing to dust. And, okay, some of the others are just... insurance, I guess. But I figure more is more in this scenario. You can sort out the security risks after Yarli's had a chance to get her team to assess them all. And maybe rank them, in terms of threat level."

Dex frowned.

He turned from me, looking at the row of holding cells behind where I stood.

His eyes scanned over the naked bodies filling those cells, lying on blankets, cement, and in some cases, on thin cots. All of them, so far at least, were still unconscious. It seemed easier that way, to tranq the shit out of them the instant I brought them here.

I wanted the security team to decide the rest of the protocols.

Not me.

It wasn't my area of expertise.

Moreover, I didn't want to.

Dex turned back to me, quirking an eyebrow.

For the first time, he dropped the polite, calm act, too.

"Are you fucking *serious* right now, doc?" The big Marine's arm went out, his hand motioning towards the unconscious, naked bodies in a kind of helpless, disbelieving, mind-blown kind of way. "I mean... are you fucking *SERIOUS* right now, doc? Are you really giving me the 'nothing to see here' *attitude,* because I'm not taking this shit in stride? You just fucking kidnapped like a hundred people. Some of them are public figures—"

"They're seers," I said, my voice hard. "Not humans. They were public figures because my uncle's people used their seer powers to manipulate and push them into those roles—"

"So the fuck what? You think this shit won't be *noticed?*"

Scowling, I folded my arms.

My eyes followed his, tracking back over the same scene in the sub-basement under Black's flagship building, located smack-dab in the Financial District of San Francisco.

Taking in the same wash of naked skin, most of it pale, most of it attached to male bodies, I firmed my lips, exhaling.

Okay, granted.

Dex had a point.

The optics weren't great.

When I looked back up at him with a shrug, the thirty-some-thing African-American with the stunning brown eyes scowled, throwing up his hands.

I knew he was tired.

I was tired, too.

I also wanted to get back to Black.

I wanted to get back to Black as soon as I possibly could.

I was getting downright anxious about it.

When I got anxious, I tended to get angry at anything making that anxiousness worse.

Right now, any delay in getting back to Black made that anxiousness worse.

I'd done my part.

I'd *done my part,* damn it.

To be fair to Dex, okay, yeah... I hadn't exactly given him or his team what you'd call "advance notice." I'd also done it with minimal explanation or direction from Black himself, whose orders they were more used to following.

All of that meant zero prep time, zero time to map out possible risk scenarios and contingency plans, zero time to think through the logistics, zero time to even get used to the idea. They were also coming off a few weeks of being trapped underground with vampires, fighting a war they'd only just wrapped their minds around having to fight.

But hell, this team was good on its feet, right?

This was happening.

It had more or less *happened.*

They needed to get on board.

They needed to get on board and deal with this.

I didn't intend to stand here and hash out all the nitty-gritty details of security and containment. I expected *them* to do that.

Without me.

As I said, it was much more Dex and Kiko's skill set, anyway.

Given all the military-trained humans *and* seers now on my husband's payroll, most of whom were experienced in multiple wars, and with all kinds of seer and human containment and sight-restraint tech, they should have this covered.

Hell, some of them, like Yarli, should be able to do this shit in their sleep.

Every one of the trained infiltrators on our team should know how to house a bunch of hostile seers so they weren't a danger to us.

I mean... right? Why wouldn't they?

Between the two teams, they could damned well figure it out.

So basically, yeah, I didn't want to discuss it.

I just wanted Dex to tell me he had this.

I wanted Yarli and Mika to tell me they had this.

I wanted them to tell me I could go.

"What would you have done?" Dex said, frowning, gazing out over the cells. "If we didn't have this holding area... where the hell would you have put all of them?"

"We do have it, though," I said, gesturing sharply towards the same rows of cells. "We had it, and Black told me to use it. He said they were built for vampires, so they're more than strong enough to hold seers."

Dex's jaw hardened more.

Visibly hardened.

It was a stroke of luck that these cells below the California Street building had already been built.

I'd remembered that, when I first proposed my idea to Black.

A carryover from when Black first went on his vampire-hunting kick, Black had the holding area built not long after he got free of that prison in Louisiana. For a few months, they even held a half-dozen vampires, back when Black and his scientific team, then mostly human, first began studying them. Black had wanted to learn everything he could about vampire physiology; he'd also done it to extract intelligence about the vampire king's whereabouts and operation.

All of which meant the cells were built to be damned strong.

With seers, the issue was less about physical strength and more about their psychic abilities. I was sure some modifications would end up being necessary, to convert them into seer holding pens.

But again... not by me.

No one needed *me* for that.

My light felt worn out, depleted.

My face was flushed.

I was dizzy.

Stepping away from the door of the cell I'd just left, I pushed on the panel to make sure it fully latched, then hit through a keypad to engage the lock. I leaned on the transparent wall with part of my back, still fighting to recover from the jump.

Dex's stare never left my face.

He kept his eyes off the rest of me, even as he basically ignored the fact that I was completely naked.

I had to be naked.

I could only do the jumps while naked.

Since I'd been doing nothing but jumps for a few hours now, transporting people from D.C. and the rest of the country into this underground cell block in Black's basement, everyone around me was utterly blasé about the fact of my nakedness.

Dex, more than any of them, barely seemed to notice at this point.

He just watched me, mouth pursed.

"You look wiped, doc," he said finally. "Truthfully? You look ill. Anemic. Like you're about to pass out." He paused for a beat. "You okay?"

Hearing all the fight gone from his voice, I felt most of mine evaporate, too.

I gave him a wry smile.

"I could use a vacation," I admitted. Hesitating, I added, "I'm pretty anxious to get back to Black. I got him out of there, then pretty much left him—"

Dex was already nodding.

He held up a hand to show me he understood.

"I get it," he said.

His eyes went back to the cells, and he exhaled.

Despite his words, I could see he was clearly not pleased with the mess I was leaving him. For the first time, I felt a little sorry for that.

I followed his eyes to the man I'd just left in the nearest of the vampire-proof cells, sleeping on the floor with the others. I could see in Dex's expression that he was still trying to wrap his mind around the enormity of what I'd done.

"So this one is...?" Dex prompted, clearly wanting me to fill in the blank.

Luce answered, from where she stood behind him.

I looked over, sharp.

I'd honestly forgotten Dex and I weren't alone.

Luce's eyes never left the tablet she carried.

"Kalri," she said, reading off the screen. "That's the seer name. His human alias is 'Jack Ranger.' Says here, in the notes, he's 'a prominent leader and agitator in the Purity Movement spearheaded by Charles in the Southern states.'"

Luce grunted, squinting at the male seer's face from the other side of the transparent, organic walls. Like the rest of the seers inside his holding cell, the male was naked and unconscious on the floor, his eyes closed.

"Aw, yeah. I got it now," Luce said, after a few seconds of staring. "I remember this guy. He was on the networks and had his own video channel, spewing crap about demons attacking our borders. He's one of those weirdo cultists from Texas or Louisiana, right?"

I nodded, still fighting a little to catch my breath.

"Yeah," I said, glancing at her, still leaning on the transparent door. "I figured we needed to take some of the figureheads, too. Lately he's been Uncle Charles' number one poster boy. He was running for state senator already, but I suspect he was being groomed for higher office given how much media time he was getting. The last thing we need is another, younger Charles popping up to take his place, or going on some kind of revenge crusade—"

"Okay," Dex cut in, frowning as he held up a hand.

That one word was clearly meant to end me and Luce's conversation.

More to the point, he wanted our attention back on him, back to what he saw as our bigger, or at least more immediate problem.

Dex stared at the crowd of seers I'd already personally transported, one by one, to our basement, most of them from Washington D.C.

All four of the vampire holding cells were nearly full.

I wondered how many people upstairs even knew this level of the building existed, under Black's garage full of expensive cars.

"Now what, Dr. Fox, am I supposed to do with all of these people, exactly?" Dex said, motioning with a frown around at all the seers I'd brought him. "Before you go off to see to Black, can you at least tell me that?"

Dr. Fox is me, in case you're wondering.

"You know," I said.

Still leaning on the cell wall, I waved vaguely down the aisle between cells.

The tiredness was really starting to hit me.

I glanced towards the door to the prison area, watching Yarli and Manny enter. They walked up to our small group, obviously listening to what I was saying. Both had their arms crossed, with similar frowns on their faces.

My eyes returned to Dex.

"...Contain them," I said. "Until me and Black get back."

"Contain them," Dex said, flat.

"Yeah. Contain them. Don't let them get out. Don't let Charles' crazy cultists find them. Don't let them tell anyone where they are. Don't let them talk to the other crazies. Keep them out of the Barrier, if you can."

Exhaling, I fingered my black hair out of my eyes.

"There's no way I got everyone," I admitted. "There will be people looking for them, like you said. They'll push humans to look for them. They'll try to get the military involved, and the local police. Brick's helping us now, and we've got people in D.C. working on erasing surveillance footage that shows me taking people... but some of that's bound to slip through the cracks. Someone's bound to have gotten me on camera, and shared it with someone else. You're going to have to oversee clean-up. The seers need to dismantle what remains of my uncle's constructs. We'll need to bury the story, at least until we figure out next steps. And if I missed anyone really critical, you need to I.D. them and get me the name so I can handle it—"

"Clean up. In D.C." That time, it was Yarli who spoke. "Bury the story."

She didn't really pose her words as a question.

"Yes," I said, giving her a look. "You'll need to deal with the media. As quickly as possible. And get some of your infiltrators monitoring the story on the political sites and conspiracy theory areas. They'll know how to send out disinformation... you need to counteract that. Luckily, it won't be hard to make anyone who actually knows or saw anything sound crazy or paranoid."

Yarli frowned delicately, exchanging looks with Manny.

The elegantly tall, dark-skinned seer then turned to stare at me with nearly-black eyes that contained glints of light like minia-ture, star-filled galaxies. She was so shockingly beautiful, I still found myself staring at her at times, and I'd known her well over a year.

Some seers were so beautiful, I found it borderline disorienting.

"Yeah," I said, aiming a warning look at her. "I shouldn't have to explain this to you guys." I looked between them, fighting annoyance. "You know the drill. You know damned well why I did this. You know how dangerous Charles was. You know the stakes—"

"Miriam," Manny began, exasperated. "I don't think—"

I gave him a hard, silencing look, without pausing in my speech.

"—So contain them," I finished. "I get the ethics of it. Get over it, okay? This isn't about a few rogue seers. It's about Charles trying to enslave the *entire human race*. Run a clean-up op in D.C., and assess the damage he's already done. See what you can do about dismantling all of the smaller constructs he built, once you tear down the big one, the one he's got over most of the country. Feed me names, if you need to, to make sure we can put the humans back in charge of their own damned government—"

"Miri," Yarli broke in, as exasperated as her older, Native American boyfriend. She waved towards the seers asleep on the floor of the holding cells. "Do you really think we can sweep this under the rug? That we can cover it up so completely that no one in the government, or the media, is going to be looking for any of these people? Given who they are?"

I frowned, staring at the same crowd of seers.

I fought with a more specific answer, then shrugged.

"Figure it out," I said, looking flatly at her, then at Manny. "This is your area of expertise, right?"

At their blank stares, I made my voice patient.

"I need to go back to Black," I said, speaking slowly, firmly. "I've been away from him for too long. I can't help you figure this out right now. You're going to have to do it without me. If you need to come up with temporary solutions... do that. Just do what you can, keep us informed, and I'll talk to Black. We'll figure out the rest later."

At their frustrated scowls, I held up a hand.

"...I need to get back to Black," I repeated, even slower. "I intend to talk to him about all of this. If he's up to it, I'm sure he'll be in touch with you as soon as he's had a chance to think it through. I need to go to him, though. Now."

I gestured at the row of cells.

"As for what's next, shit... I don't know. Check them for..."

I threw up my hands.

"...tracking devices. Get into the store of sight-restraint collars we've collected from Charles. Reinforce the sight-block from the construct. You know... the usual stuff. You guys are all military. You know the drill. Just make sure they're all clean, that they can't communicate with anyone. You know. Psychically."

"Psychically."

Again, that flat stare from Yarli.

I knew "psychic" wasn't a word seers used.

As a term, it was considered too primitive, too limited, to describe the myriad of gifts seers could employ as part of their "extra abilities."

The word psychic was too vague to be of any descriptive value to most seers... and entirely unnecessary as a term, given the far more varied and nuanced words the seers' own language provided.

"Psychic" was a human word.

It was only useful when talking to humans.

I didn't really give a shit.

"I don't know," I said, scowling. "Figure it out. I need to go deal with Black."

That time, I was done.

I really had hit the end of my patience.

Without waiting for her to respond, I geared into those structures in my light, the new ones I'd only recently discovered there, the ones I was still figuring out how to use...

...and I left.

3

TROPICAL DAMNED PARADISE

I landed in a hotel room on Oahu.

... Our hotel room.

As in, me and Black's.

The room was empty, which made me panic pretty much immediately.

I'd expected to find Black there. I'd expected to find him crashed out in the king-size bed in the suite's master bedroom, probably stark naked, like he had been when I left him.

One quick ping of my light told me he was down by the pool.

After putting on clothes that seemed more or less appropriate for the pool, I half-ran for the elevators and jammed my thumb on the button for the lobby.

Despite how enormous the pool area was, despite how many different pools it encompassed, how many snaking feet of wooden deck, how many waterfalls and slides and jacuzzis and floating bars... not to mention palm trees, deck chairs, people wandering around in bikinis and speedos and sarongs, tables covered in hibiscus flowers and plates of cut pineapples, eggs, bacon, and coffee... I saw Black within seconds of walking out onto the main pool deck.

Given how early it was, I was honestly surprised to see so many people by the pool.

It couldn't have been more than six in the morning.

Seven at most.

Once my eyes found Black, it suddenly made a lot more sense.

It made even more sense after I noticed the small crowd already gathered in his area of the pool deck, eating breakfast and pretending not to stare at him.

Black himself acted oblivious.

His leanly muscular body sprawled on a sun lounger near the largest of the main pools, right across from an island with a waterfall that fell elegantly into a volcanic rock jacuzzi. Giant stone-carved Hawaiian gods stood on either side of the island, and across from the narrowest part of the pool I saw a wall covered in carved dolphins, turtles and a depiction of the sun.

Black's face tilted towards the real sun.

He wore expensive-looking mirrored sunglasses, one leg on and one leg off the lounger, a brand new phone to his ear.

Apart from the sunglasses and the phone, he wore only black swim trunks.

To say he was getting stares would be putting it mildly.

Black was the center of attention in this whole part of the resort.

Even apart from the usual eye-draws Black got, pretty much anywhere he went, now he had people staring at him because of the news cycle of the past three months.

Maybe his flagrant exhibitionism shouldn't have surprised me, but it did.

I knew what he was doing.

I knew why he felt the need to come down here, to be as visible as he was.

It still made me flinch.

Truthfully, it scared the shit out of me... but I understood it.

Now, looking at him, I knew he'd deliberately picked the most public and visible part of the pool deck he could find. He'd deliberately posed in a way that would get stares, wearing as little clothing as possible, and situated himself close to the lobby so everyone walking out of the resort would notice the crowd and wander over.

All of this combined made it as likely as possible that Black's face would show up on people's social media feeds within seconds of him coming down here.

Even now, I saw them snapping photos and taking video of him surreptitiously.

It still shocked me, his brazenness.

What if someone had shown up, while I was gone?

I don't mean groupies... I meant law enforcement.

What if the military surrounded him out here, cuffed him, and took him away, before I'd finished doing what I was doing last night?

What if the Honolulu police dragged him in?

Again, it shouldn't have surprised me. He'd been the one to push for us to check in at this resort on Oahu, instead of hiding out at his private property on the big island, like I'd wanted, and where I'd originally taken us.

Black's property was secluded.

It had its own chef, its own private security, its own pool, a private beach, a sailboat, jacuzzis (plural), waterfalls (plural), a lake, gardeners, housekeepers, a chauffeur... not to mention all the usual Black things: weapons stashed in cubby holes, military-grade satellite phones, armed drones, body armor, a bullet-proof car, a private helipad and helicopter.

It was like a high-end resort mixed with a military bunker.

It was also extremely private.

The hotel we were staying at now had its own security, too, and better than decent from what Black told me, given who stayed here. But it was more the type of security meant to shield pop stars and A-list actors from stalkers and paparazzi... not the type of security me and Black were used to needing, especially lately.

The resort might have a helipad, but they definitely didn't have guns, grenades, body armor, or armed drones.

I hadn't been able to bring any of that with us when I popped us over here, either.

Given our method of transport, we had no choice but to come in naked, sans credit cards, phones, weapons, or ID.

For the same reason, Black gave me a specific location: one of the walk-in closets in a luxury penthouse apartment owned by a friend of his—the same friend who owned the resort where we were now staying, and where the apartment was located.

Black called first, to make sure his friend wouldn't be there.

After we scrounged up a couple of robes and left his friend's private apartment, we checked in downstairs... since Black *also* had his friend reserve us a suite... after giving him some crazy story about how he'd lost his phone and wallet and all of our clothes when our bags got tossed overboard from the deck of a yacht.

Black's friend barely blinked.

He immediately offered us the honeymoon suite of his flagship hotel for "as long as you want it," as if it was the most trivial thing in the world.

More proof, if I needed any, that the rich really *are* different.

Once we had a room, Black wasted no time in calling the staff at his property on the big island and giving them a list of things to fly over to us, via helicopter, immediately.

He then called the lobby of *this* hotel and asked the resort's personal shopper to bring us designer bathing suits, sunglasses, sunscreen, an assortment of basic summer clothes, workout clothes, several different types of shoes, socks, toothpaste, two toothbrushes, shampoo, conditioner, lotion, and a bunch of other bathroom and clothing "essentials."

I listened to him rattle off the list in near awe.

Again, the hotel staff barely blinked.

All they did was politely ask for sizes and style preferences for each of us, at which point Black gave them the number for *his* personal shopper, a man named Johan who lived in Los Angeles.

Given how Johan dressed me when I stayed with Black in Manhattan—more or less in designer, barely-there originals to distract everyone from what Black was up to at the time—I frowned a bit at that last part, but didn't argue.

As for the crazy-expensive and uber-trendy hotel, it was definitely beautiful, and definitely had amazing service and amenities... but I definitely would have preferred Black's private property on the big island.

I understood his reasoning.

It was amazing, really, how strategic Black could be.

It was even more amazing *now*, given everything that had gone down with us over the past few months.

Despite all the photographing and videoing cellphones of my husband's half-naked body on a sky-blue sun lounger, every cell in my body relaxed when I saw him there. I couldn't help smiling wryly at how perfectly posed he looked, his muscular body arranged artfully as he spoke over the phone, his deep voice booming over his part of the pool deck.

"Yeah," he said, borderline drunk-sounding as he drawled into the receiver. "I get it, man. I get it. But how is any of that *my* fault...? I can't be expected to watch the news *every* day, can I?"

Seeing me, he broke out in one of his killer smiles.

He waved me over, which immediately had all the eyes previously focused solely on him riveted to me, as well.

Fighting the impulse to both roll my eyes at him and snort openly at the ludicrousness of what he'd just said to whoever was on the phone, I ended up sighing in relief instead.

He was here, more or less intact.

He wasn't in handcuffs or being led to a van with blacked-out windows.

Moreover, knowing him, he already has his own security eyes on the resort, if not in person, then via the Barrier. Also knowing him, he likely had his own people on their way here in person as well, given that he didn't trust anyone he hadn't vetted personally.

Feeling my shoulders relax, I made my way over to where he was.

He lowered the sunglasses, raising his eyebrows suggestively at me in the brand new, dark red bikini. I wore a gauzy white wrap around my hips, and leather sandals covered in green stones on my feet. Still walking towards him, I plucked a hibiscus flower out of a bowl set on a nearby bar table and stuck it behind my ear.

New, white-framed sunglasses held back my long black hair.

Everything I wore was new.

I'd found shopping bags on the floor of our suite when I returned, and scrounged an outfit out of three of them as fast as I could, just so I could come down here to find him. Now that I *had* found him, though, I was really glad I'd found the bag with the bathing suits first.

I really wanted to go for a swim.

I wanted to wash the travel off me.

I wanted that good Hawaiian ju-ju to wash me clean.

Black pushed his own sunglasses back up his nose to cover his eyes, smiling at me as he continued to talk into his brand-new phone.

"...I get all of that," he said, his voice still friendly, booming, lazy, magnanimous. "I do, Grant... I really do. But I'm on vacation right now, brother. I get that your people are all fired up about these online conspiracies or whatever... but can it wait until I get back home with my wife? We'll only be here for another week or two—"

Someone must have cut him off on the other end.

Black paused, listening for a second.

Then he burst out in a laugh.

Heads turned towards us, staring at him openly where he lounged by the crystal-blue pool.

He was definitely in his, "suck all the air out of the room" persona.

Again, I understood why. I knew this was smart, that his strategy was smart, but I also knew what it meant for me... and for us.

Even assuming all went well, meaning neither of us got shot, arrested, or stuck in an underground lab somewhere, there were downsides to this approach.

It meant zero privacy.

It meant probably weeks of expensive resorts like this one.

It also meant parties full of celebrities, miscellaneous rich weirdos, frat boy hedge fund managers, drunken debauchery by Black, and a lot of outrageous quotes that he hoped would be splashed all over the tabloids, entertainment news, and hopefully even mainstream news outlets for the foreseeable future.

I also knew this could go on for months.

Thinking about that, it struck me suddenly, the name he'd called the person on the phone.

My lips curled in a frown.

Rather than speaking out loud, I used my mind.

Grant? I sent, a little blown away in spite of myself. *Are you talking to Grant-fucking-Steele right now? The talk show host?*

Lowering the glasses again, Black winked at me, even as he flashed his flecked gold irises in my general direction.

They looked brighter than usual.

Clicking at him in spite of myself, I sat down heavily on the pale blue lounger next to his, feeling the tiredness hit me like a ton of bricks.

Still holding the phone to his ear, he shifted his weight on the lounger, leaning closer to me. He kissed my face, sending tendrils of his *aleimi,* or living light, into mine.

I shivered, immediately feeling my limbs turn liquid.

There was so much of *him* in that curl of light, such a subtle weaving of heat, of heart, of affection, and pulling, intensifying want, my anger melted before I could even think about why.

Briefly, Black covered the phone with his hand.

"Are you hungry?" he said, soft.

Thinking about that, I nodded.

Black twisted his body around, plucking a paper menu up off a table on the other side of his lounger. Twisting back just as sensually, he handed it over to me, even as he put the phone back to his mouth.

"No," he said to the talk show host.

It hit me that Black wouldn't have called Steele.

That was far too obvious of a move for Black, and likely, it would only have the opposite effect he was going for. Calling up talk show hosts to pretend he'd somehow missed his own face splattered all over the news media wouldn't exactly be a convincing ploy.

No, Black wouldn't have called Steele.

That meant Steele had called Black.

That meant Grant Steele, the number-one-rated, late-night talk show host in the country, called my husband personally, after somehow getting his number here, where no one was supposed to know where we were, or how to reach us.

Steele found us less than eight hours after we'd checked in... and we'd checked in with zero baggage, with no reservations, in the middle of the night.

Steele must have been tipped off by someone staying at the hotel.

The hotel itself definitely wouldn't have done it, which meant one of the other celebrity guests had recognized Black and called Steele, or someone who knew Steele.

Now Steele was clearly asking for an interview.

Which again, wasn't that surprising, given everything that had happened over the past few months, but it still blew my mind a little.

"...Tomorrow's out of the question," Black was saying. "Look, I told you, I've been out of the loop. I was in Patagonia on a spiritual retreat with my wife. We were looking at glaciers. Photographing hawks. Kayaking. Contemplating the meaning of existence." Black gave me a sideways grin. "...Fucking each other's brains out."

I snorted, but Black barely paused.

"We're only now finding out about all this shit," Black added. "She and I are on *vacation*..."

He trailed, presumably because Grant cut him off.

"No," Black said, laughing again. "For fuck's sake. A *dragon?* You want me to cut short my vacation with my hot, sexy wife, in a tropical goddamned paradise, so I can answer the question of whether or not I'm actually a *dragon?* Did the entire mainstream press corps drop acid while I was gone? Because I'm beginning to think our trip was excruciatingly normal in comparison... embarrassingly normal, really..."

Steele must have cut him off again.

At something the other said, Black burst out in another laugh.

"Well, Jesus, Grant. How am I *supposed* to take this seriously? How did anyone believe this crazy fucking story in the first place...?"

His fingers curled into my hair, tugging on it.

Again, I felt a flicker of that heat on him.

Again, Grant must have cut him off.

I could almost hear the human on the other end of the line, talking earnestly in Black's ear. I could feel the intensity there as he tried to convince Black that this was, indeed, a serious story. I could practically feel his urgency, his excitement at getting to Black first.

Steele was practically pissing himself, I realized, that he might get the jump on his industry peers.

He desperately wanted to press his advantage, to get Black to commit before anyone else in the media swooped in and talked Black into some sort of exclusive.

"I can't promise you anything, Grant," Black said after a longer pause. "I'm looking at my wife right now in a barely-there, brand new bikini, and I'm telling you... you're not going to be able to compete with that, no matter how many upgrades or five-star hotels you throw at me. She's just prettier than you..."

Black listened again for a few seconds.

He broke out in another laugh, glancing at me through the sunglasses.

"No," he said, that humor still in his voice. "I doubt you'll be able to talk my wife into doing a joint interview. Anyway, she hates New York. She thinks you're all a bunch of bloodsucking vipers and Wall Street criminals..."

I quirked my eyebrow at that.

Well, he wasn't wrong.

Grinning at me, Black reached over, squeezing my thigh in one hand.

Again, I felt a flush of heat off him.

That time, it hit me in the belly.

If only to distract myself, I picked up the menu he'd set on the lounger next to me.

Exhaling in a sigh, I began scanning the list of items listed for the poolside restaurant. The longer I stared at it, the more I realized just how hungry I was.

I found myself in an existential dilemma about which thing I wanted more... to swim, to eat, or to sleep.

All three sounded heavenly.

At the same time, there was a fourth thing I wanted to do even more.

Tell me about it, doc... Black murmured in my mind.

"I'll ask her," he said aloud before I could react, still massaging my thigh, his voice openly doubtful. "But trust me, I can pretty much guarantee the answer will be an emphatic no. In a contest between scuba diving naked with me and hanging out in a studio getting dabbed at by makeup artists, gawked at by strangers, hot lights beating down on her while you ask her and me a bunch of personal questions... you see where I'm going with this?"

Again, I could almost hear Steele's voice rise through the line.

Black laughed, cutting off whatever the talk show host was saying.

It rolled out of him, another of those deep, booming laughs that got everyone around the pool to turn, staring at both of us.

Black was the only person I knew who could hold court just by existing.

All he had to do was *not* hide, *not* quash his light, *not* go out of his way to be quiet, and every eye gravitated to him like a magnet surrounded by iron filaments.

"You're an optimist, buddy," Black said, another of those killer smiles on his face. "Don't get me wrong, I love that about you. I do. But I think you're going to be disappointed this time. My wife just doesn't care about shit like that."

Settling on a few things from the menu, I looked around for a waiter.

Waving to a man in an all-white uniform, I held up the menu, indicating that I wanted to order. Breaking out in an infectious smile, the Japanese-looking human straightened from where he'd been setting down drinks by another pair of loungers.

He immediately began walking directly towards us.

He reached me a few seconds later, with a flourish and a bow.

He was so cheerful I found myself grinning back at him.

Given how tired I was, I still found myself stumbling over my words, and feeling vaguely like I'd left part of my brain in that basement in San Francisco.

I haltingly described and pointed at things on the menu: sliced mango, yogurt, granola, summer rolls, avocado, a large cappuccino, a bottle of water. My choices felt utterly random, but just the fact of making a decision allowed me to relax... finally... maybe for the first time in weeks.

Only after the waiter left did it cross my mind to wonder if I should have ordered something for Black.

No, it's fine, Black murmured in my mind, leaning over to kiss my face. *I want to look at the menu again. I'm fucking starving... I ate most of a chicken while you were gone. Not to mention a plate of grilled fish. And a plate of fried calamari. And like a bucket of shrimp.*

I laughed, shoving at his chest, which was already warm, even halfway under an umbrella in the early morning sun.

Shrimp? I teased, now rubbing his chest and bringing another ripple of heat off his skin. *Fish? I would have thought you'd be sick to death of seafood. I expected you to demand a steak or something... or more of those chicken skewers you devoured in Thailand.*

He shrugged, giving me another of those killer smiles as he reached for the menu next to my leg.

Fishies need to beware of me, he sent, kissing me on the side of the face before tugging the menu onto his lap, resting it on his bent leg. *Sushi sounds good, too. I think I still have a giant, reptile-sized stomach, where no fishies are safe.*

I laughed at that, too.

...Even as I marveled at the fact that we *could* laugh about that.

We still hadn't talked about it, really.

Not about what happened to him.

Not about how it happened.

Not about what he'd done.

He told me a few things, just in the process of us getting from the big island to here. He told me he'd been drugged when the whole thing started, that the drugs might have had a part in his loss of control over his light.

He told me, grimly, that he'd warned Charles.

He warned Uncle Charles to get out of the way, even as it was happening.

He also said he'd more or less lived on seafood while he'd been, well, not-human.

After he transformed into a hundred-plus foot animal with leathery wings, glass-like teeth, black scales, razor-sharp claws, a whipping tail... a massive creature that *breathed fire*... Black's main source of food came from the ocean.

For the most part, the ocean was also how he got around.

All of that was enough to tell me he remembered being that other thing, in part at least. He remembered the decisions he'd made. Some part of his mind continued living there, even with him utterly transformed on the outside.

I had a hell of a lot of questions.

I had so many questions, I didn't really know where to start.

Pushing that out of my mind, I lay back on the sunning lounge.

The sun beat down on my bare skin around the bikini. The warmer I grew, the more I felt myself start to relax for real.

I barely listened as Black wrapped up his conversation with Steele.

In fact, I'd nearly dozed off by the time the waiter came back with my food.

I picked up my cappuccino first, sipping at it and listening in near-awe as Black took the opportunity to order for himself: grilled scallops, a cheeseburger, meat skewers, two beers, a basket of curly fries, chocolate cake, blackberry parfait, a piece of baklava.

When the waiter walked away, I peered at him over my sunglasses, and laughed when he grinned at me apologetically.

"Hungry, baby?" I said, quirking an eyebrow.

"You're going to help me with the cake," he informed me. "And the baklava."

"Ah," I said, smiling.

Spearing a piece of the mango, I chewed on it between sips of cappuccino while I mixed the rest of the fruit, along with the yogurt and granola up in the bowl. I found myself staring longingly at the pool, trying to decide which thing I wanted to do first: swim, eat, finish my coffee, or take a nap.

What about the other thing? The thing you were thinking about before?

I glanced at Black.

You said you wanted to do it more than those other things, Black murmured in my mind. *Did you change your mind?*

As his light pulled at me, his fingers went back to curling around the ends of my hair, pulling through the strands gently to comb it out.

Closing my eyes when another plume of his heat hit my belly, I smiled, taking a bite of the mango parfait I'd just made for myself.

I thought you wanted us to stay out here for a while. Be visible, I sent, swallowing the bigger bite. *You said we needed to be seen by as many people as possible today. You wanted time for the media to come out here... for our photos to start trending on social media.*

All true, he conceded, a faint reluctance in his thoughts. *Even this much is already helping. Larry called me before this,* he added, meaning Lawrence Farraday, the lawyer who handled Black's more "delicate" dealings, both with the public and law enforcement. *He says we're trending on a few gossip sites already. Just my being here's already got a number of them speculating and doubting all the news reports.*

When I turned my head, sighing in the morning sun, he tugged on my hair harder, sending more of his heat flooding into my skin.

Farraday reverse-engineered a New-Agey meditation retreat for us in Patagonia, Black added in my mind. *So the receipts are more or less there. Even Grant seemed pretty convinced the whole thing was a hoax by the time he hung up.*

So what's bothering you? I said lazily scooping up another spoonful of the mango, yogurt and granola. *Isn't that what you wanted?*

Thinking, I added before he could answer,

Is it what I just did? With Charles and the others? Are you worried that will get traced back to you too quickly for the coverup to work?

Black shook his head, his mouth grim.

No. I've been talking to Yarli.

Given I'd left Yarli and Dex less than an hour earlier, and Black had been on the phone with Steele that entire time, I had to assume he'd been talking to Yarli in the Barrier.

It made sense. She *was* the head of Black's infiltration team; he'd talk to her to set up security for us here, if nothing else.

Still, his ability to multi-task always blew my mind a little.

It sounds like they're good, he said, shrugging. *I told them to get the vampires to help, now that Brick and some of his people are on their way up from L.A. The vamps can shield your detainees until we figure out where to move them... or if we need to move them. If we decide to keep them where they are, the vamps can shield them until we get collars on all of them and a stronger construct built over that holding area.*

My shoulders tensed as I turned over his words.

I kept it off my face, and out of my light, nodding.

I still hadn't told Black about Nick.

My husband had no idea Nick Tanaka was in the building at California Street at this very moment, or that Dalejem was with him, or Solonik.

I was definitely waiting on that conversation.

Is it D.C., then? I said, my voice neutral. *Are you worried about how to handle that?*

Black turned, his eyes mostly hidden behind the dark sunglasses he wore.

His perfect, strangely beautiful mouth twisted in a frown.

"You haven't told me anything, you know," he murmured, speaking out loud as he leaned closer, kissing my jaw. "You know that, right? I find it almost cute that you assume I know everything you've been doing... or even who had you all this time."

I blinked at him.

Then, realizing he was right, I frowned.

Thinking a few seconds more, I snorted.

"Are you going to pretend you didn't get on the phone the second I left?" I said, clicking at him faintly as I caressed his jaw. "Because I know you've probably had at least ten conversations already. With Dex, Kiko, Manny. Cowboy... probably Angel. Lawless, Alex—"

He nodded. "And Jax. And Mika. And Brick."

I started.

"Brick?" I stared at him. "You called him? About what?"

He snorted. "About you of course." At my incredulous stare, he snorted again. "Miri, I called every damned person I could think of after you left. If nothing else, I wanted some say in who you pulled out of D.C."

Thinking about that, I nodded.

That made sense.

I'd kind of wondered how Kiko and Dex managed to pull that list together so quickly.

They had at least thirty names by the time I got back with my Uncle Charles' first-chair infiltrator, a female seer named Jalisa.

Every name on the list belonged to a seer prioritized as a key member of Charles' network.

"Let me know if you missed anyone," I told him, rolling my eyes a little.

"Oh I will, sweetheart... I will."

He kissed me again, that time on the mouth.

That time, it was a real kiss.

His fingers tightened in my hair, pulling me into him as he relaxed some of his light, just enough for me to feel how much he'd been holding back. His heat flooded my chest as he let out a low sound, kissing me harder, using his tongue.

I fell into the kiss without thought, and then I was gone, my mind rippling into static as I curled my arms around his neck. The time we'd been apart really hit me, even more so when I realized I had no clear idea of how long it had been.

Weeks. Months.

He let out another heavy sound.

Wait, I thought at him, pulling away. *People are probably recording this.*

He looked up at me, his eyes glassy, shaking his head.

No, he sent. *I let them have their fun for the first few minutes. Then I started pushing them. None of them are looking at us now, doc. They won't look over. Not unless I let them. I can keep them out.*

All of them?

I turned, glancing around us, and realized he was right.

All the tourists who'd been staring at us, taking photos and video with their cellphones, were now either lying back on their sun loungers, eyes closed, or drinking coffee or mimosas, talking to their friends, eating bagels, scrambled eggs, fruit, dipping their legs in the water.

I didn't see a single one of them looking at us.

I didn't see a single phone or camera aimed in our direction.

Black's light pulled on me again, harder, with an urgency and heat that melted my brain all over again.

We can fuck out here... he murmured in my light. His hand

wrapped around my hip, his light pulling on me harder, more insistently. *No one will bother us. We can fuck, then I'll let them notice us again afterwards... it'll be okay. Promise.*

Normally, that idea would have been a hard no.

I wasn't really a have-sex-in-public type, even with my semi-exhibitionist husband.

This time, I hesitated.

Can you control your light? I sent. *Don't we need to be cautious, considering...?*

I trailed, unsure how to finish that sentence.

...do we need to worry about that? I ended finally.

He shook his head.

"No," he said aloud.

"Are you sure?" I said. "How do you know? We haven't exactly experimented with—"

I don't want to wait, he murmured, tugging harder on my light with his. *Please. Please, doc. Don't make me wait until we get a chance to go up to the room...*

When he leaned towards me the next time, I found myself kissing him back.

Then I was in his lap.

I stopped thinking. I stopped thinking about where we were. I stopped caring about who might see us. I stopped caring about anything but Black's breath, his tongue and lips, his hands growing rougher on me, his chest growing warmer as he pulled me down against him. I could maybe blame his light, or mine... or both of ours.

But I'm pretty sure that was bullshit, too.

I just didn't give a damn.

Black and I earned this. We were overdue.

Finding myself in a tropical damned paradise, with my half-naked husband, who I finally had to myself, after what felt like months of stress, fears of him dying, fears of me dying, fears of not being able to get to him in time... not to mention nonstop separation pain and loneliness... I just didn't care anymore, not when it came down to it.

I had no intention of wasting this.

I wasn't wasting this.

I didn't give a damn what anyone thought.

4

MAN VERSUS FOOD

I was still there, in Black's lap, about twenty minutes later, when two waiters walked up to us.

They didn't look at us, either.

Even so, they got close enough to our sun loungers that Black flinched, his body flushing as he pulled back from where he'd been kissing my throat. Removing his hand from inside my bathing suit, he tugged one of the hotel towels up and wrapped it around my ass, even as his eyes checked over my bathing suit, making sure I was more or less covered.

Given that we'd had our hands all over each other for the past however-many minutes, it took me another few seconds to adjust my bikini top and bottom to where I was mostly decent, despite sitting astride my husband's hard-on.

Staring up at me, watching me adjust the suit and then look down at him, that hibiscus flower still behind my ear, Black pressed up against me like he couldn't help himself.

Gaos, he sent. *You were right. We should have gone up to the room.*

Frustration seethed off him.

Maybe we could fuck in the pool, he sent next.

There's a jacuzzi on the deck of our suite, I offered.

He nodded, jaw hard.

I felt his annoyance with himself that he hadn't canceled his order of food, or had it delivered upstairs. I felt his annoyance that he hadn't pushed the waiters into not approaching us, in addition to not looking at us. I felt his hunger mix with his annoyance, mixing with both of our sexual frustration.

Now he wasn't sure what to do.

Just eat, I sent, brushing his hair out of his face and kissing his temple. *We'll go up after. I can go for a swim while you're devouring half of their kitchen.*

He nodded, but I felt that frustration coiling around him still.

His hand still gripped my hip as he watched the waiters.

Polite in that way servers are only at expensive resorts, they'd already begun silently setting up a table next to the one on the other side of Black's chair, laying out all the food Black ordered. Through all of it, they acted as if we weren't there, as if the two of us weren't half-naked and I wasn't sitting on Black's cock in full public view.

Even so, their presence there, so physically close to where we were, was impossible to ignore. It more or less snapped me out of the sex-fog.

I could tell it had done the same to Black.

When he loosened his hold on my hip, I slid off Black's lap, not really thinking about how I left him exposed when I did... not until Black dragged the towel he'd been using to shield me into his lap, and I snorted a laugh.

He gave me a wry smile, but I saw that denser frustration in his gold eyes.

I also saw him push it back with an effort.

He re-donned the mirrored sunglasses, plucking a beer off the smaller table where they'd placed an ice bucket. Sinking back into his sun lounger, he took a long swallow.

I felt the precise instant he lifted the light shield he'd put around the two of us, the one he'd been using to push humans into looking the other way.

I felt the surrounding eyes focus back on him, and on me.

I felt the resentment and jealousy in some of those eyes.

Turning his head, Black grinned that shark's grin of his at me, crossing his ankles and cushioning his head with an arm as I retreated to my own sun lounger. He continued to caress and tug on my fingers while we watched the waiters finish setting up his food.

I wondered, though.

Why didn't Black want to go upstairs?

Even with his light shield, it seemed like we'd been out here long enough, at least for now, especially after his loud conversation with Grant Steele.

Hell, our leaving would likely get us *more* media attention... not less. Especially if Black made a point of why we were leaving, and why he wanted his food brought upstairs.

Didn't Black want to have sex?

It was pretty rare that Black prioritized food over fucking.

He laughed, obviously hearing me, and turned his head, clicking at me.

Waiting for the waiters to leave, he leaned towards me again, wrapping a warm arm around my waist.

Jesus fucking Christ, doc... I want sex, he murmured in my mind, tugging on me with his arm. *I want it badly enough that I'm tempted to just fuck you and let them all watch. Or at least have you give me a hand-job while I eat.*

When I rolled my eyes, clicking back at him, he grinned wider.

Anyway, I thought better of it for now, he added. *I think we should wait. I have plans for us later. I can suck it up until then.*

I gave him a wary look. *Plans?*

Yes. He kissed my mouth. *Very important plans.*

Plans beyond us dismantling Charles' operation embedded in the government?

Far more important plans, he assured me. *Totally different plans.*

When did you have time to make even more plans?

He tilted his head, smiling at me from behind those sunglasses.

I could almost see his gold eyes in my mind.

You were gone a long time, doc, he sent, lifting my hand and kissing it.

I stared at him. I was tempted to laugh.

I also felt a sharp flash of guilt.

As I did, I found myself shielding my mind more tightly, at least the parts of it I couldn't afford to have him overhear, namely the parts about Nick. I knew Black would have liked to know Dalejem was alive, too. I specifically hadn't told him about Dalejem because it would have raised too many questions about Nick.

Maybe I just felt bad because I felt so much openness in Black's light.

Even with his frustration, he felt more open than I'd felt him in months, including in the weeks leading up to when I got abducted at the border.

I don't think he'd even been this open on *Urtre,* when we were staying with his cousin and his cousin's wife, Allie.

So, these plans of yours, I sent, quirking an eyebrow. *They definitely, absolutely, one hundred percent mean we can't go upstairs to the room for a few hours?*

His lips curled into another mocking frown.

Releasing me totally, he leaned in the other direction, swiping the beer he'd grabbed off the low table. The glass bottle was already sweating from the tropical heat, despite its bed of ice. Black took another long drink, swallowing a few times before exhaling and wiping his mouth with his hand.

He grinned at me, popping a French fry into his mouth.

A few hours? he sent, lifting an eyebrow above the shades. *With us?*

You think it'd be more than a few hours? I grunted. *You're cocky.*

Realistic, doc. Not cocky... realistic. We definitely can't be trusted to remember anything after a few hours in a hotel room. Especially given how damned long it's been. If we don't wait, we won't make it—

—To the "plans," I clarified, using air quotes.

Exactly.

I stared at him, caught somewhere between exasperated and amused.

Watching me look at him, he burst out in a laugh.

"You should see your face right now." Leaning to me, he kissed me on the mouth and pulled back, grinning wider. "You don't handle surprises very well, doc. Too bad for you. Especially since I find you wanting to strangle me adorable."

Leaning toward the table again, he picked up the plate with the cheeseburger on it, and pulled it into his lap.

I stared at it, then at the rest of his spread, in disbelief.

"Are you really going to eat all that?" I said.

"Watch me," he grunted, picking up the cheeseburger. "I'll probably lick each and every damned plate. I'd eat it *off* you, if it wouldn't get us both arrested."

I leaned over him, maneuvering around his plate as he took his first big bite of cheeseburger. I laughed when I heard him give a low groan of pleasure, snatching a few French fries and the second beer out of the ice while he complained through his mouthful.

I leaned back on my own sun lounger, taking a long drink of beer.

I popped a few fries in my mouth, glancing over as Black took his second bite of cheeseburger. He was already halfway through the damned thing, and it was enormous.

"Don't make yourself sick," I advised.

"Not possible, sweetheart. In fact, I'm thinking of just using my hands and fists on the rest of this stuff, cram as much of it in my mouth as I can before I choke."

"You sure you're not overcompensating?" I said, quirking an eyebrow and glancing pointedly at his crotch.

"When did I say I *wasn't* overcompensating, doc?" he said. "I'd much rather fuck you while I eat, but again, I'd probably get us both arrested, so that'll have to wait until—"

A voice cut through his, even as he was about to shove the final piece of burger into his mouth.

"Mr. Black?" it said. "Mr. Quentin Rayne Black?"

Both of us looked up.

We squinted into the man's silhouetted form, shadowed and haloed by tropical sun. The man was more or less invisible for those few seconds.

Black took that time to finish up the motion of bringing the last bite of burger to his lips.

He continued to stare up, chewing vigorously as the man above us spoke again.

"...I'm afraid I going to have to ask you to come with me, Mr. Black," the male voice said, its words grim.

⚜

B lack swallowed, frowned, and glanced at me.
      He looked back at the man standing there, who I could now see better, since my eyes had adjusted to the bright light and his face in shadow.

He wore a white suit.

That suit was nothing like what the waiters wore, but I still got the sense he worked here, in some capacity. Maybe it was the cautious, overly-polite way he approached us, or something about how he looked at Black, like he was waiting for his approval to say more.

Whoever he was, he looked like a throwback from another era.

Unlike the neat white uniforms of the waitstaff, with the gold buttons and mandarin collars, his suit was double-breasted with a matching vest, a white starched shirt, and white buttons. His also looked hand-tailored, if roughly forty or fifty years out of style.

He wore it with a white Panama hat with a black band, black dress shoes, a gold Rolex, gold cufflinks that were probably real gold, a black tie.

All in all, despite his dark skin tone, the man's clothing looked like it belonged on the set of some old movie about "The Colonies" featuring women in silk dresses and inappropriate footwear, where all the men smoked hand-rolled cigarettes and fanned themselves with hats just like this one while giving languid speeches about the desperate sameness of it all.

He looked to be in his sixties to me.

His curly, short-cropped hair, what I could see of it, had probably been black once, but now appeared to be almost entirely white. I suspected a bald spot might live under that hat. His face was beaded lightly with sweat despite the spotlessness of his clothes, and his dark, freckled skin looked like it hadn't been kissed much by the sun of late.

I guessed he spent most of his time wearing that hat and sitting under umbrellas.

"I'm extremely sorry to bother you, Mr. Black," the man said, giving a short bow to acknowledge me before looking back to face my husband.

Up until now, he'd spoken quietly, in a way clearly meant for no one to hear but the three of us. But now he stepped even closer, leaning towards Black to speak in a softer voice, almost a murmur, presumably to keep our conversation even more private.

"...but I am told you are a *detective,*" he said, glancing around, as if nervous he might be overheard speaking such an unsavory word. "A most *famous* detective, one who works for a highly select clientele... in addition to your other merits. I was asked to summon you, in a matter of *utmost urgency* to our property."

Black glanced at me, quirking an eyebrow.

I gave a perceptible shrug.

Humor touched his eyes, even as his lips pursed.

Then, breaking out in one of those killer smiles, he looked up.

He made his voice lazy, back into the voice of the rich dilettante.

"Now, who out here..." Black boomed, as the man's face winced in alarm. "...in this idyllic place, would be handing my name around in such a whimsical manner, my good brother? Can't a rich asshole enjoy his wife's company and the chef's bounty in peace?"

I covered my mouth, stifling a laugh.

The man didn't notice.

He glanced around in increasing alarm, lifting a hand as he scanned the pool deck for eavesdroppers. I could tell he was having to bite his tongue to keep from shushing Black.

"...My dear sir, I'm sure you're a credit to this institution," Black continued in the same oblivious voice. "But I've made it perfectly, reasonably, *explicitly* clear, that I, and my lovely wife, are on vacation. We really desire nothing but food, uninterrupted sex, uninterrupted sleep, lubricants of various kinds, a few massage therapists, occasional dips in the pool, a surfing lesson or two... and a modicum of privacy."

Black paused, quirking an eyebrow up at the man.

"If this is about another interview, I've already told the press—"

"Oh, no." The man looked horrified. "No press coverage. No... I apologize for the misunderstanding, Mr. Black. We don't want that *at all*. No, I represent the interests of Mr. Peter Yarrick."

He paused, waiting for the name to sink in.

When he saw a slight frown touch Black's lips, the man added,

"Mr. Yarrick confided in me that the two of you are friends. He asked that you might look into a matter that has arisen for us here, at the Blue Sail Resort... preferably before we are forced to involve the police."

The man took a deeper breath, as if to calm himself.

"He told me to convey to you that he would 'make it worth your while,'" the man added carefully. "He also mentioned he would 'help you with your evening's plans' as part of his compensation to you. He hoped you could attend to it quickly, however, sir, and, really, as quietly as possible."

Nose wrinkling, the man held up a palm, as if squelching an unpleasant sound.

"As you know, *discretion* is just so very important to us here at The Blue Sail, Mr. Black. It is simply *critical* for the safety and well-being of our guests."

Black tilted a look in my direction, one eyebrow cocked.

"Really, now?" he said, adjusting his back on the sun lounger.

"Pete asked for me? And he's offering gifts and promises as compensation?"

"Yes, sir. Well, sir... if I am understanding you correctly, then yes, sir."

The man in the white Panama hat looked absurdly relieved, even as he glanced around the rest of the pool area, obviously unnerved at all the people who continued to stare at me and Black, and now him, since he was talking to us.

"Mr. Yarrick thought you might be generous enough, sir, to do him a favor in this matter. He really would rather if this situation didn't disturb any of our other guests."

Black nodded, taking a few swallows of beer.

"What about all of my food?" Black said, glancing at the laden table next to him. "What are we going to do about that?"

The man in the Panama hat blinked, then turned, staring at the obnoxiously large spread to the right of Black's sun lounger.

After another beat, the man pursed his lips.

"We will of course take care of that, Mr. Black," the man said politely, still staring in obvious shock at the number of plates heaped with food. "I will have the waiters take this away. Fresh food will of course be brought to you immediately, as soon as we are finished, and free of charge." Pausing, he added carefully, "If this... favor... ends up taking some time, we will have food brought to you wherever you are."

He glanced at me, his hazel eyes reflecting nerves.

"...and for your beautiful wife, of course."

Black gave me another sideways look, his eyebrow quirked.

Well? What do you think, doc? Ready to be crime-solvers for a few hours?

I grunted a half-laugh.

It didn't contain a lot of humor.

Black seemed to have made up his mind, though.

Transferring the empty plate, now missing its cheeseburger, from his lap back to the table the waiters set up, Black exhaled, sitting up.

Then, after sitting there a beat too long, he swung his legs and feet gracefully over the edge of the sun lounger, rising fluidly to his full height.

The man in the Panama hat stepped back, a faint look of alarm flashing across his flushed face as all six-foot-five of Black unfolded in front of him.

"Sure thing," Black said, grinning down at his face, his gold eyes hidden behind the expensive, mirrored shades. "Anything for my pal, Petey."

5

A BODY

T he man in the Panama hat led us down a winding path that led to different parts of the resort's private beach.

We passed the main opening out onto the white sand, hanging a left and walking with the ocean to our right. My sandals slapped lightly on volcanic flagstones lined on either side with pineapple bushes, hibiscus, banyan, and palm trees.

I trailed a little ways behind the two of them, retying the gauzy wrap around my waist and keeping a kind of lookout as Black and Panama hat guy talked.

I looked out in the Barrier, too.

The latter included extensive mind-reading of the man now leading us away from the resort and away from the resort's largest beaches. By now I knew he was bringing us northeast, to the resort's smaller, more secluded beach, the one that mostly catered to people wanting to take surfing lessons, rent out aquatic vehicles of various kinds, or go tide pooling.

Black and I both knew by now that Panama hat guy's name was Mr. Fournier.

Beauregard "Bo" Fournier.

He was the manager of the Blue Sail.

I'd already read Fournier enough to be assured that, whatever this was, as far as Fournier knew, it had nothing to do with what was happening in California or Washington D.C. Strangely, and reassuringly, it had nothing to do with *any* of what had happened to me or Black over the past few months.

However bad this thing might end up being, it wasn't about any of that.

It wasn't about Black at all.

As for specifics, all I'd really been able to get out of Fournier was that they'd found someone (possibly some*thing?*) washed up on the beach, something that made Fournier sick when he saw the photo.

Whatever it was precisely, I caught Fournier hoping it wasn't dead.

He didn't want to think about what he would do if it turned out to be dead, or if it brought the resort negative publicity.

Fournier received notice of the possibly-dead thing from one of his employees, who was the one to find it on the beach. Fournier promptly told that employee to hide whatever it was... then, just as promptly, Fournier called Yarrick.

Yarrick told him to go find Black.

From all this, I surmised that Fournier's "dead thing" on the beach belonged more to Black's previous life, as a paid security consultant and P.I., not the life we'd been living the past few years.

Frowning as I clicked out of the deeper of my three scans into the man's mind, I shifted my attention back to my immediate surroundings, right as I heard Fournier telling Black about the exact thing I'd just been reading from his mind.

"—a body," Fournier said, his voice low.

He shook his head with a whisper of drama, scrunching his lips in dismay.

"...It is unheard of here, Mr. Black. Simply unheard of."

He glanced over his shoulder at me.

"Dr. Fox," he added politely. "I'm glad you are with us as well. I am told you are an expert in these matters. That you worked for the police, prior to partnering with your husband in his organization."

I smiled, a little surprised he got my name right.

These days, most people just called me Mrs. Black.

Fournier's serious look shifted to Black, his full lips still curled delicately in disgust.

"We simply cannot have the Blue Sail known as a place where *death* occurs," Fournier said. "Those types of associations, once they enter the public mind, they just *never go away,* you understand. Mr. Yarrick thought you might be able to do something... to declare this an accident, to find information indicating that the death occurred *somewhere else.* That it has absolutely *nothing to do with* our resort. Preferably before we are forced to involve the police—"

"You haven't called the police?" I said.

He flinched, then looked over his shoulder at me.

He hunkered down as he did so, like he was afraid I might hit him.

Granted, it was pretty clear from my tone I didn't approve.

He peered at me that way for a second, then looked away, still hunched.

"We did not," he said, a little defensively. "I was asked to handle this—"

"Discreetly," Black boomed, clapping him on the back and making the human jump about a foot. "Yeah. We know. But dead bodies..." Again, Black boomed the words. "...have a way of being conspicuous, Bo."

The man flinched a second time, blinking up at him.

I could tell from his expression he was trying to remember if he'd ever told us his name, much less the nickname only his close friends and family used. I watched him scan his memory of our conversation thus far. I watched him trying to decide if Peter Yarrick would have told Black his nickname, and if so, why.

In the end, Bo Fournier let it go.

He never stopped peering up periodically at Black, however, a wary look in his hazel eyes. Although Fournier had to be around five-foot-ten, he moved like a much smaller man.

"Yes, well," Fournier said, his lips firming. "With all due respect to both of you," he said, giving me another brief stare over the shoulder. "I do as I'm told. I was asked to have you look at this first. Mr. Yarrick wished to have some idea of what to expect, once the Honolulu authorities arrived. Also..."

Mr. Fournier lowered his voice to a whisper.

"There are... abnormalities."

"With the body?" Black boomed helpfully.

Fournier winced, grimacing delicately.

"Yes."

I frowned. Abnormalities?

I opened my mouth, about to ask, when Black's mind rose in mine.

He doesn't know. He wouldn't go near the body himself... he's blood-phobic.

Fournier spoke into the silence, even as I absorbed Black's thoughts.

"Keon, our boatman, found it," he said, again firming his lips in faint disgust. "He seemed to think there was something... unusual. Mr. Yarrick spoke to Keon directly about this, but I did not."

Black gave me another look, quirking an eyebrow.

I quirked my eyebrow back.

Are you getting any specifics? I asked him. *Any idea what he means?*

He sent me a plume of heat.

You know it still turns me on when you do that... speak to me in my mind, he murmured back. *Clearly, you don't do it nearly enough.*

Except I do it all the time, I retorted, amused in spite of myself.

Not nearly enough, doc. Not even close.

Really? I sent. *You're going to flirt with me now? When we're going down to look at a dead body?*

Black shrugged, giving me an over-the-shoulder wink. *Given how our lives generally go, doc, I figure there's no time like the present. I need to soften you up so I can seduce you later.*

I rolled my eyes at him, snorting a little, and he smiled, reaching his arm and hand back long enough to trail his fingers over my bare arm.

For a few seconds, it almost worked.

Then, thinking, realizing he'd been changing the subject again, I looked up at him, frowning.

Did you really not find anything about the body? I sent. *Or is it a secret?*

He laughed, out loud that time, making Fournier jump.

Just then, the path twisted around a last curve.

The view opened out onto a white sand beach.

It looked completely empty, stretching all the way towards a gentle green slope of steep mountain in the distance. The beach appeared to end where the mountain and its outcropping towards the ocean began.

Suddenly, the ocean seemed to surround us.

The sand dunes, pineapple bushes, palm trees, and hibiscus must have done a surprisingly good job shielding the sound of the ocean waves, since that sound got immediately louder.

I gazed out over that stretch of rolling waves with their perfect curls and white crests, noting the jetty of rocks that reached out from this end of the beach, the black volcano stone somehow making the water appear an even brighter and clearer blue.

My eyes returned to the mountain, following the beach as the island curved around, meeting the steep slope covered in jungle green where it stood out from the water, creating a sheltered cove. It was strange to see such a beautiful beach so entirely deserted. I couldn't see anyone at all, apart from a few surfers in black and neon wetsuits in the distance, surfing the waves nearer to the other end of the cove.

"This way," Fournier muttered, checking his watch nervously and glancing up and down the beach, as if expecting a stampede of rich guests at any minute. "We moved it inside, so no one would happen upon it accidentally—"

"You moved the body?" I said, having a harder time sounding polite.

Fournier turned all the way around that time, blinking at me.

He didn't look apologetic so much as startled, as if he couldn't imagine why anyone would question either his right or his need to do this.

"Of course," he said.

"You've tampered with a potential crime scene," I said, gritting my teeth. "You know that's against the law, surely—?"

Black grinned, slinging his arm around Fournier, making the shorter man in the white suit and the Panama hat flinch again.

"My wife," Black said, his eyes and voice genuinely affectionate as he looked at me. "Once a cop, always a cop."

"I was never a cop," I reminded him.

"You were *basically* a cop," he said, undaunted. "You were cop light. An honorary enforcer. Awash in proximity to cop-world. You worked for them. Your office was next door to theirs. Your coffee shop was *their* coffee shop. Hell, your two best friends..."

He trailed.

For the first time, I saw a real frown touch his lips.

Trying to head off what I saw there, knowing it was about Nick, I snorted.

"I don't need to be a cop to know it's against the law to tamper with a potential crime scene, Quentin," I reminded him. "Especially for an unreported crime. Especially when it's an unreported, potential *murder*."

Seeing the panic rise in Fournier's face might have been funny in other circumstances.

As it was, I responded to it with a level stare.

"See?" Black said, clapping Fournier on the back as he recovered his smile. "She's unable to shed her cop brain. They imprinted on her when she was young and impressionable, like a baby duck... turning my darling wife into an extension of the long arm of the law."

He grinned at me, winking.

"It's sexy as hell, don't you think? I might have to get her to handcuff me later. We all know I've been a very bad man. With any number of unpunished crimes..."

He sent a curl of heat so intense, I jumped, my cheeks and neck flushing hot.

The flickers of pain, longing, and sheer liquid sexuality I felt behind that pulse made me wonder if he was entirely kidding.

Not kidding at all doc, he murmured.

"...She's also not wrong, Bo," Black said, turning back to Fournier and making his voice serious. "I get the wanting to avoid having one of your starlets stumble onto a rotting corpse and scream their bloody head off... but the cops are going to be wagging some stern fingers in your direction for screwing with their crime scene."

"M-M-Mister Yarrick," Fournier stammered, his face reddening likely more than mine. "He instructed me—"

"I get it, friend. I get it. You were following orders. But the cops, see, they might not care. Technically speaking, you're here and Petey isn't—"

"But Mr. Yarrick—"

Black clapped him on the back, making Fournier choke on his own words.

"Worry not, dear Bo. We'll cross that bridge when we come to it," Black said.

Fournier slid out from under Black's arm, nearly stumbling in the soft sand.

"It's just up here," he said, fighting back his composure as he fumbled a set of keys out of his pocket. "Please. Both of you. This will only take a minute... then you can perhaps advise Mr. Yarrick on what we should do next."

Fournier proceeded to stumble towards a man and a blue-painted structure a few dozen yards away, walking in a zig-zagging path, his footsteps heavy in the dry sand. Pausing before following him, Black turned, his lips tilting in a faint smirk.

You're a bad man, I told him.

Only sometimes, he sent, caressing my cheek with his fingers.

Snorting a little, even as I shivered from his touch, I turned to follow Fournier to the light blue building.

The boathouse stood on a rise over the main stretch of beach.

In front of it stood the man I'd noticed before, a significantly younger man than Fournier, wearing a white linen shirt and cargo shorts. He paced in front of the building, directly in front of its red-painted door, watching the three of us approach like he'd been waiting for us for a long time already.

He had long black hair, and while I was far from an expert, he looked even more Hawaiian to me than Fournier, as in, someone who was born here, who had indigenous blood. That, or he might have more generic Pacific Islander heritage, or some combination of that and Japanese, since any number of similar combinations were common in the islands.

He looked relieved as we got closer to him, and I could see his expression.

He looked openly relieved we were there.

Checking his large, waterproof-looking watch, he looked up and down the beach, then up at the rising sun, as if envisioning the same beach full of people. He was clearly as nervous as Fournier about tourists showing up before we'd dealt with whatever it was he'd hidden away in that boathouse.

Once we were close enough that he could talk to us without shouting over the sound of the waves, he blurted out words, like he'd been restraining himself up until then.

"Thank God you're here," he said, looking straight at me, then at Black.

He was handsome.

He also looked even more like a local up close, with his dark brown eyes, tanned skin, broad nose, tribal tats—the real kind—a coral necklace, and faintly sunburned cheeks. He looked about as much like a surfer as anyone I'd ever seen.

Well, apart from Nick maybe.

I felt Black wince, then stare at me.

Even with him wearing the mirrored shades, I could practically feel his eyes boring into my face.

I shielded my mind without thought, flushing.

Gaos. I had to be more careful.

I couldn't afford to have Black picking up my stray thoughts on that subject, not now, not until I'd decided the best way to tell him.

Thinking about Nick, about him hanging out at the building on California Street, guarded only by my wolfhound puppy, and Dalejem, and possibly Angel by now, just gave me anxiety stomach. I winced a second time as the thought echoed, keeping my eyes off Black with an effort, keeping my surface thoughts utterly blank.

Whatever I'd told Angel and Cowboy, Dex or one of the seers could stumble in on him at any minute. Once they did, there was a damned good chance they'd try to kill him, regardless of my orders. Regardless of what I'd told Angel to tell them.

They'd also tell Black.

At the very *least,* they'd tell Black.

They'd tell him, and it was a damned good bet they'd leave out the part about Nick and Dalejem saving my life in Russia.

They'd conveniently forget to tell Black it was Nick's idea to come rescue me, and that Nick nearly died, trying to save me and Jem. They wouldn't add that Nick risked running into Black himself in the process, who he knew would kill him on sight.

They'd skip right over the fact that Nick knew he'd be facing everyone's wrath by coming back to San Francisco, and that he'd done it anyway.

They'd most assuredly skip mentioning *my* take on things.

They'd skip the part where I was pretty sure Dalejem was in love with him, too.

More than anything, they'd leave out the part where Nick was *Nick* again.

They'd blow right past that... assuming they bothered talking to Nick at all.

Black wouldn't want to hear any of that stuff, anyway.

Black wouldn't want to see Nick, much less talk to him.

Once Black knew, I was ninety percent certain he'd just tell Dex to deal with the problem with a foot-long piece of sharpened wood.

That, or a broadsword to the neck.

Thinking about that, I tightened the shield around my mind.

"...I wasn't sure if I should call someone," the boatman was saying, pulling my mind and eyes back to him. He looked at me, his dark eyes worried, wringing his muscular hands, speaking in nearly a mutter. "I really thought maybe I should call someone—"

"Did you?" Fournier cut in, his voice alarmed. "Call someone? Besides me? Besides Mr. Yarrick?"

The boatman looked at him. "No."

Fournier looked almost comically relieved.

"Why?" I said, turning back to the boatman. "You found the body, didn't you? Why would you suddenly need to—"

But the man was already shaking his head.

"It's *doing* something," he said darkly, hooking a thumb towards the shed. "It's bad enough when it was just a dead body, man. Now, it's like... doing things."

"Doing things?" Black stared at him, his rich, drunk guy schtick forgotten. "It's a body. What the fuck could it be doing?"

The boatman only shook his head.

"It's better if I show you, man," he said. "It's just better if I show you."

His face still scrunched in worry, he turned on his heel, aiming for the red door. Moving fast over the soft sand, he trod lightly on his tanned, broad feet, without looking back to see if we were following. His long black hair flopped on his head as he walked.

Black and I exchanged another look.

Then Black shrugged.

Stepping forward on the sand, he followed the boatman.

I followed Black.

Wringing his hands and muttering about things needing attending to back at the main resort, Fournier followed me.

6

STOP DOING THAT

I entered the interior of the boathouse, glancing back as Fournier shut the door behind us.

It was darker than I expected.

I blinked, letting my eyes adjust.

Once I could see clearly, I found I understood the lack of light, at least in part.

The building, meant to open out onto the beach on one side, was completely closed up, with no windows save one. That high window faced west, so away from the morning sun, and was crusted with salt and sand, taking up only a few feet of space below the flat ceiling and above a workbench at the back of the boathouse.

Right now, it also provided most of the interior illumination.

For reasons unknown, the boatman hadn't turned on any of the lights.

Other than the window, I could see only a faint blinking of blue light near the floor, what looked like the light from some electronic device: a monitor, a phone, maybe even a digital clock, if it was big enough.

I glanced towards the sliding doors to my right, and saw a

padlock on them, next to a combination pad that might have been for an alarm.

I didn't know why he hadn't turned on the lights.

I didn't know why he hadn't opened the sliding door yet, either, if it was because the boathouse wasn't technically open yet, given it was only around eight in the morning, or because he was hiding a dead body in here.

I suspected the latter.

Well, I suspected it more than I suspected the former.

"Is there a light?" Black said, obviously wondering the same as me.

The boatman acted like he hadn't heard him.

He looked so wound up and distracted, maybe he hadn't.

"I need to get him out of here, man," he muttered, shifting his weight from foot to foot and motioning towards a segment of cement floor on the other side of a row of brightly-painted kayaks.

I noticed it was the same segment of floor with the flashing glow of blue light.

"...I can't have this, man," Keon the boatman continued. "I can't have this in my space. I've got a whole group coming here at, like, nine o'clock. I'm supposed to take them on a trip up the coast. I can't even get the equipment ready, not with that there."

I saw Black frown.

He gave me another swift glance, then both of us walked closer to Keon the boatman, and in the general direction of the flashing blue light. Stepping around Keon on either side, we walked towards that same segment of cement floor past him, where he'd been gesturing and where he continued to stare down, shifting his weight from foot to sandaled foot.

I could already see something on that piece of floor.

Something apart from the blue glow, I mean.

A dark bundle lay there.

Paler swaths stood out on the dark heap, what I soon recognized as skin.

I realized suddenly that the blue light was coming from him, too.

He had to be wearing some kind of tech. Something around his head or neck was blinking and flashing with what I now saw was pale blue and pale green light. I saw flashes of orange and white, and even red, but the predominant colors were those pale greens and blues, making the space around him almost otherworldly.

The brighter colors had been muted by the angle of the body, particularly the head and shoulders. The face was nearly straight down on the cement, which is why I hadn't realized just how much light was coming off him until we got around the row of kayaks.

Most of the body was covered in soaking wet black cloth.

The feet were covered in what looked like combat-style boots.

Those lighter patches of exposed skin I'd noticed before lived primarily on his upper body: his face, the back of the neck, his hands, and two thick and very muscular-looking arms. His upper body was covered only in a black T-shirt, like something one of Black's team wore as part of their day-to-day working uniform.

He really looked like he could be one of Black's.

He looked like a soldier.

That, or a military contractor.

He looked like a Navy Seal, one who'd drowned in some kind of combat mission.

Now that I was closer, I could see what Keon had been talking about, too, when he said the body was "doing something." I'd assumed he meant the lights coming off whatever tech the corpse was wearing, but the body itself wasn't totally still. In addition to those strange, pale blue and green lights, the body was twitching, vibrating, jerking on the cement floor.

He seemed to be twitching and vibrating more violently as I watched.

Those eerie, ghostlike lights continued to blink and scroll dimly on that part of the floor, clearly coming from something by his face, but even up close, I couldn't see the headset.

Still, everything about this screamed organic tech.

I'd never seen standard tech that could project images like that, creating what was, in effect, a full-blown computer screen for the headset's wearer.

The headsets Black's team wore could do that, but this guy wasn't one of ours.

If he was, I didn't know him.

Could he be a seer? I murmured in Black's mind, glancing at him. *One of Charles'?*

Black was frowning down at the body, too.

I don't think so, he sent. *I think he's human.*

I glanced at him, frowning. *How do you know?*

Black gave me a sideways look, a bare glance.

I can smell him, he admitted after a pause. Before I could respond, or even give him a look, he added, *Don't ask. It's a new thing, doc.*

New? I sent. *New, as in, new since—*

Yeah, he sent, cutting me off. *New since that.*

I frowned, fighting to incorporate that into everything else.

So he... smells human. To you.

Yes. Black gave me a faint frown. *Gaos. It's not that weird. I didn't turn into a vampire or anything. I've always had that weird smell thing. I told you that. It's just... stronger now. I can smell a lot more.*

I nodded, still frowning faintly.

He *had* told me that.

Still, this was a whole new level of "weird smell thing," if he could now ID humans and seers by species, solely by how they smelled, and from ten feet away.

There was a silence where Black and I only stared at the body.

Then Black gave me another sideways glance.

I distinctly got the impression he was self-conscious about what he'd confessed about the smell-thing. When I returned his look, however, nothing showed on his face.

Without speaking, he resumed walking towards the body, moving as silently as a cat. I realized only then that he was still barefoot. He didn't even wear the thin leather sandals I wore. He'd come down here in the form-fitting black bathing suit and sunglasses and nothing else.

He reached the side of the dead body in a few strides.

Crouching liquidly next to it, he cocked his head, and I found myself wondering, not for the first time, if I was the only one who noticed how damned strangely he moved. If anything, he moved even more strangely now. I was used to it, of course, but I couldn't help tensing when he fell out of his "human suit" with outsiders present.

I watched him stare down at the body.

He reached for the chin of the corpse, turning it slightly towards him, and those blue and green lights grew brighter, illuminating Black's face, as well as the face of the corpse.

I noticed for the first time that Black had removed his sunglasses. His gold irises shone strangely bright in the blue light, looking almost silver.

He peered into the man's face, frowning.

Then he raised a hand to that face.

I watched in disbelief as Black seemed to start poking at one of the corpse's eyes.

Hey, I said, sharp, in his mind. *Don't do that.*

He stopped, looking up.

Why not?

I frowned. *Because it's gross?*

He flashed me a smile, his teeth shining in the blue light.

I'll wash my hands, doc, he sent. *Promise. Anyway, not much choice. Somehow I didn't think to bring crime scene gloves with me from the hotel room—*

—and then there's that, I sent, folding my arms. *Crime scene, Black. Remember? It's not like you haven't been told a million times. It's not like Angel or—*

I cut myself off.

—or Angel wouldn't have your head for what you're doing right now, I continued, managing to talk over Nick's name with barely a stumble. *You shouldn't be touching him. You definitely shouldn't be touching him*

with your bare hand. You have no idea how he died. He could have a damned disease for all you know. He could have been poisoned.

Black didn't answer me that time.

If he noticed my stumble over Nick's name, it didn't show on his face.

Still poking the corpse's face lightly with one finger, seemingly right smack in the middle of the man's eyeball, he frowned, as if something about the eyeball bugged him.

I had to bite my tongue, watching him do that.

I folded my arms, trying to keep the grimace off my face.

It took most of my already-frayed willpower to not smack his hand away.

At minimum, I really wanted to yell at him.

Black finally stopped poking the dead body, but he never took his eyes off whatever he was looking at in the corpse soldier's eye.

"Doc?" he said. "I need you to look at this."

I scowled.

After the barest hesitation, I walked up to him, my leather sandals slapping on the concrete floor. They sounded weirdly loud after how quietly Black crossed the same distance.

"I'm not poking that," I muttered under my breath.

"You don't have to poke anything. Promise."

I glanced at Keon and Fournier, remembering they were watching and listening to all of this. They were still keeping a healthy distance, hanging out just behind the row of kayaks. They were talking between them, barely paying attention to us, their voices quiet. I saw Keon gesturing widely, obviously upset.

They were talking too softly for me to hear any specifics.

I considered reading them, but watched them instead.

Fournier obviously didn't like whatever Keon was saying.

Keon noticed me looking at them then, and fell silent. Fournier's eyes followed his, and both of them stared at me, the whites of their eyes weirdly visible in the dim light.

It's not about us, doc, Black told me.

I returned my gaze to Black.

He gave me a pointed look. *You don't have to worry. They're not whispering about your weird, alien husband poking corpses like a lunatic... not yet, anyway.*

I fought the impulse to click at him.

Then I fought the impulse to laugh.

So what is it, then? I sent. *What are they freaking out about?*

Black gave me another swift look.

Keon wants to call the cops, he sent, matter-of-fact. *He's worried about getting in trouble for moving the body. He's worried about being accused of hiding evidence. Fournier keeps telling him he'll protect him, that Yarrick will protect him, but Keon's not buying it... and I can't really blame him. Fournier's the one pushing to keep this whole thing quiet, not Yarrick. Fournier's worried about losing guests if this gets out.*

Will he? I sent, crouching down next to Black. *Lose guests?*

Black shrugged, still staring at the corpse's face.

Could go either way, doc. Celebs and rich people are weird. They're also perpetually bored. They might decide this is "interesting" and come to stay with their friends just so they can gossip about it. I suspect that's the more likely scenario.

He motioned towards the corpse.

I don't recognize the guy. He shrugged with one hand, seer-fashion. *I don't just mean in terms of the military... I mean at all. He's a nobody. That puts his murder more in the "interesting" than alarming category. It would only freak them out if he was one of theirs.*

One of theirs? I sent. *You mean another rich guy?*

Yeah. Black gave me a grim look. *Someone rich. Someone famous. One of the chosen ones.*

I thought about that.

It made sense.

It was also irritating. It reminded me why I'd hated our time in New York so much, surrounded by those self-appointed "chosen ones" and their parasitic entourages.

Rising back to my feet from the crouch, I walked around the body and joined Black nearer to the man's head, so I could get a better look at the eyes.

For a few seconds, I only stood there, staring down at the display on the floor.

The lights coming off the corpse were brighter from here, without the man's shoulder or the cement floor muting the effects, or even Black blocking them from my view. I could see the display better from that angle, as well—well enough to confirm the projected lights definitely weren't random. I studied the lines and patterns, the scrolling characters and numbers. I saw what looked like maps, possibly schematics.

It looked like the reflection from a monitor.

It had to be some kind of next-gen, organic headset.

I still couldn't see the headset, so it must be wrapped around the ear pressed into the boathouse floor.

I was still squinting down at the display when I saw photos flash on the floor.

Most of those appeared to be of people, specifically of peoples' faces.

A fair-few looked official, as in mugshots, arrest photos, even government and other IDs. A few depicted groups of people, including what looked like official police line-ups, like the kind used for witnesses to identify individuals from a group of suspects.

Other photos looked far more informal.

Those mostly depicted people in couples or in groups.

Some appeared to be professionally-done portraits.

Some looked like military IDs, mixed in with casual shots at bases and in training camps. I saw men and women in different branch uniforms, driving or riding in vehicles, piloting air transport, using different types of equipment. In the background, I glimpsed beaches, jungles, desert terrain, mountains.

It all went by too fast for me to track much specifically, much less get a lock on faces. I thought I saw a few that looked familiar, but I couldn't scan them quickly enough be sure.

Then one face flashed by I definitely recognized.

I knew it so well, I flinched.

It looked almost exactly like—

Hey, I sent to Black, pointing at where the photograph had been. *Did you see that, just now? Was that—?*

Black talked abruptly over me.

"—I need you to tell me what I'm looking at, doc," he said, giving me a warning look. "Can you come down here? I need your doc's eyes."

Heeding the warning there, I cut off my thoughts.

"Sure." Stepping closer, I blinked at the green and blue lights, holding up a hand as they seemed to be growing brighter again. "Can you shut that off first? Whatever it is?"

Black gave me a faintly disbelieving look, then grunted.

"I would if I could, doc," he said only.

Frowning at the vagueness I heard behind that answer, I crouched down by Black, staring at the green and blue lines as they hit the cement floor.

Before I could bend down to get a real look, Black glanced at me.

"Wait," he said. "I'm going to move him. So we can both get a better look."

I shook my head. "That's not a good idea, Black. The crime scene—"

"—Has already been tampered with," Black reminded me. "Me turning him over isn't going to do shit, doc. Not after they dragged him up off the sand and over the painted cement floor and scraped on and off God knows how many pieces of evidence from the sand, the floor and whatever else."

Something in his tone and eyes still verged on a warning.

He'd also lost every trace of the drunk-acting, rich-douchebag, playboy voice.

Something about the body was really bothering him.

Studying the tautness of his expression, I nodded.

"Okay."

"Move back." He motioned me to take a few steps back. "It's probably better if only one of us touches him. It's the least we can do for the Honolulu police."

I nodded. I straightened from my crouch in one motion, step-ping back.

I watched as Black hesitated, staring at the body again, as if trying to decide the best way to manipulate the limbs and torso without disturbing the corpse unnecessarily. I was maybe three feet back when Black gripped the man's broad shoulders, one in each hand, and began to ease him to one side, pulling his left shoulder up and towards him.

The instant he did, the light flashed up, widening to splash across the ceiling.

Unobstructed, it seemed to grow brighter.

"His face," Black muttered. "Can you see it? There's something weird about it."

I frowned, looking at the man's features for the first time.

White male, maybe in his late-twenties. Brown hair. Square jaw. Squarish face. Clean shaven. Hard to tell eye color in the blue light, but I didn't see anything weird about him, really. If anything, he looked bizarrely normal, almost a textbook "military man," like he'd been cast for the role in a Hollywood movie.

I was about to say as much to Black, when the virtual display flashed brighter.

It morphed as I watched.

The stream of faces and photographs dimmed and receded, transforming into a secondary and smaller screen, a scrolling feed running in the background. Replacing the prominence of the photos, a brighter, three-dimensional sphere rotated into the fore-ground, taking up most of the space about a foot from the man's face.

Seeing an image of a globe taking shape, I blinked.

The globe morphed, showing more detail, a topographical map with lines for longitude and latitude. More lines appeared, the faint outline of nation-state borders and ocean territories, lines depicting shipping lanes, major currents in the ocean, wind speeds and directions, clouds, weather, storms.

The detail blew my mind as it continued to unfold, until the globe abruptly exploded in size, expanding into the dark space of the boat house.

The globe continued to rotate until a bright red dot grew visible.

The rotation came to an abrupt stop.

The virtual monitor zoomed in on that dot, increasing the size of the globe yet again, even as the edges faded into darkness, growing indistinct.

Noting the outline of the Hawaiian island chain, I realized the red dot was indicating where we were... as in us, as in right now.

"Some kind of homing device?" I muttered.

"Has to be."

"So that means someone must be receiving this," I said. "Presumably whoever he works for. Right?" At Black's silence, I glanced at him. "Is that what you're worried about? You think someone is on their way here? Military maybe?"

Black looked at me.

Now that he was out of the circle of blue-green light, the gold in his eyes was visible again, faintly reflecting the dim light from the boathouse window. I noted that his perfect mouth remained grim, harder than usual.

"You're kind of brushing past the main issue here, aren't you, doc?" he said.

Frowning, I looked at him.

"Which is what?" I said. "The guy's face? He looks like a G.I. Joe doll, Black."

"That was my point. About his face." Seeing me about to open my mouth, he cut me off, his voice darker, "...It also isn't what I meant, doc."

I stared at him blankly.

Exhaling, clicking under his breath, Black went back to manipulating the body.

Now he was carefully pulling the rest of the body all the way towards him, from its side all the way to its back, so it was aligned with the head. Once he had it more or less flat on its back, he set the arms down carefully on either side of the muscular torso, which looked like it belonged to a weight-lifter—or, more likely, a Marine.

Through all of it, Black handled the guy less like he was worried about damaging the crime scene and more like he worried the body might explode.

"The thought crossed my mind," Black muttered.

I frowned again.

"What did you mean?" I said. "What's the important thing about this I'm missing? If it's not the G.I. Joe thing, then what is it?"

The light coming from the dead body was growing brighter again, bringing my eyes back to his face, which looked ghostly white under all those blue and green lines.

Once I refocused on that blank face, on the empty stare up at the ceiling, it clicked.

I knew what Black was going to say.

I knew what I'd missed.

Black said it out loud, anyway.

"Where's the light coming from, doc?" Black glanced at me, still in a crouch, his arms resting on his thighs. "Any ideas?"

I couldn't tear my eyes off that pale, dead-eyed stare.

He wasn't wearing a headset.

There was nothing in either of his ears, or at the front of his neck, the only other place I'd seen my uncle's headsets rest. The light wasn't coming from his uniform, or from anything else he was wearing. He might wear an organic implant, that didn't explain all this light.

Now that I was looking for it, the answer was obvious.

His irises were lit up from within.

The projection of that massive, detailed, rotating, green-lit globe, the scrolling numbers, the occasional flash of schematics, photographs, the more cryptic symbols and lines—none of it came from any kind of tech I'd ever seen, nothing remotely like the organic machines I'd used or seen used by others, whether my uncle's people or Black's.

I'd never seen anything like this before.

And compared to just about anyone, I'd seen a *lot,* including experimental tech, both from my uncle and from Black's databases.

I remembered Black's fascination and unease with the guy's eyes.

It made a lot more sense now.

"Contact lenses?" I said, frowning.

Black shook his head. "Not wearing any."

I turned, staring at him. "Seriously?"

"Seriously." Black nodded towards the body. "Anyway, do you really think contacts could do that? Jesus, Miri. The headsets we have back at the Raptor's Nest don't have the capability to stream and crunch that much data... certainly not that quickly. I've never seen anything like that in Defense Department specs."

"So... what?" I frowned, looking at Black. "You're saying he's enhanced in some way? Cybernetic?"

Black grinned, waving his fingers at me individually.

"Woooooo..." he said. "Maybe it's an *alien,* doc. A real one!"

Before I could roll my eyes at him, another voice interrupted.

"I do not find this quipping amusing," Fournier said, his voice sharp. "Is this a military issue of some kind? Or not? And how would we confirm that?"

Apparently, Fournier had gotten over his fear of Black.

That, or a few minutes of bullying his employee revived his courage.

"What is it we should do?" Fournier went on, at me and Black's silence. "Am I correct in thinking this is some form of experimental technology? Something more in the..." Fournier cleared his throat. "...military purview? As opposed to that of the police?"

I had to admit, he had a good point.

I understood now, why Yarrick wanted Black to check this out before he called up the Honolulu police. From the little bit Black told me about Yarrick, he was some kind of tech genius. He rubbed elbows with Black at tech conventions, ones that also tended to host military contractors of various kinds, not to mention representatives from the Pentagon and the Department of Defense. Yarrick primarily knew Black in that context, as a military contractor—not as a P.I., or even as a Wall Street type.

If this dead soldier was wearing some form of experimental military tech and drowned while out on a mission... or if the tech itself killed him, through some kind of short or other malfunction... then we probably should call the military first, not the Honolulu P.D.

Given where we were, it wasn't such a crazy idea.

A good chunk of Oahu, the island, was military.

Hawaii housed the headquarters of the United States Pacific Command (USPACOM), comprising Army, Navy, Marine Corps and Air Force service components. Those headquarters lived here, on Oahu. Even the Coast Guard had a large presence here.

Whatever this was, it was a good bet USPACOM would have the answers.

That, or Schofield, the army base located more in the center of the island, or even Pearl Harbor-Hickam, the jointly operated Air Force and Naval Base.

When I looked at Black, I could see in his eyes he agreed with me.

After a beat, he glanced at Fournier.

"Okay," he said. "I'll make a few calls." He paused, then added, "I don't have my phone. I'll need to do it from the resort. Is your guy Keon here okay with keeping an eye on the body for a little while longer? You may have to close the boathouse for the day."

At the panicked look on Keon's face, Black raised a hand.

"Maybe rent some kayaks from a nearby resort. Find a way to transport your clients there. Or reschedule. Or refund their money. I'm sure you can find some way to keep them happy. After all... you're doing your duty, right? To your country? And your boss?"

By the end, Black was looking only at Fournier.

Fournier seemed to get the message.

Frowning, he glanced at Keon, then back at Black.

After a pause where he seemed to be thinking, he darted his eyes back towards Keon, his mouth curled in a scowl.

"Well?" he said. "You heard him. Call Bethal Bay. See if we can rent or purchase a sufficient number of kayaks for the day. Then call the concierge and see about getting limousine rides to and from the resort. We can offer then champagne on the ride back, as well."

Keon's expression cleared as his boss talked.

"Okay. Got it." He hesitated, his eyes darting to the body on the cement, which was still emitting blue-green light out of both eyes. "What about that thing? Should I hide it? Throw a tarp over it?"

"Don't do anything to it," Black said, making a negative gesture with one hand. "Leave it alone."

The motion of his hand was a seer gesture, and both humans followed it with their eyes, mesmerized by the graceful motion.

Black didn't seem to notice.

"Don't do a damned thing to the actual body," he reiterated. "Don't cover it. Don't go near it. For fuck's sake, don't touch it. In fact, maybe just lock it in here. Keep anyone from coming inside. Even other employees. Tell anyone who asks this building is strictly off-limits, by order of the owner."

Keon paled.

Still pale, he glanced at Fournier, as if looking for verification.

After a bare pause, Fournier nodded, his head jerking up and down sharply.

He looked annoyed now, although if it was because he heard the truth of Black's words or because Black was ordering his employee around, I had no idea.

I also didn't care.

"Do as he says," Fournier said, sounding as annoyed as he looked.

Black had already turned away, pretty much the instant he felt Fournier going along with him.

Looking at me, he motioned towards the door with his head. He didn't wait but walked around the two of them, moving purposefully now, in more of his military gait than the lazy stride he'd adopted on the way down here.

Hesitating a bare instant, I glanced back at the body.

Something about leaving it here, with Keon, made me nervous.

I didn't know what I was nervous about exactly, but the feeling lingered.

I was still standing there when Black nudged me with his mind.

Come on, doc, he murmured. *We need to get on this.*

I knew he was right.

We had our own reasons for needing to know what this was.

It couldn't only be me who wondered if this was purely a coincidence, this dead robot-soldier thing showing up here, at this resort, on this beach.

I wasn't a huge believer in coincidences.

My jaw hardening, I turned, following Black towards the one and only door leading to the beach. As I did, I found myself remembering the one photo I'd seen in the soldier's internal database, the one that looked so much like—

Black's mind rose in mine.

It was Nick, he growled, his thoughts openly annoyed. *I saw it too, Miri.*

Feeling the blood drain from my face, I glanced at him,

I immediately shuttered my reactions, shunting them off to the back of my mind.

That was still a topic for another day.

Not today. Not now.

Black opened the boathouse door, and sunlight flooded into my face and eyes, making me throw up a hand. The light still wasn't all that bright, given it was relatively early still, but after the near pitch-darkness of the boathouse, it was nearly blinding.

The humidity was already making the wrap stick to my skin, creating a sheen of sweat on my face, neck, and upper chest.

Gazing out over the shocking blue waters of the protected stretch of beach, the clear sky with only a smattering of pure white clouds, I couldn't help grumbling a bit in my mind.

I mean, seriously.

We were in Hawaii, for fuck's sake.

This was supposed to be our *down* time.

This was supposed to be our vacation.

Why couldn't we get a damned break? Just once?

Glancing at me, Black reached for my hand, squeezing it warmly in his fingers. When I met his gold eyes, I saw a whisper of pain there, both separation and the other kind.

We needed to talk.

We really needed to talk.

We really needed time alone, just me and Black.

Still looking at me, still holding my hand, he used his free hand to pull the mirrored sunglasses out of the pockets of his shorts. Winking at me, he gave me a faint, tired smile as he shoved them back on to cover his flecked gold eyes.

I felt him agree with me, though.

I felt him agree with every single fiber of his being.

7

VETOED

I followed Black back up to our suite.

He was on the phone with Dex in minutes.

I found myself sitting on one of the deck chairs of our terrace, drinking cappuccino I ordered from room service, and flipping through a brochure I'd found on a credenza in our suite. I was surprised to find there was another pool on the roof. I'd assumed Yarrick's apartments were the highest part of the building, but apparently, above him, there was a pool deck and bar, along with a raised jacuzzi for star watchers.

I wondered if Black and I should go up there tonight.

Assuming we didn't have to deal with any of this shit.

I contemplated our own jacuzzi as Black paced in the room behind me, his new phone held up to his ear.

He occasionally walked out to the terrace to update me.

After some back and forth between him and Dex, then him and Manny, then him and Kiko, and then him and Alex Holmes, Black offered to be the one to call USPACOM, given that he had a few contacts there.

That made me nervous.

It made me really nervous.

It made me so nervous, I ended up taking the phone away from him, and more or less arguing with him about what a terrible idea that was, and moreover, that I forbade him from doing it, at least until we knew more about his status with the government.

I told him to call Dex back, have Alex Holmes make the call.

Or Lawless.

Or Manny. Manny was fine.

I threatened to call Dex myself, if Black wouldn't.

I think that's the first time I'd ever done that, vetoed one of Black's decisions outright.

Despite Black's startled look, I didn't back down.

I repeated... okay, shouted... that I wasn't okay with him making the call. I argued that having Alex do it made a lot more sense, anyway. Alexander Holmes was the son of Colonel Harrison Hamilton Holmes III. He knew a lot of the same people as Black, and he wasn't a wanted *terrorist* as far as we knew.

Holmes the younger was the logical choice.

Truthfully, though, I would have been happy with *anyone* making the call other than Black. As far as I was concerned, Cowboy, Dex, Angel, Kiko, Yarli... any one of them would be better candidates to call the military command center than Black.

I was nervous enough about him getting picked up.

I was worried the only reason they hadn't picked Black up yet was that the whole administration was in chaos from what I'd done the night before. They'd just had a bunch of people mysteriously disappear, both from the Pentagon and from various political positions around the United States.

We might be in the eye of the storm.

Hell, it wasn't even *just* about missing seers.

Yarli and her people were dismantling Charles' construct even now.

I'd already noticed a difference in the Barrier space, and I was about as far away from Washington D.C. as I could be, while still being in the United States.

For me, that difference was nothing but a relief.

For humans working directly under Charles' control, it would be more of a mixed bag. Even for those humans who'd instinctively hated the construct, the radical change would still take some getting used to. It would be disorienting as hell to lose the whole framework they'd been operating under for months.

Yarli made it pretty clear her people would take a distinct pleasure in smashing that fucking thing, so I knew they wouldn't waste any time.

With most of my uncle's high-ranked infiltrators unconscious under the building on California Street in San Francisco, they wouldn't meet much resistance, either.

And yes, while I would do nothing but cheer with that thing gone, my uncle's construct coming down would leave big chunks of the country massively confused. There was the government, of course, which he'd been controlling directly. There were also militia groups operating across the country, starting riots in cities across the United States, who'd been more or less under my uncle's direct control, too.

Then there were the scattered military officials, politicians in Congress, Cabinet members, judges, bureaucrats, department heads, various state actors. There were people in the media, people on Wall Street, heads of corporations, lobbyists, even just ordinary citizens in some of the cities where there'd been big riots.

The list was long.

The seers on our team were actively ripping apart all of it.

They were breaking the psychic links connecting all of those people.

They were dismantling the mind-controlling structures my uncle had been using to control the United States government and a good chunk of its people for the past however-many months. There was bound to be confusion. There was bound to be chaos, without that unifying mental structure, holding all of them together.

I didn't want Black anywhere near any of it.

I'd only taken my uncle out of commission a few *hours* ago.

Sure, with my uncle out of the way, Black could probably use his seer abilities to push his way out of the worst repercussions he might face with the human authorities… but I wasn't really up to risking that right now.

Feeling my nerves, even past my yelling at him, Black backed down, fast.

He called Dex, told him he'd reconsidered.

He agreed it was probably better if Alex Holmes made the call, not him.

I listened to the two of them talk, feeling something deep in my gut start to relax.

I could feel it relax the longer I heard Black and Dex talk.

When he finally hung up, looking at me cautiously, I felt almost like myself again.

"Okay?" he said, his voice careful.

I nodded. "Okay. Thank you. Thank you, Black."

My voice came out strangely formal.

Given my screaming of a few minutes earlier, I'm sure I sounded ridiculous.

Black only grinned.

Gliding up and twisting his way out of the chair he'd been sitting in while he talked to Dex, he reached me in a few strides, still only wearing black swimming trunks, sunglasses, and now a matte black watch, which he'd snapped on when he was first on the phone with Dex. The watch looked expensive, and good on him, but still strange; I'd only ever seen him wear his military watch, the one Holmes senior had given him.

He coiled his arms around me, pulling me up against his warm, bare skin.

"You worried about me again?" he murmured, kissing my face.

I folded my arms, looking up at him.

At my flat, unsmiling expression, he laughed.

I grumbled, "You don't have to enjoy it so much."

He kissed my mouth, but too briefly.

"Anyway, you're probably right," he said, raising his head. "It's better if we don't push our luck with the military right now."

Grunting, he added,

"Speaking of which, I should probably agree to do the inter-view with Grant. Or someone, anyway. It's better if our showing up here hits the media in a real way before the government decides to do something about it. It'll make them a whole lot more cautious... it will also make them look silly if I'm laughing about being called a dragon in television interviews. They don't like looking silly. Which is kind of the point."

I nodded, frowning a little as I stared out the open glass doors to our terrace.

I was hungry again. I wondered if we could get Black's food sent up here, now that we were no longer by the pool.

Black nudged me, squeezing me tighter in his arms.

"Dex said he'll call back," he offered. "As soon as Alex gets off the phone with whoever he manages to contact... they'll call us. Tell us what the deal is, if we need to back out of this and let the police handle it, or what."

"Is he going to tell them we're already involved?" I said. "Is Alex going to tell whoever he talks to that you're here?"

"Dex said he'd keep our names out of it, if he could," Black said, sending me a pulse of reassurance. "He'll use Yarrick as the contact. And Fournier."

I fought to relax again, still feeling a dense anxiety in my gut.

Tugging me tighter against him, he stroked my bare back above the wrap tied around my waist. His heat started coiling into me, pulling on me, tugging at my light, coaxing me into him.

"Of course," he added, shrugging, clearing his voice. "We might need to leave this resort, if they come here. I'd probably have to push Yarrick and Fournier if we did that, make them forget involving us."

His voice grew more cautious as he studied my face.

"If we can, though, I'd prefer to stay, doc. Just suck it up and play dumb... let them question me if they want, but threaten them with lawyers and whatever else if they start screwing with us for real. I'll call Steele back this afternoon, offer him that interview if he'll let us do it from here. Have Yarli back me up with her infiltrators to make sure I can push them into letting me go as soon as they check the cover story Farraday set up for us down in Patagonia."

I nodded, biting my lip.

I was staring out the window again, though.

Something was bothering me.

It was making it hard to listen to him, to think about the implications of his words.

It was even making it hard to think about the military coming here.

"Hey." Black shook me a little. "What? What is it?"

I looked up at him.

Frowning, I held out my hand. "Can I have your phone?" Thinking, I amended my words. "Never mind. I'll use the hotel phone."

He looked openly puzzled now, but released me without question, and also without moving very far back. Folding his arms, he watched me, lips pursed, as I crossed the room to the resort phone sitting on a table under a mirror near the credenza where I got the brochure.

Black continued to watch, and listen, as I put the phone to my ear, hitting "o" for the building operator.

"Yeah," I said, when a pleasant female voice answered. "I need to speak to Mr. Fournier. Is he available?"

The woman on the line fell silent briefly.

"Do you mean Mr. Beauregard Fournier? Our manager?"

"Yes," I said, equally polite. "May I speak to him, please? It's urgent."

In my mind's eye, I saw her checking where I was calling from.

I felt the slight jump in her living light when she realized I was calling from the honeymoon suite, and that we were listed as special friends of the owner, Peter Yarrick.

"One moment please," she said, her voice noticeably more solicitous. "I will connect you to his cell phone, now."

"Thank you so much," I said, mirroring her tone.

When I glanced at Black, he was frowning, his eyes openly puzzled.

He walked towards me when I didn't speak.

Once close enough, he started poking me with his fingers, which felt both playful and semi-serious.

What's happening, doc? he murmured in my mind, still poking my sides, his fingers insistent, holding a faint jolt of light. *Why so mysterious, doc? What aren't you telling me, doc?* Why *aren't you telling me? Huh? Huh?*

I held my hand over the receiver, answering him aloud for some reason.

"I think they need to get away from the body," I told him, my voice quiet. "I want Fournier to call Keon and tell him to get out of that boathouse."

Black's eyes flinched.

His playfulness fell away, leaving him serious, his mind stripped.

"Did you feel something?" he said. "What did you feel?"

Just then, the phone on the other end picked up.

I hadn't even heard it ring.

"This is Mr. Fournier," the crisp voice said. "May I help you?"

"Hi," I said. "This is Miriam Black... Dr. Fox."

"Ah! Hello, Dr. Fox! Was your husband able to—"

"Yes," I cut in. "He has someone working on it right now. But in the meantime, we need you to call your employee, Keon. Tell him to get out of the boathouse. It's better if all of you stay out of there. Keep everyone else at least a few hundred yards away from it, too. Until we can have someone remove the body."

There was a silence.

In it, I had to bite my lip to avoid snapping at him.

I really wanted to tell him to move his ass.

"May I ask why, Dr. Fox?" Fournier said politely.

"Good fucking question," Black muttered from next to me.

I gave him a flickering glance, then focused back on the phone.

Realizing cryptic might work better with someone like Fournier, I kept my voice polite, but firm.

"It's better if you don't," I told him. "...Ask, that is. Please, just let Keon know. As soon as possible. Now, really. Right now. He needs to be at least a hundred feet from—"

Before I could finish, an explosion cut off my words.

BOYS WILL BE BOYS

I heard the explosion over the phone.

It was loud.

Loud enough I winced, jerking the phone from my ear.

I realized Fournier must still be outside, and somewhere on the beach.

My eyes darted to Black, then past him, through the open terrace doors.

Black was already looking that way.

Once I glimpsed his face, it hit me that Black hadn't heard the explosion through the phone, but through the open glass sliding doors. A beat later, I realized I'd heard the sound out there too, if quieter and a lot further away.

Realizing that gave me a much better idea of the size of the explosion.

That was kind of the good and the bad news.

I mean, it wasn't a *small* explosion, but it did seem localized to the private beach where we'd been earlier. It hadn't come from the resort itself. It hadn't touched any of the resort buildings, or any part of the crowded restaurants or pool areas.

It was still big enough to vibrate the glass of the doors and windows, even up here on the upper floor of the resort. I saw them shimmer, giving the illusion of my vision blurring as my eyes fought to adjust.

It was big enough that others definitely heard it, all over the resort.

Meaning people other than me and Black.

I even heard a few screams, but they were screams of surprise, not pain.

I heard voices rising following those scattered yells and screams, people talking excitedly from the poolside area, audible through the open sliding doors. The gauzy curtains fluttered in a light breeze, one that seemed to carry the voices inside, distinctly enough, I could even make out words here and there.

I could tell most of those guests were far more excited than scared.

In other words, it was a good-sized, dramatic-sounding explosion... but compared to the explosions Black and I had been dealing with lately, it wasn't much. It wasn't anything like the missiles we'd experienced in the California desert by the border, for example.

It wasn't anything like the missile that nearly killed me.

It wasn't much louder than the Russian grenades we'd used in Moscow.

The rumble echoed through the valley and its surrounding bay, but the sound had already mostly died by the time my eyes made it to the blue sky beyond our white-painted balcony.

I saw a small column of black smoke.

I looked at Black.

Then I put the phone back to my ear.

"Fournier?" I said, sharp. "Fournier! Bo! Are you there?"

A breathless voice rose in the receiver.

I immediately exhaled in relief.

"Y-Y-Yes," he said. "I'm here. I'm here..."

"Was that the boathouse?"

"Yes." He took another series of deep breaths, and I could see him nodding in the darkness behind my eyes, his free hand, the one not holding the phone, balancing his upper body on his thigh. "Yes... it was the boathouse. It's on fire. Half of it is gone. There's Fiberglas everywhere. Wood. The beach is covered with—"

"Keon?" I cut in. "What about Keon?" My voice was still louder than usual, maybe to counteract his panting breaths. "Was he inside?"

"N-N-No." Fournier cleared his throat, coughed. "No. He's with me. He's all right. We were watching the door from here when you called—"

"Oh, thank God." I felt my shoulders slump in relief. "I'm so glad."

I looked at Black, clutching the phone to my ear, but he was snapping his fingers now, frowning, asking me with his eyes to hand it over.

"Black wants to speak with you," I said.

I handed the phone over without waiting for Fournier to answer.

Black's message to the resort manager was curt.

"Call security," he said. "Private resort security only. Have them guard the site of the explosion. Tell them to cordon off the whole area."

I heard Fournier's voice rise, like he was trying to interrupt, or maybe like he asked Black something. Whatever it was, Black's response was equally sharp.

"You need to get up here," he said. "Now. Back to the resort. You need to calm everyone down, Fournier. And for fuck's sake... don't tell any of the guests what you saw in that boathouse. Tell them it was a gas explosion, a faulty gas tank that got ignited, a canister for a speedboat or whatever the hell you and Keon can come up with as a cover story in the five minutes it takes you to walk back up here..."

Black gave me a grim look, even as his voice lowered to a growl.

"...just whatever you do, don't fucking tell them a dead body *exploded* in your goddamned boathouse."

I couldn't hear Fournier's answer.

I have my doubts I could even hear his voice, not with my ears.

I could definitely feel Fournier's relief at Black's words, not to mention his utter and complete agreement with Black about the cover story.

"Keon can direct the security people," Black added. "Tell him the same. And get your ass up here. You're the only one who can calm everything down up here. Miri and I will go to the lobby. We can at least talk to some of the staff..."

Fournier must have broken in to say something.

Black shifted his head and neck, cradling the phone's earpiece between his shoulder and ear as he listened. I watched him stalk over to the closet, open the mirrored doors and tug a shirt off a hanger.

Still listening to Fournier, he pulled the dark gold and green shirt around his shoulders, shoving one arm into a sleeve at a time and letting it hang open over his chest. That whole time, he kept the phone receiver jammed right up against his ear.

"Yeah, okay," Black said. There was a pause while he listened, frowning. "Okay," he said. "I understand. Go ahead and call them. I'll contact my people too, let them know to modify the message when they speak to central command..."

He trailed.

Again, he seemed to be listening.

I could tell from his face that he was distracted now, though.

Even as I thought it, Black motioned with his head to get my attention as he began buttoning up his shirt. Using his light, he pinged me towards the closet, as well, following his head with a slight frown and another jerk of his chin.

Realizing he wanted me to get dressed, too, I sighed.

Black had dropped his drunken rich-boy persona entirely.

Given that, and the sudden need for us to be wearing clothes, even if they were still vacation clothes, I had a feeling I knew exactly who Fournier was about to call.

We were about to get a visit from Peter Yarrick, Black's tech genius pal.

Yarrick would be forced to act on this.

He owned the resort.

He couldn't afford to play oblivious about the body any longer.

Well, unless Black pushed him, and basically *forced* him to.

I strongly suspected Black wasn't going to do that, though.

Black had already more or less told me he wanted to get this side of things over with. He wanted to jump through the military's hoops, convince them he was just an ordinary person, that he had nothing to do with what happened at the California-Mexico border.

That meant we were probably going to get a visit from someone in a uniform in not too long a time... possibly a whole lot of someones in a whole lot of different uniforms... none of whom I had any desire to see.

৩১১

We stood next to a marble lobby fountain downstairs when Peter Yarrick breezed through one of the revolving doors that led to the parking circle out in front of the resort's main lobby.

I wouldn't have known it was him, but I happened to be standing right by Fournier.

"He's here," the resort manager murmured.

Before I could turn, Fournier straightened his shoulders, his eyes locked on the front doors as he left my side to greet his boss in person.

I watched the small, Hawaiian-looking man cross the clay-tiled floor with light taps of his Italian shoes. Fournier reached Yarrick even before the doormen who speedily intercepted Yarrick to take four or five shopping bags out of his hands.

Everything the billionaire had been carrying disappeared in a flash, leaving his hands free and open. I was quite sure those bags were already on their way up the elevators to the penthouse floor, just above the suite where Black and I were staying, and just below the pool I'd been hoping to lure Black up to that night.

Yarrick himself barely seemed to notice.

That's what it was to be rich, I'd learned.

Everything in your life just got magically taken care of.

I continued to study Yarrick's face after he'd released everything he'd been carrying into eager hands, without bothering to look at who was taking it from him.

Yarrick barely even spared a glance at Fournier.

Instead, the tech prodigy remained focused on Black.

He grinned at my husband even as he cocked his head towards Fournier, who started talking the instant he was close enough to Yarrick to not be overheard.

Still head-cocked and listening, pausing in his casual walk towards us, Yarrick held up a hand to both me and Black, more or less asking us to give him a minute.

I used that minute to assess Peter Yarrick in earnest.

He was younger than I'd expected.

His sharp, light-brown eyes never left the two of us. I saw that shrewd gaze flicker in my direction, appraise me swiftly, note my appraisal of him, all while he listened to whatever Fournier murmured rapidly into his ear.

The longer I looked at him, the more I realized everything about Peter Yarrick surprised me.

At the same time, I had to think a few seconds, about why that was, as I hadn't consciously imagined him as someone different.

Still, certain assumptions must have been baked into my subconscious. I frowned, thinking about what those were, and what I'd expected him to be.

Older, definitely. That was the easiest thing.

I'd expected someone more like Ben Frasier, Black's billionaire buddy in New York, or maybe a slightly younger version of that, someone more active, into extreme sports but still in their late forties and edging into a midlife crisis. Someone like one of the Wall Street wonder boys we met while we were in Manhattan, the more tech-y, data-oriented set.

While a handful of those guys had been young, especially the more tech-focused ones, most of the *really* rich people I'd met in New York had been at least in their forties.

Most were in their fifties or higher.

Peter Yarrick looked about twenty-five years old.

I doubted he *was* that, but he looked it.

It was honestly hard to tell; he had one of those agelessly boyish faces, and he dressed like an overgrown kid. Despite being relatively tall, he was also a scarecrow, with a body that reminded me of my high school boyfriend, who was all elbows and knees and other sharp bones.

Hey, Black sent. *No thinking about ex-boyfriends.*

I snorted, glancing at him.

He's thirty-four, Black informed me. *But yeah, he's crazy young. A mere pup.*

I snorted at that, too.

Black was already grinning at Yarrick though, walking forward and holding out a hand once he saw his friend disentangle himself from Fournier's anxious murmurs.

"Mr. Quentin Black!" Yarrick surprised me again, by having a loud, booming voice, and an English accent. "Have you sobered up yet, from your crazy yachting excursion? The one where you felt the need to toss all of your worldly belongings into the ocean?"

Black gave him a mock-offended look.

"What makes you think I was drunk?" he said.

"I didn't say *drunk,*" Yarrick corrected, winking at me as he enveloped Black in a hug, clapping him roughly on the back and shaking him.

"...I was thinking it sounded like your Patagonia trek had left you in the midst of an intense psychic crisis, old boy... perhaps even unaccountable *ennui*. I envisioned that you'd filled yourself up on painkillers and bourbon, and decided to leave the emptiness of a consumeristic existence behind you... after having your life changed by your personal shaman 'Rudy,' or 'Dharma Gosa,' or whatever the fuck his name was..."

Yarrick's voice remained dry as he pulled back, grinning up at Black's face.

"I had visions of you reaching a kind of decadent, post-bourgeois enlightenment... like a few bags of fortune cookies scrambled in your brain, only with a lot more target shooting at seagulls. As a part of that, I imagined you deciding at four in the morning, your mind loaded on prescription drugs and ethanol, your pupils swallowing those disturbing, piss-yellow eyes of yours, to give up all your worldly possessions. I imagined you then deciding to chuck it all in the sea. Really, I was just relieved you didn't decide to chuck yourself overboard, as well..."

Black snorted openly at that.

"If only I had that kind of integrity, Pete. If only."

I elbowed him, hard, and Black mock-gasped, holding his side in mock-pain, even as he coiled his arm warmly around my back and waist.

Yarrick grinned wider, stepping back to aim that smile at both of us. "You finding the suite okay? Is it to your liking?"

He looked at me that time.

"It's wonderful," I said sincerely. "And incredibly generous. Thank you."

Yarrick's smile widened, just before he glanced at Black, hooking a thumb in my direction.

"This is the poor suffering creature I've heard so much about?" he said. "The ephemeral Mrs. Black?" Winking at me, he added, "We had a pool, you know, on how soon his hypnotism of you would wear off. We figured he must have kidnapped and brainwashed you, to get you to agree to spend more than a single, horror-filled weekend with him—"

"Doctor," Black muttered, stepping back so I could shake Yarrick's offered hand.

Black said it quietly, but Yarrick heard him.

Not only that, he immediately understood.

"Ah." Yarrick's lips firmed, that shrewd look rising back to his light-brown eyes as he looked me over again. He stared at me as if he were filing the information away in some kind of organic vault locked inside his brain cells.

"Not Missus. Doctor. Yes, of course... I see."

"She mostly goes by her maiden name, too," Black added. "We haven't argued that one out yet."

Yarrick chuckled, giving Black a sideways look as he released my hand.

"No wonder you married her," he commented, aiming his smile back at me. "Is this the first person who hasn't let you bully them into total capitulation, Black?"

"Not the *first*," Black said, quirking an eyebrow at me.

I harrumphed at that, too.

Black elbowed me back that time, and I smacked his arm.

Looking back at Yarrick, I smiled. "Thanks again for the suite. And for the last minute reservation. I can't take him anywhere..."

Yarrick laughed louder at that.

"Did he *really* dump all of his belongings overboard?"

I shrugged. "Yes. Mine too... apparently he was taking that whole 'the two become one' thing a little too literally."

Glancing up at Black, I quirked an eyebrow.

"Hallucinogens and Quentin don't mix," I added, straight-faced, looking back at Yarrick. "At least in Peru, the Ayahuasca sessions were supervised. He probably would have thrown *me* overboard too, in his quest to 'streamline his life'... if I hadn't been downstairs, asleep."

Yarrick let out a startled belly-laugh.

Black turned his gold eyes on me, but I only raised my eyebrow higher.

"It's probably good he didn't," I added. "For him, too. He'd given me the keys to the boat for 'safekeeping' before he ate the last of our stash... including a bag full of psilocybin mushrooms. Too bad he didn't also give me his wallet. Or his phone. Or *my* phone—"

Yarrick laughed again, gripping my arm in a friendly way.

He looked at Black, his expression delighted.

"Seriously? You were *tripping?* I was totally kidding, by the way."

Black shrugged, giving me a sideways smile, quirking an eyebrow.

"Yeah, well," he said. "They always told me I didn't have the right temperament for those things. But you know how I am... I required experiential proof."

Yarrick laughed again, looking at me.

"I hope you took his guns away, at least," he said, giving Black a sideways grin.

I sighed. "Oh yeah. After he threatened to shoot our guide while we were canoeing on Inútil Bay, the guns all went back to San Francisco. He was convinced the guy was trying to turn him to the dark side... he was disturbingly specific as to how."

Again, Yarrick belted out one of those deep, belly laughs.

Black's arm slid further around my waist. He squeezed my hip warmly in one hand.

Oh, game on, baby, he sent, low. *Game on.*

I don't know what you mean, I sent back innocently.

I can make up some screwed-up stories too, doc. I can be very creative, in case you forgot. Very creative. Just wait.

I'm helping, I told him primly. *You said you wanted distracting stories, right? And a good excuse for us missing all the news? Why not a few ayahuasca benders in the Andes? You said we were supposed to be on a "retreat," right?*

Black grinned wider, aiming it at Yarrick.

"My wife," he said, jerking his chin towards me, even as he yanked me closer to his body with his arm. "Light of my life..."

Yarrick let out another delighted laugh.

Then I saw his face change.

I watched the light in his eyes and face alter as he remembered what brought him here. The young, boyish smile faded, that sharper look returning to his light-brown eyes.

"So what happened here?" he said. "Can we talk somewhere?"

Black nodded. "Of course. Up in your room?"

"I was thinking we'd walk down to the site. Multi-task." Yarrick glanced at Fournier, who was standing more or less at our elbow, looking markedly more relaxed, now that his boss was here. "Fournier tells me the area is cordoned off. He also says there hasn't been any guest bleed. Not so far anyway. So I think we'll be okay talking on the way."

Black glanced at me.

I could almost feel his thoughts, even though he didn't reach out with his light, or speak into my mind that time.

He was wondering who Yarrick had called.

Both of us were wondering who'd called who, and when.

I could feel Black specifically wondering who might be arriving here at any minute, to check out the scene. Not only would that disrupt Fournier's story about the gas leak... they'd see Black.

They'd see me.

In addition to my fears about Black, neither of us had any idea how much of *me* they'd gotten on surveillance the night before.

However much they'd gotten, it might be too much. Our people hadn't had time to do clean-up work to that degree, not yet. No cover story had appeared on the news, no government officials had come forward to declare the whole thing a hoax.

I wondered how Yarrick might react if a military extraction team burst down the doors of his five-star resort, looking to bring both of us forcibly into custody.

I wondered if Yarrick's celebrity guests would handle that in the same blasé fashion they'd handled the story of a faulty gas cannister causing an explosion at the boathouse.

I didn't voice any of that aloud, of course.

Neither did Black.

"Lead the way," he murmured to Yarrick, still gripping me around the waist.

Giving me a fleeting look, he gripped my waist tighter as we moved out of the way, letting Yarrick, and then Fournier, lead us to the other end of the lobby.

9

WORD GAMES

No one waited for us by the smoking remains of the boathouse.

I felt a ripple of relief off Black, along with a denser pulse of puzzlement.

I knew he'd be on the phone already, if he could be.

If Yarrick and Fournier weren't there with us, he'd be talking to Dex, and to Alexander Holmes, trying to find out what the hell was going on with the military, why they hadn't come here yet, swarmed over the beach with their bomb squad and squint-types, trying to figure out what happened, and if the dead soldier had been one of theirs.

I've been talking to Yarli, he murmured in my mind. *She says they've been called off. Not by our people.*

I frowned, giving him a sideways glance.

I wanted to ask.

For now, with Yarrick with us, I should probably keep my mind here.

I looked out over the beach, grimacing at the black pieces dotting the white sand, most of them smoldering, a few actually on fire.

The smell of plastic and Plexiglas filled my nose, but I could also smell other, more subtle smells below that. Smells that struck me as meatier.

Not quite food smells, but definitely along the lines of cooked flesh.

My eyes found Keon, who stood a little way away from us, smoking what looked like a hand-rolled joint. He was clearly decompressing, leaning against a palm tree, talking to two of the security guards who'd walked down here with us.

My eyes scaled up that tree briefly, in spite of myself.

I felt strangely protective of the young-looking Keon.

I didn't think too closely about why, or who he reminded me of, if only in a sideways, indirect way, possibly only because he was obviously a surfer and had a surfer's body. In any case, I found myself scanning that palm tree for coconuts, worried he might get brained by one while he stood there, recovering from the shock of nearly being blown up.

A few yards from Keon, Fournier was speaking into his phone.

He looked paler than I remembered, even now that Yarrick had taken over the situation. I watched Bo Fournier stare out over the mess of the beach, patting his own forehead with a white handkerchief he swiped under the brim of his Panama hat.

It was getting close to noon, and the temperature had risen.

I felt the tropical humidity thing now.

I was also feeling my night of zero sleep, what was going on days of zero sleep, of near death, of too many jumps... and the fact that I was starving.

I needed food. I needed sleep... or at least caffeine.

I was definitely getting weird.

But that wasn't why I was frowning.

I suspected it wasn't why Black was frowning, either.

Where the hell was the military? Why weren't they here?

If Yarli and Alex Holmes hadn't called them off, then who had?

As if he'd read our minds, or maybe just our facial expressions, Yarrick clapped Black on the shoulder, his voice reassuring.

"I spoke to your friends at USPACOM," he said. "They're sending a crew down tonight."

I flinched.

Black did too, from where he stood next to me.

Yarrick seemed to pick up on our reactions. I saw his scrutiny tighten as he looked between our two faces.

"...I asked them to be discreet," he added.

That didn't really clear anything up.

Why would the military be willing to leave an incident scene for twelve-plus hours, all on the request of some rich kid who happened to own a beachside resort?

Their forensics team would know the potential for scene-contamination.

Hell, the passage of that many hours would degrade the scene even if no one went near it. Wind, waves, debris washing out to sea, the salt air, all of that would affect their ability to assess what happened with any accuracy. The still-burning fires might give them additional clues about the incendiary materials used, not to mention the type of bomb mechanism.

Unless they already knew those things.

Unless soldier-robot-boy was one of theirs, and they knew why the explosion occurred, how it occurred, and who or what triggered it.

Even if that were all true, it was still strange.

If it was experimental tech, wouldn't they want to remove all evidence before the wrong person stumbled upon it, photographed it, stole pieces of it, or just started asking questions?

More to the point, who was Yarrick, that he could keep a military investigation at bay, when it might jeopardize national security? What possible reason could they have for going along with him?

My ex-military, used-to-work-with-cops brain rebelled against all of it.

Yarrick spoke up again.

Again, it was almost as if he'd heard some portion of my thoughts.

"I'm doing more military contracting since we last spoke, old boy," he said, giving Black a sideways smile. "I'm stomping in your playground pretty frequently these days, in fact. If you'd been more active with your own contracts since the old man died, you'd know that."

Black blinked.

Something in his expression told me Yarrick's words genuinely surprised him.

Yarrick was still talking.

"...I managed to use what leverage I have, plus my unparalleled charm." Yarrick widened that boyish grin. "I convinced them to call off the dogs for now. I had them talk to your people too, of course. And that lawyer friend of yours from New York, Mr. Farraday. They got your itinerary for the past few months, and that seemed to calm them down. They'll still want to talk to you, of course, but they agreed to postpone that end of things."

Looking between us, Yarrick quirked an eyebrow.

"I also *may* have told them I wished to persuade you and your lovely wife to help with the investigation on our end," the young-looking billionaire added. "They were fine with that, incidentally. In fact, they jumped at the possibility of having you assess the scene before they could get down here in numbers tonight. They know you're familiar with evidence protocols, and will keep the integrity of the scene. They plan on sending someone to help you with that... just to cover their asses, I suspect. Assuming you agree to work for me—"

"Someone?" Black interrupted. "Who?"

Yarrick shrugged.

I got the impression he found the detail irrelevant.

"Someone with a tech background, presumably, and sufficient security clearance, so they might assess whether this thing Keon and Fournier found belonged to them."

Yarrick glanced over at Fournier, signaling something to him as he finished.

Whatever he signaled, Fournier seemed to understand.

Nodding, the manager began walking to Keon and the other resort employees.

Yarrick turned his eyes back to us.

"The Honolulu police will send someone too, I suspect," he added. "I was told the military plans to involve them, as well. As a professional courtesy, if nothing else. But I wouldn't expect to see them until tomorrow."

Black and I exchanged looks.

Yarrick hesitated, looking between us, clearly attempting to gauge our reactions.

"I confess, my reasons for wanting you involved are purely selfish, old boy," Yarrick added, putting on designer sunglasses over his eyes after squinting up at the sun. "I really want someone to represent *my* interests in this, Black. They understood that. They just want your cooperation. And if you do any investigating of your own, they were hoping you'd check in with them on what you find... share any information you come up with."

They were hoping Black would check in? my mind muttered. *The military was "hoping" Black would agree to cooperate?*

Who was this Peter Yarrick, exactly?

Black gave me a darting glance.

Yarrick was watching both of our faces, though.

Seeing something in Black's, Pete smiled.

"Sorry if I spoke too freely for you, old chap," he said, giving an apologetic shrug. "Nothing's written in stone. I told them I hadn't talked to you yet. I was just telling them my own thoughts on how to organize things."

Still studying our faces, Yarrick added,

"I'd sure appreciate it, though. And I'd pay you, of course. Your usual rates, plus twenty percent? For each of you?"

He paused a second time, motioning between me and Black.

"...And, of course, everything here at the resort is on the

house. For you and your wife. Including any boats or other equipment you want to rent, horses for riding, scuba trips or other
excursions... anything run out of the Blue Sail. I figure that's fair
enough. I know dealing with law enforcement was never your
thing, Black."

I fought a grunt at that, managing to suppress it into a cough.

Yarrick glanced at me, almost like he knew, but he kept his
poker face.

"Also," he said, rubbing the back of his neck, keeping his voice
studiously light. "And forgive me for saying it... but I figured you
could use the good publicity right now. Helping the military and
the police to solve a strange crime. Doing a solid for an old friend.
It's practically screaming for a feel-good afternoon special. Well,
minus the exploding soldiers."

Yarrick smiled, aiming half of it at me.

"Given the crazy headlines of the last few weeks, I thought
perhaps a bit of mind-numbing normality might be welcome.
Remind people who you are. What you do for a living."

Peter hesitated, then went on in an even more careful voice.

"I read about all that... the nonsense being said in the papers
about you. I figured maybe you stepping back into the ring like
this, it could help. Bonus that we could spin it as a job for the military. That gives you all the *God n' Country* crap to make people love
you even more. Convince the crazies to look for a new target for
their mad conspiracy theories."

Black hid his frown.

Well, he hid it from his face.

I felt it, standing so close to him, even if I couldn't see it. I saw
the barest hint of scrutiny in his gold eyes, a faint tightening of his
lips.

When he spoke, aiming his words at Yarrick, his voice had
gone back to indolent rich-guy, despite the slight edge I heard
underneath.

"Of course, Petey," he said. "Of course. Happy to do it, buddy.
Especially after you bailed us out with the yacht thing."

Pausing more deliberately, he added, his voice as light as Yarrick's,

"I guess I'm just confused. Is this *only* a favor you're throwing my way? Not that I'm complaining, but—"

"What do you mean?" Yarrick said.

Staring at the other man for a beat, Black smiled.

Glancing at me, then back at the boyish-faced billionaire, he smiled wider.

"What do I mean? Come on, Pete."

Black's voice was still rich-guy voice, but with some of the disingenuousness dropped. If Yarrick had been a seer, Black would have clicked at him.

"You've got your own security team here at the resort," Black said. "Knowing you, they're good. Better than good. Anyway, you can't possibly believe this was some kind of hit on you, or on your resort—"

"I'm not hiring Black the security consultant," Yarrick said, his voice warning. "I'm hiring Quentin Black, Private Investigator. I'm hiring the *detective.*"

"To do what?" Black said. "If the military's already claimed jurisdiction over the body, or bomb, or whatever it was, what's the point of hiring me? You think I'd have a chance in hell of figuring out what this was before they do?"

Black seemed to weigh his friend's silence before adding,

"If they just want me and the wife to bag up evidence before the scene gets corrupted, well, fine." Black shrugged. "But you're overpaying, Petey. By a lot. I imagine you could hire a few local forensics specialists to do that for half of what I charge—"

"None that I trust," Yarrick cut in.

Black frowned. He continued to study his friend's eyes, in a way that told me he was probably reading Yarrick.

"Why?" Black said after a beat. "No offense, but why would you need someone you trust *that* much? From everything you've said, I gather the thing washing up here was just a coincidence, right? Clearly, it's pricked someone's ears at USPACOM, or they wouldn't be sending a team under cover of darkness. Just as clearly, the military wants to own this... ahead of the Honolulu police. But what's the connection to you?"

Pausing, Black winked at him, giving me a sideways look.

"You trying to pull me into something, buddy? Some contract you're negotiating?"

When Yarrick smiled, shaking his head without really saying no, Black nudged him with a hand, giving him another shark-like grin.

"You making promises for me, Petey? If so, 'fess up. Don't be shy. I'd rather know exactly what it is I'm agreeing to, before I sign on the dotted line."

There was a silence.

After that silence had already stretched too long...

Peter Yarrick smiled.

Even I could see the embarrassment there, and I wasn't even trying to read him.

"Well, you know me, Black," Pete said, holding up his hands and giving his own version of the killer grin. "I like playing in various playgrounds—"

"Yeah." Black was looking at him straight on now, the rich playboy gone. "I do know you, Peter. That's why I asked."

"Did you ask, Quentin?" Yarrick quipped back. "Was that you *asking?* Just now?"

"It was," Black said.

As they verbally sparred, my eyebrows rose higher.

Black nudged me with his light.

My eyebrows lowered back down again.

Even so, I understood what Black was asking Yarrick now. Black wanted to know if Yarrick had sold him, in all or in part, to whoever he worked with inside the military-industrial complex. Black wanted to know if the two of us were part of whatever deal Peter cut, and what that deal entailed exactly.

That would definitely explain why they'd backed down on picking up me and Black.

It was also alarming as hell, depending on what had been promised.

"As I said, I've been doing more military contracts of late," Yarrick said, squinting up at Black, shoving the designer sunglasses higher on his nose. "If you're wondering why the military's being so hands off with me on all this... that's a big part of why. Those contracts aren't small. They're significant. And we're negotiating for another, as we speak."

"They're half-assing an investigation of experimental tech to sweeten a contract negotiation?" Black said, grunting. "That's neighborly of them."

I heard the edge in Black's voice that time, too.

He knew Peter was still holding out on him.

Yarrick's voice remained unapologetic.

"They're granting me leeway because of that, sure," he said, shrugging. "Of course, I'm not saying *this* incident... or that poor chap my people found dead... have anything to do with projects I've currently got in the works. But I also can't claim to be totally *uninvolved,* either, given the R&D work we've been doing at Dark Sands over the past few years. If anything about this embarrasses *me,* it has the potential to embarrass *them*... if you get my drift."

My eyebrows wanted to go up again.

I kept them firmly in place, my expression smooth.

"That's really interesting, Peter," Black growled, his voice a touch harder. "But it doesn't exactly answer my question—"

"Okay," Yarrick said, holding up his hands with that half smile. "Okay, Black. All right. There *might* be some people who'd like to see you working again. Working *with* them, rather than against them. They *might* have expressed an interest in having me soften you up a bit, by involving you in this. They'd like an opportunity to renew ties... now that they know your name's about to be cleared."

I felt my jaw harden.

Black let out a disbelieving grunt.

"...Either way," Yarrick continued, frowning seriously at Black. "Regardless of what *they* want, I'd really like to have someone in my corner on this. Someone I can trust. Someone who understands my unique concerns."

Another of those deceptively dry smiles.

"Given the mess you've been dealing with," Yarrick added. "Having those jackals in the media knocking down your door, accusing you of all kinds of nonsensical crap... I'd prefer to have someone looking out for me on this."

Again, I had to fight to keep the reaction off my face.

I could practically feel the circular evasion living behind his words.

"So, are we good?" Yarrick said, looking between us. "If you're okay with just the preliminary, evidence-gathering side of things, I thought you and your wife might be okay with a handshake deal for now. Assuming all goes well, we could dinner together tonight. I'll have a contract written up by then... you can tell me what you think."

There was a pause.

Slowly, Black nodded.

"Sure, Petey," he said, his voice back to rich-guy casual. "I don't see any harm in me and the wife helping secure the scene, and doing what we can to help out with the investigation side of things. You're overpaying, as I said... but it's your dime."

He gave me a sideways look, briefly probing my gaze.

"...Assuming the doc's okay with it."

I returned Black's look, my expression smooth.

"Of course," I said politely, turning back to Yarrick with a smile. "We'd be happy to help in any way we can, Mr. Yarrick. You've been so generous with us, it's the least we could do." Nudging Black with an elbow, I added, "And don't listen to Quentin about the money. He's only giving you a hard time. He has no intention of charging you."

"Fat chance..." Black snorted.

But Yarrick barely seemed to hear that part.

The young tech mogul exhaled, his face transforming into a real smile, maybe for the first time. His relief was palpable.

It also felt genuine.

"That's excellent!" he said, breathing out. "I owe you one, both of you. More than one. I'll find some way to make it up to you in spectacular fashion... I promise it."

He started, blinking up at Black, as if remembering something.

"Hey!" His voice brightened. "Tonight. Given everything that's happened, I assume you'll be canceling your previous plans. But that means we'll have even more time to make arrangements for something *truly spectacular*—"

Black cut him off.

All the play dropped from his voice.

"Peter," he said. "Not now."

I glanced up in time to see my husband make the universal *shut-the-fuck-up* gesture with one hand, running that hand in a sharp line over his throat.

When he caught me looking at him, Black stopped mid-gesture, lowering his hand and trying to play it off like he hadn't been doing anything.

I let out a disbelieving laugh.

"Really?" I said.

Black gave me a warning look.

His gold eyes returned to Yarrick, right before he reached into his breast pocket, pulling out his sunglasses and using them to cover his flecked irises.

As he did, his expression smoothed.

"Yeah," Black said, clearing his throat, speaking deliberately to Yarrick, not to me. "I'll look into doing that another night. We can talk about that later, Pete—"

"When I'm not around," I muttered, blowing a few strands of hair out of my face and folding my arms.

"Yes," Black said, giving me a harder look. "When you're not around."

Peter Yarrick looked between us.

Amusement returned to his eyes, touching his bow-like lips.

"Riiiight," he said. "Well. We'll leave it there, then. Until tonight, Blacks."

Motioning up towards the resort, he added,

"I'm going to head back up. But I'll be in touch. Call me if you find anything interesting. The Naval guy they're sending should be driving down from Hickam within the next couple of hours. I believe he's already en route, but I never got an E.T.A."

"En route?" I frowned. "Isn't Hickam only about a half-hour away?"

"Closer to an hour from here," Yarrick said, glancing at me. "But that's not what I meant. They were bringing him in from the mainland. San Diego, I believe."

Again, I fought to keep my reactions off my face.

It didn't help that now I was distracted by whatever the hell Black was talking about, in terms of "plans" he'd apparently had for the two of us for the evening. I mean, he'd alluded the same to me... but he'd also told Yarrick?

Why?

And why were those plans suddenly off? Were they really that involved, or did Black plan on picking through debris for the rest of the day and night?

If so, I was definitely going up to the room for a nap.

And probably to devour a whole pizza... and maybe a few plates of sushi.

It rankled, though.

It rankled that Yarrick knew all about these plans, and I didn't.

And it damned well better stay that way, Black muttered in my mind.

I snorted my opinion of that.

Black smacked my light a little, more to let me know he was serious. When I quirked an eyebrow in his direction, his mental voice dropped to a harder growl.

I'm going to be really pissed if you read him for it, doc. Really pissed... as in, the real thing. This isn't some challenge for you to find some way to do it without me noticing. Trust me, I'll notice. And I'll be pissed.

I snorted again, softer that time, but Black didn't let me blow it off.

I'm not playing, doc. Stay the fuck out of his mind. Please.

I fought not to look up at him.

A part of me wanted to snort at him a third time, but I suspected I'd be pushing my luck. At the same time, I felt my jaw clench, maybe in reaction to the implicit threat I felt behind his thoughts.

Honestly, though, I think I was more puzzled than anything.

I could feel how serious Black was.

I could also feel his light more or less strangling Yarrick's in an attempt to keep me out of his friend's mind.

After a bare pause, I backed off.

I wouldn't read Yarrick, not if Black didn't want me to.

There was no reason for me to be a jerk about it.

But I could damned well be annoyed about it.

It didn't help that I had no idea how long it had been since I'd last slept. The time change between Moscow, San Francisco, and now Hawaii didn't help.

Or the lack of food. Or the lack of sex.

At the same time, I really, really needed to talk to Black.

The list of things we needed to talk about just kept growing exponentially.

Black gave me another darting glance.

Since he was wearing sunglasses, that one was harder to read.

"Do you need anything?" Peter said, pretending not to notice the long silence.

"I don't think so—" Black began.

"Gloves," I blurted.

Both of them looked at me.

Ignoring their stares, I continued in more of my "doc" voice.

"Surgical gloves," I clarified. "Also, tape. Sealable bags for evidence. Tongs and trowels if you have them. A good-sized shovel. Gauze for chemical samples. Tweezers. Cutting implements. Sealable bins for the larger pieces. You'll need to post guards, and establish some kind of perimeter, to keep people out. Maybe you could put Keon in charge of that, but he'll need help—"

Yarrick was smiling now though, holding up a hand.

"Of course. Of course. Pardon my stupidity. I'll have Gordon arrange it all. He's my head of security," he added. "He used to be a police officer as well. Homicide."

"It would be good to have him down here, then," I said.

"Of course, Dr. Fox. I'll get on it immediately."

Yarrick winked at Black.

The way he did it, I could tell it was as much for my benefit as Black's.

"...I forgot your wife was a cop," the boy-faced, billionaire defense-contractor added with a smile.

I didn't bother to correct him.

"I'll leave Keon for the two of you," Yarrick added. "Once Gordon gets down here, he can direct the rest of the staff. Don't worry," he said, his eyes swiveling back to mine. "I'll tell him you're my envoy, that he's to do whatever you say. As for materials, Gordon can take care of that, too. He'll know the kinds of things you need."

Pausing, he faced me directly.

"Please... let me know if you need *anything at all,* Dr. Fox. You and your husband are doing me a tremendous favor. My resources are entirely at your disposal."

Thinking about that, I looked out over the beach.

I once more grew aware of the smell.

The harsh smell of burning paint, plastic, and Plexiglas stood out the most, more or less drowning out the more subtle smells, even those coming from the ocean. I frowned, looking over the blackened shell of what remained of this side of the boathouse, the chunks of burning and blackened materials littering the beach.

"Yeah," I said, frowning. "We'll let you know."

10

YOU MUST TELL THEM

"Hey!" Angel said, sharp. "Stop that! Get down from there!"

Despite her irritation, she had to fight not to laugh when he twisted his head around, looking down at her with a dumbfounded expression on his face.

He continued to hang from the hole in her ceiling, swaying lightly from where he'd stopped midway, halfway through pulling himself up through the square opening.

Even with those odd, clear, crystal-colored eyes, he looked so much like her friend, she had to press her lips together in a stubborn refusal to even smile.

"Get down," she said sternly, motioning for the floor. "Right now, Nick. Jesus. What is the matter with you?"

"You said you put our old surfboards up here," he said, disbelief in his voice. "When my parents couldn't store mine, you said you put it up here, with yours. I was *helping*, for fuck's sake..."

"Helping?" She snorted. "Helping break my house, you mean."

From the couch, another male voice chuckled.

Angel glared at him, pointing at him next.

"You're not helping," she informed the seer, who sat cross-legged in the middle of her fabric couch, a dozing, jet-black Irish wolfhound taking up most of his lap. "You're supposed to be babysitting this shit-show. Not giving him free reign to trash my house."

"So now I'm *trashing* your house?" Nick frowned at her from where he hung on the hole in the ceiling, which he still hadn't gotten down from. "Seriously? I've barely been here twelve hours. What have I trashed, exactly? I don't eat anything... nothing you'd want," he added when she glared pointedly at him.

"I did the dishes!" he added, still sounding annoyed. "*Your* dishes, I might add... from fuck-knows how long ago, but obviously well before you and Cowboy went down to SoCal. You don't want to know the nasty shit I had to scrape off a few of them. Hell, *I* don't want to know what that stuff was originally..."

Dalejem let out another snorting laugh.

Angel glared at him. "Shut up. I mean it, Jem."

Dalejem let out a partly affected sigh, holding up a hand and tilting it in a decidedly seer-like fashion.

"What more do you want from me?" Nick complained. "Should I do the windows next? Clean the grout in the bathroom?"

"Now that you mention it," Angel grumbled.

Jem laughed again, and Angel gave him a scathing look.

That time, the seer spoke through her glare, undeterred.

"You're the one who told him he could go surfing, sister," the seer reminded her. "You didn't expect him to dismiss that as a hypothetical, did you? Vampires don't sleep. He's been trapped inside all day... and frankly, he needs to get out. He needs exercise. It's not exactly *safe* for him to be wandering the streets of San Francisco right now, when we could run into one of Black's patrols, or worse. Not to mention, you don't want him hunting... and that's what his instincts are telling him to do..."

The puppy in Jem's lap wiggled, sliding halfway out of Jem's lap.

Startling itself awake, it raised its furry head bolt upright.

It blinked, looking around the room, bleary-eyed.

The puppy sneezed then, its eyes wide awake—maybe from the brief falling sensation that made him panic, maybe from Jem talking so close to his ears, maybe from Angel's tone, or maybe from his puppy nap simply coming to its natural end.

Whatever the reason, the dog clearly decided he was missing something, that something exciting was happening.

Then the dog's dark eyes found Nick.

His ears perked up.

Letting out a delighted bark, Panther bounded off Jem's lap.

He ran over to the opening in the ceiling leading to the attic, where his favorite non-human now hung from a white-painted wooden ledge.

Clearly, Nick was doing something interesting.

Panther immediately began to bark again, his puppy voice both strangely deep and strangely loud for his size, a precursor to the *very* large dog he would become, once he grew into his adult body.

"Panther!" Angel said, exhaling in frustration.

The pup looked back at her, wagging his tail tentatively, as if not sure what to make of her tone, or if it was an invitation to play.

"Yeah, you," she said accusingly to the dog. "You're not helping, either."

Panther barked, opening his mouth in a doggy grin.

Then his dark eyes returned to the vampire hanging from the ceiling.

He barked louder. That time, Angel distinctly heard various doggy versions of "Whatcha doing, person? Is it dangerous? Is it fun? Can I help? What's that hole?"

The inquisitive barks were definitely aimed at Nick.

Still swaying slightly, Nick glanced down at the pup and smiled.

"Hey, buddy," he said. "Don't listen to the mean lady." He gave Angel a level look, his lips pursed. "It's not you she's mad at."

Angel snorted loudly at that.

"You can say that again," she said.

Nick went on, still talking to the dog, "—She's clearly forgetting *she* decided to bring us here. She *offered* to let us stay here—"

"Like an idiot," Angel countered.

Nick exhaled one of those fake vampire exhales at her, rolling his eyes. "Do you want me to get the boards down or not? Are you really that much of a control freak that you'd rather do it yourself? When I'm already up here?"

"Why didn't you use the ladder?" she snapped. "Like a normal person?"

"The mechanism wasn't working," Nick said, as if it was the more reasonable thing in the world. "I'm going to fix it, damn it. Just not *now*. I'll fix it tomorrow, while Jem's asleep. I want to go surfing now. While it's dark out—"

"It's barely dark now," she grumbled. "The sun went down like thirty minutes ago, Nick. It's not like you don't have time to fix it before—"

"—I didn't say I *can't* fix it now," Nick cut in. "I said I *don't want to* fix it now. And it'll take at least ninety minutes to get down there," he reminded her. "I want to get a decent run in. And Jem's never been surfing, so we need to factor in teaching time. Not like he won't be better at it than me by the end of the night—"

Jem snorted derisively at that.

Angel gave the seer a look, then shifted her gaze back to the vampire.

"Do you absolutely *have* to go to Santa Cruz?" she said, raising her voice, even though with his vampire hearing, he would have heard her if she whispered. "There's plenty of beach *here*, you know, in San Francisco. Not to mention a score of beaches between here and Santa Cruz, all of them closer than the lighthouse—"

"I *want* to go to Santa Cruz," he said, as if he hadn't already made that clear. "What's the big deal, Ang? You worried I'm going to crash your car?"

"Among other things," she muttered.

There was a silence.

Then Nick exhaled another of those fake vampire sighs.

"Look, I made a deal with Jem," he said, glancing over his shoulder at her. "He's going to teach me archery, and I'm going to teach him to surf. If we're going to do this, we should do it *right*. I want to take him to the Lighthouse for his first time."

Pausing, he frowned down at her, still hanging from the opening.

"Did you bring the bow for him? For Jem?"

Angel rolled her eyes. "Yes... I *stole* a bow for your boyfriend from Black's stores. I also got him a bunch of arrows. I didn't know which kind he'd want, so I got a quiver of each type. I figured that would keep you two busy for a while—"

"I saw that," Jem said, humor in his voice. "You realize some of the arrows you brought me are *explosive*, sister? You handed me a veritable arsenal—"

"One *you're* responsible for, Jem," Angel warned, aiming a finger at him. "Nick blows anything up with those, and it's entirely on you." Clenching her jaw at the thought, she added, "You should probably go up to the mountains to practice with those. Or the beach. Or at least somewhere no one will see either of you."

Jem chuckled.

Shaking his head, Nick seemed to make up his mind.

Looking away from her, he pulled his body with strange, machine-like grace up through the opening in her ceiling.

Angel couldn't help pausing in her annoyance to watch him, briefly fascinated by the way he moved, which was equally graceful but completely different from the more animal-like movements of seers, including Nick's new "boyfriend," Dalejem, the seer currently sitting cross-legged on her couch.

Angel's mind bracketed their status in quotes only because Nick himself seemed to be doing so. Weirdly, given all the other things going on with Nick right now, the newborn vampire still seemed to be in some kind of bizarre denial that he and Dalejem were a couple.

Angel wasn't harboring those delusions.

For the same reason, she should probably lose the mental air-quotes.

She continued to watch as Nick brought his feet up to the edge of the opening in the wall and leapt the rest of the way up, lightly, despite his bulk, landing on the slats holding up her ceiling, and tamping down the several layers of insulation.

Angel watched Nick's shadow as he looked around inside the storage space.

"You're not getting the car for your archery lessons, either," she called up to him. "Much less tonight. I know how you drive. I've seen you on those narrow coastal roads."

He barely seemed to hear her. He was still looking around when his voice reached her through the opening, now sounding distracted.

"Have Jem drive, if you don't trust me," he said, his words muffled by the ceiling.

Shifting his weight and turning from where he balanced on two brace-beams over her apartment foyer, he glanced down, meeting her gaze, his crystal-like eyes glowing from where they picked up a smattering of light.

"Or hell, I don't know why you don't just come *with* us, Ang," he added. "From what you've said, you could use a night off. Cowboy probably could, too. And that way, *you* can drive your precious antique—"

"I'd prefer not to *die,* thanks," she said, folding her arms tighter. "I'd prefer not to have you rope my boyfriend into your crazy bull-shit, either—"

"You don't have to surf," Nick said, back to looking around the attic storage space. "Although it's not like I'd let either of you *die,* Jesus. What a drama queen..."

Dalejem laughed.

He cut it off when Angel glared at him.

"Shut *up,* Dalejem—"

"—And stop crapping on Jem," Nick added, looking down at her and frowning. "I know you don't want me here, but don't take it out on him. He's doing a lot more babysitting than you are. And he's had to listen to me pace the fucking apartment all day."

At Angel's disbelieving noise, Nick got louder, cutting her off.

"You could hang out in Santa Cruz with Panther," he offered. "We can't leave him alone here in the apartment, anyway... not for that long. You and Cowboy could drive down with us, take Panther to the boardwalk or downtown Santa Cruz, walk around with him for a few hours. Go to one of those coffee shops you like so much. Or hell, bring him into a bar. Most places won't care. It's California."

Nick's voice got more muffled as he disappeared deeper into the crawlspace, which was tall enough to qualify as an actual attic.

"...It's that," he added, speaking louder. "Or you'll have to take Panther with you to California Street, and that's going to raise a bunch of questions. Like, 'Where'd you get the dog, Angel?' 'Whose dog is that, Angel?' 'How did Miri bring a dog here, and why is this the first we're seeing of it all day, Angel?'"

Pausing, he added,

"You could say it's yours, but again, they'd have questions. Like, 'How did you have time to get a dog after spending weeks in an underground cavern with vampires, Angel?' and 'Who's been feeding the dog all this time, Angel?' and so on. They'd also wonder, again, why this was the first time they were seeing the danged thing, when they all know you're animal crazy and would have brought it to the offices the second you got it..."

There was a crash overhead.

Angel ducked in reflex, wincing.

Then she glared up at the opening.

"What the hell was that?" she snapped.

"It was nothing," Nick's voice floated down. "A box fell. Calm the fuck down."

"You break any of my mom's antique ornaments, I'm going to *stake* you, Nick."

Jem burst out in a real laugh at that.

When she glared at him, he held up a hand in a seer's half-assed apology, but he didn't really stop laughing. Noticing the seer was wearing a dark-gray sweat suit with the Black Securities and Investigations' eagle logo on it, she scowled again.

She needed to get them both more clothes.

Which meant she probably needed to raid Jem's old room in the Raptor's Nest, and ask Miri where Nick's clothes might be, assuming Black hadn't lit them all on fire after throwing them in a dumpster and pouring gasoline on them.

She wondered if Nick kept his apartment in South San Francisco... then remembered he didn't.

He'd stored a few boxes of things at his parents' house in Potrero Hill, but most of it, meaning the stuff he was still using in the day to day, he'd moved to the building on California Street.

Nick's body had changed a fair bit since he'd transformed from human to vampire, anyway. Angel found herself wondering if his old clothes would even fit him all that great, or if she should just give up and buy him some new ones.

Scowling, and refolding her arms even tighter, she realized it was no use.

She needed to take them both shopping.

That, or she had to get a credit card for Jem, and let him handle it.

Overhead, there was another, less-loud clattering sound, as Nick knocked something over something else she'd stuck up in her attic crawlspace.

"Goddamn it, Naoko!" she snapped, yelling up at her ceiling.

A surfboard was emerging from the hole in the ceiling though, gripped by bizarrely white, muscular hands.

Nick's muffled voice arose from behind the Fiberglas board.

"Is someone going to take this?" he said. "Or should I just chuck it down onto the floor, and hope for the best?"

Angel exhaled, unfolding her arms and preparing to step forward.

Jem got there first, though, leaping up from the couch before she could cross the few steps to the opening. She watched as the seer padded swiftly and almost soundlessly to the space under the board and grabbed hold of it, taking it from Nick.

Once Nick let go, Jem pulled it the rest of the way down,

extracting it from the opening neatly and efficiently. Once he had it all the way out, he leaned it carefully against the wall, finding an empty spot between the pictures Angel had hanging in her entryway.

"See?" Angel snorted. "Jem can manage to handle the thing without *breaking my house,* Nick."

Nick gave her a darting look through the opening in the ceiling.

"I thought vampires were supposed to have super-fast reflexes," she said, ignoring his look and refolding her arms. "You sound like a drunk toddler up there, knocking everything over that isn't bolted down—"

"You put the surfboards in the back," he complained, staring back at her with a frown on his lips. His strangely young-looking face, after the forty-plus-year-old man he'd been, made her stare again briefly.

"...Couldn't you have warned me that you heaped a few dozen, open, loose boxes full of breakable trinkets in front of the damned boards?" he continued in his best complaining voice, gesturing in a way that made her think he'd gotten the mannerism from Jem. "Why do you need to keep all this crap, anyway? You're going to end up like your Aunt Leticia in NOLA. We'll have to dig you out when you die, following the smell of cat piss and crawdads..."

Angel let out a snort. "Hey. You *liked* my Aunt Leticia."

"So? What's your point?"

"—And you're one to talk," she said, ignoring his last words. "I remember your office back at the precinct. Not to mention your apartment. Where *is* all that shit, anyway? Did you rent a storage space? Or just give up and light it all on fire?"

Nick looked about to answer her.

He didn't though, looking back towards Jem when the seer clicked his fingers at him.

"Argue in the car, children," Jem said, his voice still amused, but businesslike. "There is another board, *na?* Didn't you go up there for two boards, brother?"

"Yeah."

Even in just that one word, Nick's voice abruptly changed, making Angel blink.

It grew lower, softer, his bluster suddenly gone.

"I have to go back and get the other one," Nick added in that same voice. "There wasn't room to carry both. I got it out from behind the boxes, though, so it won't take as long. Give me a sec. I'll be right back."

"...And you can be polite to *him,* I see," Angel scoffed. "*Weirdly* polite. I wonder why that is." She quirked an eyebrow at the absurdly handsome seer. "You put the fear of God in him, Jem? *How,* I wonder? And how much would I have to pay you to learn that secret?"

Again, Nick gave her a look.

That time, she didn't get the impression he was glaring at her as part of their usual back and forth.

She distinctly got the impression she'd embarrassed him.

In fact, she strongly suspected he'd be doing the standard Nick blush routine, if he wasn't currently a vampire... as in neck, ears, cheeks, the whole nine yards... and why the hell did she keep forgetting what he was, all of a sudden?

Jem gave her a sideways look, his lips twitching faintly.

"You're not alone, sister," he murmured.

Angel thought about that.

Conscious of Nick's super-good vampire hearing, which was even better than Jem's as a seer, she mouthed her next words, rather than say them.

Miri? she mouthed to Jem. *The doc?*

"I meant me," Jem muttered, even softer. "But yes. Her too."

"Her too, what?" Nick said, now sounding annoyed.

Another board appeared through the hole in the ceiling. Smiling a little, first at Angel, then up at Nick, Jem rolled his eyes, walking closer to the opening.

"You are paranoid, brother," he chided him. "Can't I say

anything to your friends, without you assuming it's something terrible I'm thinking or saying about you?"

"No," Nick said, his voice gruff.

Angel laughed.

She knew Nick meant it as a joke, that she was *supposed* to laugh, but her amusement was still less around his words and more about how utterly and completely *different* he was around Jem, how much quieter he was, how he seemed almost embarrassed to have anyone see him talking to or interacting with the male seer.

Even if Jem hadn't already told her, she would have known Nick had a thing for him, male or not, just from the way he was acting.

The more times she saw the two of them interact, in fact, the more she was convinced it was more than just a "thing." She hadn't seen Nick act like this around *anyone* before, not even Miri, not even when he was at the height of his crush thing with her.

Nick had been straight when he was human, but somehow, that wasn't all that weird, either. Angel found she barely blinked about that end of things, even though she'd known Nick since they were both little kids, living in the same shitty neighborhood in Hunter's Point.

She hadn't really had the nerve to talk to Nick about anything personal in the day or so since he'd gotten here, and become her houseguest.

She'd barely talked to him at all, really, given everything going on at the building on California Street right now. She'd only managed to get away now by making up some story about a sick friend. Cowboy was covering for her, of course—he was the only other one of their team who even knew Nick and Dalejem were here, for obvious reasons.

Cowboy wasn't exactly thrilled with that information, either.

He definitely wasn't thrilled with having to lie to the others about it, even if it was mostly a lie of omission. Cowboy understood the logic of letting Miri be the one to tell Black, since it was Miri's call to bring Nick back here... but he didn't like it.

Cowboy had been avoiding talking to Black for the same reason.

Angel strongly got the impression Cowboy wished he wasn't in the know on this whole thing at all, that he was as blissfully ignorant as Dex and the others.

Of course, Nick was fully aware of the shit-storm his presence back in San Francisco would undoubtedly cause.

It was part of the reason, she suspected, he was avoiding mentioning the whole thing, and focusing on things like taking his new boyfriend surfing.

At the same time, it was so easy to slip into a back-and-forth with him.

It was so easy for her mind to more or less erase everything that happened in the past few months, and just accept Nick, her childhood friend, as being alive again... and more or less himself, the way she remembered him.

It was definitely a lot easier to relax into that part of things than it was to, say, focus on the psychotic seer currently chained up in her garage, beneath the living area of the apartment her aunt had left her when she died.

Thinking about that, Angel frowned, in spite of herself.

"What about Solonik?" she said, still frowning. "Someone should be here, right? Watching that piece of shit?"

Pausing at the silence of the other two, she added,

"I don't want him in my car, Nick. If you get hungry after surfing, you're going to have to find some other way to deal with it."

Glancing up, she saw Nick scowl at her words.

He'd handed through the second surfboard to Jem already, and Angel watched the seer lean that one carefully against the wall next to the larger, black and red board, which had been Nick's from back when they were both in high school. Angel's was a bright, pale green.

She still remembered picking it out at the surf shop with Nick.

Back then, they spent just about every weekend surfing.

For obvious reasons, Angel hadn't been able to get Nick's more current, adult-sized and significantly more expensive surfboard for him.

There would have been a hell of a lot of questions if someone saw her drag that thing out of Nick's old room at the building on California Street, and not only because they were in the middle of a crisis after what Miri had just done.

Angel was still thinking about that, about the cages full of seers underneath the California Street building, when Nick jumped down from the hole in her ceiling.

Despite his size and probable current weight, he landed lightly, barely making a sound.

The movement, which was so obviously not-human, made her flinch.

"We're not bringing Solonik," he grumbled, as if she'd just spoken. "And I'm not going to be snacking on tourists in Santa Cruz... for fuck's sake."

"Just the locals," Jem quipped, curling an arm around Nick's waist when he got close enough.

When Nick rolled his eyes at Jem, looking faintly irritated again, the seer chuckled.

"She knows I'm joking," Jem said, tugging on Nick's long hair.

"Sure she does," Nick muttered.

Angel saw her childhood friend give her a sideways glance, but again, she found herself oddly touched. He was clearly mortified about her seeing him with Jem. Not because Jem happened to be male, but more likely because Nick knew Angel would pick up on the connection between them, not to mention Nick's feelings.

At the very least, he was definitely downplaying their relationship.

Angel suspected she knew why.

"I wish you would clue me in on it," Dalejem grumbled, looking at her.

Flinching a little when she realized the seer heard her thoughts, it occurred to her in the next handful of seconds that he must not have read her deliberately. If he had, he *would* know why she thought that, and wouldn't have to ask.

"Stop that," Nick growled, looking between them.

"Why?" Jem said, his fingers still in Nick's hair. "What is bothering you?"

Nick frowned. He looked like he was about to answer for a beat, then shut his mouth.

"We were talking about you," Jem said. "Or really, I was talking about you. She was just thinking about you—"

"I get it." Nick gave him a warning look. "Just cut it out. Both of you."

"I was about to tell you what she was thinking and I was responding to," Jem said mildly.

"I know," Nick said. "And I'm asking you not to." Not looking at Angel, he added, lower. "She'd tell me if she wanted me to know."

"Maybe," Angel said, amused again, in spite of herself. "Actually," she added. "I think I will tell you. I was thinking—"

"Please don't," Nick said, giving her another hard look.

That time, Angel laughed for real.

Then she thought of something else, and pursed her lips.

"Are you going to go see your mom?"

Nick stiffened.

Jem did too, but Angel immediately got the sense it was for a different reason. The seer's pale green eyes darted to Nick, partly in concern, partly in surprise.

Angel was a little taken aback by the tenderness she saw in that look.

"Your mother," Jem said, soft. "Your mother's alive?"

Nick glanced at him, wincing a little, then gave Angel a sharper look.

"I called her today," he said, his voice close to a mutter.

"Does she know you're back in San Francisco?" Angel said.

"No."

Jem looked openly astonished now. "Your mother is in San Francisco?"

"Both of his parents are," Angel offered, probably not so helpfully, in Nick's eyes, but she got a perverse pleasure in seeing Nick the Vampire squirm. "...and one of his three sisters. The other two live in Seattle and Los Angeles, last I knew."

Jem gave her a sideways look at that, clicking under his breath.

"You are enjoying this too much, sister," he said, his voice chiding. He looked back at Nick. "You called your mother? While I was asleep?"

"Are you going to introduce her to your new boyfriend, Nick?" Angel said, her voice openly mocking now, like they really were both human again, and maybe twelve years old. "I wonder what will confuse her more," she said, tapping her lip with a finger and pretending to think. "You being suddenly 'gay'? Or you looking like you're twenty-five years old—?"

"Shut up, Ange."

Angel found herself shutting her mouth.

She stared at him.

He'd sounded so much like Nick that time, even with that odd, extra bit of musicality to his voice that came out more sometimes than others.

Not only that, he sounded genuinely angry.

Blinking, still staring at him, she realized she'd managed to upset him.

"Hey." She walked closer to him, holding up her hands. "Sorry."

Thinking about what she'd been teasing him about, and the fact that Nick had always been extremely close to his family, to all of them, including both of his parents and all three of his sisters— coupled with the fact that Nick didn't exactly *ask* to get made into a vampire in the first place, she suddenly felt like a shit.

"I'm sorry, Nick," she said, as all of that fully sank in. "I really am. I wasn't thinking—"

"Forget it." His voice went back to gruff, even as he waved her off. "I just..." Hesitating, he glanced at Jem, and again, Angel distinctly got the impression he would be blushing, had he still been human. "...I just haven't figured out how to deal with all of that yet."

There was a silence.

In it, she felt all three of them thinking, not only Nick.

Then Jem surprised her, and not only because he was the first break the silence.

"How to deal with it?" the seer said, his voice suddenly decisive. "But of course, you must tell them. You must tell them all of it. You must tell them the truth."

Nick and Angel both turned, staring at him.

Nick turned with that inhuman, vampire grace, but other than that, they could have been pulled by the same hand.

For a long-feeling few minutes, neither of them said a word.

11

ROAD TRIP

A ngel ended up going with them.

To Santa Cruz, that is.

Cowboy opted out of the vampire outing, so Nick and Angel went back and forth about whether Angel would go out on the water with them, or wait in the car.

In the end, Angel put her foot down, saying no, and informed them she'd bring a book, a pad of paper, and Panther, and take the opportunity for a little alone time.

She didn't tell them she also wanted the opportunity to think about something else, which was the fact that her boyfriend, Cowboy, a.k.a. Elvis Dawson Graves, had asked her to marry him. He'd even sounded semi-serious about it.

Since their evening of discussing all that had been interrupted by the sudden reappearance of Miri—with Nick, Jem, Solonik, and Panther in tow—they'd put the actual, for-real proposal and any subsequent discussions regarding marriage on hold.

But Cowboy had seemed serious about it, for sure.

Hopefully, the sudden reappearance of Nick, not to mention the fact of him residing in her apartment, hadn't changed his mind.

Because Angel was pretty sure she was going to say yes.

In fact, she was almost entirely sure she was going to say yes.

Still, a night of thinking about it, like a grown up, wouldn't exactly be unwarranted.

Cowboy caught her off-guard, asking her at all.

Without ever really thinking about it consciously, she'd sort of figured he wasn't the marrying type. He's never once mentioned marriage to her, as something he wanted in the future, or considered in the abstract, much less specifically with her. He'd never mentioned friends of his who were married. He'd never mentioned marriage as something he'd given any thought to at all, or had any opinions about, for or against.

So yeah, he'd caught her off guard.

Moreover, she'd been engaged once before, and that had been pretty spontaneous on her part, again because a boyfriend surprised her. This time, she intended to think it through, as self-honestly as she could, before she said yes to another man.

She wanted to know she meant it this time.

She wanted to know she was, if not one hundred percent certain, as certain as she could be under the circumstances.

She didn't get much quiet time on the drive down to think about it, though.

"...So I'm just supposed to dump that on my parents, both of whom are in their seventies, that I'm a fucking vampire?" Nick said, exasperated, cutting Jem off, and not for the first time since they started this conversation, somewhere around Geary Street and Divisadero.

They were now on their way down Highway 1.

If anything, the conversation had only gotten more heated, but Angel didn't remember any new points really being raised by either of them since the whole thing started.

She had to admire Jem's tenacity.

Generally speaking, Nick wasn't easy to argue with, and not only because he was probably the stubbornest person she'd even met, outside of maybe Miri.

"...Do you want to kill my parents?" Nick finished, his voice frustrated. "Do you hate my aging parents, Jem?"

The seer let out an involuntary laugh.

"For the gods' sake... give them some *credit,* Nick. Do you think it will not bother them more, to know there is something strange, to know you are lying to them? You freely admit you are very close to all of them. There is no closeness based in lies. It is impossible... trust me in this. So why would you jeopardize these relationships? *Why* would you not tell them the truth?"

Nick exhaled, looking at Angel, as if for help.

Returning his gaze with a sideways look of her own, she firmed her lips, shaking her head just enough to make it clear she had no intention of jumping into this fray.

Even more annoyed by her refusal to agree with him, Nick turned where he sat shotgun, shifting sideways to stare at Jem in the back seat. The green-eyed seer sat in the middle part of the couch-like backseat of her mint condition, midnight blue with white racing stripes, 1970 Plymouth Hemi Barracuda.

Angel, of course, drove.

She didn't like anyone driving this car, truthfully.

She'd let Nick drive it before, but it definitely wasn't a regular thing.

"I can't tell them I'm a fucking vampire," Nick said, his voice hard. "I can't tell them that, Jem. I'll give my dad a heart attack. Not a figurative one... a real one. My sisters will flip out. They'll want to put me in a psych ward—"

But Jem ran over his words as easily as Nick ran over Jem's.

The seer's voice was equally frustrated, if slightly calmer.

"Vampires have been all over the news, *na?* It seems to me an opportune time to—"

"No!" Nick let out an incredulous laugh, throwing back his head. "Absolutely fucking not! I'm *not* telling them that!"

"So... what? You will just never see them?" Jem's mouth and voice hardened. "You will just keep your distance? Lie to them over the phone?"

Angel glanced at Jem in her rearview mirror as she drove.

She heard a note of hurt in the seer's words.

"...And I will *never* meet them?" Jem added. "There will just be no relationship with them any longer, apart from the occasional, cryptic, dishonest phone call?"

"I didn't say that," Nick growled, his voice warning.

"How will you explain it then, Nick?" Jem said, frowning. "How do you explain you look like this?" He gestured gracefully towards Nick. "You look very different. You must know that. You were handsome before... believe me. But you were a middle-aged human. You are now a vampire. Do you plan to simply don colored contact lenses? Have make-up applied in an attempt to age yourself? Perhaps you can add some stray gray hairs, here and there, to really sell them on their fake human son?"

Nick scowled at him. "You've given way too much thought to how old I was before."

Jem exhaled an outraged half-laugh.

"How *old* you were? Shall we really discuss age... pup? I'm practically a child molester, being with you..."

Angel let out an involuntary snort.

At Nick's disparaging look, Jem added,

"...and *of course* I remember how you looked! I wanted you. I could tell you a lot more about your physical appearance, Nick, than you probably want to hear. Towards the end, I wanted you badly enough I was more or less obsessed with your physical appearance. I could tell you details of your face and body that you yourself perhaps never noticed. I could also tell you and your friend Angel here, exactly what I was doing, while I imagined those details—"

"Hey, hey, hey." Nick held up a hand, grimacing. He glanced at Angel, his mouth still a hard line. "Too far, Jem. Too far—"

"Too far? Really?"

"Yes—"

Angel laughed. "Oh, I vote a definite *no* on the 'too far,' Jem," she said, a delighted note reaching her voice. "*Do* go on. I would be absolutely *riveted* to hear what else it is you noticed about our buddy, Nick, here." She craned her head around. "Miri mentioned you're an artist. Did you draw people?"

Jem opened his mouth, but Nick cut them both off.

"Another word," he said to the seer, holding up a finger. "One. More. Word. Just one, Jem. And I'll drown you out there. I mean it."

Angel burst out in another laugh.

Panther, apparently feeling he was missing something, let out a bark from the seat he shared with Jem.

Nick reached back, scratching him behind the ears, and the gangly puppy lunged at him, trying to crawl into the vampire's lap. Nick pushed him back gently, then looked at Jem, a slight frown on his mouth.

"You're an artist?" he said, gruff. "You never said that."

"You never asked."

"I'm supposed to *ask* that? Hey, Dalejem... are you an artist? Seriously?"

"I meant," Jem said, quieter, his voice holding a faint rebuke. "You haven't asked me much of anything about myself, Nick."

There was a silence in the car.

Nick looked at Angel somewhere in it, and she arched an eyebrow at him, an unspoken question. Nick scowled in response. Looking back between the front seats at Dalejem, he didn't speak for a few seconds more.

"You want to meet my mom?" he said, his voice gruff. "Really?"

"Of *course* I want to meet your mother," Dalejem said, clicking at him. "Why wouldn't I want to meet your whole family?"

Angel grinned; she couldn't help it.

"I soooo want to be there for that," she murmured.

Nick aimed another scowl at her. That time, even Dalejem didn't laugh.

Instead, his voice grew serious.

"I really think you should tell them," he said. "I think you should have your family's support in this." The seer shrugged with a graceful wave of the hand. "Of course, it is not for me to say... it is entirely up to you. I just think it would be a relief, to be able to talk to them. It would be a relief to have them back in your life, in a way that is not based on a lie."

When neither Angel nor Nick spoke, Jem added,

"They obviously love you. You should trust them more."

The silence deepened.

When Angel gave Nick a bare, sideways look, she saw him thinking, now staring down, seemingly at nothing at all.

He didn't answer Dalejem, or appear to agree with him.

He didn't appear to disagree with him that time, either, though.

That time she didn't tease him, as much as that younger, more evil side of her might be tempted to. It was weird, though. She'd never seen Nick defer to anyone he'd been dating before, *especially* when it came to his family.

Generally speaking, Nick's family was off-limits.

He guarded his relationship with them like an attack dog.

He was fiercely protective of his parents. He was fiercely protective of his sisters.

"Okay," Nick said, surprising her again.

She looked over, but he wasn't looking at her, he was looking at Dalejem, a frown, along with a warning look on his face.

"...I'm not saying I'll tell them what I am," he added, his voice harder. "I'm saying I'll bring you over there. We'll go see them."

"With make-up?" Dalejem said, his eyebrow quirked. "With contacts?"

"No," Nick said. Pausing, he added, "Well, maybe with contacts, but no on make-up."

"You do not think this will disturb them? Without an explanation?"

Nick frowned. "Will you just let me meet you halfway on this?" he growled. "I'll take you over there. I'm not sure what I'll tell them, but I'll take you, we'll stay for dinner or whatever my mom wants. I don't know exactly what I'll tell them, but you're going to leave that to *me*, all right? Including about you and me."

Dalejem grunted, folding his arms across his chest.

"So I am to be a 'friend,' then? A work colleague?"

"I didn't say that, either," Nick growled, his voice openly annoyed. "For fuck's sake. Will you just let it go for now?"

Pausing, he added,

"My mom will grill the shit out of you, anyway. She's not stupid. She'll know we aren't just 'friends,' all right? And I had no intention of lying to her about that, anyway."

Angel gave Nick a look.

Noticing that time, he grimaced in her direction.

"What?" he said.

"You don't think Yumi would care if you were suddenly gay, Nick? When she's watched you be a human slut with women for thirty or so years?"

Nick frowned.

His eyes darted to Dalejem, and his frown deepened.

Then, seeming to think about her words, he shrugged.

"Honestly?" he said. "I doubt it. I'm sure the family would gossip about it, but I don't think she'd freak out or anything, if that's what you mean. She'd grill the shit out of Jem, though. She'd want to know how we met, who hit on who first, what I'd promised him, how serious we were, whether he liked kids... and she sure as hell wouldn't trust me to tell her."

Dalejem let out a disbelieving laugh. "Seriously?"

Nick gave him a look. "You don't know my mom."

Angel laughed. She did know Nick's mom.

"Yeah," she said, thinking about what Nick had said. "That sounds about right."

They were coming into the outskirts of Santa Cruz.

All of them fell silent that time, and it hit Angel, as she turned into another windy segment of Highway 1, the part that hugged the cliffs, that looked out over the small beaches and tidepools along this part of the coast, what a big deal it was for Nick to promise Dalejem even this, even the small amount he had.

She wondered if Dalejem knew how big a deal it was.

Glancing at the seer's slightly hard-looking face in the rearview mirror, she found herself thinking he probably didn't... know, that is.

As it was, she found herself wishing she could read him as easily as he read her.

Clearly, something they'd just been talking about bothered him.

It seemed to bother him a lot.

12

THE LIGHTHOUSE

"You are way too good at this," Nick muttered, when the seer paddled up to him, gasping a little and smiling after he'd just caught a wave.

When the seer got closer, Nick raised his voice slightly, so Jem would hear him.

"You are way too good at this," he repeated, louder. "You don't need a teacher, Jem. You need a better board... one that fits your skill level and height. Seriously. If surfing comes this naturally for you, just ignore anything I say. Just do your thing. Trust your instincts. Anything I tell you will probably just fuck you up."

Jem blinked at him.

Then he laughed.

"You are abdicating teaching duties with me?" he said, throwing his head back and pushing the wet hair out of his face. "Already?"

Nick shrugged from where he sat on his own board.

"I really don't think there's much I could teach you, based on what I've seen. Just practice. At this rate, you'll be better than me in a week. Then I'll need lessons from you."

Jem laughed again, rolling his eyes, seer-fashion.

"I doubt that, brother," he said, smiling.

"I don't," Nick said seriously. "I'm not blowing smoke, Jem. You're on a crappy board that's too small for you and you're still holding your own. You don't need my help. You just need a better board, and—"

Jem was clicking at him though, in a way that made Nick fall silent.

The seer paddled directly up to him, until they were only a few feet apart.

When he reached his side, Jem sat up entirely, positioning his ass squarely at the balance point on the board and gasping a little in the cold air. Clenching his fingers together, he blew on his hands, which were bright pink in Nick's vampire vision.

Nick started worrying it was too cold for the seer.

It really might be too cold for him.

He was about to say as much when Dalejem looked at Nick, stopping his gaze when he caught Nick watching him.

"I've surfed before, Nick," he said.

Nick blinked.

Then, staring at the seer's face in the dark, he frowned.

"You've surfed before?" he said. "How many times?"

"Enough. It's been a few years," he added with a shrug. "But it turns out it's a bit like that human expression about bicycles. I remember more than I thought I would."

There was a silence.

Well, not a silence, but they stopped speaking.

The sound of the ocean filled the gaps.

Even those were quieter than usual. Since it was night, the sea lions, even the seagulls were mostly quiet.

Nick was still frowning when he finally spoke.

"Why did you lie to me?" he said, more bewildered than angry. Well, and maybe a little hurt. "Why would you lie to me about that? Why in the fuck would you ask me to teach you? Were you trying to make me look stupid?"

The seer stared at him with those light-green eyes, still gasping a bit in the cold.

"Make you look stupid?" he said, frowning. "No."

"Then why—"

"Maybe I wanted you to teach me?" Jem suggested, shrugging his broad shoulders. "Maybe I wanted to see what you were like, as a teacher? I am thinking now I should have waited until spring, though. Or summer."

Nick ignored the last part.

His frown deepened. "So this was what...? A test?"

"Not a test." Appearing to think, Jem shrugged then, his strangely perfect lips pulling into a frown. "Well. Maybe a *little bit* of a test. Maybe I wanted to know how you would react to me having some skill in an area where you pride yourself an expert—"

Nick let out an outraged laugh.

The outrage wasn't entirely in jest.

"Really? You're fucking serious?"

Jem shrugged, meeting his gaze with those stunning, pale green eyes. "It is a good thing to know about a partner, is it not? How they react to being the one with the power? How they react to that power being threatened in some way?"

Nick stared at him in the dark.

The waves bobbed both of them up and down gently.

Seeing Dalejem studying him back, now apparently assessing how he was reacting to this, Nick let out a snort.

"Jesus. I thought *I* had trust issues."

"Would you not want to know this?" Jem said, his voice sharper. "About me?"

Nick glared at him harder. "I thought *I* was a control freak."

Dalejem clicked at him.

That time, however, he looked annoyed.

"Says the person who didn't bother to tell me his family was alive," Jem said, speaking louder over the waves. "Or that he was close to that family... or that he'd been in contact with them since being turned into a vampire. The same vampire who doesn't want to introduce me to them as his partner. Or at all, really, since he'd rather lie to them about what he is—"

"Jesus Christ," Nick cut in. "You're *still* pissed off about that?"

He stared at the other male's face, making it out as a pale oval with detailed features, framed in hair that looked black now that it was wet, and half tied back from his face. Like the seer's hands, Dale-jem's face was pinker than usual, yet also somehow paler than usual.

Nick could see a conflict of emotions flicker across that face.

It shocked Nick still, how much he could see with his vampire eyes.

After focusing on the other male's features for a handful of seconds, he could see him almost as if it were daylight.

He saw every nuance of those green eyes, including the flicker of real anger that lived in those pale irises.

"You are," Nick said, frowning. "You really are pissed off at me about my damned *family*. About the fact that I haven't figured out what to tell them about what I am."

He grabbed the seer's board, jerking it towards him as they bobbed up and down in slow, sensual strokes from the ocean's lull between larger waves.

It wasn't fully to bring the seer closer to him.

It was the equivalent, out here, of shaking the seer by his shoulders.

"Why?" he demanded. "Is it really because I'm afraid to tell my nearly eighty-year-old parents that I *died?* I'm seriously not sure how that's hard to understand—"

"It's not that, brother."

"Then what?"

Jem looked out over the moonlit water, his long jaw hard, his eyes scanning the horizon, maybe for waves. It was getting quieter out here, now that it was getting later, the bigger waves fewer and further between.

Anyway, Nick suspected Jem wasn't looking for waves.

"You don't want to tell me," Nick said, frowning.

It wasn't really a question.

Thinking, he added,

"Is it that I never asked you about yourself?"

Jem rolled his eyes. "No."

Nick frowned more. "Good. Because I asked you about surfing and you fucking *lied* to me about it. Given that, I'd likely have been wasting my time asking you anything, at least until we're past this phase where, apparently, *absolutely everything* between us needs to be a fucking psychological test of some kind, to see how I'll react—"

"She called you a name. Angel."

Nick blinked, genuinely confused.

"What? What are we talking about now—?"

"Just how many women did you sleep with?" Jem cut in, staring at him through the dark. "As a human? This term Angel used with you... that didn't feel wholly like she was joking." He muttered, "It didn't feel like she was joking at all."

"Term?" Nick stared at him.

Then, realizing what the seer meant, he let out an incredulous laugh.

"You mean when she called me a slut?" Nick let out another laugh. "You're kidding, right? Angel was just giving me shit—"

"About something real." Jem gave him a hard look, a near-warning in his voice. "She was giving you shit about something real, Nick."

Pausing, staring at Nick's face when he was too bewildered to answer, the seer added,

"You weren't like this when I knew you. As a human. You didn't sleep around indiscriminately... at least not that I saw."

"Who says I slept around 'indiscriminately' at all?" Nick growled.

The seer ignored that, too.

"What was the difference, Nick?" he said. "Why did you stop? Was it because you were in love with Miriam?"

Nick's jaw fell more.

He stared at the seer perched on Angel's highlighter-green

board, a leftover from the color trends back when they were both kids and an eyesore now.

Jem sat on the thing like he'd been surfing his whole life.

Which, as it turned out, he may well have done.

Thinking about Dalejem's question, he fought between wanting to goad him more, wanting to laugh, and wanting to shake the seer, hard, with both hands.

"What do you want me to say?" he said in the end, making his voice as neutral as he could. Clenching his jaw, he fought to understand what he was supposed to say to this. "Are you seriously mad at me because I had commitment issues as a human? Or that I wanted people who didn't want me? Or was I not supposed to have wanted anyone at all, before we met?"

"No, goddamn it!" Jem turned on him, his pale eyes flashing colder. "You're such an *asshole,* Nick. This stupid act of yours... it is so goddamned maddening. Are you really going to pretend you don't know I'm threatened by the Miriam thing?"

"Miri?" Nick blinked, his jaw hardening. "I thought I was a slut?"

"Clearly, both are true," Dalejem snapped, not missing a beat. "I was already wondering about Miriam, about where I fit with this... and now, which is *very* nice, by the way, I'm further threatened by the fact that you burned through women before that. Which, if nothing else, makes crystal clear not only your preferences, but your probable views of me..."

"My probable views of you." Nick stared at Jem's face, fighting not to react.

He wanted to yell at him now, but he fought that, too.

He could feel an irrational heat building in his chest.

It made him want to shake the seer again, or maybe just bite him... anything to shut him up, although he couldn't fully explain that to himself either, not with his rational mind. He could feel the part of him that understood the seer feeling threatened.

Moreover, even though he hadn't bitten Jem, even though he wasn't a seer, he could feel the fear on the other male somehow.

He knew Jem had "issues," as Black would have said.

Jem as much as told him that, all the way back in Siberia.

Jem had issues, and they still hadn't talked about it.

Clearly something about Nick was setting those issues off.

Remembering something else, Nick scowled.

"Wait." His voice hardened. "Wait a minute, Jem. Didn't Mika tell me you were, like, *known* for burning through sexual partners? I thought she meant women at the time, but clearly, she meant men *and* women. I remember her giving you shit about it, on *Koh Mangaan*. She said before you fell for 'the boss's wife,' you slept with most of their—"

"Just shut up," the seer snapped.

Nick flinched.

The silence between them deepened.

Then Jem exhaled in anger, motioning sharply out over the dark water, and rolling swell of waves moving under their boards.

"You don't even *like* males," the seer snapped. "I don't know what the fuck I'm doing with you. I must be a fucking idiot. Doing this again... with someone who has no real interest in me. With someone who won't *ever* have any real fucking interest in me."

Staring out over the water, the seer shook his head angrily, folding his arms.

Nick's jaw hardened.

He stared at the male seer, now verging on angry himself.

When Jem looked at him, Nick looked away, fighting an urge to tell him to go fuck himself. His anger only worsened though, until he couldn't keep it off his face.

"What?" Jem said. "Go ahead. Deny it. Deny you prefer females, Nick. Deny the fact that you never would have *touched* me, had you remained human—"

"And yet, I'm not fucking *human*, Dalejem. Not anymore. So why does this even matter? Why do you keep wanting to take that shit out on me, like it was something I had any control over in the first place?"

"Do you really not understand what I want from you?" Jem

turned, staring at him through the dark, his eyes nearly glowing in the moonlight. "Are you playing stupid again? Because I really cannot tell sometimes, Nick. I really can't."

Nick blinked.

Then he frowned harder.

"Do you know what I want from you?" Jem snapped. "Do you?"

"No!" Nick growled back. "Other than you apparently want me to have never slept with anyone else, especially not women, or apparently to have even wanted women, or had a preference for women, before I met you. Apparently, you're going to hold shit against me that isn't even fucking *relevant* anymore. Apparently, you'd rather if I'd never been human at all, I guess, since those things only really mattered to me then—"

"Don't hide behind this 'human' bullshit—" Jem began angrily.

That time, Nick cut him off for real.

"It's not *bullshit*," he growled, raising his voice. "I'm not going to *cheat* on you, Jem! Why the fuck do you keep acting like you can't trust me, like I'm some kind of dick who's still chasing Miri around? You know damned well I'd sooner cut my own wrists than go near her—"

"That is *guilt*, Nick," Jem snapped. "I'm not interested in your *di'lanlente a' guete* guilt. Don't you see how that's not exactly helping, in terms of what *I'm* talking about?"

"What *are* you talking about?" Nick growled, louder. "Are you going to tell me? Or do you just want to fight with me for some fucking reason?"

"Maybe I do," Jem snapped, throwing up a hand. "Maybe it's the only way to get any *truth* out of you! To anger you into telling me what you really think—"

"Or maybe I need to fucking *bite* you," Nick growled, his voice harder. "Just to get some goddamned sense out of you. Because I'm not the one who's avoiding telling you what's going on... 'brother' Jem. You're one hundred percent throwing shit at me right now. Pretty much anything you can think of for why we won't work, why you can't trust me, insulting me to piss me off... really any excuse you can think of to walk."

He felt his jaw harden.

Emotion rose in him, clenching his chest.

"Is that what you want?" he growled, forcing it back. "To walk? Or do I have to bite you to get that out of you, too?"

There was a silence.

Then Jem scoffed, again sounding more angry than amused.

"As if you would," he muttered.

Nick clenched his jaw harder.

He was still fighting to control himself, maybe in part because of everything he'd just said, maybe in part because he was pretty sure some part of Dalejem *wanted* him to lose his cool.

He watched the seer's face, wary.

When Jem still didn't speak, Nick made a feeble attempt to lighten things, nudging the seer with an arm.

"I don't know," he said, gruff. "I *might* bite you. You sure as hell deserve it. And you look pretty tasty, sitting there. Glowering at me. Looking like you want to punch me in the face, just because I did things as a human you don't like—"

Jem reached over both boards, grabbing him.

The seer moved... fast.

Faster than even Nick's vampire reflexes could respond to.

Nick threw up his hands instinctively anyway, sure the seer was about to hit him, but Jem grabbed his arms, shoving Nick backwards onto his own board and leaning his full weight on Nick's chest.

Immediately, Nick felt his body react.

Aggression hit at his vampire nature differently than it had when he was human. He didn't get scared. He didn't get angry. He didn't even want to fight.

He looked up at the seer's face, and made his body go soft.

That only made the anger in Jem's eyes worse.

Gripping Nick's wrists, he shoved down on him on the board, bobbing it partway under the water. Nick got a mouthful of salt-water and spit it out, blinking his eyes as he looked past the seer's dark head and up at the stars.

Somehow, what came to him wasn't that the seer seemed to want to drown him.

Instead, he found himself thinking it was a strangely clear night.

He knew it must be cold as hell, but the cold didn't bother him anymore.

He wondered again if the seer was cold.

He was about to ask when Jem shoved at him again.

"Goddamn it," Dalejem snapped. "I don't know what you're thinking about, but stop it. Stop fucking *going away* when I'm trying to talk to you—"

"Jem." Nick coughed up more water from the seer dunking him. "I'm not going away. I'm worried it's too cold out here for you... I'm worried you're too cold."

Jem stared at him, his eyes and voice disbelieving. "What?"

"Will you just tell me?" Nick growled. "Tell me what's bothering you, damn it! Or let us get out of the water, at least... so you can warm up."

"Warm up?" Jem continued to stare. "What the fuck are you talking about, Nick?"

Nick frowned, looking up at his pale, disturbingly beautiful face.

"You know what's bothering me!" Jem said, shaking him. "I *just fucking told* you—"

"I'm not in love with Miriam!" Nick snapped. "I'm not in love with her, goddamn it!"

"Bullshit!"

"No. It's not." Nick scowled for real. "It's not *bullshit.* I love her, yes. I love her a lot. But I don't feel that way about her anymore. Whatever that was... whatever I felt at the start of all this... it's gone. I don't *think* about her that way now. I really don't."

Jem just stared at him for a beat.

Then, clicking under his breath, he looked away.

Nick watched as the seer stared out over the waves, his mouth set in a hard line. His jaw remained clenched as he gripped Nick's wrists.

"I want to believe you," he said.

"You *do* believe me," Nick said, angry. "I know you do. I can fucking *feel* it on you, Jem... even without the blood connection. So stop telling me I'm playing 'dumb' and tell me what the hell this is about. Is it about women?"

Seeing the other's face twist into an angry grimace, Nick raised his voice.

"Yeah, I liked women. I liked them a lot. What the hell does that have to do with you and me?"

Jem let out a disbelieving laugh, but Nick cut him off.

"It only matters if you don't trust me," Nick said. "Which, clearly, you don't. You don't trust me at all. Is that because of that dick you dated back on your old planet? Or that threesome thing with the dick's wife? Because I'm a little tired of you projecting that shit onto me. I'm not him. I'm not her. And I pretty much hate both of them at this point."

At Dalejem's angry scowl, Nick's voice grew colder.

"...and maybe *I'm* not the one who's still in love with someone else."

Seeing Dalejem's face harden more, Nick cut him off before he could speak.

"...If not several someone's," he added. "Since I honestly can't tell which one of them you're still hung up on. Assuming it's not both of them. Or someone else. Either way," Nick snapped. "This relationship is feeling pretty goddamned crowded, Jem."

There was a silence after he spoke.

Jem didn't loosen his grip on Nick's wrists.

He looked away from Nick's face, breathing harder inside the rented wetsuit, still pinning Nick's wrists to the board. The seer's jaw hardened before he looked back at Nick, his face in shadow as he stared down at him.

Nick was about to say more, to try and get a real answer out of him, when Jem lowered his mouth. He kissed him, his lips salty, his tongue hot in Nick's much colder vampire mouth.

The contrast shocked Nick into silence... then turned him on instantly.

It also made Nick shockingly aware of just how cold his body had gotten in the January, after-midnight, Pacific Ocean.

Guilt hit him again, as he realized he could be giving his boyfriend hypothermia...

He forgot that, too, as Jem's kiss deepened.

He strained up against the seer, wanting his hands back, but unwilling to force the issue by making Jem let him go.

He kissed him back instead, carefully once his fangs extended, groaning against the other's mouth. When Jem pulled away, only long enough to bite Nick's throat, sinking his teeth deep enough to break the skin, Nick writhed under him, clenching his jaw to keep from throwing the seer off him for real.

The seer bit him a lot.

Jem bit him a hell of a lot.

It ignited Nick's predator/prey instincts so intensely he'd been forced to stop what they were doing a few times.

He'd been forced to walk away.

Now, out here, on the cold waves, he let out a frustrated cry.

He closed his eyes, fighting to let go, to just let the seer do what he wanted. He'd almost succeeded, falling into the heat of the other's body, his tongue and lips on his throat... when Jem raised his head.

Letting out a frustrated sound, the seer slammed him down on the board again, submerging Nick in the salty water.

Nick, startled, came up seconds later, exhaling and coughing out water.

He didn't need to breathe, but having his throat and lungs fill with water still brought up a human-like reaction to drowning in him. Moreover, it reminded him of being waterboarded, in Iraq. He wasn't past all those memories either, so he panicked, fighting to get the water out of his throat, nose and chest.

He coughed out more, looking up at Jem, and the seer growled at him.

He fucking *growled* at him.

"Jesus Christ," Nick said, still staring up. "What the fuck is wrong with you?"

The words came out less angry than bewildered.

Nick honestly wasn't sure if he, meaning Nick himself, was angry at all.

He couldn't make sense of seer emotions, of vampire emotions.

He just felt frustrated and turned on, and confused enough that it was coming out as something like anger, something like frustration, something like aggression. He could feel the seer pulling away from him, and that brought up fear, along with a desire to close down, to avoid all of it. He knew, in some quieter part of his mind, that he was waiting for the seer to walk away. He was waiting for whatever this was to blow up for real.

But he couldn't make himself walk away first.

Even now, even with the seer wanting to kill him apparently, Nick pressed his now-hard cock up against the seer's hip, still fighting not to flip both of them off the board so he could rip off his maybe-boyfriend's clothes.

He was genuinely worried now, that it was too cold out here for Jem.

For the same reason, as much as he wanted to fuck the seer out here, in the waves, both of them half-underwater, maybe while holding the bastard up by the throat to keep him from drowning... he wasn't going to do it.

He wanted to get him out of the water.

He was worried Jem was going to catch pneumonia.

Before he could get far into that line of thought—

"You belong to me," Jem growled. "You fucking *belong* to me."

Nick blinked, staring up at him.

He opened his mouth to answer, but the seer slammed his weight down on him again, pushing the board partway under water. Nick raised his head, fighting to keep it up so it wouldn't go all the way under that time, but he got a mouthful of seawater anyway.

When the seer let him up, he coughed.

"You've lost your goddamned—"

"I haven't lost *shit,*" Jem snapped. "I'm telling you how it is for me. I don't give a fuck if you don't want to hear it. I don't give a *fuck*, Nick."

Nick stared at him.

He opened his mouth to speak, but Jem slammed down the board again, submerging him entirely that time.

When Jem let him up, Nick exhaled in a startled gasp.

"Don't fucking say anything," Jem snapped, while Nick spit up more water. "Not unless you're going to agree with me. I don't want to hear another fucking *word* out of you if you don't agree. I don't want to hear any stupid questions about *what I mean* and *where is this coming from* and *are you serious.* If you play stupid on me right now, I will fucking *leave* you out here. I'll make Angel leave you, too. You can damned-well walk home. Find some woman whose basement you can borrow in the meantime, fuck her and feed off her until it's dark again..."

Nick scowled, opening his mouth.

Jem cut him off.

"I'm not bluffing, Nick. I'm not *bluffing,* goddamn it. SHUT UP. If you don't agree... keep your fucking mouth shut. Don't say anything."

Nick stared at him.

He fought to think through what the seer had said.

Truthfully, he was afraid to say anything.

He was afraid to laugh, which for some reason nearly bubbled up as well.

He knew the last part was a nervous reaction, though.

He could feel the fury on Dalejem now.

It was so tangible, it felt almost like a blood connection, like he could feel him for real. Thinking about that, about what it would be like to really know the other's thoughts, to feel his emotions, the things going through his mind, he let out an involuntary groan.

He freed his wrist with a jerk in the same set of seconds.

Wrapping his arm around the seer, he yanked his body up against him, straining upwards to kiss him on the mouth. When the seer cooperated, at least enough for Nick to kiss him, Nick let out another groan.

He wanted to kiss him hard, to shut the fucker up, to silence both of their thoughts... instead he kissed him only as hard as he could, given that his fangs were fully extended, given that the goddamned seer was trying to run his tongue over those razor-like fangs even now, trying to coax him into feeding on him.

When Jem did it again, when he kept on doing it, Nick pulled away, angry.

"No," he growled. That time, it was him who shook the seer. "NO. You do that against my will and we're done. We're fucking *done,* Jem."

The seer stared down at him.

His pale, green eyes were glazed now, where the moonlight caught them.

The seer looked dazed, but he was also fighting to breathe, his thick, struggling breaths seeming to catch in that broad chest.

Nick was still staring at him when the seer's eyes abruptly brightened.

The seer let out a choking sound, his chest hitching, and Nick panicked.

He didn't think.

He grabbed hold of the seer, and without waiting, sat up, grabbing the bright green board and yanking it closer to the black one with the painted flames that he'd been using all night. He pushed Jem backwards, so that he was astride his board, his wetsuit-clad legs dangling down into the black water on either side of it.

Nick watched the seer wipe his eyes.

He watched Jem avoid looking at him.

Still gripping Jem's arm, Nick shook it, tightening his fingers on the seer's bicep.

"We're going in," he growled. "Right now. We're going in."

Still avoiding Nick's eyes, the seer wiped his eyes with the side of his hand.

He didn't argue.

He didn't say anything.

When Nick shook him again, the seer only nodded, leaning down over the board to paddle when Nick tugged his own board around, kicking off with his legs as he aimed both of them towards the shore.

13

ANGRY GUESTS

We didn't meet Yarrick for dinner that night.

Black rescheduled the check-in for the following morning.

Some of that was for me.

Some of it was for the Naval forensics guy, who'd apparently been delayed first in San Diego, then again when his flight took him through Kauai with a five-hour layover, instead of bringing him directly to Oahu.

Then there was me and Black's room.

As I'd suspected I would, I crashed before Black did.

At around seven o'clock that evening, my brain just... stopped working.

Luckily, it seemed to have waited until we'd bagged, boxed up, and labeled most of the evidence of the explosion, and had a good chunk of it stored in a locked storage shed located in the parking lot by the boat dock.

Black noticed before I did.

He caught hold of me while we were near the water's edge, examining what looked like an honest-to-gods part of the soldier's corpse. Gripping my wrist lightly in his fingers, he pulled me gently but insistently aside, out of earshot of the others and at least twenty feet away from the small team of resort staff who were still down there, helping us.

"Hey, doc." He wrapped his arms around me, brushing hair out of my face with one hand. He'd brought me under one of the periphery torches, and now proceeded to stare down at my face. "When's the last time you ate?"

I frowned, looking up at him.

I tried to think, to answer his question.

My mind was a complete blank.

"Never mind," he said, his voice softer. "I'm making an executive decision. You're calling it quits. You are officially kicked off this crime scene... for at least the next twelve hours. Possibly the next twenty-four."

I frowned up at him.

I wanted to argue with him, but I wasn't entirely sure why I wanted to argue with him.

Thinking about both things, I realized he was right. It had crept up on me over the previous few hours, but now I was having trouble focusing on his face.

"You're not going to argue with me, doc," he said softly, shaking me lightly with his hands. "You're just going to agree with me, and go upstairs."

Frowning lightly, I didn't answer.

Some part of me was still trying to answer his question from before. I couldn't remember eating.

I must have though... right?

I was still staring off to the side, focusing sightlessly on the ocean, when Black gripped me tighter.

"*Gaos,*" he said, kissing my face, curling his fingers in my hair. "I'm so sorry, honey. I should have realized how tired you were. I should have sent you up hours ago."

Hugging me against his chest, exhaling heat and light and emotion into me, he released me a few beats later, his gold eyes verging on hard as he stared down at my face.

"You're done, Dr. Fox," he said, his voice now brooking no argument.

He pointed up at the stone-lined path leading up to the resort.

"Go. Right now. Order room service... and I mean a *lot* of room service. Take a shower. Eat. Then go to bed. In that order."

I smiled, in spite of myself.

"What happens if I don't?" I said.

"You're not going to find out," Black said. "Because you're going to do *exactly* what I said, doc. You're not going to rebel against it just to get your asshole husband's goat."

I laughed at that, pushing at his chest.

"Come with me," I said, my voice coaxing. "Come upstairs with me. Make sure I remember all that."

He hesitated, looking down at where I was tugging on his shirt.

I felt him thinking about it.

I also felt him gauging my light, trying to decide if he could really send me back there on my own, given what he felt on me.

Then, just as decisive, he nodded, once.

"All right," he said. "I'll get you to the door. I'll call the kitchen so I at least know you got some food."

Hesitating, he added,

"But I'm not going to stay, doc. You need sleep, and I need to finish up down here. If I stay with you, neither thing is likely to happen."

I frowned at that, looking around the beach.

I considered arguing.

Again, I had no idea why I would want to do that.

I was just standing there, staring down at what looked like a piece of burnt leg sticking out of the sand, when Black caught hold of my fingers and began leading me down the beach, away from the portable lights and rows of torches the resort staff brought down after sunset.

Truthfully, I felt nothing but relief.

Relaxing into his light, I followed as he led me across the footprint-pocked sand, then onto the stone path, then into the resort's lobby.

He never let go of me, not once, even as we rode up the elevator.

He walked me straight to the door of our suite, used his card key to get us inside, then froze. He'd barely cracked the door.

"Wait here," he said, his body stiff.

Propping the door against his shoulder, he peered inside, reaching into his jacket.

I watched him pull a handgun out of a holster. I watched him aim the gun into our room, his gold eyes sliding out of focus as he scanned the inside of our shared suite.

I should have known he was carrying. Somehow, I hadn't.

What's wrong? I sent, quiet, when he continued to scan our room.

He gave me a bare glance.

Someone's been in here. He squeezed my arm in his hand, then let go. *Stay behind the wall, doc. Wait here. I mean it. If you hear gunshots, run for the elevator. Contact resort security as soon as you get to the lobby.*

I frowned, not answering.

I had zero intention of making a run for it while my husband was being shot at.

I also knew it was pointless to argue with him, so I just said nothing.

I stood there, by the wall, as he disappeared through the opening.

By then, I was using my *aleimi* to scan inside the suite.

I slid deeper into Black's light, using his eyes, his light, even more than my own. Through him, I felt the whisper of lingering presence that set off his radar. I felt the intent there, the strangely discordant note that didn't align with anything else I felt in the room.

Whatever it was, it felt recent.

Black didn't feel anything alive inside the suite now; neither did I.

Of course, that wasn't a one hundred percent guarantee no one was there. If they were seer, or had the help of a seer, we might not feel them.

When Black reemerged, about ten minutes later, he shook his head.

"It's clear," he said.

He didn't look happy.

Relaxing marginally at his words, I leaned a hand on the wall for support. "You're sure it wasn't just an exceptionally angry housekeeper?" I said, smiling wanly.

I knew it wasn't housekeeping.

Black shook his head. "They were looking for something."

"What?"

His eyes clicked back into focus.

He met my gaze, looking me over with a frown.

"I don't know," he said. "But I don't think they found it, whatever it was." Pausing, he added, "I'm putting someone on the door. While you sleep."

I didn't argue.

I just followed him inside.

I followed his hands, his words, his feet, his gently prodding light, as he led me into the suite, then into the shower... then into bed.

I barely even remember those last two things.

I don't think I've ever fallen asleep so fast in my life.

I may have actually been asleep before I hit the bed.

I don't remember undressing, or being in the shower, or drying off, or getting under the covers. Black mentioned food, but I had no memory of eating. Black must have helped. He must have washed me, dried me off, but I don't remember that, either.

I remember his presence.

I remember warm kisses, murmured words, heated light. I remember at least one murmured conversation on the phone, another by the door.

Then everything just blissfully...

Went away.

ॐ

S ome long, dreamless blur of time later, I woke up, sitting
upright in the massive, King-sized hotel bed.

Black was already gone.

I pinged him, and he was down in the lobby.

He was waiting for me.

I'd forgotten all about our morning meeting by then.

Feeling my unwillingness, my half-wish for him to go without
me, Black started prodding me more awake with his light, pushing
me to get moving, to get up, telling me he needed me there, that
he'd wait for me.

Start without me, I told him. *I'll be fashionably late.*

We both will be, he sent back at once. *I'm waiting for you, doc.*

Ugh. Why? I sent, frowning into the fluffy hotel pillow I held
over my face. *You're going to make me hurry, aren't you?*

Not at all, he sent innocently. *I'll just be waiting for you, that's all.*

Making an exasperated sound, I tossed the pillow off the bed.

While I dragged myself out of the bed, he reminded me about
the break-in. He promised he'd let me sleep by the pool the rest of
the day, if I'd just go to the meeting with him and help him try to
figure out who'd broken into our room. He already seemed more
than halfway convinced it had been the military.

And yes, Black said, he'd had someone on my door all night.

Through all of that, I managed to open my eyes enough to
brush my teeth and figure out how to wrangle my body into a
white bikini. Over the bikini, I threw on a long white shirt and a
skirt, shoving my feet into sandals.

I'd decided throwing myself into the pool would work better
than a shower, maybe better than a cup of coffee.

I fixated on the rooftop pool.

It was closest.

I took the elevator up the two floors—only to wriggle out of the clothes I'd just wriggled into, kicking off the sandals and leaving them under a deck chair.

Without waiting, I jumped into the pool. I swam about a dozen laps, then floated on my back, sighing up at the bright blue Hawaiian sky.

I felt human again.

I also felt more or less ready to eat anything anyone wanted to put in front of me. I was so hungry, my stomach sounded like an angry dinosaur. I just couldn't quite make myself want to get out of the pool.

Around then, Black found me.

I'd barely noticed, but the pool had half-filled with tourists and A-listers by the time Black showed up, all of whom were staring at both of us, pretty much the instant Black left the elevators to fetch me.

Even with all the gawking and surreptitious picture and video-taking, Black had to coax me out, mostly by bribing me with promises of cappuccinos and pancakes.

Eventually, the thought of coffee got me to climb out of the blue water.

After I dried off and threw on clothes, Black led me back to the elevators and down to the lobby, walking me into the resort's premier breakfast place, The Blue Orchid. It was supposedly one of the "casual" restaurants out of the four or five in total at the resort, but the brunch place abutted a garden full of gardenias, hibiscus, anthurium flowers, birds of paradise.

Wild birds filled the rafters. Tropical fish swam in a long rectangular pond below a wall fountain, and modern art light fixtures hung from the white-painted walls.

It also had a perfect view of the beach.

Inside, orchids hung from the ceiling, most of which was open, since they'd pulled back the retractable top. It was still technically hurricane season, and we were due for light showers and wind over the next few days, but so far, we'd gotten nothing but sun.

Looking around as we walked in, I was a little bewildered at how little had changed since the bomb went off.

All the brunch tables were full.

Everyone was talking, laughing, eating, wearing sundresses, bathing suits, wraps, Hawaiian shirts, sunglasses, expensive-looking sandals. They draped themselves languidly over old-fashioned wicker chairs, drinking mimosas and cappuccinos, snacking on blueberry crepes and mushroom omelets like nothing had happened.

The fact that a damned bomb went off, a bomb that may or may not have been an actual human being, and it just didn't matter, was... strange.

To me, anyway.

Apparently, the cover story was working.

Equally apparently, Fournier's concerns about the incident scaring off his rich, celebrity guests were wholly unfounded. If anything, they'd gone the other way, of the two probabilities Black outlined. The Blue Sail had become the place to be.

Given that it was the off-season, maybe people were more starved for entertainment than usual.

I'd already seen two actors and a young pop singer with bright orange-dyed hair I recognized. The singer had a whole group of people roughly her age with her, including a tattoo-covered boyfriend with long, scraggly hair and a wispy goatee, who also looked familiar to me.

Funnily enough, when Black and I walked in, all eyes turned to us.

Specifically, they turned to Black.

He had on the mirrored sunglasses again, a white shirt open in the front, black tailored pants, and slip on tennis shoes.

I knew the outfit was part of Black's attempt to "blend." Glancing around, I had my doubts he was having much success in that. He still managed to draw every eye in the place, male and female, including the waiters and other staff.

Even with his bored, rich-guy schtick, he still managed to look strangely formal compared to most of the people in the resort.

He also looked oddly predatory, even with him grinning around at everyone and changing everything about his usual manner, even the way he walked.

The *oddness* of him still leaked through.

I found I was hyper-sensitive to it again, after the dragon incident.

I desperately wanted him to look normal.

I wanted him to look *excruciatingly* normal.

I wanted the very idea that there could be something strange about Black to sound ludicrous to anyone who actually met him.

Unfortunately, he just wasn't pulling that off.

Then things got worse... much, much worse.

We walked around one corner of the restaurant, towards a tucked-away table with a beach view. I recognized Yarrick at the table, along with Fournier, Keon, a woman I'd seen working in the lobby, and a man who looked even more formal than Black.

He might have been trying to blend too, but somehow only managed to make himself more conspicuous. His dark blue windbreaker screamed law enforcement. His crisp white shirt, white shorts, white socks, and white tennis shoes with white laces made him look like a caddy at a high-end golf course, or maybe a tennis pro.

His clothes, his jacket, even his socks, were so clean and wrinkle-free, he might have just put them on, fresh from a vigorous ironing.

That man had his back to us when he stood up.

Then Yarrick saw Black's head above the brunch crowd.

"Ah!" he said, smiling. "Here he is now. The consultant I told you about."

The man, who had to be the Naval forensics specialist from San Diego, followed Yarrick's eyes.

He turned smoothly, his expression serious, but relaxed.

He looked at me, a faint smile on his lips...

Then he blinked.

I saw recognition bleed into his features, along with confusion, a kind of disbelieving horror as he took in my face, his eyes sliding down the beachy clothes I wore, stopping on my feet in the leather sandals. It seemed to dawn on him, somewhere in his bewilderment, that I was real... that I was actually there... that he wasn't hallucinating.

I watched the succession of understandings hit the rest of his brain, reflected visibly in his eyes and the loosening of his jaw, right before everything seemed to click together.

His head turned sharply.

His eyes found Black.

There was the barest pause, a faint beat while his blue eyes took in Black's face.

I saw his face transform again, that time as if in slow-motion.

The man's eyes widened, opening wider and wider as he realized exactly who and what he was looking at.

Still staring, he reached inside his blue jacket.

He ripped a gun out of a holster at his ribs.

He aimed it straight at me.

14

A BAD BRUNCH

S creams erupted from a nearby table as a woman spotted the gun.

"Get your hands up! NOW!" the man in the blue jacket yelled.

I realized in stunned shock that he was talking to me.

I started to hold up my hands.

More screams echoed in the restaurant, bouncing off the volcanic stone walls around the basin separating the tropical fish-filled moat from the beach.

Black was already moving.

He likely jerked into action before the guy's hand made it inside his jacket.

I was the one who stood there like an idiot, holding up my hands.

Maybe some of it was because I couldn't believe Yarrick hadn't told him we were coming... that no one had told him we'd be here, who we were.

Whatever the reason, Black had to snatch me out of my trance.

He gripped hold of my wrist before the reality of the gun fully penetrated my still sleep and time-zone confused brain. He yanked me down with him, forcing my knees to hit the floor, then pulled me roughly behind him.

He'd dragged us both behind a stone planter basin before I heard Yarrick's voice.

"Hey!" the tech mogul yelled. "What the fuck? Put it down! What do you think you're doing? You're not even allowed to *have* that on my property!"

I knew without looking that the man with the blue windbreaker didn't put it down.

The guy hissed words back at Yarrick, not taking his eyes or the gun off the stone planter we were hiding behind.

"This is your damned 'consultant?'" The man's voice rose, openly furious. "Are you serious? Do you even know who the *fuck* that is?"

"Of course I know who it is!" Yarrick snapped. "Have you lost your mind? Put that gun away, or I'm going to have to have you removed! And I *will* press charges..."

There was a silence.

I crouched behind the planter, still well behind Black, panting as I pressed up against his side.

I could feel Black's anger as he wrapped his light protectively around mine.

I could feel his fury worsen, his energy sparking violently around me, as he tried to decide if he should use his sight to take the guy down. Without thinking about why, really, I found myself stroking his bare arm below the short-sleeved shirt he wore, subconsciously attempting to calm him down before I even realized what I was doing.

Once I'd really thought about it, I found myself winding my light into his more deliberately, pulling it into mine.

He hadn't told me much about the dragon thing yet.

He hadn't said anything, but I strongly suspected he couldn't fully control it.

That was assuming he could control it at all.

Black losing his cool here would be a very, *very* bad thing.

He looked at me, pulsing a dense pocket of heat at my chest. Leaning closer, he kissed my face, nuzzling my neck.

I'm sorry, doc, he sent softly.

What for? I sent back, genuinely puzzled. *You probably just saved my life.*

I mean about the dragon thing, he sent. *It's not on you to keep me from losing my shit. You're right, though, we need to talk—*

"Black!" Yarrick called out.

He raised his voice when neither of us answered.

"Black! It's all right. You can come out now. He's putting it down."

"Down?" Black growled. "Then he still has it in his fucking hand?"

Black out loud sounded nothing like the voice I'd just heard in my head.

He sounded nothing like the rich douchebag, either.

Black's voice boomed out as an overt threat, making the table full of young, hipster-looking gay men next to us jump almost a foot. I saw out of the corner of my eye when one of them, a twenty-something, extremely handsome man with dark brown hair, recovered and fanned himself dramatically, smiling to his friends.

I don't think Black noticed any of that.

"Did you confiscate the damned *gun*, Peter?" he growled in the same voice. "Because I'm not risking my wife's life on the word of that trigger-happy asshole. Get the gun. Take it away from him, or I'm taking her out of here... now... and filing fucking charges—"

"He put it away," Peter said.

"Did I stutter?" Black growled. *"Take* it from him. Or we're leaving."

There was another silence.

In it, I could feel Black reading all of the men on the other side of that planter, as well as the security guards now approaching from the front of the restaurant.

Feeling my presence, Black opened his mind, showing me that security was coming, Peter's guys. Along with Black, I watched through the Barrier as the man in the blue jacket unholstered his gun a second time, handing it over with obvious anger to Yarrick.

I saw the gun exchange hands.

I saw Yarrick activate the safety, and shove it in his coat pocket.

I knew Black saw it too, but he still sounded angry when he spoke.

"Do you have it? Pete?"

Yarrick let out a dramatic sigh. "Yes, Quentin. I'm handing it to Marshall, on my security team, right now." There was a pause. "Marshall has it now."

"I got it," a different voice confirmed.

"What kind of gun is it?" Black said.

There was a pause.

"Sig Sauer P226," the new voice said.

"This guy a SEAL, Marshall?" Black asked, as if the Naval officer and Yarrick weren't standing right there.

There was a silence.

Then the security guard named Marshall grunted.

"Looks like it to me, boss," he said, a smile in his voice. "He looks mighty pissed you asked, so I'm thinking you're on the money."

"Frisk him, Marshall," Black growled. "Do a good job. And don't forget his ankles."

There was another silence.

In it, I read the minds of the group on the other side of the planter through Black, including Marshall the security guard, Yarrick, the Naval officer, and another security guy standing there, and even Fournier and Keon, who were sitting at the table, slack-jawed.

As I touched the various minds, I watched via the Barrier as both of Yarrick's security people—starting with the big, Samoan-looking guy, Marshall—patted down the Naval officer, who stood there, exuding fury, his hands and arms in the air.

They didn't find any more guns on him.

Feeling other presences, closer to me, I glanced to my right, that time primarily with my physical eyes. Once I had, I jumped, startled to see how close a group of tourists sat to where Black and I crouched.

They were all staring at us, three women and two men in their party, delighted smiles on their faces at how close we were, and how exciting all of this was.

Behind them, I also saw that we were being filmed by that same group of twenty-something celebrities and pop stars I'd noticed as Black and I were walking in. All of them had their smartphones aimed at me and Black and the Naval officer on the other side of the stone planter. The singer I'd recognized was grinning like a loon, halfway under the table to aim her phone, seemingly right at Black's ass.

I couldn't help rolling my eyes.

I'm sure at least a few of them caught my eyeroll on their smartphones, but I didn't much care.

They could have been *shot,* and here they were, gleefully antici-pating being the first to get Black's face... or possibly his ass... up on social media, as part of some kind of epic gun battle they could detail to their rapt followers.

I had no doubt they'd risk being shot again just to film the Naval guy trying to kill me or Black a second time.

Hell, they were probably disappointed neither of us had been shot already.

Black was slowly rising to his feet.

He gripped my hand tightly, so I rose with him.

Even in that, Black kept me shielded with his body, although I leaned out anyway, watching tautly from behind his arm. I had zero compunction about jumping both of us out of there if neces-sary, even if it meant sending a clean-up crew to erase the minds of every human in this place.

Of course, I knew that was primarily bravado.

I knew how unrealistic it was—not just me being able to out-think and outrun a bullet, but the idea that we could get to everyone here and erase every trace of the event, given the number of smartphones trained on us right now.

I hoped like hell Black knew what he was doing.

I do, too, he muttered in my mind.

We walked around the planter, Black now stalking as much as walking, his body and movements so predator-like, I found myself falling into the energy behind his strides, reacting to them in spite of myself.

Unfortunately, I wasn't reacting the way I should have been, under the circumstances.

I felt Black's more predatory side notice.

I felt that part of him gear into his military persona, his eyes tracking the room, looking for threats—threats other than the Naval officer in front of us.

Unfortunately, none of that helped my light's reactions to him.

Cut it out, doc, he murmured in my mind. *That's distracting as hell.*

Before I could answer, he spoke aloud.

"Are you here alone?" Black growled to the man in the blue windbreaker.

The Navy SEAL glared between me and Black, lowering his hands slowly back to his sides as the security guards backed away.

"Do you have any idea how many people are looking for you?" His blue eyes glared unmistakably at me. "...Not to mention your wife."

Black glanced at me, frowning.

He looked back at the Naval officer.

Black came to a stop as he approached an open chair, keeping me behind him with a nudge of his light and a warning look. He laid both of his muscular hands on the chair's back, gripping it tightly and staring coldly into the Naval officer's face.

"I've been talking to people at the Pentagon since four o'clock this morning," Black said, low, presumably so as not to be overheard. "They know full well I'm on this."

"Funny," the officer said. "No one called me."

"Maybe you're just not in the loop... lieutenant."

"That's *commander,*" the other snapped.

There was a silence while the two of them just stared at one another.

Then Black straightened.

He pulled out the chair he still gripped in one of his hands.

Angling himself around it, and nudging me with his light to sit next to him, he folded himself inside the bamboo chair like some kind of giant, bipedal cat.

"I don't get a fucking name?" Black growled. "How do I know who to credit, when I call my pals in D.C. to commend their officers on the front lines for their *sterling* judgment in pulling a loaded weapon in the middle of a public place?"

Black glanced around the dining area, his sculpted lips curling in an open scowl.

"Or were you about to tell me it's perfectly appropriate for you to wave a gun around in a place packed with this many civilians? To threaten my *wife.* Without so much as telling us what you believe the charges against us even are?"

"Really? You want to know what the charges are?" The commander grunted, his expression disbelieving. "You say that like every law enforcement agency in the country hasn't been looking for you for *weeks—*"

"I've been out of town," Black cut in, his voice a harder growl. "Which you would know, if you knew *shit.* Hell. Ask Peter here. Apparently, he's more in the loop with the military leadership than you are."

Black jerked his chin towards his friend, who was still standing, looking warily between the two of them. From Yarrick's expression, he was waiting for one of them to try and kill the other again.

Black growled, "Petey here made a deal with your higher-ups yesterday. Maybe you should ask someone about that."

"Where the *fuck* have you been?" the Naval commander snapped. "Are you going to explain yourself?"

"Why the hell would I?" Black leaned forward, his light growing hotter.

I felt my own light reacting to it, coiling around his, even as I glanced at him nervously.

To the other male's credit, he didn't even flinch.

"...I still don't even know who the *fuck* you are," Black added.

When the other's expression grew colder, Black looked at Peter Yarrick.

"Do I have to put up with this shit, Pete?" he said, his eyes focusing back on the Naval Commander. "Because if so... I changed my mind. I'm not charging you enough. Getting shot at by dickheads wasn't part of the deal. Neither was risking my wife's life."

I glanced at the Naval officer.

His dark blue irises were locked on my face, his mouth twisted in a hard scowl. Both reflected a loathing I could feel as much as see.

When he didn't look away, or make any effort to disguise his revulsion of me, I fought the urge to hiss at him.

"Your superiors know where I was, anyway," Black said, his voice openly warning as he looked between me and the Naval officer. "They know where my wife was. Both of us have been in Patagonia for almost two months—"

"—And you just happened to miss every goddamned newspaper, every online news source, every television in existence?" the officer snapped, swiveling his head to glare at Black. "For two months, you never once saw news about the damned border wall on fire, or dragon sightings all over the Pacific?"

"That was the whole fucking point," Black growled. "The whole damned *point* of the trip was to unplug. Our tour organizer designed it so we could—"

"Bullshit! Who does that?" the man cut in angrily. "Who just 'disappears' like that?"

"Rich people," Black snapped back.

Yarrick let out an involuntary snort.

The Naval officer glared at him.

Peter wiped the look off his face with a faintly apologetic wave, but the smile never entirely left his lips.

Black went on, drawing the commander's eyes back to him.

"Hell, did it ever occur to you that the reason we got blamed for all this, is that someone knew we *wouldn't* see it? Check our social media accounts, genius. We talked about this trip for *weeks* leading up to it. Thousands of people knew... hundreds of thousands, just based on our follower counts alone..."

The officer shook his head, his jaw clenched so that the bone protruded.

"Convenient."

"Really?" Black said. "Is it? Because it seems a fuck of a lot *less* convenient to us. We just wanted to unplug. To meditate. Hang out in nature. It was an end of year thing. It was also something we've talked about doing practically since we first met... and it kind of *sucked* coming back to all of this b.s."

Black's voice grew louder towards the end.

I knew why.

He was hoping some of his speech would end up on the smart-phone footage still being recorded all around us.

Black snapped, "It wasn't a fucking *secret,* jackass. My wife posted photos before we left... so did I... so did the social media team run by my publicist. If you geniuses would figure out how to use these new-fangled, wacky, 'computer' devices..." Black hooked his fingers in sarcastic air quotes. "...you could have found us months ago. Then maybe you'd be looking for whoever doctored those video feeds. Not us."

By the end, Black was nearly shouting.

When he finished, there was another silence.

The tables around us were silent, too.

Somewhere in that, the Naval officer turned to glare at me.

"Do you seriously expect me to believe the two of you somehow 'missed' everything happening in the world for two months, due to some kumbaya vacation you and your wife took in the Andes Mountains—"

"I don't give a *fuck* what you believe," Black snapped.

That time, he sounded genuinely angry.

I mean really, really angry.

It actually made me stiffen, made the hairs on my arms stand on end.

"...And if you don't stop looking at my wife like that," Black added coldly, leaning over the table. "You and I are going to have a serious goddamned problem."

There was a denser silence.

I have to give Navy boy props. He held Black's gaze.

"Where *was* your wife, the night before last?" the officer said. "Out of curiosity? You said you got back yesterday—"

"She was here. With me. Not like it's any of your fucking—"

"All night?"

Black stared at him incredulously. He waved at Yarrick. "Peter knows when we got in. I called him as soon as we made it to this part of the island—"

"And you can prove that, I suppose?"

"Yes," Yarrick broke in. "He can."

The Commander swiveled his head to stare at Yarrick.

Peter Yarrick returned his gaze, his mouth pinched in a hard frown. The billionaire tech prodigy looked openly annoyed.

When the Naval officer opened his mouth to speak, Yarrick raised a hand, cutting him off.

"No," he said. "Just stop."

Exhaling, he flipped his wrist over to stare pointedly at his watch.

"Can we start over?" he said. "Maybe hurry things along a bit?"

When no one answered, Yarrick motioned towards Black.

"Commander Henry Narcisse... this is Mr. Quentin Black and his wife, Dr. Miriam Fox. Dr. Fox, Mr. Black... this is Commander Henry Narcisse of the United States Navy, expert in military forensics. He's here to help us evaluate the site on the beach, and to take custody of the evidence you two did such an *excellent* job collecting yesterday."

Silence followed his words.

Yarrick exhaled again, fingering a lock of curly brown hair out of his face.

"Before you walked up and everyone lost their damned minds," he said, giving Black a humorless smile. "The Commander here was telling me they plan to loop in the police here on Oahu, but he'd like a look at any remains we were able to collect first."

Glancing at Narcisse, he added,

"He'd also like to interview everyone involved in evidence collection. And all of you who saw the evidence in its... well, *intact* form." Yarrick motioned around the table at me, Black, Fournier, Keon. "Before the explosion."

I knew he meant the body.

Exhaling in exasperation at the continued silence, Yarrick raised his voice.

"I was hoping we could have a *civilized* meal together, first," Peter said. "I'm now thinking I should have gotten us a private conference room... but I was trying to be considerate of Commander Narcisse. I thought he might be tired. And hungry."

"I'm fine," Narcisse said, back to glaring at me.

I felt Black's anger ratcheting up as he caught Narcisse's stare.

Feeling him gearing up to say something, I laid a hand on his arm.

"Did you want to forego breakfast?" I asked Narcisse, as politely as I could. "We could meet you after we eat. It might be difficult to talk in here now, anyway, given the number of cameras pointed at our table."

I glanced around us to demonstrate the point, then focused back on Narcisse, who still looked pissed I even existed on the same planet as him.

I was tempted to tell him just how easily I could rectify that.

Next to me, Black let out an involuntary snort.

When I glanced at him, I was relieved to see humor in his eyes.

Winking at me, he swiveled his gaze back to Narcisse.

"My wife is right," he said. "We can't have any kind of reasonable discussion in here now." He looked at Yarrick, folding his hands on the table. "What do you think, Pete? Should we all just meet down at the beach site in an hour? Miri and I can get something to eat by the pool. That way I can stare at her in a bikini while I eat..."

I snorted, but couldn't help smiling a little, too.

When I glanced at Yarrick, he looked relieved.

"Agreed," he said, not bothering to ask the commander, or even pretend he cared what Narcisse thought. "Keon and the security team will take Commander Narcisse through what you've collected so far. I'll have someone come collect the two of you once we've finished that much. I'm guessing it'll take longer than an hour, but keep your phone on you."

Sounding faintly annoyed again, Yarrick added,

"Anyway, the Commander here already requested a mobile science lab from the Naval base at Pearl Harbor. He can spend today going through what you've already catalogued, rather than waste your time."

When I glanced at Narcisse, his eyes held nothing but fury.

Maybe I shouldn't have, but I couldn't help it.

I smirked.

15

WHAT'RE YOU LOOKING AT?

I spent at least an hour stretched out on my sun lounger, watching Black eat.

I watched and listened to him talk to Grant Steele, promising him an interview if he could do it from here, promising I'd sit in on at least part of that interview.

I felt Black reacting to my stare.

I also started thinking again, what a bummer this whole thing was.

I just wanted to be alone with him.

The whole point of coming to Hawaii, as far as I was concerned, was to be alone with Black. Instead we were stuck with exploding dead bodies, an asshole Naval Commander, gawking tourists, and celebrities videoing Black's ass with their smartphones every time I bothered to lift my head.

Black eventually got pissy about the last thing.

Not his ass, really.

He seemed to think more of them were videoing me in the white bikini.

Either way, he called up Yarrick and chewed him out about the constant videos of the two of us. Minutes later, someone came down and started confiscating phones and deleting videos, along with actual posts on social media.

I knew there was no way they'd get all of it, but it was weirdly satisfying to see a number of those rich twenty-somethings flip out on security guards who placidly went through their phones, ignoring them as they repeatedly hit "DELETE."

When those same A-listers screeched about lawyers, the security guards pointed out signs all over the pool and lobby areas forbidding the videotaping or photographing of other guests staying at the resort.

I even saw a few of the more obnoxious guests threatened with expulsion, or having their phones confiscated for the remainder of their stay.

Only then did I jump in the pool.

I was tempted to give the raspberry to the popstar and her friends, who were still pouting on their loungers as they stared at Black, who, stretched out and shirtless on his sun lounger, was still decimating what looked like half a pig's worth of pork skewers, washing them down with bourbon and beer.

I admit, their staring at him, coupled with the blatant lust in their eyes, did nothing to improve my mood.

When I got out of the pool the second time, the big Samoan-looking security guard, Marshall, was approaching Black's lounger.

I was climbing up the ladder to the deck when Marshall stopped over Black, blocking most of the sun with his broad shoulders, and glancing over at me periodically, as if he could tell I was listening and didn't want to be rude by not addressing both of us.

"...so he'd like you to come down there now," Marshall said, his voice apologetic as he glanced at me a second time. "He wants to do those interviews. About what you found in the boathouse. He has questions about what you saw. You know, before the..."

Glancing around us surreptitiously, he lowered his voice.

"Before the... *you* know..."

He leaned closer and made an explosion gesture with both hands, mouthing *boom* rather than finishing the sentence out loud.

Why he thought either thing would be *more* subtle than just saying the word "explosion" in a quiet voice, was beyond me.

Black looked at me, his expression somewhere between amusement and irritation.

I could feel he didn't want to go down and deal with Narcisse, either.

I don't, Black sent, speaking into my mind. *But we should, doc. Now that he's seen the remains, maybe we'll get some real answers.*

Meh, I sent back grumpily. *Who cares? I mean, do we* really *need to know? Can't we just let the military deal with this?*

Black's thoughts remained grim.

Not until I know for sure it has nothing to do with us, doc.

The body, you mean?

Yes. Gauging my eyes, Black added, *Anyway, Yarrick hired Black Securities and Investigations. He's offering us cover, too. More than I would have ever asked him for, truthfully. I probably need to check in with him on that—*

Cover? I grunted. *You mean with Commander Ass-Face? Because if that's his idea of "cover," it could use some work.*

I'm serious, Miri.

So am I, I grumbled. *That fucker almost shot us. He almost shot you,* I sent pointedly.

Black gave me a hard look.

For the first time, I felt real anger in his light.

No, he sent after a pause. *He* didn't *almost shoot us, doc. And he didn't almost shoot me. But we'll talk about that later.*

Before I could wrap my head around that, Black was already pulling himself to his feet, clapping a hand on Marshall's meaty shoulder.

"Lead the way, brother," he said genially, flashing the big Samoan one of his shark-like grins.

Exhaling, and still annoyed, I snatched my wrap off the sun lounger and tied it around my waist, shoving my feet back into my sandals as I plucked my scoop-necked T-shirt off the back of the lounger and tugged it over my wet bathing suit.

Some vacation.

❧

Marshall led us down the rock-lined path towards the beach, so apparently Narcisse and the others were still at the bomb site.

Marshall told us they had the mobile lab guys down there, too.

Unlike that first morning, I could hear people on the beach all along the path where we walked. Looking through the pineapple bushes and palm trees, I could see them, too, covering the main beach alongside a row of colored umbrellas that stood over more of the resort's dark-blue sun loungers.

Marshall had already led us past a sign and a chain that blocked off this path from the general public of resort-goers, directing them to follow a different route to the open parts of the beach.

I wondered how many minor celebrities and looky-loos had broken that line already.

I found it weirdly fitting and also vaguely ridiculous that the rich and other celebrities would be as bad about that kind of thing as, well, regular, non-celebrity people.

Once we got off the path and onto the sand, we were greeted by three more security guards, all of them armed.

They scowled at us when we first emerged from the path, and immediately began walking in our direction.

Then I saw one of them recognize Marshall.

They recognized Black next... then me.

All three of them relaxed, going back to their original positions, which presumably gave them better views of the perimeter.

On the other side of the beach, I saw three more figures wearing the light blue polo shirts and tan pants worn by the rest of the security detail.

I scanned the beach, looking for any familiar face. The only one I saw was Keon, and he was staring out at the water, a frown on his full lips.

I looked at Black, who also noted Keon, before glancing back at me.

"Stay here," he muttered. "I'll go with Marshall to find the others."

"They're probably out at the mobile lab," Marshall offered. "It's parked on the lot by the main boat dock. I can take you over there, Mr. Black."

"Sure." Black gave me another sideways look, frowning faintly.

Again, I got the feeling Black wanted me to wait here, to stay on the beach, let him go ahead. Maybe he wanted to have a word with Narcisse alone. Or maybe he wanted to make sure the Naval commander wasn't going to pull a gun on him again.

On you, Black growled in my mind. *I don't want him pulling a gun on you, doc. And I want to read him before I let you anywhere near him... since he clearly has some kind of fucking issue with you. I also want to know what he's seen, in terms of surveillance footage. And what's being said on the ground in the military about those people you disappeared.*

I thought about that.

It made sense.

Yarli couldn't clear any of that up? I sent.

She's looking into it, too, Black sent. *I've asked her to devote most of our undeployed resources to clean up, at least until we can get the targets off our backs.*

I frowned, puzzled. *I thought they were doing that already? It sure feels like they have been, if the Barrier is any indication—*

They are, he cut in. *I'm just directing it more now, doc.*

"I'll call you, Miri," he said, handing me my phone, which I'd seen him scoop up off the table by the pool. "Stay here. Maybe Keon over there can catch you up. Or keep you company, at least." Kissing my temple, he flashed me one of those killer grins. "Maybe see if you can get a free surfing lesson out of him."

I nodded, still a little puzzled, but didn't argue.

Black really seemed to think I was more of a target than he was right now.

I wondered why.

I watched as he made his way towards what remained of the boathouse, walking alongside Marshall as the other talked to him, using his hands. Still watching them head towards the cement boat ramp on the other side of the bomb wreckage, I began slowly walking towards Keon, like Black suggested.

Keon was still looking out at the ocean.

Tearing my eyes off Black, I found myself studying the Hawaiian surfer's face instead. As I did, I occasionally found myself glancing towards the ocean to see what he was looking at.

I didn't see anything.

Well, maybe a shadow.

It could have been a seal, maybe a bird.

"What're you looking at?" I said curiously, once I was close enough.

Keon jumped, maybe a half-foot, before turning towards me.

His face flushed, but I couldn't tell if it was embarrassment or if he somehow felt caught.

After a beat, he exhaled, placing his hands on his hips. He pointed towards the ocean, his mouth pursed as he continued to scan the horizon.

"I saw something," he admitted. "I'm not sure what. But it glinted. Like metal or something... I can't find it now."

"Something floating?" I suggested. "Are you worried it's more debris from the explosion?"

He shook his head. "No. Whatever it was, it was moving under its own power. I know the boss's got people patrolling out there, keeping the guests off this part of the water. Keeping the surfers closer to the main resort. I was trying to figure out if I should call him."

I followed his stare, trying to see something, anything.

I didn't notice anything that might fit his description.

I reached out with my light, scanning with my seer vision, too.

When I slid into that stretch of ocean from the Barrier, I saw living glows erupt all over and under the water.

Mostly, I saw pale lights from seaweed and algae and schools of fish. I saw seals further out, what might even have been dolphins or whales, along with more plentiful glimpses of anemone, starfish, sea cucumbers, abalone, sand dollars, coral.

I got lost there, feeling a sudden urge to go snorkeling. I hadn't ever really looked at the ocean like this, not even when we were on the island of *Koh Mangaan.*

The closest I came was looking at Black's light connection to the ocean, which was deep, and intense... and strange. It also encompassed the ocean from a more archetypal level, a kind of "ocean-ness" that lay below all the creatures that made it their home.

"There!" Keon pointed from next to me. "Do you see it?"

I followed his pointing finger, now even more puzzled, since I'd been actively looking with my light, and I hadn't noticed anything.

Maybe it was a machine.

Seers couldn't see dead matter, according to Black.

When we saw things like rocks, metal, etc., it was generally in one of two ways. Either the substance was somehow covered with live-matter imprints or remnants (algae, moss, bacteria, even things like fingerprints and other remnants of contact), or else we saw them in their absence, a blank spot next to living light.

The latter was pretty rare.

Most things on Earth were smeared with imprints and living matter of various kinds.

Whatever Keon was seeing, it couldn't be alive.

"Do you see it?" Keon said, turning to frown at me.

I was about to shake my head, to say no—

When suddenly I did.

A flicker of metal caught my eyes. It flashed brighter than the reflection of the sun on the clear blue water. I saw a dark shape, moving steadily towards the shore. At first, it didn't seem to be moving very fast... then I realized that was an optical illusion.

It was definitely moving towards us.

It was definitely moving fast, faster than most ocean animals.

Stranger, the closer it got, the more it looked like...

"Is that a *person?*" Keon said, his voice baffled.

I didn't answer at first, biting my lip.

I considered calling Black.

The thing was reaching the wave break. I watched as it went from swimming, if you could call it that, to curling into itself, reorienting its body.

Then it was on its feet, walking towards us.

The waves buffeted his chest and belly at first, but the man never slowed.

It *was* a man, I realized.

It was definitely a man.

He wore all black, what looked like a wetsuit.

He continued to slog through waves and current, walking forward, seemingly straight for where Keon and I stood. The water wasn't up to his chest anymore; it was up to his waist and upper thighs.

Now it was splashing primarily against his calves and knees.

Black, I sent, alarm in my mind, bleeding sharply into my thoughts. *Black... you need to get down here. Bring Marshall. Something is going on.*

I felt Black's presence flare up in mine.

It filled me so swiftly and completely I sucked in a breath.

Black didn't bother to ask me anything. He just began looking through my eyes. As he did, I could feel everything around him so clearly, it felt like being inside his skin.

I could see Fournier, standing next to him.

I could hear Narcisse talking, his mouth curled in an annoyed frown as he addressed something Black had just said—

Then I felt a sharp spasm of reaction go through Black.

My attention flickered back to me, to where I was.

Seeing the man coming towards me on the beach, I felt a second stab of feeling go through Black.

MIRI. His mind exploded in mine. *RUN!*

But it was already too late.

16

NO THOUGHTS

T he man on the beach broke out in a sprint, the instant my
eyes clicked into focus.

My mind flared, shifting tracks, hardening to a crystal-sharp
clarity.

I scanned options in a split-second, a bare whisper of time that
seemed to last an eternity.

Run.

No. Too late to run. I'd only have my back to him when he
dragged me down. The way he was running, he was too fast for me.

Jump dimensions.

Black wasn't with me.

I couldn't always control how long it took me to come back.

I wasn't leaving Black.

Fight.

Yes. Fight.

My mind hardened around that, around standing my ground.

It was the best option. The most logical option.

The man sprinted towards me across the sand, gaining feet and
yards, seeming to glide over the surface of the beach, his feet
leaving a trail of kicked-up sand after he darted over and past the
denser, wetter section of shore.

He was almost upon me.

My eyes took in his appearance in a seer's mental snapshot, even as I reached out with one hand and arm. Grabbing Keon's shoulder, I shoved him, hard, to get him out of the way.

I never took my eyes off the man running towards me.

I heard Keon let out an *"Oof!"* of surprise.

I slammed out with my mind in the same instant.

I unleashed everything I had, aiming for the man running towards me. I watched him come at me in the scuba suit that wasn't really a scuba suit, that looked more like highly functional and flexible body armor, now that I could fully see it. I focused every bit of training I'd gotten over the last year-plus... from my uncle, from Black, from Jem, from Mika, from Yarli and Jax. I went for his light, intending to knock him out.

I hit into him, and...

Went through him.

Like he wasn't there at all.

I didn't have time to think about what that meant.

He reached me, even as I heard Keon let out a yell.

I never took my eyes off the approaching soldier's face.

His eyes burned a strange, unnatural blue, even as a knife appeared in his hand, flashing in my peripheral vision. I stepped back, blocked him instinctively, but I couldn't feel his light. Unlike how I'd been trained to fight by Black, Jem, Mika, and even Cowboy over the past however-many years, I couldn't fight the soldier like a seer at all.

I had to fight him like a human.

He was a blank wall.

Luckily, I'd originally learned to fight blind; I was back to fighting how I'd first been trained, back at the dojo with Nick and Angel, where I could only react. Only it was worse than that. It was worse than being a human fighting other humans.

It was like fighting something made of metal and stone.

Darting under his arm, I slid around behind him, but he followed, slashing forward and sideways with the knife. As soon as

I maneuvered myself more space, I kicked out, a sharp, fast, inside crescent kick I tried to use to knock the knife from his hand.

It was risky, kicking so high.

I hoped to surprise him.

I connected, hard, right in the knuckles of his knife hand with the edge of my foot.

He didn't act surprised.

He also didn't let go.

Without waiting, I leapt forward before he could pull his hand back, angling a slice downward, a move I got from our in-house Choy Li Fut instructor. I slammed my full weight into the place where his neck connected with his shoulder.

The man's body moved a corresponding few inches, but my blow didn't down him, despite the precision of it—or the fact that I'd downed seers twice his weight using the same maneuver in the ring back home.

It didn't even seem to slow him down.

When I landed on my feet, he slashed out, forcing me to leap back.

I managed to avoid getting my stomach sliced open, but didn't move fast enough to keep him from cutting across the front of my loose T-shirt.

For the next blur of minutes, I blocked seven, eight, nine... I lost track... darting blows. He switched hands with the knife, moving forward and back, switching targets and hands so fluidly I had to focus with every ounce of my attention to avoid getting hit in a way that could end with me dead.

He went for my throat, chest, belly, thighs.

I evaded and blocked, ducking and weaving.

I didn't think.

I fell into a pure no-mind state.

Knees, elbows, forearms, hard palm-hits, fists.

I pivoted and angled my body, limbs, hands, feet, to protect every part of myself I could.

He went for arteries, veins, organs.

I slid forward, back, jerking out of range of the knife, giving him something when I had to, jumping all the way back or sliding around him when I didn't.

My knuckles got slashed. My other arm. My thigh.

My chest, just below my throat.

I managed to move enough to keep him off major arteries.

I knew I was in a fight for my life.

Now I was thinking I might have to jump.

I might have to jump... but it might already be too late for that.

I needed a few seconds to jump. I needed a few seconds to gear in, focus on those structures in my light, activate each one in just the right sequence.

He wasn't giving me the space to do that.

Right now, he wasn't giving me the space to do anything but fend him off.

I'd have to find some way to knock him off balance for real.

I'd have to earn those few seconds on my own.

I heard Keon shouting, moving away from me on the beach, but I didn't dare look away from the man in front of me, or let my concentration waver for even a fraction of a second.

Even so, my consciousness split.

I felt Black, distantly, running my way.

Some other part of my mind looked for an opening.

That same part of my mind split, scanned options for weapons, for things to put between myself and him, for ways to create space, give myself a few seconds, or even just *one* second—even as he leapt at me again, switching knife-hands so quickly I barely tracked the motion.

He cut downward with the long knife, slicing my forehead before I could slide completely out of the way.

Warm wetness coursed down my face, getting in one eye, distracting me, but I didn't try to wipe it away.

I knew that was why he'd done it.

He was trying to gain a few seconds, too.

Maybe just one second, just long enough to kill me.

He was trying to blind me, distract me, lose me time... lose me reaction space.

He lunged at me again and I switched tactics, using an Aikido move to pull the energy of his lunge into me and pull him across me, flipping him over my back.

He landed on the beach, hard enough that I felt the weight of him through my feet.

He weighed too much, my mind noted.

He weighed too much for his size.

I didn't stop my movements to think about that.

I leapt onto his knife arm, pinning it with my knee, and he swung from the side with his other arm, punching me in the kidney and ribs. I gasped, but didn't take my focus off his face, or my weight off the arm with the knife.

Without thought, I gripped either side of his face, digging my thumbs into his eyes.

I was desperate.

My only thought was to stop him.

To make it stop.

Throwing my weight into him, I dug hard into his face, into his skull.

I was screaming when I finally managed to force his first eye out of the socket, half-crushing it in my clenched fist.

He didn't make a sound... not even when I dug out the second eye, using three of my fingers when I couldn't get it with my thumbs.

He punched me again, then again.

His expression didn't change.

Even with no eyes, his cheeks, mouth, forehead, lips—none of it moved.

I picked up a rock out of the sand, seeing it by his head.

Hefting it and gripping it as tightly as I could, I slammed it into his knife hand.

He didn't let go.

I smashed it into his hand, over and over again, while he kept punching me in the ribs and side and back. I heard a rib crack, then another. I gasped in pain, crying out, but didn't stop smashing his hand with the rock.

I was still hitting into his bloody hand, over and over, when a gun went off, seemingly right by my face.

I froze.

I was sure I was dead.

In that split second, I was sure I'd been shot.

Then a boot came down on the guy's other arm, and I recognized the boot.

The gun went off again.

I saw it that time.

I saw the gun lower down by my shoulder, aiming at the man at point-blank range, a split second before the man's face exploded under me. I stared down, watching it happen, even as it hit me that he'd been shot in the face once already and hadn't stopped punching me in the side with that steel-like fist.

The second shot seemed to affect him more.

His hand opened.

The bloody hand of his, which I'd almost pulped with the rock, breaking at least three of his fingers, finally released the knife.

I saw the second hand unclench next, the one attached to the arm that Black's boot dug into the sand.

Slowly, the arms unclenched, too.

Then the chest under where I knelt.

Neither of us moved, even after the man went limp.

I knelt on the man's one arm, while Black stood with his whole weight on the other arm. Black continued to aim his gun at the soldier's face, as if waiting for him to start fighting again, waiting for him to move.

A few seconds passed like that.

Maybe even a few minutes.

It felt like forever, with both of us hovering there, staring down at that broken face, which didn't even appear to be bleeding. I hung there, the rock still clenched in my fist, my fist poised over my head. I was panting, now feeling flickers and shocks of pain spreading over my body, the cuts stinging on my arms and legs and head from the salt air.

My side, where the man had been punching, felt caved in, pulped.

Then the blood on my face pooled on my chin.

It dripped down to the man below me, and I flinched.

Something in that got both of us to move.

It snapped us out, somehow.

I lowered the rock, releasing it on the sand. I gasped as I released it, the pain in my side rearing up so intensely it blinded me. I noticed only then that the whole side of the rock was covered in the man's blood.

"Not a man," Black muttered, maybe in answer to my thoughts. "Not a man... there's no way that's a fucking human being."

I struggled to pull myself backwards, to climb off him, but I couldn't get up. My side and back hurt so bad I gasped. I was still trying when strong hands caught me carefully under the arms, helping me at first, then lifting me completely off him.

Black didn't just take me off the soldier on the beach... he kept walking with me gripped tightly in his hands, more or less carrying me a good ten yards away from where the body lay crumpled on the sand.

My eyes never left the man in the black, scuba-like armored suit.

I watched him minutely as Black carried me away. I continued looking for any sign of movement, any sign of breathing... any sign he might get up and start slashing at either of us with the knife, or maybe pull a gun off some other part of his body.

Black must have been thinking the same thing.

When Keon approached the body, staring down at it in disbelief, Black barked out words, so loudly I jumped where he held me in his hands.

"Take the fucking knife," he told the boatman. "At least kick it away from his hand. And grab any other weapon you see on him. Then *move away,* Keon. Don't stand too close."

Keon turned, his eyes so wide it might have been comical, if the situation were different.

As it was, I was pretty sure Black's hands were the only thing keeping me attached to this version of Earth.

If he hadn't been holding me, I probably would have jumped dimensions.

That, or I would have started sprinting across the sand, running full-tilt for the resort.

I would have run if only to deal with all the adrenaline coursing and pumping and jerking through my veins.

Keon blinked at Black.

"Should I be touching it?" he yelled out. "This is a crime scene, right?"

"Get. The. Fucking. Knife. Away. From. That. Thing." Black spoke through clenched teeth. "Now."

Keon blinked, looking taken aback.

Then he seemed to agree.

Still being held by Black, I gasped, watching as the man in the dark blue surfer shorts with big flower patterns leaned down and gingerly plucked the knife up from the sand.

Stepping back, he held it away from his body, gripping it in two fingers like he thought the knife, all by itself, might attack him.

"Any other weapons?" Black growled, again making me tense.

"I didn't see any."

"Frisk him," Black snapped.

I saw Keon swallow, then nod.

Tossing the knife awkwardly down on the sand so it was a good six or seven feet from the body, Keon walked cautiously back and began feeling over the dead soldier's uniform and limbs. I saw him grimace as he looked at the man's face. Then he began patting him down harder, through the wet suit.

"Legs, too," Black growled, watching Keon's every move. "And his arms."

"Dude's definitely dead, man," Keon said, holding a hand over his nose as he complied with Black's instructions, feeling over the black, Kevlar-like suit the man wore. "He's not breathing. You like... fucked him up. His head's broken apart."

"Just be careful," Black said.

His voice was slightly less intense that time.

Only slightly.

When Keon finally straightened, stepping back, I heard more shouts up the beach.

My eyes darted towards the sounds in time to see Narcisse and three members of Yarrick's security team coming over the dunes between the boathouse and the parking lot for the dock.

Behind them, Marshall trod through the soft, dry sand, followed by Fournier, who was wringing his hands together, again wearing a Panama hat, only today with a bright red scarf tied around his throat above his dress shirt and white jacket.

He must switch that up with the black tie he'd worn the day before. He still wore the gold cufflinks and watch; I saw them glinting in the sun from his wrists.

Black placed me gently on the sand.

Pulling me around carefully to face him, he looked me over, wincing, his jaw clenched, his skin close to pale. I could feel a kind of panic in him as he tried to assess the damage to my body as objectively as he could. His eyes flickered from the cut on my bicep to the blood running down my other arm, the cut across my chest, the one on my thigh, the one on my forehead.

He touched my side, gingerly, pulling his hand away when I grimaced.

I saw him noting blood-flow, depth, how much blood was on my clothes, running down my neck and arms and hands and legs.

I knew he was looking for the most dangerous of my wounds.

I felt as much as saw him trying to assess how serious each one was.

I felt his terror as he tried to decide if any one of them might kill me, or the combination of them might end up being fatal. I felt him worrying about internal bleeding, damage to my kidneys, broken ribs, punctured lungs.

I shook my head, reaching out to grip his hand.

I didn't realize how bloody my fingers were until he winced.

"No," I told him. "No. I'm okay."

His jaw clenched harder.

I saw him fighting to remain quiet.

I saw the part of him that wanted to start shouting at me.

I saw the sheer irrationality of it.

Somehow, it only touched me.

"Help me?" I said, voicing it almost as an offer. "What do you think? The mobile lab? The resort? Or should we go to a hospital in Waikiki?"

Black's eyes brightened.

Meeting my gaze, he only nodded.

I could see from his face he still didn't trust himself to speak.

Before I could think about my own question, much less decide which place we should go to, he bent down, wrapping his arms carefully around my shoulders and under my knees. He made sure to pick me up so that my hurt ribs and side faced out.

Moving so fluidly I might have weighed a handful of pounds, he lifted me up to his chest, holding me tightly against him.

I didn't argue.

It hurt my side like fuck, any movement at all, but I didn't complain.

By then, the adrenaline was giving me a stomachache.

Closing my eyes, I leaned into his chest, resting my head on his shoulder and fighting back the part of me that still wanted to either fight or flee. I knew there was still some risk I could jump out of there totally.

Black being there grounded me.

Through his light—that dense, volcanic-like light—I felt myself start to relax.

I had a vague awareness of Narcisse saying something to Black, telling him we had to stay there, that he had questions for us, for me.

I don't know exactly what Black said to him.

There were a lot of swear words involved.

I heard Fournier and Keon yelling at Narcisse too, Fournier more sounding disbelieving that anyone could be so callous, while Keon sounded almost as mad as Black.

I heard someone mention the helipad.

I heard another voice say someone was already coming.

None of it mattered.

I knew Black would take care of me.

I knew he'd take me where I needed to go.

Even as I thought it, he was walking with me, his feet heavy in the sand as he brought me over the dry dunes.

Before he got to wherever he was going, before he got both of us off the sliding dry sand and onto the asphalt, I'd already started to doze off, my head still slumped on his shoulder.

The last thing I remember was the sound of a distant siren.

17

DONE WAITING

B lack didn't want to leave her.

He didn't want to leave her there.

He couldn't make himself just sit there, either, not after what happened.

He couldn't just fucking *sit* there, and wait for someone to try and kill her again.

Pulling every scrap of detail he could from his mind, he sent an info-dump of intelligence information to the Barrier construct in San Francisco.

He gave them everything.

Everything he'd seen and learned about the body on the beach that exploded, and the whatever-the-fuck-it-was that attacked Miri, which appeared to be the same thing.

He sent them the names of everyone involved, along with whatever he knew about each of them. He sent information about the Blue Sail. He sent them Yarrick's information, how he knew Yarrick, the names of every one of Yarrick's employees he'd met, all of Yarrick's various holdings and companies, the names of Yarrick's lawyers and the CEOs and other players he knew off the top of his head.

He sent them every detail of what he'd seen of that fight on the beach.

He sent them what he'd been able to learn about Narcisse.

He sent them all of his Barrier impressions.

He sent everything he could fucking think of.

Then, without waiting for them to assess any of it, he called Yarli.

"I know you're busy," he growled. "But don't tell me how busy you are. Don't argue. Just do what I'm about to ask you to do. Don't fucking *argue*. Just do it."

Yarli's light immediately grew still.

"Of course, sir."

"I just sent you a bunch of intel," he growled. "It should be accessible to all of the seers in the leadership and infiltration teams by now. I want you, Jax, Rico, and Mika on my wife. At all times. I want to know the fucking *instant* you feel anything coming near her, or pick up any intel that might indicate something's coming near her. Set up a perimeter in the Barrier. I want you to find some way to track these fucking things. Look for anything coming in from the water, from the air... anything that might already be on the island. I'll have people here, too, on the ground. And I want you to tell Ace and Michelle to get their asses over here. Now. I want you to send more of my people over here, too. Dex, Kiko, Luce, Javier—"

But Yarli must have plucked the names from his mind already.

"I got it, boss," Yarli said, her voice businesslike. "Reviewing the intel now. I got all the names you want. Unless you have any to add, they're already on their way upstairs to gear up. Dex says he'll work on getting one of the Black Hawks fueled to bring them to the airport."

Pausing, as if waiting for him to approve or disapprove, she added,

"I'm going to dedicate a jump team to Miriam's security from here, and send Jax and Holo your way along with the humans you mentioned. They'll be leaving out of SFO via your private plane in under an hour. Cowboy is calling the pilot now. Kiks is working on getting them clearance to land—"

"You can't leave her," Black growled. "She hasn't opened her fucking eyes—"

"We're watching her," Yarli said, her voice both softer and holding more of an angry edge. "Right now, boss. Mika, Jax, and Holo are working on a construct. Zairei and Kiessa want to come to Hawaii, too. I'm approving it, unless you object. I want you to have the additional backup. The others are all in D.C., but let me know if you need me to pull anyone."

Black forced himself to take in her words.

He forced himself to try and relax, to breathe.

"Someone has a hit out on her, Yarli," he said. "Someone has a hit out on my wife."

"I agree," she said. "We all do. Trust me. We're on it. We'll find out who."

"It's someone in Charles' team, I think—"

"We'll drop anyone who goes near her."

"You may not be *able* to drop them," Black warned. "I tried. Miri tried—"

"Understood. Can you get us any tissue samples, or better yet, electronic components from the thing that conducted this most recent attack? In particular, I'd like Luric to look at the tissues for organic machine components... but our tech team is highly interested in any electronics, but particularly the eyes, based on what you and Miri saw in that boathouse. From everything we got from the info-dump you sent, that's the main sign of a robotic component, right? Jax thinks we should try to hack it. If we can't bring them down from the Barrier, it might be our best bet—"

"Good." Black frowned, nodding. "Okay. Good. I'll get you what I can."

"Kiko just let me know they have clearance to land. They're fueling your plane now, boss. The pilot is less than ten minutes out."

Black nodded again, his jaw hard. "I'm looking here, too," he said, his voice a growl. "I'm going to the military base. I'll share whatever I find."

Yarli hesitated.

He could feel her wanting to argue with him.

He could feel her wanting to ask him to wait for the team she was sending him.

He also felt her exchange looks with Manny, her boyfriend and one of Black's oldest human friends.

"Can you wait a few hours, boss?" she said finally, her voice careful. "I'm not arguing. I'm really not arguing. It's just, it might be good to have backup—"

"I *have* backup," Black growled.

"I mean *seer* backup," she said, without missing a beat. "Do you really think you should go in there without that? To a military compound? Without Miri? Given everything?"

There was a silence.

Black didn't really think about her words.

He couldn't.

He wasn't even pretending to think.

He stopped talking just long enough to decide whether he should tell her the truth.

"What the fuck did I say to you about arguing?" he growled.

Before she could say anything to that, he hung up.

❦

He bought a motorcycle.

He went to the lot intending to rent one, but all the bikes they had for rent were shit.

Worse than shit.

He couldn't bear to be gone from her for even a second longer than he needed to be.

After scanning through the inventory they had at the bike shop Yarrick recommended, he picked out a black and green Kawasaki

Ninja H2R, with a 998CC liquid-cooled, four-stroke in-line four, DOHC, 16-valve engine.

It wasn't the fastest thing on the road, but it was damned close.

Right now, he needed something that could move.

He paid cash, instructing them to fill it up with gas and anything else it needed while he handled the transfer of ownership.

Marshall waited with him in the sales office.

The big Samoan had driven him out there, along with two of his guys, and that beach bum, Keon, who seemed to have taken the whole thing on the beach with Miri personally. They brought him out in a giant Jeep-thing with roll bars, and told him they'd follow him up to the USPACOM base, northeast of Honolulu.

Black nodded at first.

Then he thought about it.

"No." He turned on Marshall, scowling at him, then at Keon. "No. You'll go back to the hospital. I want you to keep an eye on my wife. There might be more of them. I don't need you at the fucking base... I can handle that. I want you protecting my wife."

Marshall and Keon looked at each other.

Then, Keon's jaw hardened.

He looked at Black, anger in his eyes.

"She pushed me out of the way, man," he said, that anger reaching his voice. "She pushed *me* out of the way, when that asshole came at her. She probably saved my life."

"So return the favor," Black growled. "Keep her safe for me."

He looked between Marshall and the other man, his jaw hardening as an image of Miri, pale and covered in blood, rose back to his mind.

It was too close to that thing on the roof.

It was way too goddamned close to the last time he'd found Miri like that.

"Keep her safe for me," he repeated. "Please. And don't tell anyone I'm not there with her. I mean *no one*. Not even Yarrick. No one needs to know that, and I don't know who's listening in on the phones. If I need to tell Peter, I'll tell him myself."

Marshall hesitated for a beat at the mention of Yarrick, then nodded, clapping him on the shoulder. "You got it, boss. I'll call ahead. Get more of my people there, too. Watching over her room. We won't tell anyone shit."

Black nodded, feeling absurdly grateful.

"Thanks." Pausing, he added, gruff, "I won't be gone long."

"Don't worry, boss," Marshall assured him. "We got this."

Black felt another rush of gratitude, feeling the warmth and determination off the big Samoan as he vowed to protect Miriam. He knew the humans' chances of stopping one of these fucking robot things on their own might be close to nil, depending on how the next one was armed, but having a wall of people protecting his wife was definitely better than nothing.

Anyway, he didn't want Marshall and the others coming with him.

He wanted to deal with this end of things himself.

He'd already checked the route. He knew where he was going.

He also knew his only real prayer of stopping this was to cut it off at the source.

Revving the bike, he flipped down the visor on the helmet he'd bought with the bike, zipping up the front of the leather jacket Keon lent him. The surfer was following them on his own bike, which wasn't exactly the Kawasaki, but decently fast for a street bike.

Black didn't wait for them to get back into the Jeep, or for Keon to climb back onto his red and black Triumph Street Twin.

He pulled out onto Punchbowl Street and gunned the new Ninja out onto the road, heading north towards HI-61, which would take him most of the way up to the base, until he could cut over to I-H-3 East.

His mind fuzzed to static as he rode.

His light stretched out, looking for cops, not because he cared about getting a ticket, but because he didn't want anyone getting in his fucking way. For the same reason, he didn't want to deal with fighting off, pushing, or running from the police—it was easier to just feel them in advance and push them into not seeing him in the first place.

He partitioned his mind.

He began methodically reading everyone who'd seen anything on that beach.

He'd already called Yarrick about the eyes, following up on Yarli's request.

Narcisse bitched and moaned about it, yelling about military jurisdiction, but Yarrick dealt with it somehow. Peter managed to handle the issue before Black even had to call Yarli in to have her infiltration team deal with it more forcefully.

Of course, it still might come to that.

For now, however, as far as Black knew, Jax and the others would get custody of at least one of those cybernetic eyes as soon as they touched down at the Daniel K. Inouye International Airport and made their way to the resort's mobile lab.

Black tried to reconstruct what happened on the beach.

He went through the minds and memories of every person who'd witnessed any part of it.

He started with the other firsthand witness to Miri's attack.

Sliding his light deep into Keon's, he watched the fucking whatever-it-was approach Miri from the water. He watched it sprint across the beach, moving strangely, running strangely—too fast, with too much precision, with too little expression, with too regular of breaths.

Guy was wearing some kind of specialized suit.

Not a wet suit, although it may have doubled as one.

It was more like an enhanced combat suit, with flexible armor, multi-pivot joints, and maybe some water-proofing built in.

Whatever it was, it didn't impede his mobility at all.

Black flicked on his phone through the helmet he wore.

"Yarrick?" he said, when the other man picked up. "Get me the suit, too, if you can."

There was a silence. Then the human on the other end sighed.

"Narcisse won't like it."

"He can have it back," Black growled. "But I've got a team that is actually qualified to assess it."

Yarrick chuckled, his words dry.

"Well, he *definitely* won't like it, if I say it like that." Pausing, Peter added more cautiously. "I've got my own lab here," he said. "I could send it over there. A compromise? Your people and Narcisse could go over there together."

Black clenched his jaw.

He fought with whether that would be a good idea.

"We'll do that next," he said after the pause. "If you don't mind. You hired me to figure out what's happening here, who these fuckers are. Let me do that. The more we keep it inside my team, the safer it is for everyone. If we bring it to your lab, that's involving a whole new group of people. We can't be sure the lab's secure. We can't be sure anything's secure right now. Including this phone call."

After a pause, he felt Yarrick agree.

"Where are you now, Black?"

Frowning, Black scanned street signs.

"I'm with my wife," he said. "Where do you think I am?"

"Ah, of course. No offense meant. I just wondered if you had a minute to come down here... to the beach. It might ease things, if you could coordinate with Narcisse in person."

Black let out a grunt, in spite of himself.

"You sure about that?" he muttered.

"No," Yarrick said, smiling over the line. "But it might make things easier for *me*. Also, I'm pretty sure Narcisse is now shit-scared of both you and your wife, so it might expedite things, as well. I suspect he's much more likely to argue procedure with me than with either of you. Even if he curses the both of you behind your back."

"I'll get there when I can, Peter. My people will be here in a few hours, too."

"Got it." Peter hesitated. "Let me know if there's anything else

I can do, Black. Anything at all. I'm dreadfully sorry about Miri, old chap."

"Thanks, Pete."

Without waiting for a reply, he hung up.

He didn't do it to be a dick.

He didn't want to be on the line for too long.

He also didn't want Pete—or anyone else who might be listening in—to figure out where he was, that he was on a bike, that he'd left the hospital, that he wasn't poised over his wife's bed, armed to the teeth and ready to start a war.

He didn't want anyone to see this as another opening.

Fighting back a surge of fear and adrenaline at the thought, he went back to Keon, to the surfer-boatman's memories of what he'd seen on the beach.

He watched as Miri reached out, as she shoved Keon out of the way.

He saw the blue, glowing eyes of the machine-like soldier in the scuba suit that wasn't really a scuba suit. He saw that... thing... run up the beach, straight for Miri.

He watched the guy fight.

He watched that thing try to best—no *try to kill*—his wife.

He watched the whole thing through Keon's eyes.

Then he watched it again.

He winced with every cut, even as his heart nearly burst with pride as he watched his wife fight. She was so good it made his chest hurt.

Ninety percent of the fighters on his team would be dead.

More than ninety percent.

Maybe Dalejem could have beaten this guy.

Maybe Black himself could have stayed alive as long.

Maybe.

He watched her mix Choy Li Fut with Muy Thai, switch to Ju Jitsu, to Krav Maga, to Wing Chun... all the while blocking or twisting away from the knife with any part of her body she could, anything that would keep him from getting in that kill-stroke he sought.

That Aikido move to get him off his feet was fucking brilliant.

She didn't wait that time, either.

She didn't stop to survey her success.

She was *on* him before he hit the sand, pinning his knife arm, positioning her weight with a precision that kept him from flipping her off. She had her fingers dug into that fucker's eye sockets before he'd stopped struggling to get his knife arm free.

Even after she got his eyes out, she didn't stop, but started pounding his hand with that rock. She didn't stop even when he started whaling on her ribs... even after he broke and cracked a few of them, even after he was clearly hurting her, crushing that part of her body.

She didn't miss a fucking beat.

She'd been fighting blind.

She'd fought like that—blind.

Anyone else would be dead.

He gunned the motorcycle at the thought, jamming his foot down on the accelerator pedal, leaning low over the bike and jacking the speed up past 170... then 180.

He split off another part of his mind, even as he kept looking for cops, even as his mind focused with laser-like precision on the road, on every car and motorcycle and truck he flashed past. He watched Narcisse look over the body of the man on the sand, frowning as he used gloved hands to carefully pick up the eyes Miri *ripped out of his fucking head...*

Again, Black's heart hurt.

Gaos. Gaos, gaos, gaos...

He pinged Yarli, using his mind that time.

Nudging her towards the mobile lab unit, and the work Narcisse was doing over the body on the beach, he sent her snapshots of what he'd seen already, the strange, blue, glass-like outer coating on the eyes, the metallic sheen, the feel of them.

He felt her acknowledge what he sent.

He felt her noticing where he was, what he was doing.

He felt her notice he was alone.

He pushed her out of his mind, focusing back on Narcisse, on the forensic analyst's mind.

Narcisse was on the phone now, with someone in his command structure.

...Draper. Draper-something.

The name slowly crystalized in the darkness behind Black's eyes.

Frank Draper.

Black didn't know the name. Someone in forensics in San Diego. He felt like Narcisse's boss, but Narcisse was yelling at him.

He wanted to know what they weren't telling him.

Narcisse felt like they were withholding information from him.

He wanted to know why the hell no one had arrested Black, or Dr. Miriam Fox.

He wanted to know why no one told him Quentin Black and his wife were just being allowed to roam around as free citizens... in *Hawaii*, of all places. He wanted to know why Yarrick had so much pull, how some "rich British schoolboy" managed to cut an illegal deal with the Justice Department, and with the military hierarchy.

Black felt his jaw harden, the longer he listened.

The fucker didn't give a damn about Miriam.

He didn't care that she'd nearly died.

Hell, he still seemed to think they were behind what happened in some way.

Narcisse seemed to think the fight was staged... or maybe that the soldiers had something to do with what happened at the California-Mexico border.

Black could feel Narcisse trying in any way he could to pin all of this on them.

On Miri, especially.

Asshole had a real hard-on for Miri.

Black listened harder, until he could make out the words the human was speaking into the phone.

What do you mean, 'classified'? Narcisse sputtered furiously. *Why the hell did you send me out here, if I'm not even allowed to examine—*

Whoever was on the other end cut him off.

Are you saying they had NOTHING to do with this? That this isn't *about all of those people disappearing? How is that possible?*

Black frowned.

He wanted to trace the connection from Narcisse's mind to the man on the other end, but he didn't dare concentrate that hard, not while he was doing 190 m.p.h. on a windy, winding, mist-slick freeway on a brand-new bike.

He skimmed the male human's mind instead, feeling the surface thoughts, thinking he'd go in deeper when he was back at the resort.

He'd give the asshole credit for one thing.

Narcisse was scared.

He was also pissed off.

Narcisse didn't know if the man on the other end knew anything about the two dead cyber-soldiers who showed up at Yarrick's resort, but Narcisse increasingly suspected *someone* in his command structure did. He also increasingly suspected Black had been right that morning, when he told Narcisse he was out of the loop.

The forensics officer could practically feel it.

Black was going to have to have a little talk with this fucker when he got back to the resort and the mobile lab.

Even as he thought it, Narcisse started yelling at Frank Draper about the fact that he'd been more or less "ordered" to hand over vital evidence to Black and his team, as a condition of Yarrick allowing the military sole access to the crime scene.

Focusing more of his attention back on the road, Black pinged Yarli, again pointing her to Narcisse, to whoever this Frank Draper was, on the other end of the line.

Yarli pinged him back, assuring him they were on it.

He hoped like hell they were.

He hoped like hell Yarli would stay with the two humans, and find out everything she could about Draper and Narcisse, and whoever was behind Narcisse being sent out here. As far as Black was concerned, all of them had already more or less made his list of suspects, in terms of who wanted Miri dead.

He wanted to know why.

Was it really about what Miri had done last night?

How could they have organized all of this so fast, given Miri only disappeared those people the night before?

Who was pulling the strings now, with Charles out of the picture?

Whoever was behind this, they were about to get a big fucking message from her husband about why trying to kill his wife was a *really, really bad idea.*

Black didn't care if he had to erase the minds of every goddamned soldier in Central Command. He'd go through all of them, one by one, if that's what it took.

Hurry, his mind and light urged him. *Hurry, hurry, you worthless fucker...*

He didn't say the rest of it in his mind.

He didn't even let himself think the rest of it, not in so many words.

He knew what he was racing against.

He knew.

He needed to get back to his wife before they realized he wasn't there.

He needed to get back to his wife before they sent the next one.

"Do we have eyes on it yet?" Yarli said.

Her voice was crisp, businesslike.

Angel could hear the thread of anxiety underneath, what verged on fear.

She watched as the female seer, who was more or less in charge of things here at the Raptor's Nest right now, turned around, focusing those odd, near-black eyes of hers on Alexander or "Lex" Holmes, son of Colonel Harrison Hamilton Holmes III.

The elder Holmes, who'd been Black's mentor as far back as the Korean War, was dead. Since that Holmes' murder, probably at the hand of Charles, his middle-aged son had been with them, more or less living at the California Street building with the rest of them.

The Colonel's son frowned at Yarli now.

His eyes reflected the kind of irritation that told Angel he had a good idea Yarli already knew the answer to her own question.

Angel could sympathize.

It was frustrating sometimes, being a human surrounded by highly psychic seers.

"It's almost up," Lex said, that annoyance reaching his voice. "You realize I'm breaking more than one law, letting your team tap into the surveillance feeds at USPACOM in the first place? Not to mention putting friends of mine... and Black's... in danger."

Muttering, he added,

"...That doesn't even get into the national security implications."

Yarli tilted her head in acknowledgement, seer-fashion.

"We need to see in there," she said simply.

"Black didn't order it," Lex pointed out, giving Manny a harder look. "You could just *trust* him. Trust him to get what he needs, and get out... without anyone being the wiser. Let him contact us when he knows more."

Yarli frowned.

Those dark, galaxy- and nebulae-filled eyes of hers flashed like volcanic-glass mirrors, looking even more alien than usual.

"I understand," she said after a pause, that strange seer accent coloring her voice. "Under normal circumstances, I would likely agree. But Black didn't feel..."

Yarli glanced at her boyfriend, Manny, then at Cowboy, who stood on the other side of the conference room table, then at Angel herself.

Angel distinctly got the impression the female infiltrator was remembering that all three of them were close, personal friends of the Blacks.

Both of the Blacks.

Lex was close friends with Quentin, even if he didn't know Miri well yet.

"...Stable," Yarli finished bluntly. "The boss didn't feel stable."

On the comm, Mika, who'd joined them virtually from Black's private plane, which was currently crossing the Pacific Ocean, let out a loud grunt, obviously in agreement.

"Moreover, his wife is unconscious," Yarli added, speaking louder over Mika's commentary. "He has no backup on the ground at all right now, and won't until our team lands there, in approximately four and a half hours."

Glancing around the conference room table, she gave them all, including Alexander Holmes, including Angel herself, warning looks.

"But it's more than that," Yarli added. "As far as we know, the doc is the only one who can really help him control his light. We have to bear that in mind, under the circumstances. She's neither conscious nor with him at the moment. I think we need to consider the possibility we might need to take him down... knock him unconscious, using Miri's light, if that's at all possible... if it looks like he's going to, you know..."

"Turn into a dragon again?" Alexander Holmes grunted. "We all know what you mean, cousin Yarli. No need to be coy about it."

Everyone exchanged uncomfortable smiles, shifting their weight.

Only Cowboy's face remained stoic.

"Yeah, well." Yarli looked flustered, which was unusual for her.

"Then you know why I'm not just taking the boss's word for it, that he can handle this on his own. And why I'm kind of anxious we get eyes into that compound before Black gets there."

Lex held up a hand impatiently, nodding his understanding.

Even so, Angel saw the middle-aged man's face relax somewhat.

Clearly, Yarli's reasoning made sense to him, despite his own military background.

Everyone in this room, just about, and everyone listening-in virtually, was ex-military.

They were also pretty hardcore believers in the chain of command.

Lex was not only ex-military himself, but he grew up in a pretty intensely military household. Colonel Harrison Hamilton Holmes III was more or less a legend at the Pentagon, and not only for his "special projects."

His son, who looked a hell of a lot like him, despite the distinct differences in the two men's style, must have grown up under that shadow, at least to a degree. He'd also grown up seeing Black off and on for what must have been close to the entirety of his life, and without seeing Black age, or change in any way really, at least not physically.

Angel couldn't help wondering what young Lex had thought of that, growing up.

She wondered what his famous dad's explanation was, for Black's "condition."

She was still looking at the forty-something, African-American man with the dreadlocks bound in a ponytail, when she realized he was on the phone, presumably with someone over at the Pentagon. She could see from his headset light that the connection was live.

Even as she thought it, relief came to the man's face.

It immediately reached his voice.

"Great, Minh. Thanks. And thank Yuzo and Verne for us, too. Can't tell you how much I appreciate it. I'll let Black know…"

He trailed briefly, listening with a frown.

His expression cleared again.

"Okay. Got it." He continued to frown. "That would be great if you could, as soon as the feed finishes on your end. We can make any recordings we need here..."

He trailed into another brief silence.

"I'll tell them," he said next. "We'll send someone on Black's team your way, too, make sure your area's clean, now that they've got those people out of there..."

He trailed, listening.

"Yes," he said, grimly. "Definitely. Have them check the phones too, when they get there. I know you said this line's secure, but it's probably better that we give it another look. You know how Black is..."

Trailing again, he laughed at something the other said.

"Yeah. I will. Thanks."

His headset light clicked off, and he looked at Yarli.

"You should have access to all the cameras over there now. Minh's team hooked it up. They'll erase the feed as soon as it plays, anything with his face on it, and replace it. So if you need a record of anything we see... you'd better record it here."

Glancing at Angel, then at Manny, Lex returned his gaze to Yarli, adding, "I figured it was better if we didn't have a record of him over there. Under the circumstances."

Yarli nodded.

Angel felt some of the tension leave her own shoulders, even as she noted the relief on Yarli's face.

Angel recognized the names she'd heard Holmes speak over the line; they were what remained of the Colonel's "special unit" within the Pentagon, the one that studied seers and vampires before any of that information entered into the public awareness.

Angel felt a little guilty that'd she'd forgotten all about that crew.

She was relieved at least a few of them remained working on the inside, even after Charles' takeover of most of the United States government.

Hell, she was relieved they were still alive.

She also knew the likelihood that their minds hadn't been tampered with at all during that time was next to nil.

Yarli would be aware of that too, of course, so Angel didn't bother stating the obvious.

They would have people over there, checking the entire team out.

Hell, they were probably on their way already.

Still, it was unlikely Charles bothered with a lot of mind-to-mind control or tampering with that team, since they were all human. Charles had that whole place psychically wired, as soon as he'd put that damned construct thing in place. From what Angel understood, the construct warped human minds collectively; Charles didn't need to waste time going after individual humans.

In the end, Charles would've tried to cover the whole world with that net.

On the monitor over Yarli's shoulder, Mika let out a humorless snort.

When Angel and the others glanced at her, the small, Chinese-looking seer smiled at Angel and Cowboy before motioning with one hand towards Yarli.

"This crazy *jurekil'a* sister thinks we actually have a prayer of stopping Black, if we can just keep visual contact once he reaches the compound." Pausing meaningfully, she grunted again, half in amusement, half in derision. "...'Cause that worked so well for Charles, the last time Black was inside a government building."

Manny looked between them, frowning.

"Is that the plan?" the older Native American man asked. "To stop Black? I'm not sure that's such a good idea—"

"It's really not," Mika agreed cheerfully.

Yarli frowned at the monitor, making a motion with one hand in Mika's direction.

Angel strongly got the impression that gesture meant "shut up."

Alexander Holmes only scowled.

"It should be coming up on the screen now," he said, once more holding his earpiece in one hand. "Jax says Minh already has them linked to their video and satellite feed."

Angel gazed up at the second monitor over the industrial-style conference table, folding her arms over the thick, dark-green sweater she wore.

It hadn't occurred to her until just that instant that the sweater she wore was Nick's. She was still trying to figure out how to smuggle his clothes and surfboard out of here without anyone noticing.

She'd even considered soliciting Yumi Tanaka's help, Nick's mother.

If she could claim it was some family thing—

Angel cut off her thoughts, noticing Mika staring at her.

Mika wasn't even in the room, she was in the monitor, but there was no question the Chinese-looking seer was staring right at her.

Like Yarli—like most seers, really, including Black, even including Miri to a degree—Mika had unusual eyes. Dark blue, almost black, with a white-gold rim, the smaller seer's irises seemed to bore through Angel's head, seeing her every thought.

Fuck. Why was she thinking about Nick in here? Was she stupid?

Mika's eyes flickered away.

Maybe Angel was being paranoid.

No one in the actual room seemed to be looking at her. All of them had turned at Lex's words and were staring up at the monitor. Angel cleared her throat, following their stares, refolding her arms tighter as she felt her cheeks warm.

Damn it. Damn it. Damn it.

Hopefully, if Mika heard her, she wouldn't say anything.

She was still fighting Nick out of her mind, fighting not to think about the craziness in her apartment the night before, when a third monitor above the table switched on, went to static, then abruptly righted itself. Angel fought to concentrate on that, watching as the image split into numerous smaller screens until they filled most of the wall, around forty-six separate views on the Command Center in total.

Angel's eyes took in the various angles on the UPSACOM building, including the parking lot, the front gates, the main entrance.

Then Black's motorcycle got tagged.

Yarli must have somehow gotten the make and model of his new bike.

The program responded to the information by increasing the size of one of the screens, making the others into smaller rectangles around the edges. Angel glimpsed the front of the Kawasaki motorcycle as it first reached the gate.

The bike moved forward a few feet, and Angel made out a tall, muscular man astride the black leather seat. It had to be Black. He wore a brown, beat-up leather jacket she didn't recognize and dark pants, his head encased in a black helmet with a mirrored black visor.

She barely had time to see him before he gunned the engine of his motorcycle, sliding through the security gates and into the main parking lot.

Given how fast the guards raised that gate, Black definitely must have pushed their minds, and probably pretty hard, to get through.

"Yeah," Mika muttered from the other monitor, glancing at Angel, making it clear she'd heard her that time. "Not exactly points in favor of the boss approaching this thing with measure and calm. He didn't even bother to mirage credentials. We usually do that, especially at an entry point where there's known surveillance. Looks better to the cameras."

Angel frowned.

Her eyes returned to the larger screen.

She also fought to ignore the increased scrutiny she still felt Mika aiming her way.

Everyone else stared up at the wall monitor, too.

The guard post screen diminished in size, bringing up a second camera angle.

This one, facial-rec must have tagged.

Black had removed the helmet and left it with the bike. He now strode up to the doors of the compound. Angel noticed he kept his face turned away from the cameras.

He stood there, by the front doors, for a long-feeling few seconds.

Then the doors opened.

Two uniformed Marines walked through.

One wore double-silver bars on their shoulders. Captain? Angel was pretty sure that put him at the rank of captain. The other had the golden oak leaf, which she was pretty sure put him at the rank of major.

Whatever rank they were, Black must have taken control of their minds.

One of them, the major, walked right up to Black, removing his security access card from his lapel where it had been clipped and handing it to Black without a word.

For a few seconds, both officers just stood there, presumably while Black read him, probably to learn the basic security protocols and layout of the complex.

A few seconds later, the other male soldier, the captain, handed Black his badge, too.

"Different levels of security clearance?" Mika mused aloud.

"Different areas of the building," Yarli corrected, her voice grim. "One is aid to a Brigadier General. The other works with defense contractors."

Angel let out a half-outraged snort.

When Yarli turned to look at her, Angel couldn't help giving the seer a cynical smile, shaking her head, although she couldn't have explained the mixture of emotions going through her head. Normally, she might have been slightly offended by Black's blatant disregard for the sanctity of human free will, but given where

Black was going, looking for his wife's assailant, most of Angel's irritation was aimed at the military itself.

Clearly Black thought these "super soldiers," or whatever the fuck they were, came out of some kind of experimental military tech.

If so, it was something Charles commissioned.

Maybe something meant to kill vampires faster.

When Angel glanced at Cowboy, her boyfriend's gray eyes met hers.

From the look reflected there, and the frown on his mouth under his dirty-blond hair, she strongly got the impression Cowboy was thinking along the same lines as her.

Refolding his lean arms over his chest, he returned his eyes to the screen, his face set in a colder-looking mask. Studying his expression, Angel found herself thinking Elvis was one hundred percent cheering for Black.

She couldn't exactly blame him for that.

She more or less felt the same way.

Cowboy was mad about what happened to Miri.

At this point, after everything that happened in that California desert, after everything Charles had done, and those people who kidnapped Miri, not to mention what happened to Nick, Cowboy was just plain mad, period.

It wasn't really Cowboy's way to get mad in a loud way.

Moreover, as much as Cowboy was not thrilled about having Nick staying in his girlfriend's apartment above Divisadero Street, Angel knew his feelings about that were more complex than he generally let on, too.

Cowboy and Nick had been friends before Nick got turned.

That time, when Angel's eyes left Cowboy's face, she caught Yarli staring at her.

Angel blinked, again feeling the blood drain from her face.

The dark-skinned seer didn't look away. Her full lips pulled into a faint frown as she studied Angel's face openly.

Clearly, like Mika, she'd heard something.

Angel had a sinking feeling she knew exactly what she'd heard.

Impulsively, she thought at the African-looking seer.

Don't tell him, she thought, aiming her thoughts at Yarli, and in a lesser way, at Mika. *Don't tell him, please. Let Miri talk to him. Let Miri be the one to tell him.*

There was a silence.

In it, Yarli went totally still.

She didn't move, didn't blink.

Then, a small frown touched the edge of her lips.

Angel panicked. She was about to try again, to try reasoning with the seer, to beg her, really, not to tell Black that Nick was here, in San Francisco, much less that he was here with Miri's full knowledge and blessing...

Yarli exhaled.

Still frowning slightly, she nodded perceptibly.

Then she pointed at her mouth, right before she pointed between herself and Angel.

It wasn't normal sign-language for humans, but Angel got the message.

Yarli wanted to have a little chat with Angel.

Privately. Likely as soon as possible.

Likely as soon as this meeting was over, and the immediate Black emergency was more or less handled, and Yarli could spare more than thirty seconds.

When Angel glanced at Yarli that time, the tall seer nodded again, her eyes holding an overt warning.

Feeling her face flush with heat, and again pushing the whole topic from her mind, or at least filing it away for later, Angel saw movement on the screen in her periphery and turned, just in time to see Black ascend the cement stairs up to the compound doors.

Once Black reached the landing at the top, he paused long enough to press one of the two badges against the security panel.

The panel's light flickered, then Black jerked open the heavy metal door.

He disappeared into the building.

There was a slight pause.

Facial-rec caught him again on the other side.

The board reconfigured.

Angel watched Black walk down the corridor.

The camera angles switched a few more times as he made his way deeper into the complex, turning right down one corridor, then left, then another left. He walked gracefully, deceptively fast, seemingly without a single hesitation, pushing every human he encountered into simply not seeing him, at least if the looks on their faces were any indication.

Angel frowned, wondering where he would go first.

Clearly, Black had a specific destination in mind.

As she thought it, Black entered an elevator.

The board reconfigured again.

The angle showed him from above, his dark head aimed down, his long body leaning against the elevator's back wall, gripping the handrail with both hands. He must have known about the camera, since he didn't look up.

It struck Angel that he hadn't looked at any of the cameras.

So he hadn't forgotten himself entirely, in terms of the risks around what he was doing. He also clearly didn't know Minh was erasing all traces of his visit in the surveillance log. That, or it was such a habit for him to avoid cameras, he did it entirely in rote.

"Probably the last of those," Mika muttered.

Angel ignored that.

Still, it was yet another reminder, as if she needed any, that both Yarli and Mika were watching her like damned hawks right now, and likely listening to every thought running through her head.

She almost understood why.

It still annoyed her.

"Damn," Cowboy said. "Here we go."

Angel looked back at the monitor, shoving the two peeping-Tom seers out of her mind. Once she did, she saw that Black had left the elevator, and was stalking down towards a reception area, and what looked like a large office on the other side.

Black didn't even pause at the reception desk, and the man sitting there, obviously some kind of administrative support person, didn't so much as glance at him.

Black walked straight for the office door, and flung it open.

"Shit," Yarli muttered.

The image didn't change, since there were no cameras inside the office itself.

Still, there was no mistaking what happened through the open door.

The camera aimed straight through, at a low enough angle to capture the desk, the man sitting there, and Black approaching that desk.

Before Angel could get a good look at the man's face, Black was already walking purposefully around the desk, walking directly up to him. Without a pause, Black bent down, catching hold of him by the throat.

"That's not a human!" Mika said then, her voice sharp. "It's a seer!"

Just then, the screen blurred into static...

Right before it went dark.

18

CLASSIFIED

B lack lifted him up by the throat.
Without thought, he slammed the other male against the wall.

Yarli's thoughts rose in his, panicked-sounding, distracting.

He's a seer! Boss, he's a seer—

No shit he's a seer, Black sent back, irritated. *Tell me something useful, why don't you? Like who the fuck he is. Like his goddamned sight rank. Like how long he's been one of Charles' butt monkeys. Like what the fuck he's doing, putting out hits on my wife—*

Working on an ID now—

Work faster, goddamn it, Black growled.

He'd known what this joker was before he walked through that door.

He'd more or less known when he first read his identity off the Marine Major he'd stopped outside the compound. Something about the way the male looked, through the mind of the Major. He'd seen the contact lenses, even via the human. He'd noted the muting colors, not to mention the male's height, his odd mannerisms, the fact that he was known for odd silences and stares.

Definitely all seer stuff.

The fucker got lazy.

He'd done just enough to camouflage himself from humans who had no idea seers were a thing, but nowhere near enough to camouflage himself from other seers. Even in just a few months of living on this version of Earth, he got lazy, playing God.

Black slammed him against the wall again, still holding him by the throat.

"You know me, brother?" he hissed between his teeth.

The male seer's eyes widened, staring at him as his fingers grasped at Black's hand around his throat.

The seer was tall, with the odd, half-Asian, half-Eastern European features of a lot of seers from Old Earth. He wasn't particularly muscular, despite the military uniform he wore, and Black found he could hold him up easily, one-handed.

"You might want to answer me," Black growled. "You won't like me when I'm angry."

"I was under orders!" the other blurted, lurching violently to get away, then simply twisting and writhing in his grasp when he couldn't. He gasped, fear in his eyes, fighting to breathe past Black's tightening grip.

"Brother... I was under orders..."

"Of that fascist prick?" Black growled. "You think that's going to save you?"

When the seer only stared at him, wide-eyed, still struggling like a rabbit in his grasp, kicking out feebly against Black's legs, Black shook him, violently.

"Was it Charles?" he growled. "Did he give the order?"

The seer's eyes widened more. "Ch-Ch-Charles...?"

"Yes," Black snapped. "Was it him?"

When the seer just stared at him blankly again, Black shook him, even more roughly than before, slamming his head up against the wall.

"Who the fuck was it?" Black snarled, louder. "Who put the hit out on my wife? I want a name! Now! Or I'll snap your goddamned neck, find someone else to ask..."

Black watched as his words seemed to click into place behind the other's eyes, as what he was asking seemed to penetrate.

"N-N-No," the seer said, shaking his head, his whole body shaking now. "No! It wasn't Faustus. He was already gone. The female... she had already taken him. He never would have approved a hit. Not on his own niece—"

"Right," Black growled. "Just on me."

"N-N-No!"

But Black was already losing patience with this piece of shit.

You getting anything? he asked Yarli, his mind hard in hers. *I can't feel much of a construct out here. You should be able to get past his shields—*

We're past them, sir, she confirmed, breaking into his thoughts. *He thinks he's telling the truth. It wasn't Charles. Not as far as he knows.*

Who the fuck was it?

There was a silence.

It was brief.

Black knew it was brief, because he was about to slam into her light, to let her know just how fucking serious he was about getting an answer... when she answered him before he could gear up his light to hit out at hers.

I don't think he knows, Yarli sent. *Holo agrees with me. So do Mika and Kiessa, at least on our preliminary scan. We read through his mind while you were... err, scaring him, sir. We saw the memory of him receiving orders. He was informed of the drop. He was told it was coming. He was told he might need to cover up any deaths that occurred. He was told to make sure any incidents fell under military jurisdiction... preferably before they hit the public, and to manage public relations with the Honolulu police. But he was also told all the details around the exact deployment were "need to know." Classified, sir.*

Black frowned, thinking about this. *Did they come from here? The soldiers?*

Yes, the fucking soldiers! Black snapped. *Did they come out of here? Were they deployed out of one of the bases here on the islands?*

Mika's mind rose, speaking in place of Yarli's.

We don't think so, sir, the younger seer sent, her thoughts matter-of-fact. *It appears they were air-dropped off the coast, originating out of the mainland. We're looking for the origination point now. It appears to be somewhere on the East Coast, but not the Pentagon or anywhere in D.C. It looks like Virginia, maybe. Possibly further south. Jax is working with Minh and Verne on getting the exact location of the site—*

How long before you can pinpoint it? Black growled.

We don't know for sure, not yet—

Guess. Give me a ballpark.

Mika hesitated.

Black could almost hear her consulting with someone else. He was about to snap at her again, when her focus returned to him.

Give us an hour, Mika sent, her thoughts apologetic. *They're going at it from two angles, sir... the site codes, and the flight logs for planes that were in the area at the times your General was told they'd be deployed. Minh says it's going to take a little time to break into the flight logs. They'll have to look at a bunch of them, since they aren't sure which is the right plane, and they haven't yet verified the origination site. They're working on it now, out of the Colonel's old shop. For now, all I can tell you is that Minh and the others aren't familiar with the ID codes on the site where the actual weapons came from—*

You mean the soldiers?

Yes. Mika confirmed, correcting her words. *The soldiers. They have them classified as "enhanced special assignment units" in the manifest we're looking at, the one they think belongs to the flight that dropped the last one. Minh says they're using an ordnance code, not one normally used for personnel.*

Are they sentient? Are they people at all?

Another pause.

We don't know, sir, Yarli said, sounding as apologetic at Mika.

How many are there?

We don't know that either, boss, Mika said, even more reluctantly. *Hopefully, once we pin down the site, we can send someone down there—*

How many are here? On Oahu? Black growled. *Do you know? Did anyone tell the General here how many would be coming?*

Another silence.

It looks like he was expecting a few waves of attacks... Yarli sent warily.

When? Black growled. *When were these waves supposed to start? Today? Yesterday? With the first dead guy who washed up on the beach?*

We're working on that, sir, Mika sent, her thoughts even more apologetic, although Black could hear her attempt to calm him woven through her light. *It's clear he was expecting two different drops. That might cover both bodies you found. Both drops were supposed to occur in the ocean, but at slightly different locations off the coast, presumably to stagger their deployment—*

Could there have been more than one body dropped in each deployment?

There was a silence.

Then Yarli's mind rose, reluctant.

It's possible, sir, she admitted. *Minh's concerned about that, too, given the time difference between the appearance of the two bodies you found.*

Black's jaw hardened, enough to hurt his teeth.

He refocused on the seer he held against the wall.

The male was starting to lose consciousness.

Black knew he had to let go of him.

He knew he had to give the other seer air, put his feet on back on the carpeted floor... but it took every ounce of his willpower not to snap the fucker's neck where he held him.

After a pause where the other seer's eyes began to roll back in his head, his face going slack, Black forced his fingers open, letting him drop to the floor.

The male seer's knees crumpled, unable to hold up his weight. He fell to the carpet and promptly slumped against the wall, gasping, holding his throat.

Black was still staring down at the male seer as the General began to cough—deep, wracking coughs that arched his back, contorting his body.

"How many did they send?" Black growled. He prodded him with a booted foot. "How many, goddamn it?"

The seer shook his head, still coughing, still holding his throat.

"I don't know," he managed, in half gasps.

"Why her?" Black growled. "Why the fuck were they trying to kill *her?* Why not me?"

The male shook his head.

"Not kill," he managed, his voice still breathless, weak. "Not kill..."

"What?" Black growled.

When the other didn't answer him right away, Black's jaw clenched. He didn't just prod the General with his boot that time. He kicked him, hard, right in the ribs.

The seer let out an agonized groan, cringing under Black's height.

"Speak!" Black growled. "What the fuck did you say?"

The male seer held up a hand, a weak plea for mercy.

"I promise you, brother," he said, still trying to regain his breath. "I promise you. It was my understanding they wouldn't hurt her. I was told *specifically* they weren't to kill her. I was told they were to take custody of her. Live capture only. No exceptions. No contingencies. They were to let her go if they couldn't get her alive. They were insistent on this, on this need for her to remain alive. For research—"

"Research?" Black's jaw tightened all over again. He had to restrain himself from kicking the bastard a third time. "Like the kind of fucking research Charles wanted to do on me?"

The male seer shook his head.

"I don't know," he said in Prexci, the seer tongue, still holding up the hand, wincing, a silent plea for Black to stop hurting him. "I really don't know anything about that, brother... I'm sorry. I was not granted access to know these things."

"For someone who claims to not know shit, you seem to know a lot," Black said, his teeth still gritted. "How do you know someone didn't go rogue? Try to take her out?"

"I don't!" the seer said, holding up his hand again, a silent plea for Black to stop. "All I know is, someone was really angry she was nearly killed. I heard this through the network. From someone I know at the Pentagon. A friend."

Are you hearing this? Black growled to Yarli.

Got it, boss, the female infiltrator affirmed. *We're sending it on now. Jax thinks he's already got an ID on this so-called "friend" at the Pentagon. He read it through that* dugra-te di aros *you're questioning. Jax traced his words and light to a female seer working for the N.S.A. He's verifying now, but it seems she is a consultant. Jorji and his team are already heading over there, to have a talk with her.*

Pausing, Yarli added,

I've ordered him to take this "consultant" into custody if it turns out she has information we need... as well as anyone higher on the food chain who might be issuing the actual kill or capture orders against the doc. That's assuming Jorji is able to read her well enough to be able to ID them. Right now, it's difficult for us to determine who's actually calling the shots for any of these moves. Most of the players ID'd so far are either human, or relatively lower-level within the hierarchy at the Pentagon—

Because that's all that's left, Black broke in with a growl. *Miri got everyone else.*

There was a silence.

In it, Black felt Yarli agree with him.

He felt it clearly, even before she sent specific thoughts.

Yes, she replied. *That's exactly it, boss. We're working on rounding up the seers who are left, but it's going to take some time. We don't know their exact succession order yet, so we can only guess in terms of priorities. In the meantime, we should probably assume this is retaliation for what Miri did. That's likely why they're targeting her.*

Black scowled.

He knew Yarli was right.

It still made him feel sick.

He'd expected them to *want* to go after her.

He just hadn't expected them to be so damned successful, not this soon.

Like Miri herself, he'd hoped Miri's purge cleaned out enough of their leadership that Charles wouldn't be able to hit back, at least not before they could assess who was left out of Charles' hierarchy who might pose a risk.

Black thought they'd have more time.

Then again, he supposed that was the point.

With more time, they could have cleaned out D.C. for real, including any shadow pockets of loyalty left over after Miri's first sweep. Charles would know this. In order to be effective at all, any retaliation would have to be more or less instantaneous.

Black should have realized this.

He should have fucking *realized* this.

He also should have known Charles would have some kind of failsafe in place—some way to retaliate if his new dictatorship was threatened.

Charles was the very definition of vindictive.

Black still wouldn't have expected it to be aimed at Miri, though.

Truthfully, he would have expected something more dramatic from Charles, anyway.

Something like a nuclear bomb hitting D.C.

Or possibly a bomb hitting Moscow... or Beijing. Or a whole lot of bombs, wiping out a whole lot of human metropolitan areas.

Something to leave the human world a complete fucking mess, if only for the unforgiveable crime of anyone daring to oppose him. Charles felt this was his divine calling, after all. He would be furious that anyone would dare to question his absolute right to enslave every damned human on the planet, if he decided that would benefit the seer race.

Even so, Black never thought he'd go after Miri.

Him, sure, Black himself... but not Miri.

Grimacing, he stepped back from the seer groveling on the carpet.

"Why were you supposed to provide clean up?" Black growled. "If no one was supposed to be killed... why would clean up even be necessary?"

The seer blinked at him in confusion.

"Well, it was likely there would be c-c-casualties," the seer stammered, looking at Black as if he were surprised by the question, as if this were a given. "We were told to expect collateral damage. Perhaps a lot of it. But it was clear this was meant to be *human* casualties. Not seers. It was thought it would be difficult to get her alive... that she'd have protection."

"Me?" Black growled.

"Not dead," the seer gasped, shaking his head, still clutching his throat.

"Because it would kill my wife?" Black said.

There was a pause, then the seer nodded, reluctant.

"In part, yes, brother. They knew it was not safe for her—"

"So just humans," Black said, his voice cold. "You were just expecting a load of dead humans, while your fucking robot army blasted its way into a nearly-full resort populated by nothing but civilians."

The seer frowned at him.

From the confusion in his eyes, he clearly didn't see the problem.

Then again, given who he'd sworn his allegiance to, the fucker probably *didn't* see the problem. One didn't follow Charles if they valued anything about human life.

"You disgust me, brother," Black told him, meaning it with every ounce of his being. "You fucking repulse me."

"Brother, I—"

"How could you follow that piece of shit?"

He didn't know why he asked it.

He didn't know why he bothered.

Who cared what this asshole told himself, in terms of reasons?

Who cared why the weak-minded looked for a savior?

The seer blinked up at him, his confusion deepening, changing.

Scowling, Black took another step back, giving the male a last look.

"You might as well have stayed on Old Earth," he told him in disgust. "You might as well have stayed there... with a human collar around your neck, brother."

The seer blinked at him from his place on the floor.

The look in his eyes wasn't anger... or shame.

It was utter and complete bewilderment.

Somehow, that confused, blank-eyed stare only made Black angrier.

Before he got tempted to do something with that anger, before he succumbed to the part of himself that wanted to take it out on this piece of shit, hurt him for real, make him pay for having to see his wife covered in knife cuts and blood...

Black forced himself to look away.

Aiming his feet for the corridor, for the elevator, for the bike he'd left parked in the lot outside... he walked without looking back, without once slowing his pace.

He needed to get back to Miri.

He needed to get back to his wife right fucking now.

19

YOU ARE DIFFERENT

Angel didn't get back to the apartment until late that afternoon.

Really, it was early evening.

The sun had set. There was still light in the sky, but it was red and orange, with even the yellows and lighter blues fading, leaving indigo and purple along the line making up the horizon, reflecting in the windows along the street leading up to her flat at the top of the hill.

She'd just come from a talk with Mika and Yarli.

The two seers took mercy on her.

Really, they took mercy on Nick... and, possibly more so, on Dalejem.

Angel couldn't help feeling guilty at how obviously relieved both of them were to hear that Dalejem was alive—not dead or enslaved via Nick's bite or venom, like they'd all quietly assumed when he went missing the same time as Nick.

Still, they hadn't been thrilled.

They hadn't been thrilled about any part of this situation.

They clearly weren't thrilled at Angel's request to keep Nick's being here quiet.

At the same time, they obviously understood the logic of not telling Dex, or Kiko... or really, any of the humans on Black's team who were friends with one or both of them. Dex would definitely want to kill Nick. Kiko would probably have a full-blown PTSD reaction to the news that Nick was alive, much less that he was back in the city.

Yarli and Mika also seemed to agree it should be Miri who told Black, since it was Miri's decision to bring Nick back to San Francisco.

More than anything, the two seers seemed to respond to the fact that Miri voiced the whole thing as an order. Angel told them Miri had given her and Cowboy an *order* not to harm Nick. She'd *ordered* them not tell anyone Nick was alive and in San Francisco, not until Miri had a chance to talk to her husband.

Mika and Yarli both looked at one other, once Angel pulled out the "order" word.

Angel saw it in their faces, before either said a thing.

They weren't going to disobey a direct order from Miri.

They saw Miri as their boss, just like Black.

Which, fair enough—Black was explicit that he and the doc were co-owners of Black Securities and Investigations now. He'd changed all the paperwork to reflect that; it even showed up on the company website, under the masthead.

He changed it not long after they were officially married, according to Miri.

Funnily enough, Angel still wasn't sure exactly when that had been. She'd first been made aware of it when Black got shot at Stow Lake, but as far as she knew, they'd never had any kind of ceremony, not even at a Justice of the Peace.

They must have, though... right?

At some point, they must have made things official.

Pushing that from her mind with a frown, she unlocked the front door of her apartment, pushing that same door inward once she'd undone the bolt.

Holding three stuffed-full grocery bags of Nick's clothes, along with an equally-stuffed backpack of other things she'd found in his old room at the California Street building, she craned her neck around the corner of the entryway into the kitchen, looking for movement.

Seeing none, she kicked off her low flats, dumping the clothing-filled bags on the entryway carpet, and tossing her keys on the low table. She dumped the backpack next to the bags.

"Nick?" she said.

Shouldering off her coat, she hung it up on a hook in the foyer, and ventured into the living room, listening for any sign of movement or voices.

She stood in the middle of her living room, staring around at the empty couches and the spotless tables and counters. She frowned, hands on her hips.

Nick *must* be bored, during the daytime hours.

It looked like he'd actually vacuumed.

Exhaling in a sigh, she let her hands fall to her sides, turning around to head for the kitchen...

...and nearly jumped out of her skin.

Nick stood there, watching her, a faint frown on his face.

She hadn't heard him.

She hadn't heard a damned thing.

Now she found herself staring at him, even as she tried to re-swallow her heart.

He stood there, shockingly white-skinned and shirtless, wearing nothing but dark gray sweat pants, his bloodless feet made even whiter by the contrast. He continued to frown, looking at her like he was trying to figure out what her problem was.

Angel couldn't help looking back at him, at the perfect lines of his chalk-white, disturbingly well-defined chest. He looked like his whole body had been hewn out of marble and somehow breathed into life.

"What are you doing?" he said, that puzzlement reaching his voice. "You're looking at me like you think I'm going to bite you."

Pausing, he added,

"Thanks for bringing that stuff. I put it in the bedroom. I hope that's okay."

Stepping forward, she moved without thinking.

She smacked him, hard, in the chest.

"Don't DO that!" she said, hitting him again. She fought a half-laugh, but her voice was shaking. "Jesus. You scared the living shit out of me, Nick!"

He held up a hand, frowning as he glanced over his shoulder, aiming those colorless, cracked-crystal eyes back in the direction of the bedroom.

"Hey," he said, his voice still low. "Don't fucking shout. I finally got him down. Don't wake him up now, or I really *will* bite you."

Angel blinked.

Then she realized what he meant.

Exhaling, she stepped back, then let her legs bend, letting her weight slump into the powder blue couch and the quilt she still had from her grandmother.

Smoothing the braids out of her face with her hands, pushing a few behind her ears, she looked up at Nick, and it hit her how hungry she was.

She might need to order a pizza.

"Has he really been up all day?" she said, looking up at Nick.

He was still staring at her, that faint frown on his lips.

"What happened?" he said, not answering her question.

"You mean besides a vampire and a seer keeping me up all last night?" she retorted. "Screaming at one another from my bedroom?"

Nick's expression barely flickered. "You're deflecting," he said.

"Am I?" She lowered her hands to the couch, looking up at him in exasperation. "What the hell is going on with the two of you? Are you going to tell me?" Pausing at his silence, she added, "Because you know how you used to say Miri and Black were a dysfunctional mess? Well, guess what, Nicky-baby? You and Jem are worse. You're a mass of crazy I don't even know how to penetrate at this point—"

Nick was frowning for real now, holding up a hand, asking her to be quiet even as he looked over his shoulder again, towards the bedroom, and sank down into the chair closest to the couch.

"Okay, okay," he said. "I get it."

"You get what?" she snorted. "That you and your boyfriend are nuts? Because seriously, Nick... you are. I was worried you were going to hurt one another last night."

Lowering her voice to a grumble, she admitted,

"...Or, really, based on what I could hear, I was worried he might hurt you." Her eyes met his, her voice a touch harder. "What the hell happened at the Lighthouse, Nick? You guys just... melted down after that."

Nick frowned, his lips pulling into a delicate expression that was somehow both exactly like the old Nick and nothing like him at the same time.

"He's going through something right now," he said. "It's not his fault."

"What?" she said, frowning. "What is he going through, Nick?"

There was a silence.

Then Nick leaned back in the recliner, exhaling.

Like the dark gray sweatpants did with his feet, the purple recliner somehow only highlighted just how white Nick's skin really was.

After another pause where he seemed to be thinking, Nick frowned.

"I'm honestly not sure I should tell you," he said.

Letting out another of those strange, airless exhales, he met her gaze.

"I would like to talk to you," he admitted. "I really want to talk to someone. But it's kind of... personal."

"Since when do we not do personal, Nicky?" she said dryly.

His eyes flinched.

The look there startled her, until she realized she understood that, too.

"Nick," she said. "Things might not be exactly the same... but they don't feel as different as you seem to think. Not anymore. Even with..." She waved vaguely in the direction of her bedroom. "...the weirdness. The you and Jem thing. The you drinking blood thing. The creepy dude you've got chained up in my garage thing."

She motioned at his bare chest and shockingly white face.

"...The you looking like *that* thing."

Nick rolled his eyes, glancing down at his chest.

"Blindingly white, you mean?" he said.

"That," she admitted. "And just all of it, Nick. The way you move. The way you look twenty years younger. The way you look like you... and *nothing like* you... at exactly the same time. Your mannerisms, which are some weird combination of the old Nick, vampire Nick, and now seer from you spending so much time with Jem. Your eyes—"

He was waving her off though, scowling.

"I get it," he muttered.

"Maybe," she said. "And maybe you don't. My point is, you're still *you*, Nick. Even under all that, I still see more you than not-you."

He gave her another of those delicate frowns.

"Now you sound like Jem," he said.

For a second, she just studied his face.

Then, exhaling, she placed her hands on either side of her on the couch.

"We're going to talk about this," she announced, her voice brooking no argument.

"Are we?"

"Yes," she said. "I'm making an executive decision. But first I'm getting a beer. And ordering a pizza," she added. "Or you're going to be talking to me while I'm slurring drunk. I haven't eaten a damned thing today, apart from a handful of chips and way too much coffee."

Pulling her phone out of her back pocket, she didn't wait for him to answer, but used her phone to reorder her usual, after checking that it would be going to the right address.

After she punched through the order, adding a few caffeinated sodas since she couldn't order beer, along with an order of hot wings and one of oven-baked garlic bread, figuring she could chew on those later if the pizza ended up not being enough, or she and Nick ended up being up all night... she set the phone down on the coffee table.

Leaning into the couch with a sigh, she folded her arms.

"Well?" she said. "Talk. What's going on with you and Jem? Why the hell was he yelling at you all night... so loudly my neighbors were probably ready to call the cops?"

Nick frowned. Thinking, he propped an ankle up on one thigh.

"What about your beer?" he said, nodding towards the kitchen. "This might take a while."

"I'll get one when the pizza gets here."

Nick's nose wrinkled. "Let me guess... extra pepperoni. Anchovies. Sliced tomatoes. Garlic."

She quirked an eyebrow at him. "Are you garlic-phobic now? Like the myths?"

He snorted a laugh, surprising her enough that she jumped.

"No," he said, smiling as he shook his head. "No, it just smells like shit. That whole combination is probably going to make me pass out, given my highly-sensitive and infinitely more discerning vampire nose..."

That time, it was her turn to laugh.

"You eat *people,*" she reminded him. "Don't even get me going on the yuck factor around the yummy things I decide to put in my tummy."

"Yummy?" He gave another of those wrinkle-nosed scowls. "Even my human nose had nothing but *ick* to say about your taste in pizza—"

"Are you going to tell me what's up with your boyfriend?" she said. "Or are we just going to play *this* game all night? Because right now, you definitely win the prize for being one hundred and ten percent the Nick I remember... with all of his avoidance games and anti-intimacy bullshit wholly intact."

It was meant to be a joke.

It was supposed to make him laugh... smile.

Roll his eyes, at least.

Instead, he winced.

He winced like her words actually hurt him.

"Now you really do sound like Jem," he muttered.

She frowned back.

Making a snap decision, she pushed herself up off the couch, still frowning faintly as she looked over Nick's facial expression.

"I guess I will get that beer," she muttered, making her way for the kitchen.

❦

Nick watched her go.

He frowned, wondering if he should really talk to her.

She seemed to really want to know.

Jem might be pissed.

Most of what he wanted to say was personal between the two of them.

Some of it was only personal to Jem himself, really. Some of it was just shit Nick theorized about what was going on... in some cases with Jem, in some cases with himself, in some cases with both of them.

Then again, they'd more or less forced their personal problems into Angel's face the night before, after that surfing trip to Santa Cruz.

Jem hadn't stopped yelling at him even after it got light out.

Truthfully, Nick was pretty mortified when he saw Angel stretched out on the couch that morning. He'd assumed she would have left, given all that, but maybe she really had been worried one of them might hurt the other.

Nick felt more or less obligated to tell her *something*.

His vampire eyes followed her as she made her way back to the kitchen.

His vampire ears followed her to the fridge, hearing her open the door.

He hadn't told her, but she looked different to him now, too.

It wasn't just that he could hear her heart beating in her chest, or hear the blood pumping through her veins, a fact that no longer distracted him, at least. He could see more of her, with his vampire eyes. He could see every micro-expression that flickered and flashed across her face. He could see every bead of sweat, every clenched and unclenched muscle.

He could hear every hitch or stop in her breath.

He could feel her temperature change when she was worried, or annoyed, or angry... or even aroused, the one time Cowboy had been here, and Nick caught Angel looking at him, likely wishing the two of them could be alone.

He knew he'd stolen a lot of alone-time with her boyfriend away from his friend.

For that reason alone, he wanted to talk to her.

He'd been so focused on his own shit, those last months and even years he'd been human, he'd missed a lot of what had been going on in Angel's life. He'd more or less missed most of the developing relationship between her and Cowboy, a relationship that was clearly serious, definitely a lot more serious than he'd let himself notice before he got turned.

He'd listened to her through all of that, of course.

He'd listened to her when she broke up with her fiancé, Anthony, back when Angel and Cowboy first got together.

He'd heard her describe her guilt and confusion about Cowboy, her guilt at not feeling about Anthony the way she thought she should feel about him, her anger at Black for calling her out on both things... but Nick hadn't really *listened*.

Truthfully, he'd been a little judgmental about the whole thing.

He'd figured she was having a commitment-phobic moment, one that had her jumping ship due to her impending marriage to Anthony.

He figured Cowboy was incidental.

He figured Cowboy was an excuse.

If it was anything at all, Nick figured it was a lust thing with Cowboy.

He'd found himself reevaluating that, even in just the past few days.

Now, when Angel came back into the room, slumping on the couch in front of him, he could practically feel how tired she was.

Something had happened at the Raptor's Nest today, something she clearly didn't want to tell him.

Her heartbeat was uneven, bordering on thread-y, but that was probably partly because of the lack of food, which he could also sense on her.

The vampire side of him wanted to bite her.

Not to feed on her, but to calm her down with the venom, to comfort her.

Somehow, he doubted telling her that would comfort her all that much, though.

The thought almost made him smile.

Almost.

"Jem doesn't trust me," he said, matter-of-fact, as Angel brought her legs up to sit cross-legged on her aunt's old, saggy but super-comfy couch.

She stopped where she'd been using a bottle opener to crack open her beer.

Blinking at him, once, she finished the motion, popping off the cap and setting it on the glass-covered coffee table with the opener. She leaned back, beer in hand, letting the powder blue couch halfway swallow her. Lifting the bottle to her mouth, she took a few swallows, then rested it on her thigh, waiting for him to go on.

She really was a beautiful woman.

It was strange how one ceased to notice that kind of thing after a while, when it involved an old friend.

But he knew he was avoiding, even now.

"Do you know anything about Jem?" Nick said, cautious. "About what happened to him on that other world?"

Angel shook her head, taking another sip of beer.

"No," she said. "Do you?"

He shook his head, mouth pursed.

"Not enough," he admitted. "I've gotten a few things out of him, but not much." Hesitating, he added, "I know it's still hurting him. I think it's hurting him a lot. Something about the thing with me and him is bringing it all up. I know it's embarrassing him, but I want him to let himself feel it... I just wish I understood it better."

Angel was watching him, a faint wonder in her eyes.

He fought to understand what the look meant.

In the end, he gave up.

"What?" he said. "Why are you looking at me like that?"

"You," she said, not bothering to elaborate. "Are you in love with him, Nick?"

The question threw him.

It more than threw him.

It completely blanked out his mind.

He closed his mouth, fighting to think about it rationally.

"I don't know," he said after a beat, exhaling, or pretending to, at least. "Honestly, I'm not sure I even know what that means anymore."

There was a silence.

Then Angel let out a disbelieving laugh. "Bullshit," she said. "You don't want to say it. Is that why he doesn't trust you?"

Nick scowled, in spite of himself.

At the same time, her words hurt.

He still wasn't used to how intensely emotions hit him at times, seemingly out of nowhere, as a vampire. It still felt like being jabbed in a raw wound, one that had no shielding, no protections or bandages whatsoever.

"He's still in love with them," Nick said, that pain stabbing harder at his chest. "One of them... both of them, maybe. I think he was in love with the male one, first. Then he fell in love with both of them. Now I think maybe he's just confused. They left him, both of them. They completely shut him out... abandoned him. He felt really used."

Realizing tears were running down his face, he wiped them away with the side of his hand, embarrassed.

He avoided Angel's eyes at first, but then, feeling her looking at him, he found himself returning her gaze.

She was staring at him, her expression completely stunned.

"Sorry," he said, gruff.

"Don't be sorry, Nick," she said, seeming to snap herself out of her own shock. "Jesus. You do love him. You really love him. You think he doesn't love you?"

Nick shook his head, frowning.

Even so, he fought to tell her the truth.

"I honestly don't know." Feeling a flicker of paranoia, he glanced over his shoulder towards the bedroom.

Hearing and seeing nothing, he looked back at her.

"He says he wants to be with me. I believe him. I don't think he's lying to me, not intentionally. I just think he's... you know." He made the sign for crazy by his head. "Not right. He's not quite right in the head... maybe in his heart. I think he cares about me, I really do. He cares about me enough that it's bringing all this shit up for him. Whoever those fuckers were, they made him feel really used... and betrayed."

Angel nodded, taking another drink of beer. "So he's waiting for the shoe to drop with you," she said, matter-of-fact.

Nick met her gaze, nodding. "Yeah."

He exhaled, human-fashion, motioning vaguely over his shoulder.

"He thinks I'm in love with Miri. He's positive I'm going to leave him for a woman... any woman, really. He keeps accusing me of being confused about him. He says I've got Stockholm Syndrome or something. He doesn't use those exact words, but he seems to think my feelings for him are temporary. Some form of psychological transference, since he took care of me when I was going through all that. With the transition and everything..."

He trailed, seeing her staring at him again.

She had that odd look in her eyes again, the one he couldn't read.

It wasn't quite confusion.

It was closer to disbelief, coupled with a kind of shock.

He also saw understanding there, a kind of knowingness that threw him.

"What?" he said again. "You're doing that thing again."

She paused, as if unsure if she should answer.

Then she shook her head, leaning towards him, her eyes serious.

"I take it back," she said. "You *are* different now, Nick. Or maybe you're more yourself now, so it seems different." Pausing at his rolled eyes, she added, before he could make a crack, "Okay. Well, at least with this, you're different. Just the way you're talking about this whole thing. The Jem thing. I don't think I've ever seen you this open, Nick. There's like, zero b.s."

Pausing, studying his face, she quirked an eyebrow, taking a few swallows off her beer as she leaned back in the couch.

She looked about to say more, when her phone began to ring, signaling the pizza guy was there. Glancing down at the face of it, she leaned forward again, setting down her beer with a clunk on the table and scooping up the phone.

"...and you've stopped acting dumb," she added, before putting the phone to her ear. "You tend to dumb-down your speech, Nick. You've done it since high school, to hide the fact that you got straight A's. You did it as a cop, too. I always figured it was a way to get people to underestimate you. But you even did it with me and Miri."

She added, the phone still ringing in her hand,

"I got used to it. It's kind of a trip, though, to hear you just talking, without any of that as cover."

Before he could answer, she swiped her finger across the glass screen of her phone and put it to her ear.

"Hey!" she said. "Yeah, I'm here... coming to the door now."

He watched her get up off the couch, still talking to the pizza guy as she climbed out of the squishy cushions and made her way to the front door.

He found himself thinking about her words.

He heard her open the door, heard her talking to the person standing there.

It struck him that they'd gotten here awfully fast.

Even for pizza delivery... that was really fast.

Too fast.

Before the thought had fully sunk into his mind, much less turned into a full-blown logical sequence of facts—

He was on his feet and darting for the door.

He moved fast.

He moved faster than he'd trained himself to move, at least when he was around humans and seers. He reached the entryway in a human heartbeat, rounding the corner of the hall in time to see the vampire standing there, on the other side of the entryway, crook a finger towards his childhood friend, coaxing Angel to come outside.

20

BLOOD RIVAL

"ANGEL!" Nick threw every ounce of thrall into his voice he possibly could. "STOP!"

Her foot halted, midair.

It stopped just where it would have crossed the threshold of her doorway.

"STEP. BACK."

Nick's fangs extended in his mouth, his vision clouding red as every ounce of the fighter in him roared to the forefront of his being.

"COME. TO. ME."

Angel's foot and leg wavered in the air.

She turned her head, slowly, blinking at him in confusion.

Seeing Nick's face did something, though. Something about looking at him, really seeing him, finally began to snap through the fog of the other vampire's thrall. It worked on her more viscerally than Nick's voice alone.

She blinked, refocusing on him.

Then, after a beat, she was staring at him more intently.

More importantly, he saw the black of her pupils recede, bringing back the brown of her irises. He saw those familiar, coffee-colored irises emerge from that darkness, even as emotion and color returned to her face.

Relief hit him, more than he could express.

"Get behind me," he growled. "Now."

He put thrall in that too, almost without meaning to.

She moved like he'd threatened to hit her, or maybe like he'd grabbed and shaken her.

Jumping back, she ran around behind him. Gripping his back and one of his arms, she actually crouched behind him, as if to hide herself from view.

"Can he come inside?" Angel said, panting. "I didn't invite him. I didn't say he could come in. That counts for something, right—?"

Nick's frown soured. "That's a myth, Ang."

"Then why hasn't he come in?"

Nick didn't take his eyes off the vampire on the other side of the door.

"Probably because he knows I'll attack him the instant he crosses that threshold," he said, his eyes locked on the taller vampire.

"But before. Why didn't he come in before?"

"I don't know," Nick said, still staring at the other vampire's face. "I can guess. Brick probably ordered him not to do anything to harm the treaty. He knows you're close to Miri and Black. He probably doesn't want to piss off Brick any more than he has to... by killing some human he doesn't care about. He was probably trying to get you out of the house, Ang."

Her fingers tensed on his skin where she gripped his back and arm from behind.

"Oh," she said, her voice small.

"It's okay." Nick continued to stare at the vampire standing there. "Go into the bedroom, Angel. Lock the door. Bar it with whatever you can find. Wake up our friend. Tell him I need him to do the thing we discussed. Only with you, instead of with me—"

The vampire in front of him finally spoke.

"I know who is here," he said.

The voice was musical, disturbingly familiar.

Nick shifted his entire focus back to him, to the shock of white-blond hair, the perfect, nearly cherubic features, a face that belonged to a bygone era.

"Why are you here, Dorian?" Nick said.

"You know why I am here, my love," Dorian said gently.

The older vampire's lips twitched, curving into a smile as if the vampire could not help himself.

"It is so very good to see you, Naoko. You are looking so well... I cannot tell you how well you look. This makes my heart and blood sing."

The sheer delight in the other's voice made Nick flinch.

He found himself taking in every detail of the male in front of him, from the shock of his pale, expensively-cut hair to his blood-red irises. His eyes lingered briefly on the perfectly sculpted jaw with just a smattering of blond beard.

Dorian strode right up to the very edge of the door's opening, staring inside.

"Gods of the source... I confess I did not expect to see you looking so well, brother," he said. The cold, bright-scarlet eyes flashed at Nick, even as yet another rare smile touched that bow-like, pale pink mouth. "You are positively... mouth-watering."

Nick scowled.

The vampire kept talking.

"We were sure you were being held prisoner here," Dorian said. "We were sure Miriam had kidnapped you... forced you to return to her husband, so that he might mete out judgment on you. Punish you for your transgressions before you had finished the change."

When Nick didn't speak, didn't move, Dorian poked his head inside the door, looking around, taking in the pictures on the wall, the coatrack, the row of hooks for keys.

"Why did you come back here?" Dorian said. "Why would you risk such an insane thing, my dearest pet?"

Nick's scowl deepened.

He'd never been fond of being referred to as "pet."

Now, he could hear the unmistakable message in the word.

He could hear the possessiveness Dorian infused into the way he said it, the claiming behind it. He could hear the colder anger underlying it, too.

It hit him only then that the other vampire was still staring at him, like he was trying to reacquaint himself with every aspect of Nick's essence and physicality, with his eyes and vampire senses alone.

He stared at Nick with that possessiveness, but not that alone.

Nick saw wariness there, too, coupled with a more covert measuring, like Dorian wasn't sure who Nick would be now.

Which, of course, made a sick kind of sense, now that Nick thought about it.

He hadn't seen Dorian since he really was a newborn.

"Go," he said to Angel. "Do as I asked. Please."

Nudging his friend gently with a hand, prodding her towards the bedroom, he waited until she followed the prod, until she released his back, running for the bedroom, where Dalejem presumably still slept.

Nick knew the seer would be groggy, even apart from being woken up by a panicked Angel. He'd left Panther in the room with Jem too, leaving the puppy curled up against Jem's back, as deeply asleep as the male seer.

Both of them had been exhausted.

Panther had stayed up with him and Jem all of the night before, maybe disturbed by the tenor of their voices, likely agitated from their argument.

When the argument died down, the puppy crashed.

He fell asleep before Jem.

From what Nick had been able to tell, Jem hadn't closed his eyes once the night before, and he'd slept fitfully most of the day. Just about every time Nick went into the room to check on him, the male seer had been staring up at the ceiling, wide awake, despite how exhausted he'd felt.

Nick needed to buy them time.

He needed to at least buy Angel some time to get Dalejem into full consciousness.

Of course, knowing the damned seer, he might not want to leave.

Which meant he needed to buy time for Angel to make him see reason.

"What are you doing here, Dorian?" Nick said, staring at the other vampire. "Did Brick send you?"

The blond vamp straightened to his full height.

Looking Nick over more critically now, and hiding his scrutiny less, he lost most of the startled expression Nick had first seen on his face.

It struck Nick with a kind of shock that he still felt Dorian through their blood connection. The feelings definitely weren't as strong as they once were, not even close, but Nick could feel enough of his old teacher's emotions that he found he understood more than he wanted to about why the older vampire had come.

He hadn't come for Angel, as Nick already surmised.

Now Nick knew Dorian hadn't really come for him, either.

Not really.

As the thought sank in, Nick felt his body tense.

His fangs extended, even as the rest of him went utterly still.

Dorian looked him over warily, his scarlet eyes flickering over Nick's chest and the pose of his body. From his stare, he might be assessing a feral animal.

"I would not hurt you, little brother," Dorian said. "Why do you look ready to attack me?"

Nick's jaw hardened. "You already said I knew why you were here. Why would you pretend otherwise now?"

"I would not hurt you," Dorian repeated, his voice warning. "I would never hurt you, my love. Never."

"It's not my body I'm worried about."

Dorian tilted his head, gesturing fluidly towards the back room.

"I will not hurt your human. I wished only to free you. We thought you must be a prisoner here... we were concerned."

Nick didn't dare take his eyes off the older vampire, not even for an instant.

"No, you weren't," Nick said, blunt. "And no... you didn't."

"You doubt me?"

"I am calling you a liar," Nick returned evenly, unapologetically. "If you were so concerned about my wellbeing, why did you not simply feel me, through the blood? You would have felt no panic in me... no cry for help. You would have felt no part of me that needed rescuing, Dorian—"

"Unless they had you drugged, little brother," Dorian said, his voice chiding. "Unless they confused you. Unless they did something to alter your mental state."

Dorian's face went as still as carved marble.

He assessed Nick openly once more.

"Am I to be accused of being too loving?" Dorian said. "Too concerned about the fate of one so dear to me? You must have known how worried I would be, Naoko—"

"Nick," Nick corrected, speaking without thought. "And I didn't accuse you of any of those things. I called you a liar."

The blond vampire flinched, a frown touching those bow-like lips.

He looked as if he wanted to comment, although if it was Nick's correcting him about his name, or the other thing Nick said, calling him a liar, Nick didn't know.

Whatever it was, Dorian seemed to change his mind.

"I have been looking for you for months now, little brother—"

"I called Brick," Nick growled. "I told him I was fine. I told him to call you off. I told him I had no need of rescue. Not anymore."

Dorian stepped into the house.

Mirroring the other vampire, Nick took a corresponding step forward.

He made his movements as casual as Dorian had, even as he

deliberately positioned himself so that he blocked more of the entryway. He did it as much to send a message to the older vampire as he did to place himself there strategically, squarely between Dorian and the back room.

"We could not feel you," Dorian said, his voice another rebuke. "When you were in Siberia, we could not feel you clearly, brother. For a long time, we could not feel even where you were. If I had not had so many of Black's agents following me, trying to use me to get to you... I would have come for you much sooner."

"And yet," Nick growled "There still would have been no need."

"You miss my point," Dorian said, his voice a sharper warning. "We could not *feel* you, brother. How can we know if you are okay, when we cannot feel you? How could we trust anything about what we felt, given that? Particularly now, given where you are, in the city of your enemies?"

At Nick's scowl, the blond vampire frowned, his voice verging on hurt.

"...Surely, you must know our love for you would not permit such a thing?"

"Brick sent you?" Nick said, still wanting an answer on that point. "You keep saying 'we,' so I have to assume—"

"Where is the new one?" Dorian cut in. "He is here. Yes?"

Nick felt his body tense.

If Dorian noticed, not a flicker showed on his angelic face.

The blond vampire's voice turned silky smooth, holding a near-thrall as he glided the rest of the way through the doorway, facing Nick from only a few feet away.

"I am told it is a male, yes? A seer?" Dorian paused, staring down Nick's body. "So it is not the female I just saw. It is someone else."

Nick felt his jaw clench more.

He felt his whole body harden, even as he fought with words, with how to calm Dorian down, when he was obviously in the midst of a hunt.

He knew there was nothing he could say.

All he could do was try to stall him.

All he could do was try to slow him down.

Dorian came here for one reason, and one reason alone.

The vampire was clearly looking for blood.

"You cannot have him, Dorian," Nick said, raising his voice in spite of himself. "I was clear with Brick on this. I was crystal clear. He belongs to me. He is entirely under my protection."

Dorian glided forward another step, so that he was less than a foot from where Nick stood. Reaching out with a hand, the vampire stroked his fingers down Nick's bare chest, tenderly tracing muscles with his fingers.

Nick hated the ownership he felt behind that touch.

He hated the memories it evoked.

He took a long step back.

"You cannot have him," Nick repeated, his growl turning harder. "Or me. The situation is changed."

Dorian repositioned his weight, the balance between his legs, his feet.

The movements were subtle, barely discernible, but Nick caught every incremental shift, every change in posture and orientation.

His eyes never left those scarlet orbs, which now glowed faintly in the foyer lights.

For an instant, neither of them moved.

Nick felt his muscles bunching up.

He felt himself waiting for the vampire to strike, to leap at him, knock him over, bite him, or simply to shove him out of the way.

Dorian wasn't finished talking, though.

"So, he is greedy, then?" the vampire hissed softly. "Your new friend?"

Before Nick could answer, a voice rose from behind him, making Nick tense more.

"He is," Dalejem answered, his voice cold. "Very."

Nick looked back, turning his head before he could stop himself.

The seer stood there, a compound bow in his hand, an arrow nocked in the string. He had the bow drawn all the way back. He aimed it steadily, his whole being focused.

Nick had zero doubt Jem had the arrow aimed at Dorian's heart.

If he hadn't, Dorian would have leapt by now.

Nick hoped like hell Jem remembered the vampire anatomy lessons Black taught, all those months earlier. Nick hoped like hell Jem didn't believe all those fucking myths about vamps, about wooden stakes, holy water, garlic, whatever other b.s. he'd read or heard back on Old Earth. Nick hoped Jem remembered all the ways he could *actually* kill one of them.

An arrow in the heart would slow Dorian down.

It wouldn't kill him, though.

Briefly, Nick considered saying as much aloud.

He didn't.

He didn't because it might be enough to get Dalejem killed.

Turning back towards the vampire... slowly, carefully now, he gauged the blond vampire's face. He already saw the change in it, just from Dalejem being here, more or less in the room with them. He saw the heat in his old teacher's eyes. He saw the desire there, the satisfaction, the near-gloating look, that this had suddenly become so easy.

Inside, Nick fought not to curse Jem out for not listening to a *goddamned word* he'd said, as usual. It wasn't just what he'd sent Angel back there to tell him. It wasn't just that Nick specifically told him, via Angel, to get them both the fuck out of there.

He'd warned Jem against going after vampires, period.

He'd fucking *warned* him.

He'd warned him about Dorian, specifically.

He'd warned him about Dorian because Dorian was a killer, even among vampires.

Right now, Nick wanted to throttle Jem for that reason alone, along with a few dozen other, related reasons, all of them having to do with Jem's general stubbornness and refusal to trust him on a goddamned thing he tried to tell him.

But he knew yelling at Jem now would only distract both of them even more.

Well, assuming that was possible.

"I wouldn't test his aim, Dorian," Nick said instead, gauging the scarlet eyes of the blond vampire. "It's good. It's better than good. I've seen it."

"And you let this creature... this toddler... aim his little stick at me?" Dorian said, that desire and satisfaction bleeding into his silky voice. "Is it not enough that he stole the lover right out of my bed? Out of the rightful bed you *should* occupy?"

Nick grunted at that.

Not a muscle in his body managed to relax.

"I don't belong to you, Dorian," he warned.

"He belongs to me," Jem said, from behind him.

Nick felt his jaw harden.

He didn't look back when he hissed through his teeth.

"Not helping, brother Jem—"

But Dorian didn't appear to listen to either one of them.

"You belong with your own kind," the vampire said. "Not with this... animal."

Dorian's scarlet eyes left Dalejem for the first time since the seer entered the space. He looked at Nick, and now anger more than affection shone from those bright red eyes.

"Brick tells me you are not even feeding on it," he said, his voice openly accusing. "Is this true? What purpose is one of these creatures, if not for the lure of their blood?"

"He. Belongs. To. Me." Nick growled at the other male, hammering each word. "You are not here for Brick. You are not here for Brick's family. You came here to kill my *mate*. That is against our laws... and theirs, incidentally. Brick would never forgive you for this. He would never forgive you for the rift you would cause in his alliance with Black."

Dorian's lips turned in a slight smile.

The coldness never left those eyes.

"Because Black would defend the death of your... what did you call it? Your 'mate'?" Dorian paused, staring at him meaningfully. "Are you so sure of that, brother?"

"I am," Nick growled. "Not for my own sake, maybe... but for his."

Dorian gauged his face.

Nick did the same back.

He could already feel he hadn't moved Dorian's mind, not with any of his words. He hadn't made a dent in the blond vampire's decision, or his motives for coming here.

More than that, Nick saw the denser look there.

He wasn't wrong.

Dorian had come here to kill Jem.

He came here for the sole purpose of killing Nick's boyfriend.

Dorian intended not to leave until he'd killed him.

Worse, Nick knew he couldn't take him. The vampire was at least three hundred years older than him... if not closer to five hundred.

"If you harm him," Nick warned. "I will *kill* you, Dorian. Maybe not today. Maybe not in the next six months. But I *will* kill you."

At the faint smile that rose to the other's lips, Nick stepped further between the two of them, holding up a hand.

His voice came out harsher, louder.

"Remember the snare," Nick growled, his voice openly warning. "Remember *that*, Dorian. I could have killed you already, brother. All it would take is time. Eventually, there would be a trap you wouldn't see coming. Eventually, I'd manage to surprise you again... and I wouldn't be merciful next time."

"You would never kill me," Dorian said.

He hissed the words, infused them with a warning of his own, despite the dismissive certainty behind them.

"You would never do it, Naoko," Dorian repeated.

Emotion rose to his voice.

Real emotion, maybe for the first time.

"Not with my venom in your blood," the vampire said. "Not with my blood in your blood. And believe me, little brother, you will be getting a lot of both. I may not let you out of my chambers for years after this. Clearly, you cannot be trusted on your own, if this is your childish means of rebellion... making your elders worry about you to the point of illness, for months and months, with no word, while you shack up with this... *thing.*"

"Get out of the way, Nick," Jem growled from behind him. "You can't reason with this thing. You can't—"

"I'm aware of that," Nick cut in, warning.

"Then get out of the fucking way," Jem said.

"Fuck off, brother," Nick growled back, without turning his head. In spite of himself, he found himself snapping at the other male anyway. "...One fucking thing. *One fucking thing,* I asked of you, and you couldn't do it. One. Goddamned. Thing."

Jem didn't bother to answer.

Nick could smell the seer behind him.

He could hear his heart beating in his chest, his veins throbbing with blood. All of it turned him on, even as it heightened his hunting and protective instincts, both of which were already screaming in his chest, throat, limbs and muscles, to the point where it was difficult to remain still, to even think.

He knew if he lunged at Dorian first, it would only hasten this.

Worse, it would set the older vampire off.

It would ignite Dorian's possessiveness even more.

Nick refocused on those scarlet eyes.

"I do not wish us to be enemies, brother," he said, his voice softer, but still holding a warning. "I wish us to be friends. You need to accept this. It won't change."

Dorian looked at him, his blood-red eyes somehow cold as ice.

Nick saw the knowing in that look.

"It won't change," Nick repeated, harder.

"You are young, little brother," the vampire said. "Everything changes."

"This won't," Nick said. "This won't change."

"Things such as this change fastest of all, my dear, sweet, and *very* young brother."

Nick shook his head. "You're wrong. Not when it's real. When it's real, it never changes. It never goes away. Never."

Dorian's eyes flickered off Dalejem, resting back on Nick.

Another of those knowing smiles curved the pale, bow-shaped lips.

"You speak to me of love, Naoko?" he mused, his smile reaching his voice. "My darling boy... how young you truly are. We are not built to love these creatures. Not *real* love."

"What would you know of it?" Nick growled.

Dorian held up a hand, cutting him off gently.

"—More than you could imagine," the blond vampire said. "The infatuations we maintain with our food... even with those of slightly longer lifespans than that of a human... they are but a kiss in the wind, my very young boy. These things, they are not meant to last. Such infatuations *never* last. You are too young to know this sad truth."

"It's not my truth," Nick said, his voice colder. "You refuse to hear me on this at your own peril, Dorian." He put thrall into his voice. "I will never forgive you, brother. Never. This is no infatuation. Brick understood. Brick agreed to order you—"

"Brick is not here," Dorian said, dismissive.

Silence fell between them.

"You would disobey him?" Nick growled. "Your king?"

Dorian's eyes flickered past Nick's.

Nick could again feel him staring at Dalejem, measuring him with his eyes, through his scent, through the tremors and pulses he could hear through the seer's skin and blood.

"I protect what is mine," Dorian said, his voice soft as a whisper. "You may have claimed this creature... but I claimed you first. You belong to *me*, Naoko. This creature cannot have you. I will not permit it."

Every muscle in Nick's body hardened to rock.

He heard the truth in the vampire's words.

He knew Dorian meant every one of them.

Fear shocked his system, igniting whatever vampire equivalent to adrenaline lived inside him. That fire burned painfully, spreading through his veins, shooting through his limbs, flooding and sharpening every nerve ending.

"Dalejem," he growled. "Run!"

"It's too late for that," the seer said, his voice eerily calm.

Nick knew he was right.

He knew it, but every part of him screamed in terror.

The fear wasn't for himself.

"Dorian." Nick refocused on the blond vampire. When his view of the vampire blurred, it hit him that tears were running down his face. "Don't do this," he whispered. "Please. You're wrong. You're wrong about how I feel. It's not an infatuation. I love him. I really love him. Don't do this to me—"

Dorian reached out to him again.

This time, his touch was even more tender.

The vampire caressed Nick's jaw, his fingers trailing down his neck.

"I know this will hurt, my love," Dorian whispered back. "I know it will hurt like fire. I know you will be angry with me... possibly for years... possibly for centuries. But I will bear this anger from you. I will bear it, for what I do today will save you in the end."

Bending forward, he kissed Nick's face.

Nick endured that, too.

He didn't move, didn't dare to move.

"You will not be able to withstand the pull of his blood forever," Dorian murmured by his cheek, caressing Nick's jaw with soft fingers.

Tears ran down the white-haired vampire's face now as well, flowing freely, even as love rose to those scarlet eyes, coloring his low voice.

"Trust me, my love," Dorian whispered. *"Please trust me* in this.

These creatures bring nothing but pain. They are beautiful poison... sent by the gods to humble us. They come only to teach us, to ruin our pride. Eventually they make us wise, too... but only if we overcome the power they have over us. Please, my love. Please do not let this one destroy you. Let me help you with this."

Nick stared into those scarlet eyes.

He could see the wall there.

He knew he couldn't reach him.

He also knew what would happen next.

He knew it even before that faint, tell-tale clench of muscles he felt in the vampire's fingers.

Dorian lunged.

Nick was a millisecond behind him.

From a human's view, Nick would have lunged with him, throwing his body into his path in the exact same instant... but Nick felt the other's movements ahead of his.

Even knowing it was coming, it stunned him how fast the older vampire moved.

Dorian was like liquid skin and flesh and bone, flying through the air with a speed that probably wasn't even visible to Dalejem, or to any non-vampire who may have been watching.

Desperate, Nick tried to get in front of him.

He lurched sideways, following the motion of his elder, snarling as he leapt, his hands out in hooked claws.

The taller, older vampire still managed to evade him.

Dorian twisted his body in a strange arc, walking up the wall to Nick's right, stepping on Nick's shoulder even as Nick fought to grasp at his limbs, to slow him down in any way he could. He fought for purchase on Dorian's legs, fought to grab hold of his knees, his calves, his ankles. He fought to stop him or slow him in any way he could.

Dorian slid through his fingers, writhed away, kicked him off.

Nick found himself grasping at air, even as he leapt up and back, trying again to stop him.

Dorian more or less mowed him over.

The blond vampire threw his considerable weight behind his long body, leaping from the wall onto Nick, kicking off him so hard, he slammed Nick into the opposite wall with a jarring slam that clicked Nick's jaws together and knocked pictures down all along the entryway wall.

Glass and ceramic shattered as a row of animal plates fell off a small shelf.

Dorian began crawling over him like a lanky cat, but Nick lunged after him again, grabbing his leg as the vampire slid forward.

It was like trying to grab hold of a snake... or possibly smoke.

He felt the vampire getting away and sank his teeth into Dorian's thigh, if only to slow him down, to force the vampire to face him, or at least drag him along with him.

He sank his fangs in deeper, pumping him full of venom, trying to reach him that way, to force Dorian to feel him—to acknowledge his feelings in any way he could.

Dorian let out a cry.

Nick felt pain on him—more than one kind of pain.

He felt Dorian's anguish as Nick's emotions rushed into him via the blood.

He felt Dorian's grief, his anger, his worry... his jealousy.

He felt the decision there, his decision to kill Dalejem, against Brick's orders. Nick felt Dorian rationalize that killing Dalejem was the only way. Nick could feel the rationale there, the cold logic coloring the other's thoughts.

He also saw through it.

Logic had nothing to do with Dorian's desire to kill Jem.

It was pure anger, pure possessiveness, pure jealousy... pure *rage* that Nick had been taken from him.

He didn't take me, Nick sent through the blood. *Goddamn it, Dorian... he didn't take me. It didn't happen like that.*

He took you stole you I saw it I saw all of it he stole you from us... he wanted to make you over like himself. Make you human again make you into his mate. He knew you'd be vulnerable... he hunted you like the animal he is...

No, Nick sent back, angry. *No... it wasn't like that. I wanted him. I still want him. He's mine. He belongs to me...*

You belong to me.

No, I don't.

You do. I claimed you. I claimed you even before Brick turned you—

Nick sank his fangs deeper into the blond vampire's thigh, his teeth grazing the bone. He gripped the wall with one hand, dug his bare feet into the floor, doing everything he could to hold him back, to at least force Dorian to drag him along with him.

The whole time, he kept injecting more venom into the older vampire.

He was about to try to reason with him again—

When he felt another, more concrete pain.

That felt like physical pain.

It wasn't his. It was Dorian's.

The vampire came to a dead stop, right before he let out a furious hiss.

"Get out of the way, Nick!" a voice boomed. "Let go of him!"

Someone grabbed hold of Nick's ankles, dragging him back.

Whoever they were, they half-dragged Dorian back with him, from where Nick still had his jaws clamped around the vampire's leg.

Nick managed to turn his gaze towards his feet without releasing his jaws. He focused back in bewilderment to see Angel, who was somehow behind him now.

How the fuck had she gotten behind him?

He looked forward, back at Dorian, and saw Jem standing there in the living room, shirtless, an arrow still nocked to the string... then Nick realized it was a new arrow, that two were already sticking out of Dorian's chest, right in the area of his heart.

Dorian hissed at Dalejem.

Nick heard nothing but murderous rage.

Nick felt the blinding hatred behind that hiss through Dorian's blood.

Then Nick found he understood.

He opened his jaws, releasing Dorian's thigh before he'd really thought about whether that was a good idea, either.

"NO!" Nick yelled, fighting his way free of Angel's hands. "NO! Jem! That's a myth! It's a fucking myth! Wood doesn't kill us! Wood in the heart doesn't do shit!"

"What about explosives?" Jem snapped, even as let fly another arrow.

That one hit Dorian in the chest, just like the other two, only this time, Jem ran backwards even as he let go of the string.

His pale green eyes met Nick's even as Jem held up a black device in one hand.

"Get back, goddamn it!" the seer snarled. "Get back! Both of you!"

Nick's eyes widened in shock.

Realizing what the seer meant, he hesitated only as long as it took him to blink.

Then he jerked back from Dorian, pushing off the vampire and rolling free.

Seeing the open front door, he unfurled his body, leaping to his feet and running for Angel without thought.

He caught hold of his friend around the waist, lifting her up as she let out a shocked cry. He wrapped his arms and body around hers, even as he forced her backwards.

Then he carried-dragged her out the door.

He gripped her tighter once he got her outside, pulling her around the wall of her porch, jamming her into the corner under the doorbell. He wrapped his arms around her legs, crushing her into the space where the two walls met, and shut his eyes.

Dalejem must have hit the detonator.

A low boom echoed through the doorway, followed by a sharper, higher explosion. Nick tensed around Angel, right as debris blew out the front door, hitting the front step and all of the plants around the entryway.

He heard harder pieces smack against the inside of the wall where he crouched with Angel, felt the tremors of impact through the wood, particle board, plaster and paint. He tensed, wishing he'd brought her further down the wall of her flat, or even out into the landscaped front yard with all of its trees and bushes... but the wall seemed to hold.

Despite the hard thuds and intensity of some of the shrapnel hits he felt through the wall, none of them went all the way through.

Even so, he yanked Angel off the wood, twisting his body around and replacing her back with his, and holding her in his arms. He held her tighter, even though the sound was dying down now, the pieces of debris finishing falling to the ground.

He heard wetter pieces rain down inside.

The bigger ones smacked into the tile of her entryway.

He glanced over to the trees and saw red drops and clumps sprayed over and falling from the leaves and branches, coating the grass and bushes below.

Grimacing, he looked away.

Angel writhed in Nick's arms, letting out a shriek when he abruptly released her, sliding up the wall to his feet. He caught hold of her arm and elbow once he was more or less steady, and pulled her up to standing beside him.

It was quiet inside her flat.

Then Nick heard Panther.

The dog howled, barking manically, in obvious distress.

Smoke still puffed through the entryway, making Nick worry about fire.

"Jem?" Nick called out.

There was another crash inside, then the seer's voice rose.

"Yes!" he called out. "You are both all right?"

Nick had to bite his tongue to keep from snarling at the seer.

Clenching his jaw briefly, he looked at Angel, who was huddled next to him now, looking paler than he'd ever seen her, her legs and arms shaking.

He got the sense she was holding onto him to keep from collapsing on her own stoop.

He looked back towards the doorway.

"We're not dead," he said finally, after that too-long pause.

21

A BLOODY MESS

I t took them hours to clean it all up.

Angel's pizza came... which was awkward.

Jem and Nick went back and forth on how to deal with it.

In the end, Nick bit the delivery guy where his shirt would cover it, and wiped the memory of everything he'd seen from his mind. They'd done it that way simply because it was faster, and just as clean, just as effective... apart from the small evidence of the bite mark itself, which shouldn't matter in this case.

Angel also gave the poor guy a good tip, via the delivery app.

Jem stood there, watching Nick feed on the poor bastard, exuding anger, which again forced Nick to nearly swallow his tongue to keep from snapping at the seer.

Not now, he told himself.

Not fucking now.

He had to fix this for Angel, first.

He had to fix it as well as he could... at least for tonight.

Initially, he took the outdoors while Jem and Angel started with the indoors.

When the pizza came, after they'd dealt with the delivery driver, Nick led Angel semi-forcibly to the living room, her arm in one hand, her pizza in the other.

He sat her down on the somewhat dusty and smoky couch.

He put the pizza down in front of her, and opened the card-board box.

Seeing the fine layer of ash in her old beer, he replaced the lukewarm bottle with a new one from the fridge, dumping the old one in the sink, then tossing the bottle in recycling.

He returned to the living room, handed her the new beer, and commanded her to sit there, until she'd eaten the whole damned pizza.

He put the hot wings and garlic bread in the oven, with the heat on low.

He intended Jem to eat that, once they'd made a dent on the mess in Angel's foyer.

When Nick first walked inside the apartment, he almost didn't know what he was looking at.

The walls were painted in scarlet and black.

Liquid ran chunkily down the walls, along with fragments of bone and skin.

Larger pieces and skull fragments stuck out of the walls.

Black smoke still pooled on the ceiling, although it was already starting to dissipate, even in that handful of seconds after the blast died down.

Jem stood at the other end of the foyer, waving smoke out of his face, his expression twisted in a grimace, that damned compound bow still gripped in his hand.

Nick wanted to throttle him.

He knew the reaction wasn't wholly rational.

He also wanted to do other things to the seer, things that were a lot *less* rational.

He shoved all of it out of his mind, at least for now.

Instead, he focused around at the wreckage of Angel's entry-way. He wandered through the middle of it, after carefully disen-tangling Angel's grip on him, leaving her by the open door. He winced as he passed what remained of Dorian's body in the middle of the scorched black carpet runner. He walked up to where Jem stood, but didn't stop.

He walked past him, into the beginnings of the living room.

Once he could see past the foyer wall, he looked around, scanning the state of the kitchen, and the wider common space, as well as the hallway leading into the rest of the two-bedroom, two-bathroom flat.

Luckily, apart from smoke, which was already settling a fine coat of white and black particles and powder over much of the furniture, most of the damage seemed to be limited to the hallway and the front porch.

Probably due to the position of the explosives, the debris appeared to blow primarily backwards, towards the open door—not into Ang's living room.

Exhaling, Nick looked at Jem only then.

"There're buckets in the garage," he said, his voice gruff. "I'll start on the outside. I can use the hose out there. Put all the pieces in garbage bags... I'll get those. They're in the kitchen."

Jem blinked at him.

Only now, seeing him up close, seeing his pale face, the wideness of his pale green eyes with the violet rings, did Nick see the shock on him.

For the first time, his anger softened.

It softened dangerously, all at once.

He had to fight the impulse to envelop the other in his arms. After a bare pause, he reached out, gripping his shoulder instead, as briefly as he could.

"Go on," he said, his voice gruff still. "Get the buckets, Jem. The sooner we take care of this, the better."

There was another strange silence, where they only looked at one another.

Then Jem blinked, as if closing his eyes with an effort.

When he opened them again, he clenched his jaw.

Only then did some of the tension leave his shoulders.

"Okay," he said, nodding.

"Put down the bow, Jem," Nick said. "Just put it down."

The seer looked down at his hand, which clenched on the bow, white-knuckled.

He released his hand, letting the weapon fall to the carpeted floor.

Without another word, Jem turned around, and walked towards the hallway, and the door that led down to the garage.

⚜

They finished around five in the morning.

Well, more or less finished.

Nick was able to do a more thorough job now than he would have been able to, back when he was just a human cop.

Dalejem was a help in that respect as well. While the seer's physical vision didn't encompass as many bands in the light spectrum as Nick's, Jem could see even more with his seer's sight. Anything organic shone like an iridescent flashlight to him from that space.

Nick went to the store for bleach, so it wouldn't be attached to Angel.

Even so, he hid his face and even his outline from every camera he saw, well aware that they might have a facial-rec tag out on him still, meaning Black's people at the Raptor's Nest.

Truthfully, though, it bothered him more to leave Jem.

He didn't like the thought of more vampires showing up there, maybe on Brick's orders, maybe feeling that something had happened to one of Brick's most beloved and loyal subjects.

But Dorian wasn't direct bloodline to Brick, as far as Nick knew.

He was a loyal servant of Brick's—well, within limits, apparently, as tonight definitely proved—but Dorian wasn't one of Brick's actual children.

Nick happened to know Dorian was quite a lot older than Brick.

Unlike a lot of older vampires, Dorian hadn't resented a younger vampire as his king.

Nick had never gotten the full story there, in terms of how the two of them became so close, or how Dorian grew to be so devoted to Brick.

He supposed he might not ever hear that story now.

Pushing the thought from his mind, along with the crawling nerves that wanted to overcome him when he thought about Brick's possible reactions to what just took place, Nick just tried to hurry, plucking bottles of bleach and scrub brushes off the shelves of the only twenty-four-hour grocery store he could find near Angel's place.

After paying in cash, he more or less ran with them back to Angel's.

Nick also dealt with the bags of "Dorian" they pried out of the walls, picked off the carpet, and washed off the trees and bushes outside.

He buried them in the park, scattering the remains in at least six or seven different burial holes.

In the end, it felt like his job to do.

Angel cried over the glass animal plates, which had been given to her over the years by family and friends. She cried again when she saw the state of the hand-woven rug her mother had given her, after bringing it all the way to California from Louisiana.

In the end, though, she'd numbly put all of it in more garbage bags, along with the wooden shelves, which were blackened and broken along with the ceiling and walls.

The door, thankfully, having been open during the blast, survived strangely intact. It still swung smoothly on its hinges, and the lock and both bolts still worked.

As for the rest of it... the whole entryway essentially needed to be ripped out and replaced. For now, for tonight, Nick contented himself with cutting out most of the drywall and stuffing that into more bags.

He could replace and repaint it all tomorrow.

Luckily, there wasn't any major structural damage he could find.

A few studs would need replacing. He would need to replace the shelves, and one of the glass panels in the front door. He would need to sand and repaint the door itself—

"Can we stop now?" Jem asked, breaking into Nick's thoughts.

He'd turned off the vacuum cleaner, and Nick hadn't even noticed.

Nick turned to find Angel sprawled on the couch in the living room, which had also been vacuumed of dust and other particulates.

Panther, who'd finally calmed down and stopped barking at the vacuum cleaner, not to mention the explosion and all the frenetic cleaning, was curled up by Angel's legs, looking as unconscious and wiped-out as she was.

All the windows were still wide open, despite it being a cold night, and already, it smelled better in here. Still smoky, still with the faintest tinge of blood and the much sharper, more pungent smell of bleach... but the worst of it was gone.

It could be explained away now as a housefire, one they managed to put out before it engulfed the whole house.

Thinking about that, Nick remembered something else.

"Fuck." Panic ran through him, a kind of debilitating fear. "The neighbors—"

"I took care of it," Jem said, dismissive.

Nick turned, staring at the seer.

Jem frowned back. "Don't look so surprised. I did it when you went for bleach the first time. I checked the rest of the neighborhood for who might have heard the explosion when you went to bury the body... well..." His nose wrinkled. "The parts."

"The rug?" Nick said, gruff. "The rest of the materials?"

"Weighted and dumped in the Bay," Jem said. "Angel did that. Also while you were gone, dealing with the grosser bits. We divvyed up the rest, after you said you'd bury the remains."

Nick felt his shoulders start to relax.

Of course. Angel was a cop, too.

She would know what to do.

And Jem... Jem was...

Nick turned on him, his eyes hard.

"I need to talk to you," he growled.

Jem exhaled, sounding tired. Exhausted, really.

Black marks smudged his neck, his hands, his face, his bare chest. He looked at Nick, his eyes glassy, and all the fight seemed to go out of him, maybe for the first time since they'd gotten in the car to go to Santa Cruz.

"Now?" he said.

"Yes," Nick said, still scowling. "Right fucking now."

He more or less dragged the seer to the bathroom, and into the shower.

He didn't really think that through, either.

He yanked the half-full quiver of arrows off Jem's back, noticing only then that the seer still wore it. Some part of his mind must have still been working, well enough to remember that the arrows had explosive tips, because he set the quiver down carefully, and outside of the bathroom door.

He then took off the seer's pants.

Jem didn't fight him.

He leaned on Nick instead, gripping his shoulders as Nick yanked the pants down to Jem's ankles, leaving them on Angel's bathroom rug after Jem stepped out of first one leg, then the next.

Nick extricated himself long enough to turn on the hot water.

He undressed himself while Jem watched.

He felt the seer's eyes on him, and somehow that only frustrated him more.

He more or less picked Jem up, despite the seer being a few inches taller than him, and deposited him in the shower.

He followed him in, and proceeded to scrub every spot of ash, vampire blood, bone dust, bone fragments, flecks of flesh and paint off of the other male. He didn't talk to him, barely met his gaze, and pushed the seer's hands away whenever Jem tried to touch him. He ignored Jem's reactions, too, shoving them out of his mind even when he felt the other's breath catch, or the few times he groaned.

"Gaos," the seer said finally. "I want to punch you in the face."

"The feeling is mutual, brother," Nick growled back.

For the first time, he looked, up, meeting Jem's eyes.

The green looked even lighter, more glass-like with his slicked back wet hair, but something about the vulnerability there made Nick's jaw clench.

"You're going to talk to me about them," he said finally, going back to gripping Jem's shoulder, rubbing the last of the ash off Jem's chest with a dark blue washcloth. "About that asshole and his wife. You're going to tell me everything about them. What they did. What you did. What you feel about them now—"

"No."

When Nick looked up, Jem shook his head, his eyes hard.

"No, Nick."

"Why the fuck not?"

"Because that's not what this is. You and me... we have nothing to do with that."

"Bullshit," Nick growled, staring him in the eyes. "You think I don't know a fucking trauma reaction when I see one, Jem? I was in three wars. Try again."

"Trauma?" Jem blinked at him. "What the fuck does that have to do with—"

"I don't know," Nick snapped, his voice even more warning. "Not exactly. Not yet. Which is why I want you to tell me *every-thing.* Every goddamned thing. Because whatever this is, it has something to do with the two of them. I know it does."

Jem stood there, looking confused as Nick finished rinsing him off.

He was still just standing there when Nick turned his back on him, and began washing off his own body.

The seer didn't move.

He just stood there as Nick washed his own hair, scrubbing everything out of it, shampooing it three, then four times, even though he knew he was already clean. Some part of him wanted to wash away every speck of memory of Dorian exploding in Angel's foyer. Some part of him couldn't even think about it yet.

He definitely couldn't think about how Brick might react.

Would Brick kill him for this?

Would he blame Dalejem?

Would he try to kill Dalejem, too?

Nick didn't know the answer to those questions, either.

He was rinsing off the last handful of shampoo, when Jem broke the silence between them, making Nick jump where he'd been lulled by the sound of the shower.

"Do you wish I hadn't done it?" the seer said. "Do you wish I hadn't killed him? The blond one?"

Nick looked over, sharp, and found Jem watching his face.

Jem's jaw hardened. "I know the two of you were... involved."

Nick stared at him a beat longer.

Then he let out a disbelieving grunt. "Jesus. No. I'm not mad at you for *killing* him. I'm mad at you for taking on a fucking five-hundred-year-old vampire... when I told you it was likely to get you killed."

He watched in semi-disbelief as Jem's expression relaxed, even if the wariness didn't disappear entirely from those green eyes.

"Goddamn it," Nick growled, staring at him. "And you wonder why I want to know about those two? Even now, you're *looking* for ways I'm lying to you. Sometimes I think all you do with me is look for reasons to not trust me. Why are you with me at all, if you feel that way?"

Jem frowned harder.

Watching him, Nick got the impression the seer was actually thinking about his words.

Like he was trying to answer that question, too.

When Jem didn't speak after a few seconds more, Nick exhaled, more mannerism than need, and leaned down, shutting off the water.

He'd clean the tub later, too... after Angel and Jem were asleep.

He waited for Jem to climb out of the shower, then followed, grabbing one of the clean towels out of the cupboard under the sink, and handing it to the seer before taking his own.

He'd deal with the laundry later, too.

Jem looked around even as Nick thought it, a frown touching his lips.

"The bathroom—"

"Leave it," Nick said, dismissive. "It's on the list. After you're asleep."

Jem turned, scowling at him. "You're not coming with me?"

But that was fucking enough.

Nick was done. Finished.

He was fucking *done*.

22

BLOOD

He didn't remember picking up the seer.

He didn't remember making any kind of decision.

Nick remembered throwing him on the bed, both of them stark naked.

He remembered pinning him there, and growling at him, even as the seer let out a groan, fighting to get free of Nick's hands and the weight of his knees on his thighs.

By then, it only turned Nick on more.

He wanted the fucker to fight.

He wanted Jem to scream at him, to hit out at him.

At the same time, he didn't want Jem to tell him to stop.

He didn't want Jem to say stop and mean it... and not only because he didn't entirely know what he would do if the seer said those words.

He wanted to believe he would stop.

He told himself he would stop.

He hoped he would stop.

He didn't entirely trust himself, though... not with how fucked up and wound up and screwed up he felt right then.

He felt like his mind and heart had been ripped apart over the past few days and reassembled backwards inside his chest.

At this point, he was so strung out on emotion and worry, and attempts to control all of it, he felt drugged. Tonight, it felt like it all came crashing down on him—with Dorian nearly killing Jem, with Dorian nearly killing Angel, with Dorian nearly kidnapping Nick and locking him into another goddamned cage, starving him and feeding on him and venoming him until he'd forced him to submit.

Nick barely knew where he was.

He didn't care anymore.

Bending down to Jem's throat, he *did* stop though.

He hung over him, and let out a groan of his own.

"Do it," Jem whispered in his ear. *"Gaos.* Do it... please. *Please,* goddamn it."

Nick gripped the seer's wrists, tight enough he might be hurting him, but Jem only closed his eyes, longer than a blink, pressing up against him.

"Gaos, please... please..."

"Do you need to read me that bad?" Nick growled.

"Yes." Jem looked up at him, tears in his eyes. *"Yes,* goddamn it."

But fear was winning out.

Fear was winning in Nick's mind, paralyzing him.

"Because you don't trust me," Nick growled, his voice an open accusation. "You want to read me because you don't fucking *trust* me, Jem. This isn't about intimacy. It's about you thinking I'm a piece of shit—"

But Jem cut him off, his voice suddenly harder, verging on cold.

"No, he snapped. *"No.* I'm not doing this again. I'm not."

Nick tensed.

He stared down at those green eyes, focusing briefly on that perfect mouth, those lips twisted now in a hard scowl.

Jem didn't just look angry. He looked distant.

Nick heard the finality in the other's voice.

"I mean it," Jem growled. "I'm not doing it again. This is the last time I ask. Then I'm done. I'm not chasing after you, trying to *convince* you to share yourself with me. I did it with her. I did it with him. I won't do it with you."

Nick flinched.

Fury rose in him, so intensely he bit his lip.

Jem might have even seen it, because he paused, staring up at Nick's eyes.

The next time he spoke, his voice only grew colder.

"Either you want me or you don't," the seer growled. "Either you're willing to take that step with me, Nick, or you're not. Make up your mind. *Now,* Nick. Or I'm gone. I'll go back to the California Street building. I'll have them work on my light... do whatever they can to separate us. Then I'll ask them to transfer me to Europe... or to Asia. You'll never fucking see me again."

Nick stared at him, half in disbelief.

"I mean it, Nick," Jem snapped. "If I leave, you won't see me again."

"I'll find you."

"You won't," Jem warned. "I've never tried to hide from you before... but trust me, you won't. You won't find me, Nick."

Rage rose in Nick's chest. It hit at him so intensely, he didn't trust himself to answer at first. He didn't trust himself to make a sound.

It wasn't just rage.

He felt the fear there, even more intensely than the rage.

"Was anything you told that piece of shit actually true?" Jem said, his voice the same hard accusation. "Was *any* of it real, Nick?"

"We've only been together a goddamned *week*—" Nick growled.

"Fuck you," Jem growled back, raising his voice. "That is utter and complete nonsense. And you know it."

Nick's jaw clenched.

Again, he didn't trust himself to speak.

Jem stared up at him without flinching, his green eyes reflecting hurt, but also a complete immovability.

It was the second thing that scared Nick more.

"So this is about that asshole and his wife," Nick said. "This is

still about them. All of your anger at me, your distrust, and now
these bullshit ultimatums—"

"No," Jem said, his voice even more warning. "It's not. You
know that, too."

"The hell I do." Tears came to Nick's eyes, blinding him briefly,
shocking him into looking away. "You just fucking said it—"

"I said I'm tired of chasing after people who don't want me,"
Jem cut in, warning. "I said I'm tired of chasing people who don't
belong to me, Nick. I'm done being the consolation prize for those
who truly want someone else. Or... in your case... people who want
some*thing* else, or perhaps who don't yet know what they want. I'm
not doing it anymore, Nick. I'm not."

When Nick clenched his jaw, the seer's voice grew sharper.

Nick flinched at the emotion he felt there.

"I'm not trying to talk you into shit anymore, Nick," Jem said.
"Do you understand? If you need me to talk you into this, then it's
wrong. Whatever it is for me, it's *wrong* for you. Why is that so
hard for you to understand? It is too soon for you, perhaps... the
timing is wrong... or what I feel is unreciprocated. Either way, it is
wrong. And I won't stay for that. I'll go. It's not a threat... it is
simply how it is for me."

"No," Nick growled. *"No,* goddamn it. That's not how relationships work. Things aren't that black and white. For fuck's sake, we
still barely *know* each other."

When the seer clicked at him, anger rose in Nick's chest, again
growing briefly uncontrollable.

He found himself speaking through it.

"You want to be like Solonik?" he said, gripping the seer tighter
when Jem started to move away. "Is that it? You want to be a
goddamned *addict?* A mindless slave to whatever vampire will fuck
you and feed off you?"

Jem shook his head, his mouth grim. "It won't be like that. You
know it won't."

"Bullshit!"

"It won't. But again. I won't talk you into that, either, Nick."

"Why would you even say that?" Nick snapped, shoving off the last thing the seer said, even as it stabbed at something in his chest. Even he heard the fear in his voice. "How would you know anything *about* that? *I* don't know. I'm a goddamned vampire, and *I* don't even know how the venom works—"

"I'm not saying I know how venom works," Jem said, warning.

"You *are* saying that!"

"No. I'm not."

The seer's voice grew strangely calm, his face still set in that immovability that terrified Nick when he let himself see it.

It felt like Jem was already halfway out the door.

Like he'd already left.

"I'm saying it wouldn't be like that for *us*," Jem clarified, his voice strangely distant. "I don't know how I know that. I just do. Just like you know it, Nick."

"Bullshit!"

"Except it's not bullshit. You know that, too."

"How could either of us *possibly* know that?"

"I don't know."

"Then why the hell would you try to convince me—"

"I am *not* trying to convince you," Jem said, his voice angry again. "Are you listening to me at all? I'm done convincing you, Nick. I'm done. I'm telling you what I feel, because I owe you that—"

"*Owe* me?" Nick said, incredulous. "Now you owe me? What the fuck does that mean? Why would you *owe* me anything—"

"Because you're my mate," Jem said, glaring up at him, his jaw hard. "Because I felt that, even when you were human, and I feel it even more now. I feel it more all the time. Which is why this feeling, this being *rejected* by you... you not wanting this with me... is getting worse all the time. It's getting *worse*... do you understand?"

"No," Nick growled.

"No. I see." Jem's jaw hardened. "Just like you *don't know* that this thing with us won't be like how it is with Solonik. Even though

I can feel it in every part of me... in every part of my light... that you *do* understand these things."

"You believe all that, and you're still threatening to fucking *leave* me?" Nick snapped. "How does that make any kind of sense?"

Jem's expression didn't move.

After a pause, when Nick didn't speak, the seer shrugged.

"If I have to go away, I will. Like I said, I'll try to make it easier on both of us. I really will try to obtain help from Yarli, from Mika, Kiessa, Jax or any other combination of the others. Hopefully, they can assist me in getting you out of my light. It's not what I want, but I swear by the Sword and Sun... I won't drag you kicking and screaming into this, Nick. I won't be in a one-sided relationship again. If you want to think it's some kind of idle threat, that I'm fucking with your head, or throwing a temper-tantrum, then I likely can't convince you otherwise. I can only tell you what I will do... and why."

Nick fought to think about his words. He really tried.

He couldn't...

God, he couldn't fucking think about this.

Not now. Not tonight.

"You say all this crap about us, about the venom and you and me, like it's somehow 'proof' that we should go forward with it," he growled, going back to their earlier argument.

When Jem clicked at him, again half turning to his side, as if to climb off the bed, Nick gripped the seer's wrists tighter, holding him in place. He stared down at those pale green eyes, the odd violet rings, fighting not to scream at him.

"You say it like your compulsion... *my* compulsion... like these are *good* signs for either of us," he said. "Like you *already* wanting it, like some kind of addict, even without my having bitten you, is some kind of 'logical reason' for me to endanger your life."

Jem stared up at him, his jaw hard.

Nick could see the frustration in the seer's eyes.

He could practically feel that frustration, the seer's desire to make him see it the way he did, to make him *feel* it the way he did.

He could also see the grief.

He could feel the bottomless fucking sadness there, in Jem's eyes.

Worse than that, he saw the resignation.

Jem wasn't bluffing.

He really was done.

Nick didn't know if Dorian made that worse.

He didn't know if it was what happened that night, or if it was just everything: Dorian, the lack of sleep, Jem's trauma from that fucking *asshole* he'd been involved with before, the one Nick increasingly wanted to punch repeatedly in the face... the asshole's wife... or if it was something about Nick himself.

He didn't know how much of it had to do with Jem's biological make-up as a seer.

Nick saw the emotions intensify on the seer's face as the silence stretched. He saw Jem's grief and frustration and sense of rejection worsen, and some part of him just wanted to shake the seer, to shake him and scream in his face until he stopped this.

At the same time, he could feel what Jem was saying.

It infuriated him, but he could feel it.

Somehow, the seer's words felt true.

They made no goddamned sense... but they still felt true.

"Will you tell me about them?" Nick growled. "Will you tell me *everything* about them? Including how you feel about them now?" Seeing the other hesitate, his green eyes flinch as he stared up, Nick growled. "Will you tell me the goddamned *truth,* Jem?"

After another beat, the seer nodded. "Yes."

"Only if I do this?"

"Yes." Jem's jaw hardened. "I mean, I can tell you anyway, but I suspect it won't mean anything to you. It won't mean much to me, either, in terms of calming either of us down. But either way, I'll tell you... if you really think it matters that much."

"It does," Nick said, frowning. "It matters to me."

Dalejem shrugged. "Then I will tell you."

"You don't think it matters?" Nick said, still frowning.

There was another silence.

Then Dalejem exhaled.

Again, Nick heard nothing but defeat in that exhaled breath.

"I have no idea," Jem said, his voice frank. "I think a lot of my paranoia isn't about them at all... it's about you not letting this connection between us happen."

Nick scowled.

He was about to argue with that, but Jem cut him off.

"Nick," the seer said, warning. "I said I would tell you. I meant it. I'll tell you anything you want to know about them... about anything in my life. If we stop playing these damned games, I can actually *show* you. I can show you everything that happened with Revik and Allie, and it will actually *mean* something to you... and to me. You'll be able to see and feel all of it. Assuming you want to. Assuming the blood connection works anything at all like a light connection."

Pausing, the seer added,

"I think it does. It feels like it does."

Nick frowned.

He wanted to argue with the seer more. He wanted to point out how insane it was, that Jem would think he would know anything about any of this.

He wanted to repeat again how short a time they'd actually been together.

He wanted the seer to see how fucking *unreasonable* he was being.

He didn't, though.

He also didn't move.

He could feel his own hesitation now, the part of him dragging his feet.

He could feel the stalling.

He could almost hear the parts of his mind freaking out, wanting to throw up any excuse, any insane justification, to not go through with this.

He could feel the fear.

That fear was slowly being eclipsed by a deeper terror, though. Nick could feel his terror that Jem really would leave him after this.

He could feel his terror that he really might not be able to find him.

He could also feel the part of him that wanted to do what Jem asked, that wanted it so intensely he could barely think straight. He'd stopped letting himself even contemplate it, but a part of him contemplated it now... not only contemplated it, savored it, rolling the thought, the temptation, the imagining, over his tongue like good liquor.

He'd wanted Jem like that for months.

He'd wanted it as soon as he woke up and found himself staring into Dalejem's face in that cabin in Siberia.

The wanting only made the fear worse.

Both things warred in his mind and blood, paralyzing him.

And despite everything Jem was saying to him, Nick couldn't help but think it had to be wrong, to do that to Jem. It had to be wrong. If he did this, even if Jem wanted it, or thought he wanted it... Nick really *would* be the bad guy.

He would be the bad guy again.

Angel would hate him again.

Miri. Mika. Jax. Holo. All the seers who loved Jem.

They'd never forgive him.

If he enslaved Jem, if Nick wiped away Jem's mind with vampire venom, he would lose everything.

Most of all, he'd lose Jem.

He'd lose whatever remained of his own damned soul.

"Nick."

Nick refocused on the seer.

He realized only then that his whole body hurt.

His fangs had extended, nicking at his tongue and lips when he didn't stop clenching his jaw. It felt like his skin was on fire, his throat. Every fucking thing hurt. It hurt like hunger, but Nick knew that was only a fraction of what he was feeling. Hunger, pain, longing... and an emotional pull that was too intense to be able to put a name to any part of it.

It made him want to scream.

All of it made him want to scream.

It made him want to scream, maybe punch the seer in the face.

Why couldn't Jem have a normal sense of self-preservation?

Why couldn't Jem be the one saying *no*... instead of constantly making it clear the answer was yes?

Seeing the other male studying his face, the understanding there, Nick swallowed.

"It'll be all right," Jem said, his voice low, soft.

Nick felt his jaw harden more.

Would it, though?

Would it be all right?

"Nick," the seer said, his voice harder. "Are you going to run away from this thing with us forever? Dorian was right in that one thing... this is part of it. This is part of who we are to one another. If you can't accept that—"

"Shut up," Nick growled. "Just shut the fuck up, would you?"

Jem's eyes narrowed.

He stared up at Nick, anger in those stunning eyes, and something in Nick just... stopped.

It stopped thinking.

It stopped giving a shit about any of it.

"I want to fuck you while we do it," he said, his voice gruff.

He saw the seer flinch, and Nick's eyes closed. His teeth hurt now.

"I want to be inside you the first time," he said.

He felt Jem flinch again.

He felt shock expand off the seer's skin.

When Nick opened his eyes, Jem's fingers had clenched into fists. Those green eyes closed, longer than a blink, and Jem was nodding, even as he writhed under him, his skin suddenly, tangibly hotter.

"Yes," he said.

His voice was as gruff as Nick's.

Nick released one of the seer's arms... then the other.

He hung there, supporting himself on his hands as Jem reached for the table by the bed. Nick watched, still clenching his jaw, as Jem pulled out a tube of oil they'd been using, closing his eyes only when the other started massaging it all over him.

He felt sick now, half out of his head.

He forced his mind to just stop... to stop fucking thinking.

He couldn't handle thinking about any of it.

By the time he was inside the other male, he couldn't even pretend any of this was rational, that his mind was involved with any part of it.

He listened to the seer let out a low sound, felt Jem's hands clench on his shoulders. The seer's hands were massaging him again, pulling him closer. Nick saw those green eyes focus on his chest, on his abdomen, down to his cock... right before Nick arched into him harder. Jem's hands and arms slid around Nick then, gripping him at the small of his back.

"I can't wait anymore," Nick told him.

His voice was thick. He couldn't look at the seer now. He could barely see.

He didn't know what he expected Jem to say.

He didn't know if he was still looking for permission... maybe waiting for the seer to ask him again, to beg him to do this.

But Jem wouldn't ask again.

He definitely wouldn't beg.

Lowering his head, Nick kissed him. He nipped at his lips and tongue that time, pulling drops of blood off him, making the seer groan.

He felt something in Jem react almost violently. He heard Jem's heart stop and stutter in his chest, his breath catch, even before the seer arched under him.

Nick's mind fogged into blood-want.

It went from something abstract to something visceral...

painfully, immediately, shockingly visceral... a sick, animal desire he didn't even try to hold back.

He was hunting now.

His cock hardened more at the thought.

Holding down the seer, he nipped at him again, marking his chest, his shoulders, his arms, his abdomen, sliding down him to mark his legs, his feet, then gliding back up him to score his chest, his ribs, his arms some more.

"Fuck," Jem cried out, half-fighting him, but Nick had him pinned under him completely now. "Fuck... *gaos*... Nick..."

Nick sank his weight, holding him to the bed.

Once Jem fell still, once Nick felt him submit, Nick nipped at him more, scoring him with his teeth, marking his skin. He let out an involuntary groan that turned into a growl when the seer cried out, fighting again to get free.

"Do you want me to stop?" Nick said, pausing.

His voice came out velvety that time, low, an animal's cajole.

"No." Jem gasped the word without hesitation, shaking his head. "Gods... no. Let me touch you. Let me fucking touch you..."

Nick ignored that.

He kissed him and bit him lightly, even as he went back to fucking him.

He couldn't quite feel him yet...

He couldn't quite feel him...

Groaning, he arched into him violently that time, again nipping at and sucking on Dalejem's tongue. The seer chased his mouth when Nick pulled away, crying out in frustration.

Dalejem was sweating now.

The seer's eyes had gone glassy, half-blind with desire and frustration.

Nick watched him like that, with marks from his teeth over him, and felt his cock get harder still, growing inside him. He marked him more, watching the seer react, feeling Jem lose control, watching those green eyes close, then roll back in his head.

Nick knew he was on the verge of coming, but he wasn't going to do that yet, either.

He sure as fuck wasn't going to let Jem come.

He might not let the seer come for hours.

At the thought, he let out another groan.

His control slid away from him in the same set of seconds.

He lowered his mouth...

He barely kissed the skin...

...and sank his fangs into the seer's throat.

He didn't bite into him halfway that time. It was no gentle nip, or lick, or taste, or even the harder marking he'd done in foreplay. He bit long, and hard, letting his fangs slide through muscle and flesh, gripping him with a possessiveness that made his cock hurt, that nearly made him come right there.

He took his first, long drink, and his whole body turned liquid, melting into the seer. He injected venom as he drank, half-sick with want now that he let himself feel it.

"*Gaos.*" Jem gasped the word, writhing, fighting to free his hands. "*Gaos...*"

Nick heard the seer say more words.

He heard the seer talking to him.

He realized again, he'd heard Jem talking to him for a while.

He'd bit and cut him with his fangs, listening to him react.

Even so, some part of him was lost, already halfway in a trance.

He was so lost in this... God, it scared him, how lost he was already.

Jem was right.

This was different.

It was different with him... it was different with them.

It didn't feel anything like it had with Solonik, with Dorian, with his first vampire lovers back in Paris. It didn't feel anything like it had with Brick.

...with Miriam.

The thought made him flinch, falter.

But this wasn't like that.

It wasn't *like* that.

He could feel the difference, even if he couldn't make sense of it.

He could feel how it terrified him, that difference.

At the same time, some part of him understood that difference all too well.

He felt the part of himself that knew exactly what it meant, what he wanted. That part of him had known for months, maybe longer... maybe before, maybe back when he'd still been human. That part of him already belonged to the seer. The seer already belonged to him.

He remembered Jem in the cave... on that island.

He'd been so afraid the seer might die. He'd been afraid those prehistoric cultists would kill him, that they'd beat him to death, thinking he was a demon. Nick tried to protect him. He'd done everything he could to protect him, without even knowing why.

He'd told himself it was guilt.

It wasn't guilt.

Jem writhed under him, gasping. "Gods... Nick. Nick. I... Gods. Stop. Stop for a minute. Please. Please."

Nick unhooked his fangs, raising his head.

He kissed the seer's face, listening to him pant, listening to his heart pound behind his ribs. He kissed the seer's mouth, and the seer melted against him, fighting to get closer to him, his body and blood pulling on him, fighting him closer, begging him...

Gods. Why do you have to kiss like this... why like this. I swear to the gods, this thing, it might kill me... it might really kill me. This time, it might actually kill me. Gaos, if you leave me... if you leave me, Nick...

Nick listened to the seer as Jem continued to talk to him.

He listened to his thoughts, his words murmuring through the blood.

He wondered if Jem even knew he was talking to him, if the seer felt the connection between them yet, or if it was still too alien to him, too different from connections with his own kind.

The thought brought Nick's possessiveness up in a heated rage, mixing with his hunting instincts, his desire.

All three things slammed into him so intensely, filling his chest, he groaned involuntarily.

That part of him wanted to not just take him... but *take* him.

That part wanted to own Jem, to put his mark on him for good.

That part had no intention of sharing him.

He wasn't going to share him with anyone.

He wasn't going to share him with other fucking seers.

He fought not to think about any of that, because it scared him. He fought not to think about anything Jem said to him, because that scared him, too. He fucked him, and after a while, he drank again too, holding back his orgasm with what little willpower he had left.

When Jem writhed, he gripped him tighter, ordering him still with his hands.

He pinned him, hard, injecting more venom.

He drank harder, even as he began to feel more of Jem there, as the seer's presence grew more and more tangible, so intensely there and tangible he had to fight not to inject him again... and again, and again. Nick felt Jem there, and his body went liquid all over, even as his presence slid deeper through the blood.

He murmured to him there, claiming him there, too.

You're mine, Nick told him. *Goddamn it... you're mine. You're not leaving. You're not fucking leaving me. You're not threatening me like that again. That asshole and his wife don't own you. I do. I do, goddamn it. You belong to me—*

"*Gaos.*" Jem moaned the word weakly, gripping his hair. "*Gaos...*"

Nick barely heard him.

Closing his mind, closing his eyes... he finally let go.

He let it all go.

23

BLACK WAVES

W hen I lifted my head, the first thing I saw was a shock of black hair.

It blurred briefly, a dark shadow coloring a background of mostly dark beige and yellow, mixed with blue, mixed with gold and pink.

A warm breeze flowed over my skin.

It smelled like flowers... like salt.

It was sunrise.

I blinked until my eyes came fully into focus, staring into that growing light, realizing I could hear the sound of ocean waves.

I heard birds overhead, and on the beach.

I was outside.

I wasn't in the hospital, like I remembered.

I was outside, in the open air.

For some reason, the realization brought an overwhelming feeling of relief.

My hands and fingers were already reaching for him, knowing it was him who brought me down here, knowing it was him curled up against me in a second dark-blue sun lounger, one he must have dragged across the sand so that it leaned up against mine.

It was his warmth I felt, his breath, his slowly beating heart. I knew he must have brought me down here, only to fall asleep next to me, resting his head on my lap next to one of his brown arms, which was also coiled around me.

I noticed every part of him managed to avoid leaning on, gripping, twisting, or even touching a part of me that was bandaged, taped up, stitched, or otherwise hurt.

Weirdly, I felt almost absurdly better.

Even my taped ribs, which hurt more than any other part of me —apart from maybe a stitched up cut on my upper chest, which burned uncomfortably in the salt air—felt so much better than I remembered before I fell asleep.

I wondered briefly, if someone stuck me with a syringe full of painkillers.

I had a vague memory of leaving the hospital with him.

I remembered that... almost.

I'd been pretty out of it.

Even so, some part of me found it mildly strange, verging on amusing in a dry, unamusing kind of way, that it didn't bother me at all, being out here. Here I was, totally relaxed, lying on a sun lounger—no guards or weapons anywhere in sight—even after what happened to me the last time I was on the beach.

Was I stupid?

Then again, Black was with me.

I always felt safe when Black was with me.

I was more surprised Black let himself doze off, given everything.

Then again, knowing him, he had at least twelve seers watching us from the Barrier, ready to wake him up at the slightest hint that some unknown danger might be coming our way.

The thought allowed me to relax all over again.

Black would be armed, too.

He likely had at least one gun sitting in a bag under the lounge.

More likely, he had three or four... plus grenades.

Whatever he'd done to secure our little nap here, out on the private beach in front of the Blue Sail Resort, I felt illogically safe.

Maybe it was simply knowing he was there, with me, that he would have taken care of any risks, without my having to ask.

Maybe it was that inexplicable feeling of safety I retained *whenever* he was there, even when it made no sense.

I mean, it's not like Black had been immune to danger in the years I'd known him.

He'd been imprisoned... multiple times... tortured, attacked, beaten, shot at, stabbed, raped, blackmailed, collared.

I flinched, gripping his hair tighter in my fingers.

I felt some more paranoid part of me try to talk myself out of that feeling of safety. It urged me to worry about him, if I couldn't worry about myself. It urged me to remember that if I was being targeted, that him being with me put him in the line of fire.

I wasn't able to maintain that paranoia for long, though.

It was too nice out here.

I relaxed back into the lounger, examining my different wounds with my light as I lay there, gazing up at the rapidly lightening sky, at the tiki torches burning silently overhead, a dark red umbrella protecting us from a sun that hadn't yet fully risen. I listened to birds chirp and fuss from the largest of the nearby banyan trees, with its wide spread of tentacle-like roots.

I closed my eyes and inhaled the flower-fragrant salt air, the smell of the sand, listening to the waves crash on a nearly-pristine beach still empty of people.

I could have stayed there...

Well, for a long time.

I fell back into the comfort of knowing he was there, with me. I thought about the fact that some part of me knew he was there before I remembered who I was, much less where I was, or what happened to me the day before.

I wanted to wake him up now.

Despite all the bandages, the cuts and broken ribs, I wanted him awake.

It had been too damned long since we'd been together.

My light was starting to hurt, just thinking about it.

My fingers hurt, my tongue, my hands, my skin.

My fingers curled deeper into his hair...

That time, he jumped.

I immediately felt guilty, realizing I'd woken him up.

I'd wanted him awake, and now I'd woken him up.

I should have remembered what a light sleeper he was.

"It's okay, doc." Lowering his head, he mumbled against my skin, burying his face into his arm. "I plan to sleep out here all day. You might have to just roll me onto the sand when you want to get up. Leave me for the crabs and the sand beetles and the seagulls. Just spray me with sunscreen or stick an umbrella over me... otherwise I'll get whiny."

I chuckled, combing my fingers through his hair.

Exhaling into me, he tightened his arms around my back and side, still careful to keep his arm below my hurt ribs, and above the cut on my thigh.

"...I expect you to protect me, doc," he muttered next, exhaling. "If anyone comes wanting to show us dead bodies, you're to fight them off with a stick. Or maybe a sword, if I can get Cowboy to airmail us one..."

I chuckled again, shaking my head.

"So we're still doing this Hawaii beach thing?" I mused, still stroking and combing my fingers through his hair, noting it was already gritty with sand. "Damn, you are stubborn."

"Stubborn?" he mumbled into his arm.

"Yeah," I said. "I figured I'd be on a plane to Thailand by now. Instead you brought me back here, to the beach... even after yesterday. We're still at the same resort. Don't pretend you simply 'tightened security,' although I'm one hundred percent certain you did. This is you, insisting on having your vacation, goddamn it. Even with people trying to kill us on a daily basis."

"Name one place that *doesn't* happen, doc," he mumbled against my skin, still not raising his head. "Do that... and I'll give you a million dollars."

"I already half-own your million dollars," I reminded him. "California law. You signed away half your fortune with that marriage license."

"Only on paper, doc," he said, still not raising his head. "Only on paper."

I frowned, fighting between amusement and puzzlement.

Only on paper?

What was that supposed to mean?

"You should have gotten a prenup," I scolded him. "Like a normal rich person. As it is, I'll take payment in backrubs. And in other assorted... favors. But you giving me your millions is redundant at this point, Quentin."

"Billions," he mumbled. "Or so my accountants tell me."

"Sure. Have you asked recently? You have half the seer population of this world living at one of your properties. Not to mention on your payroll... and eating out of your seer soup kitchen at the Raptor's Nest."

He shrugged his broad shoulders, his face still pressed into his arm.

"So, backrubs, then?" I pressed, nudging him. "Can we bet with those?"

"That's hardly something you're going to have to barter me for, doc." Thinking about my words, he snorted. "Prenup. Jesus. Why in the gods would I do that? Waste of lawyer's fees."

"Still cocky," I mused, pulling a few flower blossoms out of his hair that must have fallen from one of the trees. "I could be plotting right now, how to take all your money. Planting stories in all the tabloids... getting private eyes to follow you."

"You're welcome to it," he grunted, resetting his head on my belly. "Even if you divorced me, sweetheart, you'd still be stuck with me. That's what you get for life-bonding with a hard-to-kill fucker like me."

He snuggled deeper into my side, exhaling a sigh.

"You might as well face it, doc. You're screwed. If you take my money, you'd just get stuck supporting me... and supporting all those freeloading seers you just mentioned. Not to mention the human orphans we keep taking in."

Gripping my calf in one hand, he massaged the muscle there.

"...Just remember, I expect to be spoiled at the level to which I've grown accustomed. And I have expensive taste, love."

I snorted at that.

"Ain't that the truth," I muttered.

Still, his *only on paper* comment nagged at me a little.

Black rarely said anything that didn't mean *something*.

If anything, the things he said usually had three or four layers of meaning crammed into them, even if no one understood most of those layers but him.

"Don't overthink it, doc," he murmured. "You know your husband's a cryptic weirdo."

"Sure," I said, tugging on his hair. "But what does that have to do with what you said?"

He raised his head.

Blinking at me, he settled on keeping his eyes closed, rubbing his face with one hand as he pulled himself further up my body, resting his chest lightly and carefully on mine.

"Is this okay?" he murmured, looking down at my bandages.

I nodded. "It's fine. My ribs feel surprisingly okay. The one side hurts."

"Which side?"

"The right." I winced a little, pointing. "The side where he kept punching me."

He nodded, his eyes sliding perceptibly out of focus. I could feel his light flicker over me, assessing my injuries like I had earlier, when I first woke up.

"How're you feeling?" he said, as his eyes clicked back into focus. He squinted at me, assessing me with his eyes that time, looking over the thin T-shirt I wore and shorts. Supporting himself on one hand, he carefully turned over my bandaged arms, holding them away so he wouldn't put pressure on the cuts there.

Glancing up, he narrowed his gaze at my face.

Seeing the focus of his gaze, I lifted my hand cautiously, touching a bandage on my forehead, remembering the cut I'd gotten there, the one meant to blind me.

"You sure you're okay?" he said, gruff.

"Don't I feel okay?" I said, puzzled.

"You do." He continued to study my eyes, frowning slightly. "You feel better than you should, honestly. It's making me paranoid that I'm missing something."

He glanced up at my eyes, and I saw his pupils dilate as he looked at me, as he watched me examine my own wounds.

"I didn't lay on anything wrong?" he pressed, his voice lower, gruffer now. "Nothing that hurts? I kind of crashed out, after I got you down here. I wasn't laying on you this much when I first got here."

"I'm okay."

"You sure?"

I nodded, gauging his expression, even as I leaned forward, kissing him on the mouth. I felt a ripple of heat go through him, even as he clenched his jaw, a pained look coming to his face before he looked away.

I felt more pain in my own light, reacting to his.

I really wanted to ask him if anyone was watching us out here.

"Yes," he said, his voice that deep, heavy tone that drove me crazy.

"Can you tell them to go away?" I said.

"No." He studied my eyes, frowning. "Miri... *gaos*. Don't do this to me right now. You're wounded for fuck's sake. You almost died."

"So?"

"So? Do you have any idea how hard it is right now? Keeping my hands off you? You're not fucking helping... at all."

"I'm not really interested in helping you with that," I informed him, caressing his jaw.

He moved back though, pulling out of my reach.

For a moment he only stared at me, a faint scowl on his face.

Giving up, I let out a sigh, placing my hands on the lounger.

"Okay," I said. "So distract me, then."

He frowned. "Distract you?"

"Yeah," I said, watching his face. "Tell me things. What did you find out? About the robots," I added, when he quirked an eyebrow at me. "I'm assuming you went looking? Once I passed out from all the painkillers at the hospital?"

Glancing around at the empty beach, I added sourly,

"No way you'd be able to sit still for that long. Not after someone tried to kill the two of us—"

"*You,* you mean," he grumbled. "You keep saying *us,* but you should be saying *you,* doc. No one's tried to kill *me* yet, not *directly,* far as I can tell. I don't know if you've noticed, but everyone we come across appears to be trying to kill *you* right now. Including that asshole Narcisse... who I might need to dangle out of a window later. In fact, I think I'll pencil that in for after breakfast."

I nodded, dead-pan.

"You mean you haven't already?" I said.

"I had more pressing things on the list, doc." He nudged me with an arm. "Are you going to admit that you're the damsel in distress this time? That it's up to my manly prowess to save you from the demons and robot assassins swirling in our general vicinity? Or are you going to keep playing dumb, pretending it's *both* of us they're trying to kill?"

I folded my arms, wincing a little, and fighting the urge to roll my eyes.

"Nice distractions, Quentin... but I'm right, aren't I? You went somewhere. Was it USPACOM? I figured you'd go there first."

Black exhaled.

Despite his gentle teasing, I could feel a realness behind his words.

He really was frustrated I wouldn't acknowledge that I was the target.

Not like it mattered, really.

Like he always said, we were a package deal. If someone managed to kill me, he'd likely die not long after.

"Likely?" he muttered darkly.

I glanced over, frowning.

His pupils were still too large, too dark. I could feel him trying to stop noticing my bare legs, my eyes staring at him, which had a tendency to set him off for some reason (he called staring "seer foreplay" once, when I asked him about it)... or the fact that I wasn't wearing a bra under the thin T-shirt I wore.

I hadn't even noticed that last bit, not until I caught his furtive looks at my chest.

"Can we just fuck?" I said, exasperated. "I mean... how long has it been?"

"No."

"Why not?"

"Because I don't want to break more of your ribs," he growled, glaring at me. "And stop looking at me like that. I mean it, doc."

He wasn't really kidding that time, either.

I could hear it in the faint edge of his voice, see it in the perceptible tightening of his lips, even as anger infused his light, coiling through it in a series of orange and red sparks, veins of glowing, fire-like light. Watching it take over his seer's living light, or *aleimi*, I almost regretted pressuring him about the sex thing.

I almost regretted teasing him about my near-murder, too.

At the same time, I couldn't help but notice how different his light was now.

It was so much brighter now.

It was more than just the brightness, though.

Something about it struck me as quasi-physical.

"Stop it, doc."

"I can't help it."

"Do you need me to leave?"

"No," I snapped. "Maybe."

There was another silence between us.

Then I forced myself to sigh, gazing out over the beach.

I could still feel that hotter, denser light of his flickering over mine. Watching it coil around my legs, pulling at me, turning sensual in the hotter areas of my light, I found I understood something else.

"Are you afraid you'll turn?" I said finally. "Is that it?"

Black scowled, glaring at me. "It's not *not* it."

There was a silence where I thought about that.

"Can you control it at all?" I said.

Without thinking, I reached for him, going back to stroking his black hair.

When he looked over at me, scowling a little, I exhaled in frustration.

"Just talk to me about it," I said, meeting his flecked gold eyes, noting how much light shone in them, even with his too-large pupils. "I'll stop trying to seduce you, okay? But at least *talk* to me about why you're nervous. We haven't talked about it at all... not just in relation to sex, but not *at all*. We should. If only so I know where and how I can help you. And how fast I need to potentially move out of the way, if I trigger something."

I smiled, trying to make a joke of the last.

He didn't smile back.

Pausing at his silence, I prodded him again.

"Is it hard for you to remain... you know... human-ish? Or is it just sort of comfortable being static, whichever form you're in?" Thinking about my own question, I added, "You never really told me how it happened. The first time."

Black scowled, rubbing his face again with a hand.

I couldn't help wondering if he was buying himself time to think.

"This is a longer talk, doc," he said, his voice a faint warning.

"I figured," I said, exhaling as I refolded my arms. "I wasn't really asking for the long version. Just the short, I'm-okay-so-you-don't-have-to-worry-about-me-spontaneously-turning-into-a-giant-lizard version... or conversely, the I-have-no-clue-if-I'll-turn-back-into-a-giant-lizard-or-not-or-even-how-it-happened-the-first-time version. Or even just some indication which of those versions is *likely* to be more accurate than the other..."

Watching his face, I trailed off at the end.

His expression wasn't difficult to read.

"It's the second one," I said. "Isn't it?"

He looked at me, turning from where he'd been staring out at the ocean, watching the sunlight shine over the curl of waves near the shore.

The sun was fully up now, the sky turning a deeper blue.

"Pretty much," he admitted, meeting my gaze before turning back to the ocean. "Like I said... it's complicated, Miri."

"Because of Coreq?"

Again, he paused, only to look at me and give a reluctant nod.

Then, seeming to make up his mind, he sighed.

"Honestly?" he said. "I'm not sure I had a damned thing to do with any of it. It felt a lot more like being possessed than it did like me *doing* something. Like, I was talking to him, to Coreq... and talking to Charles... and translating Coreq for Charles... even as *he* was talking to Charles. It was really schizophrenic. Not to mention unnerving as hell."

"Coreq?" I clarified. "Coreq spoke to Charles directly?"

Again, Black nodded.

"Through you?"

Black nodded.

Looking away, seeming to think about that, he grunted.

"Your uncle thought I'd lost my fucking mind."

My lips pursed. "Yeah. Well, he's not exactly the best judge of sanity." Pausing, I added, "You have no idea what set him off? Coreq?"

Black let out a half-laugh.

It didn't contain a lot of humor.

"I dunno, wifey-kins. Maybe me waking up to find myself strapped to a metal table in a basement lab under the Pentagon? With a bunch of hospital-masked seers crouched over me, holding syringes and cutting implements? Just a guess."

Frowning at the mental image, I could only nod.

I knew Black was probably right.

From what I'd felt off the "Coreq" presence that seemed to share some part of Black's light, Coreq wasn't particularly fond of labs.

He wasn't particularly fond of seers who experimented on other seers in labs.

He'd had pretty horrible experiences in scientific settings, period.

"Why is he so much stronger now?" I said. "Coreq. He was barely a whisper before, when I first felt him in your light. He was just this faint presence... like a smell. When he talked to me, it was like he was a million miles away. He doesn't feel like that now. He feels close. He feels like he might even be listening to us, right now."

He is...

I swallowed, not sure which of them answered me.

I didn't want to ask.

Still staring at the ocean, Black let out a humorless laugh.

"I don't know, doc."

"You don't?" I met his gold eyes again when he turned. "Is it because of what Revik and Allie said? About us bonding?"

Black threw up his hands, holding my gaze.

"No idea," he said, his eyes and voice serious. "I know pretty much exactly what you know. But yeah, it occurred to me that this is probably what my cousin and his wife and that witch-doctor lady warned us about. About the bond somehow 'awakening' latent parts of my light. How it could be dangerous. And unstable."

Frowning he said, "I just thought it would be more 'me' than 'not-me.'"

Still thinking, he exhaled, frowning.

"All I can tell you is, when it took over... it *took over.* I couldn't do a fucking thing."

He met my gaze, his gold eyes even more serious.

"It's why I didn't try to talk to you about it. I didn't want to scare you. And yeah, it's why I'm kind of nervous about us fucking. I don't exactly have the best self-control when we're doing that.

And Coreq is a little too... eager. To have us fuck, I mean. I get the sense he really wants us to, which isn't exactly reassuring."

I frowned at that.

I tried to make my voice reassuring, though.

"It's okay, Black."

"Is it?" he grunted. "Well, it scared the shit out of me. It's like, any minute, I could have a serial killer driving my body instead of me. A serial killer, incidentally, who really wants to fuck my wife. It's not reassuring, Miri. At all."

I frowned harder at that.

I couldn't help it.

"Is that what it was like?" I said cautiously. "In D.C.?"

Black scowled, staring back over the water and sand. "It wasn't *not* like that."

I grimaced, about to make a crack about how we could probably do without all the double-negatives, but Black wasn't finished.

"...It was like suddenly, I wasn't in charge of my own body. Or my own light," he added, giving me a dark look.

"I could see everything Coreq was doing. I could see everything happening to my body, and my light. I could even feel what was coming, at least to a degree... but on the outside, I couldn't do shit. All I could do is narrate, and tell people to get the fuck out of the way. I couldn't reason with Coreq himself at all... even after I felt what he intended to do. He more or less blew off everything I said. He barely seemed to register me at all. It wasn't a democracy. It wasn't even a power struggle. It was a full-blown coup."

Pausing, he added,

"I didn't know *what* was coming, of course. Not the *how* of it. I felt the intention, but only in the abstract. I knew a shit-ton of energy was coming. I felt heat... power. A willingness to kill. To destroy things. I thought it would be something like what my cousin does, his relatively *less*-insane telekinesis thing. But I'm not sure I was thinking even that rationally about it, to be honest. Not at the time. At the time, I just knew Charles' people were probably going to die if they didn't give Coreq what he wanted. Or at least get the hell out of his way."

His eyes turning inward, he muttered,

"Fuck. I tried to warn him. Charles."

I slid more of my light into my fingers, stroking his face, his hair.

"It wasn't your fault," I said.

I saw the doubt in his eyes, in the tightening of his lips.

"I don't really blame Charles for thinking I'd lost my marbles. From his perspective, nothing I said made much sense." Clicking humorlessly under his breath, he added, "He thought I was *threatening* him, of course."

I grunted.

Of course.

My uncle would see it that way. It was who he was.

"And when you changed?" I prodded. "And after? Did you still know who you were? Did you still have no control?"

Black frowned, staring back at the ocean.

After a silence where he seemed to think about my words, he shook his head.

"No," he said, as if his answer surprised him. "Strangely, not much changed, after I changed. I mean... after the initial *physical* side of things, after the transformation itself... I was more or less myself again. I couldn't change *back*. But after Coreq broke us out of the building, and got us to the shore of the Potomac, he gave me back control. I was steering the ship again. I knew who I was. I knew enough to get the hell out of there."

Frowning, still staring at the ocean waves, which were growing bluer and bluer in the morning sun, he added,

"...It was weird as fuck, though. At first, a lot of my problem was figuring out what to do with a body that size, one I had zero familiarity with. I was pretty freaked out. My instinct was, get in the water and get out of there. Figure out the body thing later, when tiny people weren't *shooting* at me... or aiming missiles in my general direction. I didn't even think about trying to fly, to use the wings I had, until later. It's probably good I didn't."

He turned, meeting my gaze.

Seeing the faint worry in his gold irises, the uneasiness with what he was telling me, I slid my fingers into and around his, tugging on him gently, sending faint tendrils of my light into his. I curled them around his heart, pulling him gently into me.

After a few seconds, I felt him exhale.

I felt that tighter grip around his heart begin to relax.

His fingers wrapped around mine, pulling my hand up against his chest.

"I was looking for you," he said, kissing my fingers. "Somehow, I knew... even like that. I knew I wouldn't be myself again... not until I found you. I was pretty desperate by the end. I don't know if you felt that, but I was pretty much *screaming* for you in the space. I'm surprised I didn't blow out your mind, with how loud I was screaming. I did my best to follow your light. Even like that, I was still a seer somehow, so I tried to follow any trail I could of you in the Barrier. My light was different though, which made it harder. I also knew someone had you collared, so I was pretty frantic, scared they might be hurting you..."

I gripped his hand tighter, tears coming to my eyes.

For a few seconds, I couldn't speak.

He gripped me back, watching my eyes.

Wiping my face after a few seconds, I nodded.

"I felt you," I told him, wiping my eyes again. "I felt you. I just couldn't reach you." Sliding my other hand under his shirt, massaging his shoulder, then his chest, I watched his eyes close. "You were getting close, though. They told me you were in Japan. You may have even been on the coast of Russia. So you were getting close."

Black nodded, his eyes distant.

Then, abruptly, he frowned.

Turning, he looked at me.

"Wait. *Who* told you that? When?"

Feeling caught, without having any idea why at first, I froze.

Then, as his words sank in, I flushed.

Before I could stop myself, I averted my gaze.

"Yarli. It was Yarli, I think." I pursed my lips. "Yes. It must have been her."

"When?" Black said, his voice pointed. "When did she tell you that, doc?"

I fought to think.

Black went on before I could answer.

"...Because I was under the impression you hadn't talked to her at all yet. Or much of anyone in California." Frowning faintly, he added, "From what she told me, I fed them the lists and they fed the names to you, and you went back and forth... and that was more or less it, in terms of interaction. The last time I spoke to her, she mentioned *wanting* to talk to you. She wanted to fill you in on everything that happened while you were gone. She told me Angel was asking to speak to you, too."

There was a silence while I fought to think.

The painkillers they must've fed me definitely weren't doing me any favors right then.

I could feel Black's eyes on me.

I'd already been quiet for too long.

Still frowning as he looked at me, he broke the silence again.

"I still haven't heard the whole story on how you got away, doc," he said, his voice holding a harder edge. "In Moscow. I know you said those assholes had you. Alexei and Uri. But how did you get the collar off? How did you get out of there?"

"Maybe *they* told me?" I said, glancing up with a frown. "Uri and Alexei? Maybe it was them who told me about you being sighted in Japan? Honestly, I can't remember, Black—"

"You're a seer, Miri," Black growled. "Photographic memory."

I stared at him.

Then I looked away.

When he saw me hesitating, fighting to think, he sharpened his voice.

"How did you get free? How did you get out of the collar? Are you going to tell me?" Pausing, he added, "And why *haven't* you told me? What the fuck are you hiding?"

Exhaling in frustration, I looked at him.

"I had help," I said.

"Clearly."

His gold eyes hardened more, turning to glass when I didn't go on.

"Help from *whom,* doc?"

"You're not going to like it."

"Clearly," he growled, louder. "Will you just fucking tell me? It can't possibly be worse than where my mind is already going—"

"Nick," I said, staring at him. "Nick helped me. And Dalejem."

Black froze.

I watched his face change.

It was slow at first. I saw his mouth contort, caught between expressions, his eyes flash and widen and harden as my words sank in.

I saw the explosion building.

"...and Dalejem," I repeated, my voice warning. "Did you hear that part? They came together, Black. They *are* together, Black. As a couple."

Black sat up, abrupt.

He moved off me so fast, I gasped, shocked in spite of myself.

He stared down at me, the rage building in his eyes and light as he stared at me. More than rage, more than the building fury I could see there, I saw disbelief, a disbelief verging on denial, like some part of him couldn't accept what I'd said.

Seeing the heat building there, I folded my arms, wincing at the injuries under my bandages, but doing my best to hold my ground.

I blew the hair out of my face, a nervous tic.

"I know it sounds crazy—"

"Sounds. Crazy," Black repeated. *"Sounds. Crazy."*

"Black," I warned, my voice low. "Calm down."

"Calm. Down."

Black spoke each meaning as if in a trance.

The words came out slow, deliberate, flat as metal, but also distant, like they felt strange in his mouth, like they made no sense to him.

"Nick didn't kidnap Jem," I went on, my voice still warning. "Jem kidnapped Nick. To keep Nick safe from us... and from Dorian and Brick. Mostly, he did it so he could weather the transition with him. To be with him while Nick finished regaining his memory. He was hoping Nick might be himself again, once he'd gone through that."

Black blinked, not speaking.

Frowning, I added, "I guess he followed him out of the California Street building. That person we saw Nick holding? That wasn't Jem... it was Solonik. Nick ran into him while he was trying to escape. He bit him, and took him out of there. In his weird vampire-mind, I think he thought he was protecting me."

"Solonik."

"Yeah." Staring at Black's face, I fought nerves, in spite of myself. "He was there, too. In Russia. He's harmless, though. He's more or less Nick's slave now. He's completely addicted to Nick's venom."

Thinking about that, remembering Solonik's face as he glared at Jem, I grunted, refolding my arms.

"Honestly, Solonik barely remembered who I was. He's completely obsessed with Nick. I'm a lot more worried he might try to kill Jem than hurt me... even though Nick ordered him not to. Nick will probably have to kill him, one of these days..."

Trailing as I watched Black's face, I swallowed.

Black was staring at me, his gold eyes like flames, his face frozen.

Every muscle in my body tensed as I added, sharper,

"Nick is *Nick* again, Black. I wouldn't have believed it either, but I swear to you... he isn't anything like how he was on that roof. You would be completely stunned if you actually saw him... much less spoke to him. Hell, if you just watched him and Jem interact for more than a minute, I think your head might explode. I know *mine* did. I could barely tell the difference between how he is now, and how he was when he was human. Well... apart from the him and Jem thing. He was never into guys before."

I refolded my arms, blowing my hair out of my face again.

"Even my *dog* liked him," I muttered. "Panther practically adopted Nick, within seconds of meeting him." I stared past Black, adding, "Nick always did have that weird dog thing. Dogs friggin' *love* him. Small dogs. Medium-sized dogs. Large dogs. Even dogs that normally hate people. They all love Nick."

"Your... dog."

"Yeah." I clenched my jaw, glancing at him nervously, resetting my back in the lounger. "Yeah. I brought a dog back with me. Alexei gave him to me, but there was no way I was leaving him behind. He's still a puppy, so I left him with Nick and Jem. I didn't want to leave him alone... and Angel and Cowboy are too busy."

"Angel and Cowboy... are too busy. For your dog." Black paused. "So you left him. With a vampire. With Nick."

I scowled at him.

"Are you just going to repeat everything I say?" I said.

Black's gold eyes darkened.

Seeing the look growing there, I immediately regretted my words.

For a moment we only stared at one another.

Then Black removed himself from the sun lounger totally.

I watched him straighten, standing over me.

Swallowing, I forced myself to hold his gaze.

"Black," I said, my voice a harder warning. "You can't hurt him. You sure as fuck can't kill him. You can't. You would devastate Dalejem, for one." Swallowing, refolding my arms, I stared up at him. "...and me. And probably Angel by now."

Black's eyes and expression darkened more.

His face grew so hard, so angry, he was almost unrecognizable.

"He saved my life," I added, sharper. "And by extension... yours.

He's the *only reason* I got out of there. He's the only reason I got out of that collar. Dalejem wouldn't have been able to do it on his own. I wouldn't have been able to do it on my own. We didn't have any cutters that worked, and no way to get to the person who could have opened it."

Swallowing, I added,

"...Nick had to chew through the collar to get it off me."

Black's expression flinched.

I felt pain off him, real pain that time.

Clenching my jaw, I refolded my arms.

When Black remained standing there, as if frozen, I went on, my voice an open warning.

"If he hadn't done it, Black," I said. "I wouldn't have been able to jump out of there. I wouldn't have been able to jump to *you*. I'd still be there. In that damned castle in Moscow. Fending off Alexei. Trying to convince them to let me go. And you'd either still be a dragon somewhere... or you'd be dead."

But apparently, Black had heard enough.

Maybe his brain shorted at that point.

Maybe he was just afraid it would.

Either way, before I'd even finished speaking, he was already walking away.

I watched him turn his back on me and just walk, without saying a word, his bare feet stalking through the dry sand. I didn't call after him, although a part of me wanted to. I just sat there, biting my lip in worry, in fear, in what might have even been disbelief.

I watched him until he reached the path leading up to the resort.

I watched him disappear around a turn, grow invisible in the pineapple bushes that lined the path, and the palm trees that hung over it.

He didn't look back.

❧ 24 ❧

I ONLY HAVE EYES FOR YOU

"Yeah... Well. Just send someone down there."

There was a silence.

Black saw Mika, Kiko and Jax exchange looks.

Then Mika, who stood closest to him, spoke up, her voice cautious.

"Who?"

Black scowled. "I don't give a fuck who. I want someone down there. A seer. In person. Or bring her back up here. Just not to me. Not right now. I've got..." He clenched his jaw. "...shit to do. I want her to rest. She doesn't need to be involved in this crap right now."

The silence deepened.

Then the short, Asian seer nodded. "Okay, boss. I'll go down. I'll call ahead... see if she wants me to order her any breakfast."

"Go down now," Black said, warning. "Call up, if you need breakfast."

Mika nodded, still obviously trying to hide her puzzlement.

She was doing a shitty job, as far as Black was concerned.

"Where's Angel?" he said, turning his glower back on Kiko, then Jax. "She didn't come out here with you? Or Cowboy?"

Kiko frowned, exchanging looks with Jax. She shook her head.

"She wasn't on the list, boss. You want me to call? Get her out here?"

Black scowled.

He hadn't put her on the list.

Then again, he hadn't known Angel was babysitting Nick-fuck-ing-Tanaka back in California... and probably Solonik, too.

When Black made that list, he'd been reluctant to pull her and Cowboy over here, worrying about their safety, especially Angel's, since she'd want to stick close to Miri. He'd decided to leave them where they were, so he'd have a few people he really trusted helping out Yarli and Manny at the California Street Building.

Now the thought made him grimace.

People he really trusted, his ass.

Cowboy must know about Nick, too.

Yet neither one of them got on the goddamned *phone* with him, the very fucking second Miri came traipsing back to California with Nick and Dalejem in tow.

Hell, Black still had people out looking for Jem.

Worse, he wasn't even sure if he could pull them back right now, not without alerting everyone in California that Nick was there... or at least without raising a lot of difficult-to-answer questions.

He knew Miri meant it, when she said she didn't want Nick killed.

Black almost didn't care.

Almost.

"Fuck," he snapped, at no one.

"Do you want me to call them, boss?" Mika said, frowning. "Or not? I think Angel would jump at the chance. She was already worried about both of you."

Thinking about that, realizing he had some damned questions of his own for Miriam's best friend... and apparent traitor to him... Black scowled harder.

"Yeah," he said finally. "Send for them. Both of them. Get someone to drive them to the airport, and have them bring weapons, if possible. Commercial is fine. Talk to Kiko... she can arrange the permits. But I want them in the air before noon."

"Will do, boss."

Mika walked away.

When Jax and Holo continued standing there, looking faintly puzzled at whatever they saw on Black's face, Black waved them away, too.

"Get to that mobile lab," he said, his voice dismissive. "I want you looking at the guy who attacked Miri. You're the hacker team I've got. Right?"

Jax hesitated, exchanging another look with Holo.

Holo ended up being the one who spoke.

"We got custody of the eyes, boss," he said. "We're heading downstairs to look at those now. Your friend, Yarrick, gave us a private room to work from."

Hesitating, Holo added,

"About the armor, we had some questions. From the design you described, there's some chance it has organic components. We wondered if any kind of assessment had been done already, of its possible properties."

Black frowned, jerking his eyes and attention back to the other seer.

"Assessment?" he growled. "What the fuck do you mean?"

"A safety assessment, sir," Holo clarified patiently. "We had concerns."

"What kind of concerns? It's dead."

"Yeah," Holo said, frowning as he glanced at Jax. "We know the unit is dead. It's just... the last one was found dead, too. We were wondering..."

Holo hesitated, once more glancing at Jax.

Jax jumped into the breach, his words frank.

"Is this one going to... explode?" the East Indian seer said. "Has a risk assessment been done of that possibility, sir?"

Black frowned harder.

It was a valid question.

If he wasn't mostly thinking of creative ways to disembowel while strangling his wife's vampire rapist, he might have thought of that possibility himself.

Still, the second cyborg soldier didn't have any flashing lights left after Black smashed its face in with three, point-blank bullets to the head. The first body they'd found, the one that washed up dead, still had live components when Fournier and Keon dragged it into the boathouse.

Well, Black assumed it had live components.

Based on the flashing, blue-white, virtual screens that clicked back on, elements of the electronics were still live, even after the human part was dead. That must have included whatever caused the body to self-destruct a few minutes later.

"Better do a scan of it," he said after a beat. "Long distance. I'll get Narcisse to send photographs, to assist with a Barrier track. You can go pick it up after you've cleared it... or we'll put it in quarantine, if you note any instabilities that concern you."

Jax and Holo both looked visibly relieved.

"Thank you, sir," Holo murmured, bowing.

"You've already done that with the eyes?" Black said, frowning. "They aren't volatile? I know they're small, but there's still some chance—"

Jax shook his head. "We don't think so, boss. They came up totally inert in our scans."

"Ok. Good."

Black wrestled back and forth, fighting to think about what he should do next, even as he fought to *not* think about Nick. His mind kept flickering back to San Francisco, though, the part of him that felt like a hypocrite and an asshole that he hadn't gotten on the horn right away, warning Manny, warning Yarli, warning all of them that they had two major security risks within striking distance of the California Street Building.

Not just Nick, but Solonik.

Jesus.

Just the thought of the two of them, working together, brought up such an intense rush of rage, he struggled to suppress it before it turned into something more.

He couldn't even calm down enough to decide whether his people were safer with Angel there, in San Francisco, keeping an eye on that fucker, or if Black would be putting her life in danger, leaving her there.

Someone should be watching him.

If Nick was feeding on Jem regularly, the seer would be worse than useless.

He'd more or less be Nick's slave.

Black hadn't even thought to ask Miri if Nick had fed on her, while they'd been together in Moscow.

But just thinking about that made his jaw clench, his fury sliding past redline and into nuclear... so he consciously, deliberately blanked his mind.

He'd wait until Angel got here.

He'd wait until he could talk to Cowboy *and* Angel.

Assuming that piece of shit wasn't feeding on both of them already.

But there were ways of checking that, at least, when they got here.

For now, he needed to find whoever was sending these fucking soldiers to kill his wife. Given that he had no idea if a new one might be on its way, he didn't have a lot of time.

Realizing Jax and Holo were still in his suite, still staring at him, Black turned on them both with a scowl.

"What the fuck are you still doing in here?" he growled. "Get working on those eyes. Now. I'll get those photos to you of the armor and the rest of the body within the hour."

Jax nodded.

When Holo didn't move, Jax grabbed his friend's arm.

He half-dragged his friend back to the door of Black and Miri's honeymoon suite after executing a seer's salute. Holo continued to stare at Black's face as he let Jax lead him out, not bothering to hide the puzzlement in his eyes, but not arguing with Black, either.

Let them be fucking confused.

Right then, Black didn't much care.

More than anything, he wanted everyone around him to leave him alone.

A big part of him just wanted to lock himself in the suite, drink heavily, and keep drinking until he ended up naked and passed out in the terrace jacuzzi.

Maybe put his fist through the wall a few times, first.

But he didn't have time for that.

He didn't have time for any of that.

Someone on *this* side of the Pacific still wanted to kill his wife.

He'd worry about the fucker who raped her when he got back to California.

⛓️

"Something's going on with the boss and the doc," Jax said, looking up from the flexible monitor he unrolled on the room's long table. "Did you notice? He's avoiding her. He *never* avoids her. Never. Not unless they're fighting."

Holo grunted, rolling his eyes. "No shit."

"Especially not when he thinks she's in danger," Jax added.

Holo grimaced in his general direction, but didn't look up from where he was hooking small connectors to the back of one of the "eyes" that had been extracted from the thing that attacked Miri on the beach.

"Is it an implant?" Jax said, changing the subject when Holo didn't comment on the thing with Black. He grimaced, watching his friend work. "The eye. Is it mostly real, with an implant? Or is it dead metal?"

Holo had the camera on his headset switched on, so Jax could watch everything the other seer was doing on the monitor once he'd connected the two devices.

It made him nervous, though.

Even with the encrypted channel, he would've rather used a non-wireless link.

Some habits were hard to kick from the Old World, and from decades of being at war. On Old Earth, they'd avoided networked machines like the plague. Since most computers there had organic components, they were too easy for seers to hack.

"So?" Jax prompted, when Holo didn't answer. "What is it? Any ideas?"

"It's not a real eye," the other said, frowning as he picked through the organ with tweezers and a thin light rod with a camera at the end. "I'm guessing it's mostly dead metal. But there are organics where the dead metal was fused to fully living human tissue. My guess is, they still aren't advanced enough with the organics here, to make the actual processors that way. They're being used for simple things, like with this headset, giving it more virtual capabilities, higher memory storage, increased bandwidth... but they haven't graduated to fully thinking machines yet."

Jax thought about that, remembering some of the "machines" they'd come across in the Old World. Some of those fucking things were terrifying, more like alien lifeforms.

"That's the good news, right?" he said hopefully.

Holo nodded slowly, giving him a sideways look.

"It's definitely not the bad news," he said.

After a pause, Holo's eyes shifted sideways again, aiming grimly at Jax.

"But they're getting there, brother," he said. "I have zero doubt Charles has labs somewhere, working now, as we speak, to advance organic tech. Already, what I'm seeing in terms of the detailed connection in this..." He pointed the light at the nerve endings behind the eye. "...It's much more advanced than anything in the headsets or guns they've been producing for the past year or so."

Jax nodded, a sick feeling growing in his gut.

He knew Holo was right.

They'd known for a while Charles was bringing that tech here. Charles's fears of a repeat of the seer-enslaved authoritarianism of

Old Earth had ironically done little but advance that timeline here, on New Earth.

"Ironic indeed," Holo murmured from next to him.

Pausing, the Chinese-looking seer, who they used to jokingly call "One-Half" on Old Earth, because he looked like he was roughly half of their commander, Wreg, stared at him. Holo's pale, amber-colored eyes glowed in the increased illumination from the portable lab lights as he appeared to contemplate something in Jax's face.

"Hey," he said. "Are you ever going to tell me about Kiko? What is going on there?"

Jax felt himself stiffen.

The reaction was swift, unthinking.

He immediately regretted it.

Still, Holo was his oldest friend. It had been decades, maybe more than a century, since they'd been able to hide much from one another.

"Nothing's happening, brother," Jax said, his voice neutral.

"But you like her?"

"No." Jax frowned, not looking up from the monitor.

"No?"

"No. I wouldn't say so. We're just friends. Well... sort of. I don't know her really. But someone had to look out for her. In that mess at the border."

When Holo didn't speak, Jax glanced at his friend, fighting to keep his expression blank, although he knew it was probably a waste of time.

Holo quirked a faint smile at him.

Jax didn't have to read the other's light to know what he was thinking.

"Okay," Holo said, exhaling. Looking back down at the lit lab table, he shrugged, his voice indifferent. "In that case, do you want to fuck? We haven't in a while. I'll need to take a break between working on eyes. We could go back to my room."

There was a silence.

In it, Jax felt his jaw slowly harden.

He stared down at the screen, fighting not to scowl at the other male.

After more than a few, long-feeling seconds, Holo chuckled.

"That's what I thought," he murmured, his amber eyes returning to the half-electronic eye that lay on the lit table below him.

"A bulk of the programming definitely comes from both of these," Holo explained, motioning, seer-fashion, towards the electronic eye projected on the screen in the hotel room wall. "I think, from what I can tell, organics are communicating between the brain and the microchips in the eyes to transmit the majority of the commands."

Moving closer to the wall, Jax pointed at the left eye, adding, "We think most of the commands come through here."

Jax glanced at Holo.

When the Chinese-looking seer nodded, motioning for him to go on, Jax turned his gaze back to Black. "They seem to have broken out the functionality and memory between the two eyes. The left eye is commands, tactical downloads, targeting info. The other seems to contain the bulk of their standard memory. Skill sets. Environmental scanning, assessment, and modification—"

"What are the skill sets?" Black said. "Do you have a list?"

"Partial," Holo said, jumping back in. "Most of it is the stuff you'd expect. Weapons training, hand-to-hand... even some advanced vehicle training, including piloting and driving a list of boats, cars, trucks, airplanes, helicopters. It's pretty crude though, boss."

"It didn't seem that crude when this thing was fighting," Black muttered, folding his arms as he leaned back in the white leather chair of his suite. "What do you mean by crude? You mean in terms of the tech itself?"

Holo nodded. "Compared to the stuff on Old Earth, it's pretty basic connecting and enhanced memory work. The mission-specific stuff came in through processors located mainly in the left eye. The right eye handled a kind of 'base model' package. We're pretty sure this is some kind of prototype. It's even got a number... and we think it's an assembly number. Whoever released this, they must have been desperate. I get the feeling the product wasn't ready or probably technically cleared for use in the field."

Black frowned harder. "What makes you say that?"

Jax gave Holo a sideways smile. "Besides the fact that the serial number we found was 'CYNEX-000-0000-006'?"

"Yeah," Black growled. "Besides that."

"To put it colloquially," Holo said, his voice more serious than Jax's had been. "It's glitchy, sir. Buggy. We think there's a good chance the first one died right after the drop... maybe even from the salt water corrupting some element of the dead metal electronics. This isn't a finished product, sir. It's likely they sent them out as a kind of Hail Mary."

"That still sounds like Charles," Black commented, folding his arms.

Jax nodded. "Him, or perhaps one of his subordinates. They might have activated them after Charles was captured. That might explain why they were programmed to take out the doc. They must have captured her on surveillance, disappearing people from their hierarchy. And with Charles gone—"

"—No one would care if the doc got killed," Kiko murmured, from the leather lounge chair next to Black's.

Black scowled.

Kiko's words felt true, though.

Looking away from his second and back at the two seers, still scowling, Black saw Jax's dark purple eyes slide surreptitiously towards Kiko's face, then down her body, which was encased in a flowered pink and white sun dress, presumably so she'd blend in more at the resort.

Kiko sat sandwiched between him, meaning Black himself, and Dex, who also sat to Black's right, but one chair down.

Black wasn't sure he liked having that fucker stare at his second.

He liked Jax.

Truthfully, he liked Jax a lot, but he wasn't sure he wanted anyone staring at Kiko right now. His protective instincts went into fucking overdrive, anytime someone so much as stood too close to her, anyone apart from him or Dex.

Just thinking about someone hunting his friend made him want to beat the shit out of that person. That was true even with Jax, even if Jax's desire to court Kiko was wholly sincere, even if Jax's intentions were well-meaning, even protective... even if Jax's motives stemmed from a genuine state of infatuation and affection.

Black still kind of wanted to beat the shit out of him.

Even if Jax didn't harbor a predatory bone in his body, Black wanted to yell at him to back the fuck off, to leave Kiko alone.

But thinking about that brought up his rage at Nick all over again.

It brought that rage back so intensely, Black found himself biting his tongue to keep from snapping at Jax, hard enough to taste his own blood.

Kiko herself didn't even appear to notice Jax's furtive stare.

She was frowning up at the screen, staring at the robotic eyes with a slightly disgusted look on her delicate features.

Dex definitely noticed.

Like Black himself, the big Marine scowled at Jax, folding his muscular arms.

Only now, Black found himself thinking Dex's interests weren't wholly related to protecting Kiko from harm, like he'd been assuming. Black felt a strong flavor of possessiveness on Dex now, not to mention what might have been out and out jealousy.

Jesus, Black thought in annoyance.

He looked between the three of them, noticing new elements

in the way their lights interacted, realizing he'd missed things in the last few weeks and months. He wondered how long this little fucking dynamic had been going on.

Was there anyone on his team not losing their damned minds over either cock or pussy?

And why the *fuck* wouldn't they leave Kiko alone?

Black glared at her, at the thought.

With her arms folded across her chest in that light sundress, Kiko looked both too fragile to him, and too feminine. He wasn't used to thinking of her as a particularly small or vulnerable human. She was one of the best fighters he knew.

A part of him wanted to snap at her now, like some kind of deranged father-figure, demanding she go put on combat gear and strap on at least four guns, maybe one or two swords, a few knives and hand-grenades for good measure.

From his other side, Mika chuckled.

Turning his head, Black gave her a scathing look.

The female seer only smirked back, winking at him.

"What the fuck are you doing up here?" he scowled, looking her over in her dark green bikini top, dark green and yellow tie-dyed skirt, leather sandals, and seashell necklace. All she needed was a fucking flower in her hair. "Why aren't you with Miri?"

Mika stared back at him, unflinching.

After a pause, she shrugged.

"I wanted to hear this," she said, refolding her arms and sinking deeper into the leather chair. "Kiessa's with the doc. So are Ace and Miguel. And that big Samoan guy, Marshall. And the surfer with the cute ass... Keon. Last I saw, the doc was passed out on the sun lounger. After eating about four bowls of mangoes... and downing a few mimosas... she was out cold."

Black's shoulders slowly unclenched as he verified Mika's words.

He scanned his wife, determining that she was, indeed, asleep under the umbrella.

Kiessa sat to her left.

Ace sprawled on the sun lounger to her right.

Both the seer and the human looked almost humorous in their black armored pants, armored shirts, each of them wearing two sidearms under the light over-shirts they wore. Those Hawaiian-style shirts must have been purchased in the hotel shop, and were their only concession to the location at all.

Knowing Ace, he had two more guns on him, one at his ankle, and another at the small of his back. Ace was like Cowboy in some ways. He didn't much care if he blended or not, especially when he was on the job.

Behind them, Marshall and Keon shared a table, drinking fruit smoothies while Marshall spoke animatedly about something, moving his hands a lot.

Miguel sat in front of them on a fourth sun lounger, staring out at the ocean, not even bothering with the light shirt, but wearing his usual uniform of a biker jacket, black jeans, combat boots, and a black T-shirt.

The thirty-something human wore two guns at his ribs, and Black knew he'd have multiple knives on him, too. Knowing Miguel, after that mess at *Koh Mangaan* and what happened to Nick, he might be wearing a sword under that leather jacket, too.

Miguel wasn't a fan of vampires.

It was amazing he wasn't dripping with sweat, but Miguel always seemed to do okay in the heat.

Miri was literally surrounded.

His wife was surrounded by their people.

Peter Yarrick had his own security team patrolling too, of course, even apart from Marshall, who Peter had more or less assigned to Miri full time. The rest of the Blue Sail's security team would be walking the perimeter, keeping an eye on the water, but also on who came and went through the lobby and other public areas.

Black had them all connected with his team, as well.

Assessing the environment around his wife, Black managed to make himself relax.

Marginally, at least.

Even so, he started wondering if it was stupid to leave her outside.

He took her out there because he knew his wife; he knew she'd be happier outside than locked indoors, even with the windows open.

He could have parked her on the terrace, though.

That might have been smarter.

He needed to go down there.

Even being this far from her made him nervous.

He was beginning to think his avoiding her was only making everything worse. Moreover, once Angel and Cowboy got here, it would be even harder to get her alone.

Remembering what he'd had planned for that night... for the last three nights, really, ever since they'd gotten here... he scowled harder.

He'd thought it would be a small thing.

Just the two of them.

But now, with a chunk of their team either here or on their way, that was pretty much impossible, too.

As if she were reading his mind, or his light, Mika spoke up.

"Angel and Cowboy are on their way," she said. "I just heard from Larisse, who opted to travel with them, so they'd have a seer on board. Larisse says they just left the airport. They should be here in about ten minutes."

Black frowned, refocusing on her abruptly.

"*This* airport?" he said. "As in the Honolulu-fucking-airport? I just told them to get on a plane."

"That was..." Mika looked at her watch. "...more than six hours ago, boss. It wasn't even seven a.m. when you told me that. It's almost two o'clock now. And we found them first class seats on a commercial flight that left at a little after ten o'clock, their time."

Black frowned, doing the math in his head.

That made sense. Sort of.

It still bewildered him.

Thinking it over, though, he felt his jaw harden to granite.

"I want to see them the *second* they get here," he growled. "Don't let them go outside. Don't let them go to the pool. Don't wait for them to take a single goddamned picture of the hotel, or of a pineapple, or the water. Don't let them anywhere near my wife. Take their bags out of their *fucking* hands and send them up here. Right away."

"What about their rooms—" Mika began, getting to her feet.

"Did I stutter?" Black growled. "Have someone else check them into their rooms."

Mika blinked that time, her eyes verging on incredulous.

She didn't argue with him, though.

She simply nodded, once, and headed for the door.

Black turned back to Jax and Holo.

"You get out, too. I got you the armor," he added. "It's being transported to that room you're using as we speak. You're getting the body, too."

When they all just stood there, staring at him, Black's voice hardened to metal.

"Get the fuck out," he growled. "Now. All of you."

That time, after a few more exchanged looks... they did.

25

BYGONES

"Did that sound like a request?" Black growled.

The two of them stared at him, their eyes mirroring almost identical confusion.

"Strip," Black snapped, clicking his fingers. "Now. Both of you."

Cowboy's normally difficult-to-read face twisted into a kind of grimace, right before he glanced sideways at his girlfriend, Angel.

The exchanged looks that whispered between the two of them verged on a seer's exchange. Either way, Black found himself both annoyed at being unable to read it, and reasonably certain they had a good idea why he was asking them to do this.

"Don't make me ask again," he growled.

Exhaling in a sigh, Cowboy reached for the front of his shirt, beginning to unbutton it with obvious annoyance and resignation.

"Can't you just do me?" he grumbled. "Then have me do my bride-to-be?"

Black blinked at that, in spite of himself.

Bride to be?

He saw Angel flush at his words, too.

"Elvis," she muttered. "...this is hardly the time."

"When would be a better time?" Cowboy retorted, still unbuttoning his shirt. "Pardon me for not exactly being thrilled my boss wants to take a gander at my woman naked."

He scowled at Black, tossing his outer shirt down on the carpet and pulling up one foot, balancing his ankle on his thigh to yank off a snakeskin cowboy boot.

"...And probably have her bend over and show him everything," the human retorted. "Just to reassure his fucking paranoia that we aren't pawns of no goddamned vampire."

Angel swallowed, looking from Cowboy to Black himself.

She hadn't started undressing herself yet.

She just stood there, even as more understanding bled into her eyes.

"She told you," Angel said, her coffee-colored eyes nervous. "Miri."

Black's jaw hardened, even as he folded his arms.

He didn't bother to answer her.

He aimed his next words at Cowboy.

"Would you tell me the truth, if you did find a bite on her?" he said, frowning down at the male human, subduing his voice with an effort. "Or would you just go back and stake that fucker yourself?"

At Cowboy's silence, Black scowled harder.

"Then you're just going to have to suck it up," he growled at his friend. "And trust me that I'm not deriving any fucking pleasure out of this. Believe me."

Frowning, Cowboy looked at Angel.

When she returned his gaze, quirking an eyebrow, Cowboy exhaled, motioning towards her as he yanked off his second boot.

"Up to you, darlin'," he said, still obviously displeased.

Exhaling in annoyance, Angel dropped her arms to her sides.

Then, seeming to resolve herself, she tugged the sweatshirt she wore up over her head, tossing it to the carpet on the other side of Cowboy and Cowboy's pile.

Black stood there, gazing out the window at the surf, while the two of them undressed.

When he could see them finish in his peripheral vision, he motioned towards Cowboy.

"You first," he growled, low. "Come here, brother."

⚜

"Satisfied? Cowboy grunted, standing on the other side of the room.

His voice was probably the closest to hostile Black had ever heard it, at least aimed at him.

Black could feel the other male giving him the stink eye, too, even before he turned, and saw the gray-eyed glare in the flesh.

"Yes," Black said, suppressing the smart-assed remark that first wanted to come to his lips. "At least in the way you mean," he said, lower, unable to suppress it entirely.

The truth was, he was relieved.

He was too relieved to really mind Cowboy's hostility all that much.

Turning his back on Angel while she began to tug on her underwear, then her pants, he folded his arms, keeping his eyes on Cowboy when he next spoke.

"Okay," he said. "Now speak. Both of you. Where is that piece of shit now?"

Cowboy frowned, his eyes moving from Black to behind him, presumably focusing on Angel.

"You wanna tell him, darlin'?" the human with the dirty blond hair asked drily. "Or should I share the happy news?"

"He's staying with me—" Angel began, reluctant.

"—And doin' a fair bit of remodeling, from what I can tell," Cowboy jumped in, in spite of what he'd said. His voice remained openly sarcastic. "Him 'n his vampire pals, that is. Just about killed Ang here. Blew up half her apartment—"

"—Not exactly," Angel said, her voice annoyed. "And it wasn't exactly his fault—"

"—Because up until now, it was *me* invitin' vampires over to party," Cowboy said, his voice still an open growl. "Tellin' 'em to smash up the place, after trying to thrall my wife—"

"Are either of you going to tell me what actually fucking happened?" Black growled, cutting through the back and forth between them. "Or am I supposed to figure out how to crack this genius code you're both using?"

After a few seconds of them glaring at one another, Angel walked around from behind where Black stood. Plopping herself down on the suite's couch, fully clothed now, the elegant black woman with the long braids gave Black a level stare.

"How about you ordering us some damned lunch, first?" she snapped, sounding irritated herself for the first time. "If I'm going to have two men yelling at me, more or less simultaneously, for crap that's not even my fault... I'd at least like to experience it with a full stomach. We got on that plane before I got anything in me but a cup of coffee."

Black stared at her for a moment.

Then, scowling, he walked over to the table, picked up the room service menu, and walked it over to where Angel sat. Tossing it on her lap, he motioned, over-dramatically, towards the phone.

"I await your pleasure, my queen," he grumbled.

Angel glared at him, flipping open the menu, then paused to glare at Cowboy.

"You're damned straight, you do," she muttered back.

❧

B lack heard the whole story by the end of the next hour.

Well, he heard part of the whole story.

He heard the parts Angel and Cowboy had been there for, the things they knew about.

Cowboy and Angel alternated on describing their experiences so far with Nick.

They ate bacon sandwiches with avocado, drank coffee, shared pieces of cake, and talked pretty much nonstop, once Black started asking them questions.

They did most of their talking on the balcony, overlooking the ocean.

Black indulged all of this.

He ordered food himself, if only to keep himself calm, and to fuel up before he went down to deal with his wife in a real way.

The story, from Angel's and Cowboy's point of view, was pretty simple.

Nick went from being a newborn vampire—a highly-volatile, sociopathic rapist, torturer, and murderer—back to being Nick again, more or less like he had been when he was human.

Only he drank blood now.

Mostly Solonik's blood, from what Black could gather.

He also didn't sleep. Or tolerate much in the way of sunlight.

It had only been a few days since Miri popped back to San Francisco with that fucking vampire in tow. Dalejem, Solonik, and Miri's dog arrived at the same time, and the four of them had more or less stayed together in the time since, although it sounded like Solonik had been chained up in Angel's garage for most of it.

Black couldn't quite get that initial image out of his head, though.

The four of them appearing out of nowhere, naked—on the roof of the California Street building—apparently minutes before Miri went to find Black.

The last place Black saw Nick, the place where Nick raped Miri, where Black put a bullet through the vampire's chest, where the fucker nearly *killed his wife*...

That's where Miri chose to bring him.

She brought him back to the roof of Black's flagship building.

Angel and Cowboy hadn't kept Nick and the others at the California Street building long.

They both knew Miri's word, especially second-hand, wouldn't be enough to keep Nick alive, not once Dex knew where he was.

Rather than chance that, or try to hide them somewhere in the building, Angel and Cowboy brought all four of them, the dog included, to Angel's apartment. They smuggled them out through the elevators while everyone was still in the process of returning to the Raptor's Nest from the desert, while no one had recovered enough from that ordeal to even be thinking about security.

Cowboy drove them over in one of the Black Securities and Investigations vans.

Angel checked in on them after that, at least once every day.

She spent a lot of time talking to Dalejem at first, then, after the first day or so, she spent even more time talking to Nick.

She took the dog for walks.

She avoided her own garage, and the seer chained up down there like some kind of sentient blood-bag.

She brought Dalejem groceries.

She brought the dog puppy food, along with a leash, a new dog-bed, some doggy toys, even a small crate for him to nap in, which they ended up keeping in the bedroom since the dog often came out of it at night and wanted to sleep with Nick and Jem.

The whole thing was fucking surreal, from Black's perspective.

Like a vampire version of a bad sitcom.

Black heard about Dorian's visit, too.

He heard about that psychopathic, old-school, skater-looking blond fuck showing up and more or less demanding Nick hand over Dalejem. He heard about Nick refusing, Nick trying to stop Dorian from killing his new "boyfriend"... and Dalejem firing exploding arrows into Dorian's chest.

Black didn't bother to ask where Jem got the arrows, or the compound bow... but he could guess. Angel must have brought those to the apartment on Dalejem's request, pilfering them from the weapon's stores at the Raptor's Nest.

Fucking Dalejem and his fondness for archaic weaponry.

Black didn't ask about the arrows, but he asked a lot of other questions.

He asked a fuck of a lot of questions.

Angel answered all of them.

She didn't hesitate. She didn't pause to think. She fired out answers to every question Black asked, like he was giving her an oral exam. She seemed to think Nick's life hung in the balance, or her job, or maybe both.

She seemed convinced Nick wasn't a threat.

Cowboy was definitely more skeptical on that point.

He let Angel do most of the talking, though, since she'd clearly spent a lot more time with the "New Nick" than he had.

Cowboy also obviously let Angel hang out with the vampire alone, which was an indirect vote of confidence for this version of Nick, whatever skepticism Cowboy voiced aloud. Angel even spent the night at the apartment with Jem, Solonik, and the vampire there.

The night Angel drove Dalejem and Nick down to Santa Cruz so that piece of shit could *surf,* of all things, Cowboy stayed behind that time, too.

Clearly, Angel wasn't afraid this new Nick would turn on her.

Cowboy had no real fear of Nick killing his girlfriend, either.

Dalejem obviously trusted him.

Unlike Cowboy, Angel insisted outright that Nick wasn't a risk.

She fully believed Nick was "Nick" again.

According to her, New Nick no longer acted, spoke, or even looked much like Naoko the Newborn. In her view, Naoko Tanaka, deadly vampire, was one hundred percent back to being Naoko "Nick" Tanaka, ex-SFPD homicide detective and all-around decent guy.

Angel also insisted New Nick wasn't interested in Miri.

She seemed to think Nick retained nothing but disgust, self-loathing, shame, and guilt about what he'd done to Miri *and* Kiko. According to her, New Nick appeared to be entirely wrapped up in Dalejem... to the point where she'd left her apartment in the middle of the night a few times, having been woken up by the two of them fucking, possibly fighting, possibly both at the same time. She said the relationship weirdness with the two of them had gotten even more intense after the Dorian thing.

None of what she said really made Black's desire to rip the fucker's heart out of his chest with his bare hands any less.

He also had trouble fully believing it.

Still, he read Angel, and Cowboy... and he knew *they* believed it.

Cowboy believed it, even if he wasn't as willing as Angel to let bygones be bygones.

Worse, Black's wife believed it.

Miri believed this bullshit.

She seemed to think she even owed this new Nick her life.

After more than an hour of that crap, he could tell Angel was getting impatient. She'd already mentioned going swimming more than once. Cowboy wanted to check in with Kiko and Dex, and find out where they were with those "fucking robots," as he put it.

Black realized he'd more or less exhausted this line of inquiry anyway.

He'd read everything he could off of them.

They'd answered every question he could think of.

He needed to go back downstairs.

He needed to go talk to his wife.

26

STOLEN THUNDER

"Go away," he grunted, motioning at all of them vaguely in seer.

"...I'd like to be alone with my wife," he added.

Kiessa opened her eyes.

Miguel turned his head, craning his neck around from where he sat up to frown at Black, then exchange looks with the female seer. Ace, who'd been smoking a cigarette near the large banyan tree a few yards from where Miri's sun lounger sank into the sand, glanced over, too.

Once Black's words penetrated, the tall, muscular human put the cigarette out with his boot, then bent down, plucking the butt out of the sand with his fingers.

Kiessa snorted, once Black's words sank in for her.

Uncrossing her ankles, she sat up, pulling herself off the sun lounger in a single motion and stretching her arms overhead.

"Don't go far," Black muttered, glancing at Miguel as the male human regained his feet. Black frowned faintly, watching Miguel's eyes linger on Kiessa. He wondered if the two of them were sleeping together, or if Miguel just wanted them to be.

Black added, "The pool maybe. Stay outside, if you would. Or get a replacement, if you need a break. Take Marshall and Keon with you, too," he said, nodding towards the two humans sitting at a table just up the hill, sharing a plate of nachos.

Kiessa winked at him, saluting with one hand, seer-fashion.

"Aye-aye, Cap'n," she said.

Miguel glanced at Ace, tilting his head sideways to indicate they were going up the dirt path leading to the resort's main pool area.

Black had just left Angel and Cowboy there, amid a sprawling mass of sun loungers, umbrellas, neon bathing suits, palm trees, fake coconut-smelling oils, naked butts aimed at the sun, designer sunglasses, red lipstick, diamond rings, four hundred dollar hair-cuts, fruit plates, cannabis chews, alcohol-soaked fresh pineap-ples... not to mention six different pools, three jacuzzis, a poolside massage area, four different cafés, two of which had their own bars.

There was also a pool that *was* a bar, where one could sit on submerged stools under a thatched roof bar near tiki torches, or float around on inflatable chairs, cocktail in hand, and soak up the tropical sun.

From what Black could feel on a lot of the guests, cocaine was flowing pretty freely with this crowd, as well... and ecstasy, if in smaller quantities.

Something had shifted in the vibe, for sure.

The celebrity crowd was more noticeable here now.

Word must have gone out on the grapevine that Black himself was here, that exciting things were happening, that at least one exciting occurrence had taken place here already.

Although, from what Black could tell as he skimmed through a random selection of minds in his weaving between sun loungers, palm trees, and tables, most of the guests staying here had all of their facts wrong, or at least heavily distorted.

Pushing all of that from his mind, he focused on his wife, real-izing only then that he'd avoided looking at her while the others were there.

She lay sprawled on the lounger, her thin T-shirt clinging to her body even more tightly than he remembered when he'd first woken up with her down here.

Her white shorts looked shorter, too.

She was watching him, her hazel eyes holding a dense scrutiny, a wariness he could see on the surface. Seeing that wariness, mixed with the tiredness he could see on her face, along with faint pain lines visible around her mouth and forehead, the last of his anger evaporated.

Instead, he found himself kicking himself for not bringing her painkillers—or at least sending some down when Mika first came down here.

Still watching her face, he touched his headset.

"Hey," he said, not waiting for a greeting. "Could you go into my room? There's a bottle of painkillers for Miri on the bathroom counter. I forgot to leave them with her. She's a few hours overdue for her next pill—"

"Of course," Kiko said, her voice warm. "I'll bring them right now."

Black nodded, mostly to himself.

Hanging up, he glanced at Miri.

Some of the wariness had faded from her expression.

"It's okay, Black," she said, when he didn't speak. "It's only been bothering me for a few minutes, and it's really not that bad. I would have called if it was."

Black grunted, walking around the foot of her sun lounger.

Without waiting for an invitation, he threw himself down on the lounger next to hers, which was still sitting, frame-to-frame, from where he'd shoved the two chairs together early that morning. Rearranging his long form, he leaned his head against the cushion, staring at her.

"Angel and Cowboy are here," he said.

She started a little, then smiled.

The warmth and relief in her eyes made him glad as hell he'd flown them out.

A faint humor touched her eyes and mouth next.

"Did you strip them naked already?" she said.

"Yes," he said, without a pause.

"I bet Cowboy loved that."

"He wasn't... thrilled."

The amusement faded from her stunning, hazel eyes. "Did you tell Kiko?"

Black shook his head, once. "No. I haven't told anyone."

"But you talked to Angel and Cowboy about it. Obviously."

"Obviously."

She nodded, her eyes studying his again, wary.

"You're not going to kill him, Black," she said. "I'll send them away, if you don't want them around. I would absolutely understand, if that's what you want... if that's what Kiko and Dex and the others want. But I can't let you kill him. It's not up for debate, as far as I'm concerned. Nick's life isn't something I'm going to let people 'vote' on. If you never want to see him again, fine. But—"

He held up a hand. "I get it, Miri."

Her eyes grew skeptical. "Do you?"

"I do."

Still frowning, she pressed, "You're not mad? Angel must have been damned convincing."

Heat filled Black's chest, making it briefly difficult to see, much less speak.

"Not mad?" he said after a too-long beat. "Did you just ask me if I'm 'not mad'?"

Her gaze flickered over his eyes, his face, and she frowned, then sighed.

"I'm sorry," she said. "So, what, then? What are you thinking? What happens now?"

He shook his head, clicking softly under his breath.

"Not today, doc," he said. "I don't want to talk about Nick today."

Thinking about that, he scowled out at the ocean, trying to decide if he should say more, or if he should postpone his plans for the night yet again.

If he asked her, it kind of defeated the whole purpose of the surprise thing.

Cowboy and Angel were here now.

That supported the doing it now plan, having the two of them here, along with Kiko, Dex, Mika, Holo and Jax, all of whom Black knew Miri had grown increasingly close to since they appeared in that cave under Ship Rock in New Mexico.

Of course, out of all of them, she was closest to Dalejem.

The thought made Black scowl.

Even with most of her current friends here, the timing was iffy at best.

Not to mention, Miri might not be up for it, given she was still healing, and had bandages, butterfly closures, taped ribs, and stitches on her arms, chest, and thighs. He might be able to speed up that healing process somewhat, if he fed her enough light, but that would likely make her tired, too.

The more he thought about it, the more he realized he should call it off.

The gods obviously were fighting him on this one.

"One what?" she said. "What are the gods fighting you on?"

He turned his head.

Her eyes were shining again, reflecting depths in those green and gold irises, even in the shade under the dark red umbrella.

"The gods are fighting you on what?" she repeated, prodding his arm after a pause.

Looking at her face, studying the tiny expressions he could see there, he sighed.

He was about to answer...

When Kiko appeared, standing over Miri's sun lounger, holding out a prescription bottle of pills. She shook it briefly to show them, then set it down on the table by Miri's side of their two sun loungers, where two bottles of water already sat.

Kiko had obviously brought those, too. They looked ice-cold, and were already bleeding condensation from the heat.

"You lovebirds need anything else?" Kiko teased. "I can have real drinks brought down. Kiessa said Miri should probably eat. She hasn't eaten anything since before she fell asleep, so it's been at least three or four hours. And all she had then was mangoes."

Pausing at their mutual silence, Kiko prodded,

"Do you want sandwiches? Waffles? Meat skewers? Fish tacos? A giant burrito filled with shrimp?"

Miri grimaced a bit at that last, giving Kiko serious side-eye.

Kiko laughed. "How about some avocado toast?"

Miri shook her head, clicking at the human, making something in Black's light react with a flicker of heat. He fought it back, but it only seemed to get worse as he watched his wife look up, smiling at his second.

"Are you guys really that bored?" she said. "Is Jax up there, smashing avocados?"

"No. He's dissecting robot eyes with Holo."

Miri burst out in a laugh. "Gross."

"Says the woman who popped those eyes out of the robot's cybernetic head with her thumbs." Kiko grimaced mockingly back. "Much grosser, doc. Much grosser."

"You're way too cheerful about it, in any case," Miri informed her.

"Weddings are always a reason to be cheerful," Kiko shot back.

She didn't see Miri flinch, but Black did. He saw his wife's eyes widen too, swallowing more of her already-pale face. Kiko was looking at Black, though.

"You know, I think Cowboy and Angel might get married with you guys?" she said, grinning at him. "He's trying to talk her into it right now, while he plies her with cocktails by the pool. A joint wedding. He's got a ring and everything."

Miri choked on the water she'd been using to swallow down two of the painkillers Kiko brought down. She spit some of the water up on the lounger, and kept coughing.

Black rubbed her back, frowning.

It wasn't really the reaction he'd been going for.

He looked up at Kiko, quirking an eyebrow. "I was just gearing up to ask my blushing bride if she wanted to do this tonight," he said, a faint warning in his voice. "Given she nearly got killed yesterday, I'm thinking we might need to postpone—"

But Kiko waved off his words, unimpressed.

"That's just a Tuesday for you guys," she scoffed. "We've been talking about security. Between who we have here now in terms of seers and humans, not to mention drones, and your pal Peter's security team, we're good. Safe as houses."

"Houses with homicidal robots someone is aiming at my wife," Black muttered.

Kiko laughed. "Exactly like that."

"Kiko," he said, exasperated. "She's wounded. She probably doesn't want—"

"Maybe you should ask me?" Miri said.

Black turned, only to find her quirking an eyebrow at him, watching the back and forth between him and Kiko with obvious amusement.

"Especially since this is the first I'm hearing about any of it," Miri added.

At that, Kiko flinched, glancing at Black.

"Seriously?" she said, sounding equal parts outraged and disbelieving. Leaning down, she smacked Black on the chest, making him jump in spite of himself. "What the fuck is wrong with you, boss?"

Black scowled at her. "Maybe it's because I'm surrounded by employees who won't leave me the fuck *alone* with her long enough to ask her a damned thing—"

"Oh, no," Kiko said, holding up a hand and shaking her head. "You asked me to come down here, boss. Just now."

"She's got you there," Miri informed him.

Black turned, staring at his wife.

The amusement in her eyes was warmer now. Studying the look there, he found himself relaxing marginally, in spite of himself.

"Go away," he told Kiko. "Let me talk to my damned wife. I'll let you know if the party's happening or not."

Kiko rolled her eyes at him, winking at Miri.

"What... *ever*," Kiko said, making the "loser" sign on her forehead in a pretty convincing imitation of a high school student, right before she flounced off.

Kiko didn't *flounce*.

Miri burst out in a laugh, as if she couldn't help herself.

She winced an instant later, still chuckling and smiling, even as her hand pressed lightly on her taped ribs.

Once Kiko was halfway up the dirt path back to the pool, Black looked at his wife.

She looked back at him, still smiling, even as she downed a few more swallows of water. He waited until she'd actually swallowed them that time before he spoke.

"It's up to you," he said finally, hearing the frustration in his own voice. "I've had it lined up for three days in a row now... and I've had to cancel it every time. We could wait and do something in San Francisco."

"You still haven't told me what the *what* is, Black," she said, her voice musing.

"A ceremony," he said, blunt. "You must know that by now. I was going to have a ceremony on the beach."

"What about the legions of reporters?" she said, still sounding mostly amused. "I thought you were going to do a giant, blowout event? *The party of the decade...* isn't that what you said? Wasn't this all supposed to be part of some huge publicity stunt you and Farraday cooked up? Cameras on us from all sides? Solidifying your reputation for eccentricity, and out-and-out weirdness... presumably because this will throw them off the scent of how much of a mutant, alien weirdo you *really* are?"

He shrugged.

Studying her eyes, he tried to decide if he should be offended by how funny she found this whole thing.

"I thought we could compromise," he said. "Have a small-ish bash in a high-profile place... like, say, here. At an opportune moment... like, say, when I'm still getting the stink eye from the military, and there are a bunch of people at the Pentagon who'd like to see me strung up. Peter's invited a number of our mutual friends to fly out. I figured there's already enough press hiding out at the hotel, aiming smartphones at us any chance they get, I wouldn't have to actually *invite* any journalists, per se. We could just let the story leak out."

"When did you plan this, exactly?" she said, still sounding faintly incredulous. "While I was jumping back and forth from the California Street building? Or before that?"

He shrugged, seer-fashion.

"Well. You like Hawaii." He cleared his throat. "You like the beach."

When she burst out in another laugh, his voice grew defensive.

"I had this planned before, you know... when we were just going to come here for vacation. I told most of the team. They were going to meet us out here. Surprise you. Kiko was in charge of all that, and getting all your friends here. Her and Angel. They picked out a cake and everything. They had the flowers picked out. Your dress..."

Miri laughed again, still sounding like she could barely believe it. "So is this happening tonight? Really?"

He felt his ears warm.

"Only if you want to." Clearing his throat, he said, "Honestly, I was just about to cancel it again. I didn't think you'd want to do it like this..." He motioned towards the bandages on her arms and chest. "I figured it could wait for San Francisco. We could do it on the beach there. Or go to Santa Cruz, do it at the beach house."

Seeing her open her mouth, about to speak, he cut her off.

"We should wait, doc," he said. "We should wait until we've confirmed they're not sending any more of those toy soldiers after you."

Muttering under his breath, he added,

"I'd at least like to know who sent the fucking things before we go nuts with a big public event. I thought if we could pinpoint who that is, you could pop over, grab him or her, put them in with the others."

Glancing at her, a faint worry in his voice, he said,

"We need to move all of them soon, doc. I talked to Manny about that again today. He and Yarli think we should pinpoint a site outside of the United States. He's got a few black sites in mind, things we've used before. South America, mostly. Also a few in Eastern Europe. Yarli's also setting up shell companies so we can purchase something, if none of the existing sites are suitable. In some ways, that would be ideal, if only because it would be harder to trace back to us. It would cost more to set up, of course, and likely take longer. We'd need to hire architects, put in medical facilities, a kitchen, not to mention staff it in some way, but—"

"Oh, no," Miri said, frowning, shaking her head, then her finger at him. "You're not changing the subject that easily—"

"About my private prison camp?" Black said, quirking an eyebrow.

She grunted. "Because that's a totally normal thing to do, Black." Pausing, she added, "We can't keep them forever. We need a long-term solution. A real one."

He scowled. "I know. You think I don't know that?"

"Have you thought of anything?"

"A few things," he admitted grudgingly. "One, really. But I'm not sure how I feel about it. I'm not sure how you'll feel about it, either." Pausing, he added, "Where's Charles, speaking of solutions to difficult problems?"

When she looked away, frowning, he prodded her with his light.

"Yarli said she couldn't find him in any of the cells," he added.

Looking at him in exasperation, she exhaled loudly. "You are impossible. I said you wouldn't derail me... and here you are. Derailing me."

"Where's Charles?" he said, studying her eyes, her lips. "Do you not want to tell me?"

"I took him... somewhere else."

"Somewhere else?" He frowned. "Wanna be more specific, doc?"

She frowned, folding her arms.

He winced when she did, feeling the sympathetic pain of her arms and ribs when she moved so abruptly without thinking.

He also felt a flicker of guilt off her light.

It was brief—so brief, she must have quashed it at once. It was still strong enough for him to feel it, and wince a second time.

"Doc?" he repeated.

She sighed in frustration, glaring at him.

"You know what I mean. I took him to another dimension. Somewhere else. He was the first one I took. Out of D.C., I mean. I was worried someone might try to rescue him before we could dismantle the rest of it. So I took him... somewhere else."

Black frowned, in spite of himself.

"Where?" he said, pointed.

When she didn't answer immediately, he found himself thinking about possibilities.

He snorted a laugh. It burst out of him before he could stop it.

"Did you take him to Revik?" he said, grinning. "Did you take him to Revik and Allie's house? Because I would fucking *pay* to see that. Hell, one lunch at the Dehgoies residence, with Uncle Charles seated between my cousin and that kid with the freaky stare... that would probably make my fucking year—"

"I didn't take him there," she said, exhaling. "I wouldn't do that to Allie. And Revik would probably throttle him." Frowning, she stared out at the ocean, her light eyes distant. "I took him somewhere else."

"Where?"

"I don't know," she admitted, giving him a sideways look.

"You don't know?"

"Not really," she said, pressing her lips together. "It's not like any of the other places have names. Allie and Revik's dimension is the only one where I spent any real time."

He felt a cloud of worry leave her light.

"Could you find it again?" he said, cautious.

After another pause, she nodded, glancing at him. "I've been there before."

"What was it like?"

Thinking about that, she winced.

For a second time, Black felt a curl of guilt leave his wife's living light.

"Charles won't like it," she confessed, that wince still visible in her eyes when she glanced at Black. "He won't like it at all."

Black opened his mouth again, about to press for more—

When a hard crackle came out of a speaker somewhere overhead.

Black looked up, feeling Miri do the same right next to him.

The sound was low at first.

It keened higher, growing louder as it rose, until it pierced through every other sound of the resort and beach.

It grew loud. Then it was deafeningly loud.

It was also shockingly familiar, even though Black hadn't heard one like it in years.

It was an air raid siren.

27

BROKEN TOYS

B lack didn't warn me.

I'd barely wrapped my head around the siren.

I'd barely made sense of it was... what the sound even meant.

Some part of my mind was thinking we were about to be hit by a tsunami, a giant wave, maybe from some monster earthquake from Japan or San Francisco.

...Then Black had me wrapped in his arms.

He picked me up off the sun lounger. He held me upright at first, then, gauging my face, he seemed to make up his mind.

Sorry, honey, he sent, his thoughts soft as silk, exuding apology, a tenderness that caught in my chest. *I'm so sorry.*

Bending down, he threw me into a fireman's carry before I could take another breath, much less decide why he was apologizing.

It hurt my ribs like fuck...

I let out a shocked, half-blind cry, grasping his back...

Then he got me situated, and the pain immediately lessened.

Then I was just hanging there.

After I managed to take a full breath, I realized he was being careful to hold me so that my ribs weren't hitting any of his bones or muscles at angles. If I pressed against him, gripping him more tightly from behind, I would hang more or less flat against his back.

Something about the compression, the inversion of my weight and organs, the pressure of my upper thighs against his muscular shoulder, still made me cry out in panic.

I clung to him tighter.

I felt him wince, worrying about me.

He didn't stop unholstering his gun.

Then he was running up the dirt path towards the pool area, gripping the gun in one hand, my legs in the other. He ran like a panther, frighteningly smooth, so graceful, I grimaced and clenched my jaws for jolts and slams that never came.

Even so, it wasn't comfortable.

It wasn't comfortable at all.

It still scared me.

I had visions of my ribs cracking and breaking as he ran, ripping into my lungs, into my other organs. I knew Black was terrified of that, too. In the same second, I realized I might actually be picking up a lot of those images and fears from him.

By then, he'd run, darted, and leapt through most of the pool area.

From where we were, what I could see where I hung behind his back, he was running, all-out, for the back doors of the resort.

He'd been silent that whole time.

His silence didn't fully sink in for me until he ran through the automatic doors, and into the lobby.

Voices immediately grew audible all around us, more than half of them worried, even panicked. Even so, without the full volume of the screaming air raid siren, it sounded and felt relatively quiet inside the building. I found myself looking around as Black continued to run, now making a beeline to the main elevator bank.

He slid to a stop, and I almost felt him considering the stairs, wondering which thing would be faster.

Tourists milled around us, also waiting for elevators, staring at us.

I could feel Black leaning towards taking the stairs—

When a loud ping signaled a set of elevator doors opening behind us.

Without waiting, he turned and brought me inside, despite the eight or nine tourists who crammed themselves into the elevator car with us.

Black ignored all of them, staring up at the numbers while I stared at his ass, fighting to catch my breath. By then, I could feel that he was talking to other people—likely groups of other people, likely via his headset as well as through the Barrier—and I didn't want to interrupt whatever he was doing.

The elevator seemed to stop on every floor.

Eventually, we were the only ones left on it.

The doors pinged a last time, and opened slowly to the foyer before our suite, one floor below the living apartments of Peter Yarrick.

Black brought me straight to the door, fumbled briefly with the key-card, then got me into the room.

He laid me on one side of the suite's living room couch so gently, I might have been made entirely of glass. The Fifties-style couch with its dark orange fabric was probably the most comfortable couch I'd ever sat on, but right now, it was difficult to navigate. The cushions sank under my weight, making me feel briefly trapped as I fought to assess our current situation.

I struggled to sit up, as soon as he got me down.

He held up a hand, cautioning me to take it easy, even as he clicked his fingers, pointing at a side table to my left.

I turned my head towards the driftwood and glass table, and saw my headset sitting there, right next to a seashell-covered lamp.

He must have brought it back from the hospital.

Reaching over awkwardly, wincing as I pressed a hand against my taped ribs, I scooped it up and fumbled to get it in my ear.

Once I had it in, I used the visual prompt to switch it on.

Immediately, sound seemed to explode in my ears.

"...I'm counting sixteen... no seventeen..." Angel's voice said, speaking loud over the sound of the air raid siren in the background. "Are you getting the drone feed?" she half-shouted. "Is it coming through?"

"I can see it," Black growled.

Black was already in motion, making his way swiftly to the largest of the suite's two walk-in closets. I watched him yank open the double-doors, enter the cavernous space and bend down to grab the two hard, wheeled cases Michelle and Ace put in there a day or so earlier.

Black began dragging them out, even as he continued to talk on the headset.

"How many drones do we have up?" he said. "All the footage I see is of the ocean. What about the land side?"

"We've got two over there," Cowboy cut in, sounding breathless, but not as loud as Angel. "Ace thinks they've got people moving to flank us inside the building, but nothing's come up on the screens yet. Soon as it does, feed'll show it with a new screen. Don't want to clutter your visuals until then."

Grimly, Cowboy added, "Looks like they dumped the whole lot of 'em into the ocean this time, boss. Jax says they got a bunch o' others sinking... captured on the scanners, that is. Ones that didn't make it to the shore at all."

"Is he able to hack any of those that aren't completely broken?" Black growled, still speaking via sub-vocals.

"Not yet." Jax's voice rose, sounding strangely pale, and equally grim. "Working on that now, boss."

"How the fuck did you see them, then?" Black said. "The ones that sank?"

"We've found an ID tag... of sorts," Holo said, before Jax could answer. "We caught the signal as they started to sink. It's in the eyes. Some kind of tracking signal. There's another one on the suits they wear, but the eye one seems tied to the specific unit. All of those we've got visuals on now are wearing the same kind of suit—"

"Where does the signal go? Do you know? Who's on the other end?"

"We don't know that yet, sir," Jax said.

"Have you fired on any of them? The functioning units?"

"Small arms only, sir." Kiko that time, sounding even more intense than Jax. "We did throw one grenade from a hide, slowed at least two of them down that way. But that was when they first came out of the water. It was an empty stretch of beach. Now that they're closer to the resort, there are too many civilians. They're moving fast. We're working to set up a perimeter, but—"

"Where the fuck is Peter's team?" Black snapped. "We need someone to evacuate the damned tourists. Most of them were still by the pool when I was down there. A lot of them are drunk as shit. At the very fucking *least,* they need to be brought inside the building. Get them locked in their damned rooms—"

"I've got Ace working on that—" Kiko began.

"Goddamn it," Black growled. "We *need* Ace. See if you can get Marshall and Keon on it. Get them to find someone else to do it... not one of ours."

"We tried." Mika that time, also sounding frustrated, and apologetic. "They weren't really... scary enough, boss."

"Then use a goddamned seer," Black snapped. "A few of you, partition your lights and push them the fuck out of there."

"But where, Black?" Angel said, her voice clear, firmer than the others, but obviously afraid. "You brought Miri inside the resort. If you put all the tourists in there, won't they just be between these damned cyborgs and—?"

Black realized where she was going halfway through.

"You're right," he said, cutting her off. "Mika, you heard her. Get them out of the resort. Push them to leave, but not towards the beach... and don't let them all call for transport, or they'll clog up the damned driveway."

Still thinking, he clenched his jaw.

"Have them walk," he said, decisive. "Have them put on shoes and walk out to the road. Get them from Kahala to Diamond

Head... push them to walk all the way to Waikiki. They can call a
damned ride service once they get a mile or so down the road. Tell
them there's a big fucking party in Waikiki. A happening. Tell
them some big star will be there."

"You want them to walk in their bathing suits, boss?" Mika
said, doubtful.

"Yes," Black snapped. "I want them to walk in their damned
bathing suits. Trust me, if a few of them are baring a bit of ass to
the traffic, they won't mind. Have them put on flip-flops, or whatever the hell is convenient and push them the fuck out. It'll keep
them alive, at least."

Already, I could feel the lights of at least three or four seers on
the line complying with Black's orders.

It was a strange, distant, but somehow mechanical feeling in
the space.

I watched as they partitioned their minds, clicking over some
part of their consciousness to slide into the human lights by the
pool, urging them to walk out of the resort, convincing them it
would be fun and cool to walk all the way to Waikiki Beach, where
apparently something exciting was happening.

The stories the different seers fed different humans swirled
around the Barrier over the resort—until, at some point, they
solidified into a single, coherent narrative.

I felt that instant; I felt the exact moment the many stories
became one.

I saw when a confused whirl of faces and events, of rich people
and celebrities, solidified into a consistent roster and a single location on Waikiki Beach.

I watched in a kind of awe as all the disparate whispers and
waves clicked into place, becoming a single wave, pushing all of
them more or less in the same direction.

Like it always did, the human susceptibility to this kind of
thing unnerved me.

It really made some humans feel like animals, like a mindless
herd of highly-suggestible, easily manipulated... well... sheep.

Since I still more often than not identified as human myself, even though I wasn't one really, watching it happen always made me feel queasy.

I'd spent most of my adult, professional life, trying to convince human beings they *weren't* powerless of their own existence.

Watching seers feed ideas directly into human minds, like they were impressionable children, not much smarter than gerbils really, seemed to call into question everything I'd ever been trained to believe as a psychologist.

At the same time, and as much as I'd always resented the idea, I'd known for a long time that humans were herd animals, at base.

No time to worry about that now, doc, Black murmured at me. *Feel bad for the state of human evolution after we come out of this not-dead.*

Should we jump? I asked him. *I could get us both out of here. Those robot things might fall back, if they can't find either of us.* Thinking about that, I added, *We could make sure they saw me go. You and me, we go out in the open, let them see me disappear—*

Black was shaking his head.

His thoughts turned grim.

You're assuming they'd stop, and not just blow the fucking place up and kill everyone on our team.

Staring off to one side, clearly thinking about that, he scowled.

I don't think these things are that bright, he admitted sourly. *Their processing systems strike me as primitive, based on what we've seen so far. They're more like weapons than people. I haven't seen a ton of critical thinking skills on display. It's possible they were human once, but their regular, organic intelligence was stripped in the process of whatever was done to them. I'm guessing they'll assume you must be somewhere near wherever they last saw you... and they'll just destroy everything in the area in the hopes of getting you.*

I frowned.

I'm tempted to have you jump, Black added. *Alone.*

When I stared at him in disbelief, he frowned back.

"You're injured, doc," he said out loud. "And they're not targeting any of us. We have a better chance of catching them by surprise if you aren't here. We can set up decoys, or even project a holographic version of you—"

"Or I could stay, and you could actually use *me* for that, since it's unlikely a hologram would be good enough to fool them," I cut in, annoyed.

When he immediately scowled, shaking his head and clicking at me, I cut him off.

"You know what I mean. I don't have to put myself in direct danger, but you could use me to set a real trap. Have me lead them into a kill box, if you can find a good location for something like that. Take out most of them in one go."

"Absolutely fucking not," he growled, glaring at me.

"Why not? You just said you'd do essentially the same thing, only with holograms—"

"I was *lying*," he growled louder, still glaring.

"Boss?" Cowboy's voice rose cautiously in the headset.

Black and I both flinched.

I don't know about Black, but I'd completely forgotten the rest of the team could hear us. Probably wasn't helping them much, in terms of group coordination.

Or confidence that their leaders knew what the hell they were doing.

"Boss?" Cowboy repeated, when neither of us spoke. "Looks like they know where the doc is, that you brought her into the resort. They're reconfiguring their team. Before, they were all convergin' on the beach, but now they're changing positions. Looks like they're movin' to surround the main resort building itself."

Black grimaced in my general direction, even as his words focused back on the team in his headset.

"Any idea how they're tracking her?" he said, still watching me.

"No." Jax that time, sounding distracted. "Unknown. But Cowboy is right. They definitely seem to know you're inside. They must have eyes on one or both of you... whether it's something seer-like, something vampire-like, or just old-fashioned tech, we can't tell yet. But they're getting ready to converge on the hotel—"

"Bionic eyes?" I muttered, pursing my lips. "Maybe they can just *see* farther than we can, even with the amplification in our headsets."

Black gave me a dark look, then focused back on the headset.

"What about weapons?" he said. "Do you have a list of what they're carrying yet? Is it just knives again, or—"

"No," Ace said, speaking up for the first time. "No, these are definitely better armed than those first two you saw. Main weapons seem to be M27s, firing as semi-automatics so far... but every unit we've seen appears to be carrying grenades, multiple sidearms, knives, and backpacks, presumably with ammo, but maybe also more toys. Drones seven and fourteen picked up two swords, worn over the back in scabbards. Kiessa also spotted one of those claw-like things Charles was developing, hanging from the belt of one of the soldiers they hit with explosives on the beach. Between the swords and the claw, looks like they're equipped for a potential vamp encounter, not just seer and human."

Thinking aloud, I muttered,

"If they're still clustered, and if they're carrying explosives, maybe I can thin out the herd a bit. I could jump in, pull the pins on a few grenades—"

"Miri, no." Black turned, cutting me off and gesturing angrily in seer. "Are you out of your fucking mind? *No,* goddamn it!"

There was a silence on the line.

Then Angel exhaled.

"So... what, then?" she said, sounding annoyed. "We close ranks around the building, try to keep them from coming inside?" Pausing meaningfully, she added, "Because you know that's a fool's wish at best, Quentin."

"You want to sacrifice *your* damned boyfriend?" Black snapped. "Go right ahead. On second thought... don't. I happen to like Cowboy."

There was another silence.

That time, Black exhaled.

"Ideas?" he said, his thoughts moderately subdued. "Come on. We're smarter than this. Do we pull out and go for drone strikes?" Muttering, he added, "Peter won't be thrilled if I fuck up his buildings too badly. But presumably the place is insured. At this point, I doubt he'll be inviting me back to one of his properties anytime soon, regardless..."

I snorted.

Black glanced over, giving me a cautious look.

The look wasn't quite an apology, but I could see him trying to gauge if he'd stepped over the line with me, yelling at me in front of the others the way he had.

Don't worry, I sent to him, rolling my eyes. *I'm sure they're used to you being a control freak weirdo by now.*

Before he could react, I held up a hand, going on out loud.

"What kind of weaponry are the drones equipped with?" I said. "Do they all have those mini-drones on them? The beetles? Those can be programmed to explode, too, correct?"

Feeling everyone's attention shift towards me, I added,

"I think Black's right. Drone strikes are probably our best bet, but I'm wondering if we can get more precise than just a blanket hit. Since we don't know exactly what gunshots will do, given how hard they were to kill before, what if we had those beetle drones land on their necks? Take them out that way? I know it means using up a lot of drones, but it might be worth it, just to keep casualties down, if nothing else. We know that they pretty much short out if you fuck up their heads enough..."

"What about the one that exploded?" Cowboy said, his voice skeptical. "We really want to be in the vicinity to test out what might set *that* off? If a bunch of 'em go off at once?"

All of us grew silent.

"Where are Yarrick's people?" I said then. "Has anyone warned them? Moved them off the beach? It'll be a bloodbath if they try to fight those things hand-to-hand."

"We told Marshall and that other one to stand down—" Kiko began.

"Where are they now?" I said.

"Inside the resort," Holo said. "Keon and Marshall are with us. I'm not sure about the rest of the security team. Okay, wait..." He paused, obviously listening to someone else. "Okay," Holo went on. "Marshall says he ordered them all inside. They're armed, but with sidearms only. They're on standby."

"Where's Peter?" Black asked, frowning. "Is he on site?"

Holo spoke up. "Marshall hasn't heard from Mr. Yarrick. Neither has Keon. They think he's probably not on site. He's usually pretty involved with security issues. Marshall says he definitely would have called by now, if he knew anything."

"I'm not feeling him," Black growled after a pause. "But he could be asleep. Send up one of his people. Have them check on the penthouse apartment. If he's here, I don't want him waking up to fucking explosions—"

"What do we tell him?" Holo said, his voice a frown. "I mean... what do we tell Marshall to tell him?"

Black hesitated, glancing at me.

Then he scowled.

"Fuck. Go up with him, Holo. Knock Peter out for now. I hate to do it, but I don't want him getting himself killed. And it's better if he's out of harm's way."

The silence deepened.

"Boss?" Cowboy said. "Those things are getting damned close—"

Black's jaw hardened.

I saw his irises slide out of focus as he went into the Barrier.

His vision clicked back, and his jaw firmed more.

"We have shooters on the roof?" he said. "They're in position?"

"Ayuh," Cowboy confirmed. "They've been on hold. Because of the possible exploding thing."

"Are most of the civilians out?" Black said.

"Ayuh. Well. The pool area is clear. There're a lot still inside the building. And on the driveway out front. Kiessa's pushin' 'em through now—"

"Good enough," Black cut in. "The rifle team is on point. Start whenever you've got a clean shot. Head shots. Through the eyes. Have the drones on standby. We try Miri's way next, if the rifles don't work."

"Got it, boss," Ace said.

I could tell Ace was already on the roof with the others from the ripple that went through his light. I caught a glimpse of him staring down a scope at the beach below the pool area. Mostly, what I felt on him was relief.

He was nervous as hell about how close those things were.

I couldn't say I blamed him, after my last encounter with one.

Then again, I'd been unarmed.

I hoped we were all overreacting.

I hoped this whole thing was over in a few minutes.

"Me and Miri'll be firing from the balcony up here," Black added, glancing at me and bending down to unlatch the long case at his feet. "Jax? See if you can penetrate their defenses enough to shut down the orders behind this. I know it's a long shot—"

"On it, boss," Jax said. "Do you want Holo to stay with me? You know, after the Yarrick thing? Or should he go outside after, help out with—"

"Let him stay with you for now. If you manage to hack these fucking things, it's all over. Send him out to Kiko on the ground floor only if you can't use him, or if Kiko gets swamped and needs the backup."

Black added in a growl,

"I don't want any humans approaching these things, not on the ground. That goes for our team, too. I saw the last one fight, through Miri... a regular human wouldn't have much of a chance in a hand-to-hand situation, so keep your distance, I mean it. Even if you manage by some miracle to hold your own, we can't afford to have them accidentally detonating."

Thinking about that, he scowled,

"And if anyone sees Narcisse, I want him knocked out and stashed somewhere, immediately. You don't have to be particularly gentle about it, either. Just call a seer... any seer... or hell, call me. That fucker is a loose cannon. The last thing we need is him calling for a military strike on the resort—"

"Got it," Angel said. "I think he went back to the base, boss. We'll keep an eye out, though, just in case—"

"You'd better," Black cut in darkly, lifting the rifle out of the padded case on the floor and propping it up on its stock on the carpet. "We get a bunch of F-35s raining hellfire down on this beach, and this really *will* be a fucking bloodbath."

28

THE CLOSET

As soon as he switched his headset to background, Black nudged me with his light.

When I looked up at him, he pointed at the second gun case on the floor.

"You helping out here, doc?" he said. "Or not?"

I didn't wait, but climbed up off the couch with an effort, using the side table and the couch's arm for balance. My arms and ribs hurt like hell as I unfolded my body, but once I was upright, my ribs stop complaining long enough for me to get a few full breaths.

I approached Black, keeping my expression calm with an effort, keeping the pain out of my light as much as I could so he wouldn't feel it.

I knew if he did, he was likely to order me to jump out of there at once.

Truthfully, despite how sore I was, I was weirdly relieved he was going to let me help him with this.

I wasn't a sharp-shooter, per se, but I wasn't bad.

Black grunted, giving me an annoyed look.

"Not bad," he muttered. "You're probably the third best gun on my team. And that includes the fucking snipers, doc. That includes me. And Dalejem."

At his mention of the green-eyed seer, Black flinched, visibly.

I pretended not to see it.

He motioned me towards the second case on the floor, avoiding my eyes now as he began pulling apart the rifle inside the black, hard-plastic case he'd already opened.

I knelt down next to the longer, chrome rifle case, unclasping the two buckle snaps and flipping up the cover.

A second rifle lay inside the dark-grey foam cutouts that made up the interior of the case, a Remington MSR precision sniper rifle.

I whistled, smiling at Black.

"I get the good gun, huh?"

"You get the *new* gun," he corrected, hefting the rifle he'd just finished pulling apart into components and reassembling back together.

He'd done it so quickly, I was both disturbed and impressed.

It was easy to forget these days... that used to be his job.

Killing people.

I watched as he tugged open a hidden compartment in the rifle case in front of him, and pulled out a box magazine. He checked that it was full before he slammed it into the bottom of the rifle's barrel.

Without waiting, he yanked back on the bolt, chambering the first cartridge.

Glancing at me only then, he aimed a quirked eyebrow and pursed lips in my general direction.

"You okay with that gun, doc?" he said. "You could use mine, if you'd rather."

I saw now that he held a British model, a L115A3.

It was different from the last sniper rifle I'd seen him use, in Thailand.

This one looked a bit more beaten up, like it'd seen a lot more use.

I knew the L115A3 had a comparable range to the Remington I

held. I could also tell it was the gun he was a lot more familiar with.

"No," I said. "This one's fine. I'm just surprised. I would have guessed you'd be more likely to go for the American gun. Isn't that more your thing, Army boy?"

Grunting, he finished loading two more box cartridges with .338 Lapua Magnum cartridges, setting them on top of the foam cutouts in the gun case.

"American sniper guns were shit until recently," he remarked, his hands and fingers still agilely loading magazines. "And the Chinese guns are weird. Not intuitive. Not for me, anyway."

He rose to his feet as he spoke, walking for the closet.

He came out what felt like a bare handful of seconds later, wearing an armored shirt over black pants that were probably armored, as well.

He was carrying two armored vests.

He tossed one to me, his mouth still curled in that half-frown.

"Put it on, doc," he said, unnecessarily, his voice annoyed. "That's not a request. In fact, put on an armored shirt, first. If you don't mind."

I rolled my eyes, but rose obediently to my feet, setting down the Remington before I walked to the closet myself.

Walking into the dim space, I rifled through the military duffle that had mysteriously appeared on the floor, sometime in the last forty-eight hours.

Inside, I found a pile of armored clothes, as well as gun-grip and knuckle-protecting fighting gloves, two electric extendible batons, a few cases of colored tranquilizer darts—probably vamp caliber, knowing Black—assorted upper body and side holsters, an ankle holster, sized for Black, and an extendible baton without the electric charge.

I was still going through it when gunfire erupted from outside, echoing through the suite.

It was deafening, loud enough to make me jump.

The rifle team on the roof.

They must have gotten visual contact, not just drone feed.

That probably meant the robot soldiers had reached the pool area.

I dug through the bag with more purpose.

Finding a shirt my size, I tugged it over my head, twisting it around over my T-shirt, wincing when it rubbed against my bandages on my arms and chest.

I fought to keep the pain out of my light, knowing Black would feel that, too.

Once the shirt was on, it felt good though, on my taped ribs. The added compression was strangely reassuring.

After a bare pause, I decided to put on pants, too.

The gunfire was growing more intense outside.

No explosions yet, but when I partitioned my light, looking at the view through Ace and Michelle's eyes, I didn't see any fallen soldiers, either.

I didn't stop looking through the eyes of the human rifle team as I shucked off the loose shorts I'd worn and slept in all day. I finally saw one of the soldiers go down, falling into the pool when Ace got him through first one eye, then the other.

Still watching through his eyes, I tugged on a pair of armored pants. I immediately wondered if it was a mistake when I realized how hot they would be in this weather.

Fuck it.

If my being fully clothed calmed Black down, it would be worth it.

His mutters about my gun prowess aside, I strongly suspected he only wanted me to shoot with him to decrease the chance I would jump out in the midst of our tin soldiers, try to detonate some of the explosives they were carrying.

Knowing him, he was probably worried I still harbored some back-pocket plan to try that, if our other plans didn't work.

I still thought it wasn't a *terrible* plan.

Well, providing I did it in a way that caught them by surprise.

You're wrong, Black sent to my mind. *It's a terrible fucking plan, Miri. And would you hurry the fuck up? I need you to—*

His thoughts cut off strangely, causing me to frown.

I finished pulling on the pants, doing up the front zipper and tugging the armored shirt out over the waist band.

Only then did I glance towards the closet doors.

I saw Black walking towards me when I did.

He wasn't looking at me, but in the direction of the front door of the suite.

The gunfire made his motions, his stare, strangely silent.

I saw his mouth moving.

I realized he was talking to someone standing there.

I just hadn't heard him, with the gunfire going on outside the window.

I stared in disbelief as he shut the closet doors on me, still not looking at me. When the doors snapped all the way shut, I was left in near-total darkness.

Honey? I sent, straightening. *Something you want to tell me—?*

Don't make a fucking sound, he sent.

I froze.

I stood there, my heart thumping in my chest, fighting panic. I couldn't decide what to do. Anything I did, even just talking to him with my mind, even extending my light, had the potential of getting him killed, depending on what was on the other side of that door.

Black's mind rose back in mine.

Miri, he sent. *It's Peter.*

There was a silence.

In it, I puzzled over his words.

Peter? Why the fuck would Peter merit me hiding in the closet in the dark?

I was trying to decide if I should ask, when Black's mind rose again.

His thoughts felt distant, strangely detached.

It felt like he was doing a dozen other things with his mind and light while he was speaking to me.

He's got six of those soldiers with him, he sent, his thoughts entirely stripped. *I can't feel him at all. I can't push him. I can't reach Holo, who I sent up to look for him. And he wants to know where you are, Miri.*

Black paused, a bare breath.

You need to go, he sent. *Now.*

Realizing what he was saying, even as the pieces fell together in my mind, I receded deeper into the closet, looking around as I tried to decide what to do.

I couldn't jump with a weapon.

Everything that wasn't part of my body got left behind, including my clothes.

That meant nothing in here, nothing in the canvas bag, would help me help Black. I could try to get behind them, surprise them, but that wouldn't do much either, not against six of them, not if Black and I had no way to push Peter into calling them off.

I'd just get both of us killed.

I could jump out, get help, jump back.

That might be my best bet.

But then, Black would have told the others already, via his headset, and via the Barrier.

Clearly, if he'd been looking for Holo, he had access to the Barrier still.

So they weren't blocking his light. That meant Black likely had help on the way already, even if it was just a set of drones.

So what could I do, exactly?

I knew what Black wanted me to do.

I could feel it, even before he said it outright. I knew the only reason he hadn't said it more than once, shouted it, threatened me, made me agree to it in some way that satisfied him, was that his hands were full with whatever was happening on the other side of those doors.

I knew my husband.

He probably wanted me to jump to San Francisco at this point.

Looking up, I gauged the shelves, the ceiling, the racks only a quarter filled with clothes. The closet was mostly empty, so there wasn't much point in trying to hide.

Staring up, I fought with what to do.

Black was probably right.

I should leave.

Staring around the insides of the dark closet, I felt every part of my being protest at the thought. I knew it was probably the right thing, the only thing that would really help Black... but I couldn't make myself do it.

I stood there, instead.

I stood there, paralyzed, fighting to make myself do what I needed to do.

29

ROBOT ARMIES

You're wrong, Black sent to his wife's mind, frowning in spite of himself. *It's a terrible fucking plan, Miri. And would you hurry the fuck up? I need you to—*

The sound of the door to the suite opening cut off his thoughts.

He turned.

He'd already been walking towards the closet.

He'd made up his mind he wanted more magazines by him on the balcony, and decided to go in there to see what the hell his wife was doing, what was taking her so long.

He was halfway to the closet doors when the door to the suite opened and seven figures filed into the room.

They moved so calmly, it took Black a fraction of a second to comprehend what he was looking at, what it meant. His eyes swept over the strangely uniform line of blank faces, noting the six unfamiliar men who entered the suite after his friend.

The men walking behind Peter Yarrick wore black, armored suits, what looked almost like scuba suits, but weren't. Their jointed, armored outfits hugged uniformly muscular bodies, covering them from their boots up to their necks. The same material covered their arms down to their wrists, meeting their hands, which were dressed in fitted combat gloves.

Noting the strange uniformity of even their features, the cold blue tint of their eyes, Black kept the reaction off his face with an effort.

He immediately tried to get into Yarrick's living light.

He tried to push his mind.

When he couldn't do that, he tried to push the minds of the six soldiers.

In every instance, he hit up against a blank wall.

It surprised him less with the soldiers than it did with Peter.

He went back to Peter, focusing more intently, trying to sense what was keeping him out of the human's light. He felt a kind of force-field around Peter's whole head, seemingly emanating from around his neck, almost like the human wore an invisible sight-restraint collar.

Black tried to get past it a few more times, in quick succession.

He couldn't.

He pinged Yarli, sending her a snapshot of what he felt around Peter's neck.

Before Yarli could react, Black clicked back, focusing on Yarrick's face.

Barely two seconds had passed.

Black hadn't stopped walked towards the closet doors.

"Did they tell you what's going on?" he asked his old friend.

He spoke louder than usual, so Yarrick would hear him over the gunfire through the open balcony doors. He continued moving with deliberate strides, casually, his eyes still on Yarrick's as he made his way across the beige carpet on booted feet.

"I sent a few of my people up to fill you in," he went on, still speaking loudly. "I didn't want to alarm you, but it appears we have a situation here. I think my people can handle it... but we've called in the military for assistance, in case we can't. We already took steps to evacuate most of your guests."

Still moving deliberately, excruciatingly slowly from his own perspective, Black shut the closet doors.

Feeling Miri react, he sent to her without thought.

Don't make a fucking sound.

He used only a fraction of his mind and light.

Without a pause, without changing expression, he turned easily on his heel.

Still focusing his eyes on Peter, he walked back to the gun cases open on the carpet, mirroring his slow, casual pace of before.

"I'm glad you're here," Black added, his voice just as calm.

He made it slightly louder now that he stood closer to the balcony doors.

"I'm glad you brought your security team, too. I have an extra rifle here." He motioned towards the Remington, which sat on top of its chrome case. "I could use the help. If any of your guys have sniper training—"

"Where's the doctor?" Yarrick spoke loudly too, but Black reacted more to the tone. The human's voice vibrated with angry impatience. "Where's your wife, Black?"

Black pinged Holo.

Silence.

Using a sub-vocal control, he turned the headset on, so everything happening in here would be audible to the rest of the team.

He had to hope at least a few of them would be listening in.

Given what was going on outside, he knew they'd be distracted, but hopefully someone would hear him and Peter talking, and they'd catch on to what was happening. He had to hope at least one of them, Angel maybe, would pick up that he needed help.

He didn't dare risk the sub-vocals.

There was a good chance Peter would notice.

Black continued to stare down at the gun cases as he thought and did all of it, his face blank, as if he hadn't heard Yarrick speak.

He could feel Miri's panic from behind the closet doors.

Realizing he still hadn't told her a damned thing, he bit his tongue.

Miri, he sent. *It's Peter.*

He felt her fear shift, still there, but now colored by puzzlement.

Black walked to the balcony and closed the glass doors, muting some of the gunfire, and buying himself a few seconds. His mind continued to churn around and past hers, fighting through options, seeking a plan, any plan.

In the middle of that, he managed to send her a more detailed message.

He still dared use only the barest fraction of his mind to do it.

Mind-partitions slowed seers down in all of the requisite "parts." They slowed down reaction times, reflexes, ability to concentrate, mental agility.

He couldn't afford to lose anything in reaction times now.

He couldn't afford to lose even a fraction of a fraction of a second, not if Peter's soldier boys decided to attack.

He's got six of those soldiers with him, he sent to his wife, watching the soldiers in the reflection of the glass doors. *I can't feel him at all. I can't push him. I can't reach Holo, who I sent up to look for him. And he wants to know where you are, Miri.*

Black paused, taking a breath.

You need to go. Now.

He didn't wait for her to respond.

He couldn't afford that distraction, either.

He swiveled his eyes back to his old friend.

Through all of it, the bulk of his mind remained focused on the six men in black armored suits who stood between him and the suite's front door.

He hoped like fuck Miri had already jumped.

He hoped she'd jumped, and filled the others in.

"Where is she, Black?" Peter repeated, his voice sharp, if less loud with the balcony doors closed. "Where is your wife?"

Black refocused on Peter's face, making his expression puzzled.

"I sent her out of here, Peter," he said. "After what happened, are you surprised? I had her rest up while we got the plane ready and fueled. Once this started, I had two of my people bring her out to the airport." Checking his watch, he added, "She's probably over the Pacific by now. I told them not to wait—"

"Bullshit," Yarrick snapped.

His strangely young-looking face twisted into a scowl. If anything, he looked younger now than he ever did, his tall, gangly, tech-guy body still dressed in jeans, a salmon-colored T-shirt, and matching name-brand running shoes.

"You were seen bringing her inside this building," Peter said. "That was less than twenty minutes ago, Black."

Black frowned, making his voice more confused.

"Peter, calm down. Miri's fine. I put her in a car—"

"You carried her into the goddamned *elevator*," Yarrick cut in, his expression twisting even more. "You brought her up here. To this floor. Where is she?"

He snapped his fingers, motioning to the soldiers standing behind him.

"Check the bathroom," he told them. "Check the back bedroom when you're done."

Keeping the puzzled expression on his face, Black watched two of the robot-soldiers peel off. They walked past him, eerily close, stepping with an uncanny-valley kind of uniformity towards the largest of the suite's two bathrooms.

Black watched in the mirror over the suite's fireplace as they opened the bathroom door. He saw them walk past the double-sink counter, open the shower door, look in the jacuzzi tub. Then they started opening cabinet and closet doors.

Miri. Black's mind whispered towards his wife. *Are you gone? They're starting to search the apartment. You need to get the fuck out of here. I already sent Yarli the specs. Tell them what's happening. I can't afford to split my consciousness right now.*

Silence.

I'll be okay, Black added. *It's you he wants. You need to go. I'll stall him. Tell the others what's happening. Tell them not to get me killed.*

Again, only silence echoed back.

Was she jumping right now?

Had she already left?

Black continued to track the robot-soldiers in the mirror out of the corner of his eyes, even as he returned his primary focus to Peter.

"What's going on, Pete?" Black said, letting his voice grow a faint edge. "Why are you so hung up on the location of my wife? You must know why I don't want her whereabouts to be common knowledge right now. I'm pretty sure someone has a hit out on her. Given what's happening outside, I would think it would be obvious—"

"Cut the shit, Black," Yarrick snapped. "Your 'dumb guy' routine is even more tired than your pathetic attempts to pretend you're nothing but a rich, drunk playboy. Although it's cute you have your wife spreading those lies about you now—"

"What do you want with her?" Black's voice lost the last of its friendliness. "Are you going to tell me? Or do I have to get impolite?"

Yarrick let out a disbelieving laugh.

Reaching into his jacket, he pulled out a Beretta M9, pointing it at Black's head.

Black took a step back.

He put his hands up slowly, frowning.

"Peter. What's with the gun—"

"Take out the earpiece, Black," Peter snapped. "Now. Throw it to me."

Black hesitated a bare second.

Yarrick clicked off the safety, aiming more pointedly between Black's eyes.

"Don't make me kill you, Quentin," he warned. "I will. Believe me... I will. I'll kill you and your wife. But I'm still hoping it doesn't have to go down like that."

Lowering one hand slowly, palm facing forward, Black reached into his ear, pulling out the earpiece without switching it off. He tossed it to Peter. The human caught it, one-handed. He handed it to one of his toy soldiers, without taking his eyes off Black.

"Destroy it," Yarrick told the soldier, raising the gun back to aim at Black's head. "I'm sure he's got someone picking up every word we say right now."

"Peter," Black said, his hands still up. "What the fuck is this? What is it you think I've done, exactly?"

"Done?" Peter smirked. "You're kidding, right?"

Black grimaced when the robot soldier closest to Peter crushed his headset in one fist. The soldier continued to stand there, expressionless, grinding his fingers together so that the broken pieces fell on the carpet.

Glaring at Peter, Black growled, "That was an expensive fucking toy."

"I'm sure you can afford a new one," Peter sneered.

"What do you want? Are you going to tell me? And what does any of this have to do with my wife?"

"Gee, I don't know... pal. What could I possibly want with you?" Yarrick's voice grew colder as he aimed the gun. "What could I *possibly* want with your wife?"

When Black didn't answer, the human raised his voice.

"I know what you *are*, Black." Peter's mouth twisted in another humorless smile. "I've known for months. Hell... everyone knows. Everyone in the Pentagon. Everyone with a security clearance in the White House. Probably ninety percent of the defense contractors who've had contracts picked up in the last twelve months. Everyone who's been helping to rid the whole damned establishment of your kind—"

"My *kind?*" Black frowned. "What the fuck am I supposed to be, exactly?"

"Don't even go there with me, Black," Peter warned. "I know, okay? I've seen the specimens. I've seen the lab reports. I know everything."

At Black's silence, Yarrick rearranged his grip on the gun, keeping it aimed at Black's face.

"You're not human," he sneered. "And you're not the only one."

At Black's silence, Yarrick shook his head.

He gave Black another of those humorless smirks.

"Did you really think you would keep it a secret forever? When you never fucking *age?* When weird, unexplained shit just 'happens' around you, all the damned time? We used to joke about you being a vampire, you know. Even back when I first met you, people would talk about how weird it was, that you still looked like this—"

"You want to kill me because I have good genes?" Black snorted. "That's new. You want to shoot my dermatologist, too? They deserve at least part of the credit—"

"Cut the shit," Yarrick snapped.

Still glaring at Black, the human demanded,

"You think no one saw those files after Holmes died? There were *photos,* Black. I saw the negatives, so I know they weren't doctored. You were in the Vietnam War, for fuck's sake. You were in the *Korean* War. And you looked exactly the same as you do now."

Black's gaze narrowed.

He stared at the other male, all pretense of confusion gone.

"What do you want, Peter?"

"I want to know where the rest of your alien pals are. I want to know what you did to Charles Vasiliev... who was actually helping us *address* this issue. Finally." Clenching his jaw, Peter snapped, "We want him back. Today. Now. In pristine condition."

"Charles?" Black smiled, in spite of himself. "All this bluster and outrage is over *Charles?* Because you think Charles was *helping* you protect the sanctity of the human race? Jesus Christ. You really don't have a clue, do you?"

Peter's jaw hardened more.

"Of course he's helping us," the tech mogul snapped. "He's the one who opened our eyes to the threat. He helped us learn how to spot creatures like you. He taught us how to kill your kind... head and heart, right? He showed us how your kind already infiltrated all levels of our government... how your species was the *real* Deep State. He talked the President into building that wall to keep your kind out. He gave us specimens to study, samples of your venom. He taught us about your strengths, your weaknesses. He told us we needed an army to fight creatures like you, that you'd destroy our whole race, if we didn't—"

But Black's jaw had dropped.

"Vampires." Black stared at him. "You think I'm a fucking *vampire*, Peter?"

Yarrick scowled. "That's the fairytale name for them. We know the truth now. We know you're a separate species—"

"You can say that again," Black said, his voice still holding that disbelief. "Did Charles happen to mention he's the same species I am? Or that he fought in the Vietnam War, too? Only for *Spetsnaz,* instead of the United States Army, like me? Or did he leave that out of your little gatherings of the stupidest conspiracy theory ever?"

"Bullshit." Peter glared at him. "You're reaching, Black."

Black laughed.

He knew it wasn't particularly smart, not at that moment.

He couldn't help it.

He lowered his hands, at least until Peter took a step towards him, brandishing the gun.

Black raised his hands again slowly, still smiling.

"Fuck," he said, clicking under his breath. "Charles really did a number on you and your whole 'in the know' posse. I've got to give him credit. Telling you idiots that every seer who opposed him was actually a vampire... that's brilliant. Genius, really."

"Where. Is. He?" Peter said through gritted teeth. "We know you have him. I don't know how your wife got to him, or exactly how she got him out of the building... but we know she did it. I'm sure she brought him straight to you."

When Black didn't answer, the anger in the human's eyes grew.

Taking a step deeper into the room, Yarrick glared at Black, his pale hands clenched around the gun.

"Bring him back here," Peter snapped. "Now!"

"And here I was, thinking it would be other seers coming for him. Not stupid humans who got suckered into Charles' dumb cult—"

"Bring him back here!" Peter said, louder. "Now!"

Black gave him a flat look. "No."

"No? What did your wife do to him, Black?"

When Black didn't answer, the human scowled, pressing his lips together as he glanced towards the robot soldiers in the other room.

"Do you want me to spray your damned brains all over this wall?"

"I couldn't bring him to you, even if I wanted to," Black returned mildly, his eyes level. "And I don't want to," he added.

"Could your wife?" Yarrick snapped. "Could *she* bring him to us?"

When Black didn't answer, the human raised his voice.

"We know about the teleportation device, Black," he snapped.

Black blinked.

Then a smile grew over his face.

"Teleportation?" He smirked. "I guess you think I can turn into a dragon, too?"

Peter rolled his eyes at him, clenching his jaw as he re-aimed the gun.

"Don't be stupid," he snapped.

"But you think I can teleport? How is that any less fucking crazy than—"

"I didn't say *you*," Peter sneered. "I said your wife."

Black laughed. "And my wife being able to do it... instead of me... that's less crazy *how*, exactly?"

When Black continued to smirk, the human rolled his eyes.

"Black, I saw it. I *saw* the surveillance. It came from a system my people designed, so I know it wasn't tampered with. That dragon shit was all a big, bullshit lightshow to scare the hell out of our troops at the border... and, knowing you, likely to distract us away from the *real* tech you've got. Either way, don't talk to me like I'm a child. I'm not Joe Public. You can't scare me with your stupid pyrotechnics..."

When Black shook his head, that faint smile on his lips, Peter raised his voice.

"I don't know how you got the tech, or *where* you got it, but we want it. Stop playing games and give it to us... now... and we won't kill you or Dr. Fox. Since I haven't been able to find it on you, or anywhere in your room, I have to assume the device operates as some kind of implant. Given what we saw on surveillance at seven different government facilities, not to mention the Pentagon... Dr. Fox is the only one wearing it."

Black continued to stare flatly at the human, his expression unmoving.

Peter clenched his jaw when the silence stretched.

After a few seconds more, he clearly couldn't take it anymore.

"We got her on surveillance in at least *three* of those sites in under an hour, Black," he snapped, waving a hand angrily. "Some of those sites were hundreds of miles apart. I know you wouldn't have sent her, not if you could have taken care of it yourself. Hell, from what I've seen of the two of you, you wouldn't have sent her if there was even *one other person* who could have gone in her stead."

Yarrick's mouth twisted back in that furious scowl.

"It *has* to be her. She's the only one you gave the tech to. God knows why. To keep her safe? For some biological reason, because her body was the only one that didn't reject it? Because you thought no one would suspect her? Whatever your reasons, I know she's behind it, Quentin. I know she's the one who disappeared all those people. I know she's the one who knows where Charles Vasiliev is."

Peter added angrily under his breath,

"Then those *idiots* sent all those damned assassins here... nearly killing her before we could figure out how she was doing it, much less where you've got Charles."

Black's eyes flickered to the mirror.

The two soldiers had just finished going through the suite's master bedroom and were re-entering the living room area.

Noticing the direction of Black's stare, Peter glanced at the mirror, frowning, then turned towards the two soldiers entering the room.

"Check the other bedroom," he snapped at them. "Look under all the beds, in all the cabinets and closets. Check everything. Knowing this fucker, he's built a hidden compartment somewhere in here... so use infrared on the walls."

Black felt his muscles tense.

He had no idea whether Miri was still in the closet or not, or if she could hear any of this, but he hoped like fuck she jumped before they opened that door.

And before they saw her with their infrared, robot eyes.

If she was still in there, he knew she wouldn't just be standing there, doing nothing. She'd probably be loading up on grenades, knowing her.

He hoped like fuck she'd jumped.

He really, really hoped she'd jumped.

At the very least, he hoped she'd jumped to another part of the apartment when she heard them approach.

He knew she wouldn't want to leave him.

He knew, because there was no way in hell he would leave her.

At the thought, a hard pain grew in his chest.

Why hadn't he taken her out of here, like he'd told Peter just now?

It was a useless thought now, though.

He gave Peter a half-smile, one stripped of humor.

"You think my wife teleports?" Black grunted.

"I know she does, Black."

"And you're searching for her here? In this suite? With your robotic morons?" Black grunted another half-laugh. "And you say I'm the stupid one?"

"She wouldn't leave you," Yarrick said, angry. "And we already know, when she jumps, she can take others with her."

Yarrick pointed at the second rifle on the chrome case.

"I know that was for her... not some 'extra person' you were hoping I would bring. So, I'm thinking she can't jump right now. Maybe she got too injured on the beach yesterday. Maybe the device she uses got damaged in the fight with our Cyber-Guard..."

"Cyber-Guard," Black muttered. "Jesus Christ."

Yarrick talked over him.

"...Maybe the teleportation device needs to recharge," he said, his voice warning. "Whatever the reason, she clearly couldn't jump the two of you out of here. Which tells me she's not far. You probably just hid her, hoping we wouldn't look—"

"How do you control them, Peter?" Black cut in, blunt.

His brow furrowed as he motioned with a dismissive flick of his fingers at the soldiers. Fighting to ignore the gun aimed at his head, he continued to watch the two soldiers going through the hallway closet in his peripheral vision.

"These 'Cyber-Guards' of yours," Black said. "...oh, and *really* fucking stupid name, by the way... how do you control them? Do you have some kind of remote control you use to tell them what to do? Who to kill, or—"

"I have my ways."

"Those ways aren't exactly foolproof though, are they?" Black said, quirking an eyebrow. "If you didn't send those first two, then how are you—"

"I fucking *created* them," Yarrick snapped. "Of course I can control them. Who do you think detonated that one on the beach, before that idiot, Narcisse, or any of the other drones at USPACOM could get their hands on it? I would have blown the other one up, too, if you hadn't taken out its fucking eyes."

Black sent a hard ping to Jax.

Get away from those fucking robot eyes, he sent. *Now. Put them in a bomb-proof container... or, better yet, get rid of the fucking things. Throw them in the ocean, if you have to. The explosives are in the eyes. He put them in the eyes—*

Who? Jax sent.

Yarrick.

Feeling bewilderment on the East Indian seer, Black cut off the thoughts he felt forming in the other's mind.

Do you have anyone coming to help me? he snapped. *Or should I draw you a fucking map? Leave a trail of breadcrumbs spelling out "HELP ME"?*

Boss, we're working on it. They cut off the elevators. Most of our team is trapped and can't get inside the resort at all—

Send a fucking drone up here, to the west-facing balcony.

Boss. Your wife said—

Tell Miri to get the fuck out of here, Black sent angrily. *Now. If you're in contact with her, tell her to jump back to the Raptor's Nest. Yarrick's got six of his tin soldiers in the suite, and they're looking for her. I'd rather if they didn't find her.*

He felt Jax nodding vigorously.

We know. We're on it, boss. Miri said—

But Black couldn't afford to get distracted by this, either. Not now.

He clicked out before Jax finished, fighting to focus back on the room, to re-center himself in the present.

Yarrick was still talking.

"—I've been working under contract for the Pentagon for almost five years, Black. If you were still in the game the way you used to be, you would know that—"

"Let me guess," Black growled. "Charles Andrey Vasiliev. He ran the contracting."

Peter's brow furrowed.

"I don't know what you think you know about Charles," he snapped, now sounding offended. "But he's been a damned *hero* to the human race. He's the one who fast-tracked this whole project, to produce stronger soldiers to fight your kind."

Pride entered Yarrick's voice when he added,

"They had a bidding war," he said. "We beat out four other top-tier research teams on repeatable, reliable results... including Silver Industries, and I was told they had some pretty exciting things happening, using some new form of synthesized 'smart blood' to power their units." His pride grew more audible. "But we were the only ones to successfully fuse machines with our human subjects."

"And what a favor you did to them, too, Peter," Black said, frowning at the blank faces standing behind Yarrick. "I'm sure this would totally pass Geneva Convention muster. Illegal experimentation on 'volunteer' soldiers you more or less lobotomized in the process of grafting low-tech machines all over their various body parts—"

"The survival of our *race* depended on it!" Yarrick snapped. "The Geneva Convention isn't worth *shit* when you're talking about species annihilation. A little bit of collateral damage is to be expected."

"Cool for them, I guess?" Black grunted, half in anger, half in disbelief. Shaking his head, he stared at the black-clad, flat-faced thugs standing behind Yarrick. "Yeah. Bang up job, Dr. Frankenstein. Really instills confidence in the military-industrial complex, looking at your little creations there—"

"Fuck off, Black." Yarrick glared at him. "Don't get morally righteous with me. I know what you are. I know what you've done... what your little 'securities' firm has done in the name of God and country over the years. Even if you were human, your hypocrisy would be positively staggering."

Exhaling angrily as he looked at the four soldiers standing behind him, Yarrick added,

"Anyway, we're only in the prototype stage. The process will improve. The long-term damage will be less, once we perfect the fusion methodology. We were up against the clock. Charles had his own people doing research inside the Pentagon, too—"

"No doubt," Black grunted. "Knowing him, he probably killed a few dozen, if not a few thousand subjects all on his own. But I guess you're cool with that, too. Since he's such a 'friend' to humanity, and all—"

"You don't know what the hell you're talking about with him!"

Yarrick snapped, raising his voice. "Your bullshit psychological tactics aren't going to work on me, Black."

"Because you're such a genius," Black grunted. "Got it." Pausing, he added, "Tell me something, Peter. How do you block the mental stuff? Charles must have told you. We tricky 'vampires' can also read minds. Right?"

Yarrick smirked at him, tapping the back of his neck.

"Implant."

Black nodded, again fighting a perverse desire to laugh. "Brilliant. Let me guess. Charles gave it to you?"

Yarrick's eyes hardened. "Meaning what?"

"Meaning... he'd want to be able to switch it off every now and then. An implant-generated sight-restraint field's not much use if he can't switch it off to push your mind when *he* wants to. After all, how else is he going to get you to believe all this idiotic crap?"

"You really must think I'm an idiot, that I'd fall for these mind-games—"

"Oh, you're an idiot all right," Black affirmed. "It's a little depressing, honestly."

Peter raised the gun, glaring furiously into Black's face.

"Last time I'm asking, Black." His voice grew cold. "Hand her over. Now. And you'll both live." He firmed his lips, still aiming the gun at Black's face. "That, or I kill you now and look for her on my own."

Looking into the deranged face of his ex-friend, Black believed him.

Clearly, Peter was all-in on the Charles crazy-train.

Thinking about that, Black fought not to make another crack.

He tried to ignore the noises coming from behind him as the robot-soldiers finished tossing the connected, smaller bedroom. He knew they'd check this room next, probably starting with the closet.

Miri, he growled into the space. *They're coming. And I can't stall him much longer.*

He prayed she wasn't still in there.

His fingers began slowly and carefully moving towards the gun he wore at the small of his back, under the vest—

Black, don't. Miri's voice whispered in his. *It's all right.*

Is it? Black's mind growled back. *Are you still in that goddamned closet?*

Yes.

Jump... now, damn it! What are you still doing in there?

It's fine, she sent calmly. *I'm talking to Coreq.*

As her words sank in, he fought a reaction off his face.

We may have to use him, she added, her voice eerily calm. *Is that okay?*

Feeling her meaning, he felt most of the blood drain from his face.

30

IN HARM'S WAY

Angel stared at the drone footage, holding her breath.

She fought not to blink, not wanting to miss even a fraction of a second as she strained to see through the balcony window into Black and Miri's suite.

They were on the roof.

Most of their team was up here now.

They were more or less in a standoff with Yarrick's cybernetic soldiers.

Those soldiers had the whole resort covered now, at least on the ground floor. The elevators were all shut down.

All the exits were blocked, keeping them inside.

Well, unless they decided to rappel down the walls.

A majority of their fighters were up here now.

Everyone, really, apart from a few who were trapped in various rooms inside the resort, and a handful with Dex and Travis in a hide over the beach, too far away to help them much. They were all in a holding pattern, waiting for orders on what to do next. They'd managed to take out maybe a half-dozen of the robots in total, with only one of them exploding, taking out part of one of the poolside bars.

Since the rest of the robot-soldiers made their way inside the resort, they'd been forced to wait. It was that or make a suicide rush down the fire escapes to the lobby level.

Yarli ordered them to wait.

So did Dex and Mika, who were more or less running things here on Oahu.

"We've definitely lost all contact with his earpiece," Cowboy said grimly.

He'd just returned from where he'd been talking with Mika, Kiessa, Ace, and Michelle. Bending his knees, Cowboy got down on the rooftop deck beside her, leaning on the stone planter she'd been using as cover from the roof's edge.

There was a pool up here, along with potted palm trees, a floating bar, a jacuzzi, a scattering of tables with umbrellas, even some misters to keep it from getting too hot.

Thanks to the bar, they had bottled water, at least, if not much in the way of food.

They also had a lot of alcohol, but Angel figured that was for emergencies at this point.

As in, they were all going to die emergencies.

Cowboy plunked down and scooted closer to where she sat before he leaned on the planter, his leather-jacketed shoulders touching hers.

He spoke to her directly, not via headsets.

They were all avoiding talking on headsets right now.

"Jax thinks it was crushed," he added. "Black's earpiece."

"Did someone find Holo?" she said, speaking as low as him.

Cowboy's voice turned grim. "Yeah."

Focusing away from the view through the drone's cameras for the first time, Angel felt her throat tighten when she saw her boyfriend's face.

"God," she said. "Is he dead?"

"No." Cowboy shook his head, his jaw firm. "Not dead. But he's hurt real bad. They're trying their best to fix him up in that conference room. The same one they've been using as a lab... where Jax and A.J. are holed up."

"What's wrong with him?"

"He's been stabbed multiple times." Cowboy paused when Angel winced. "A bunch of broken bones," he added. "They don't think he got hit in any major organs, but he's lost a lot of blood. He's also got a big knot on his head. He was out cold when they found him."

Angel felt sick.

Thinking, she switched off her headset.

Refocusing on Cowboy, she said, low, so it wouldn't be picked up by his headset either.

"What about Miri? Is she still in there?"

Yarli had ordered them not to mention Miri over an open line. They were worried Yarrick could have hacked their transmissions.

There was a pause.

In it, she saw Cowboy shut off his own headset.

"Yeah," he said then, exhaling as he leaned himself against the white stone. "She's been listening through the closet doors. She's also been using the Barrier to communicate with Mika and Yarli. She says she's got a plan."

Cowboy gave her a wry smile.

"She said it might blow Black's whole PR strategy here in Hawaii. That don't seem to be her primary concern at the moment, though. She's worried anything else will get him killed. The doc's pretty sure Yarrick's gonna shoot Black, if she doesn't act soon."

Angel's mouth firmed.

"Well, Black *is* extremely charming," she muttered sarcastically. "Totally not likely to goad someone into wanting to kill him."

At Cowboy's amused grunt, Angel rested her arms on her thighs, hiking the rifle back behind her.

"So what's this plan of hers?" she said, frowning. "Use those beetle drones we sent through the back bedroom windows? Black's standing awfully close to Yarrick and his toy soldiers for that. Isn't she worried he'll get caught in the blast?"

"Yeah, I don't reckon that's her plan... not unless she can

convince Black to jump out the window first. Or maybe into the pool."

"Then what?" Angel frowned. "Is she just going to burst out of the closet and yell 'Surprise'? Hope she can distract them long enough to jump Black out of there?" Grunting, she added, "Or is she just going to poke Black with a big stick? Find some way to annoy him enough that he turns into a dragon again?"

Cowboy winced.

When Angel looked at him, quirking an eyebrow, he tilted his head sideways in a noncommittal gesture, an unconscious imitation of something seers did to say yes without really saying yes.

"Jesus," Angel breathed. "Seriously? She's going to try and turn him into a dragon?"

"She implied something along those lines to Mika, yeah."

"Jesus."

"Ayuh. But I get her reasoning," Cowboy said a little defensively. "We can't get to either of them where they are. Not without risking killing both of them. Miri can't get to Black, not quick enough to jump him outta there without him getting shot. Those robot assholes have us pinned down... both up here and on the ground floor. We're going to lose people if we don't act soon. As it is, I suspect Yarrick's ordered his cyborg tin soldiers into a holding pattern until he makes up his mind if he'll get what he wants outta Black."

Cowboy's mouth curled in a narrow frown.

"Those robot boys won't be able to do much against Black, I suspect... not if he transforms. Ayuh, it's dramatic all right. But it should do the trick."

Angel shook her head in disbelief, touching her ear to turn on the headset.

Keeping it on mute, she focused back on the drone feed.

"Hadn't we better get out of the way, then?" she said drily, glancing at Cowboy. "Or are we just supposed to rappel down the side of the building when he explodes up through the ceiling?"

Cowboy frowned, staring at her.

From his expression of slowly-dawning understanding, that hadn't actually occurred to him.

Which meant it likely hadn't occurred to Mika, either.

Even as she thought it, Cowboy was scrambling to his feet.

Angel called after him, a dark flicker of inappropriate humor rising in her voice.

"Maybe have Miri give us a head's up which side of the roof he's likely to incinerate first," she said. "I'd prefer not to be standing right in the middle of ground zero. Not unless he's going to give us a ride, at least."

Cowboy didn't answer.

Scowling, he just made his way with fast strides over the wooden deck, aiming his booted feet for where Mika stood by the pool.

Before he'd made it there, Angel heard the first faint rumble under them.

The vibration was slight.

It stopped.

Despite how slight it had been, Angel froze like a rabbit on a dark highway. All of her inappropriate humor evaporated. Her breath stopped. Then she was panting, adrenaline shooting through her blood, making it hard to think.

She stared down at the wooden deck.

Still breathing hard, fear thudding in her chest, she swiveled her gaze back to her boyfriend and Mika.

Cowboy hadn't yet reached them.

From his back, Angel couldn't tell if he'd noticed the building's tremble.

Angel focused on the female seer's face.

Ace stood beside her, looming over Mika in a way that might have been funny under different circumstances, if only because it reversed the usual seer-human disparities in height.

Mika was unusually short for a seer, even a female.

Ace was unusually tall for a human, even for a male.

The lanky ex-Ranger stood next to the short, Chinese-looking seer, feet apart, his muscular arms folded, his rifle slung over his back as he frowned, staring around the pool deck.

Earlier that day, Angel had found herself thinking that the two of them, Mika and Ace, had been working together a lot lately. Kind of like how Jax and Kiko had been working together a lot lately. Like Kiko and Jax, Ace and Mika had gradually morphed into a "paired set," one that seemed to be growing more and more entwined.

Angel knew she wasn't the only one to notice, even if no one mentioned it to her, not in so many words.

She hadn't seen anyone ballsy enough to tease Ace about it yet.

It might just be friendship. If so, it felt unusually tight.

Like right now, she saw Ace frown, staring out over the pool deck. She felt the same alarm tremble through Mika that she'd seen reflected on Ace's face, almost like it started with him and rippled over to her.

Mika had been talking before it reached her.

She'd been standing there, talking, her brow furrowed in worry—

—when abruptly, she went silent.

Angel saw Mika's face blank, her eyes slide out of focus.

For a few seconds, Mika didn't move.

Ace, who appeared to be growing accustomed to that kind of thing in her, and probably in seers in general, remained silent.

Refolding his arms, the big ex-Ranger waited.

Then Angel saw Mika seem to come back.

The female seer's eyes slid back into focus.

Understanding bloomed over Mika's face as she seemed to be digesting what she'd just seen, or possibly heard, or more likely both.

There was a split second before that understanding fully clicked in.

Then it turned to fear.

"RUN!" Mika shouted, making Ace jump, and Cowboy, who

had nearly reached them. "MOVE YOUR ASSES! TIME TO GO! NOW!"

The words burst out of her.

"MOVE!" she snapped, louder. "STAIRWAY. EVERYONE. NOW."

Mika started waving her hands towards the opposite side of the roof, where the door leading to the stairs lived. Unlike the glass doors into the roof's elevator lobby, all that lived there was a plain metal door, with the words "Emergency Exit Only" on it.

Still, Angel immediately understood the logic.

"ARE YOU DEAF?" The female seer was screaming now. "THE STAIRS. NOW. EVERYBODY. *MOVE YOUR ASSES!*"

Ace was speaking into his headset, motioning sharply for Mika to follow as he began loping towards the stairs himself, his long gait wolf-like.

Cowboy turned, looking for her, Angel.

His gray eyes held fear when they found hers.

Seeing her sitting there, he motioned sharply for her to get up.

Realizing she was just sitting there, watching all of this unfold, even as her ass sat on the deck right above Black and Miri's suite, Angel yanked herself up, using the stone planter for balance. Hoisting the rifle further over her shoulder, she began to run.

Cowboy stood there, waiting for her, motioning her faster.

"RUN, BABY... C'MON NOW..."

As soon as she was close enough, he reached for her arm, maybe to reassure himself, then he was running with her, sprinting with her across the wooden deck.

They ran with the rest of the human and seer rifle team that had been scattered around the pool area. Most of them had a head-start on Angel already, so she could see them running in front of her and Cowboy, weaving around lounge chairs, tables, umbrellas, around the pool and the jacuzzi, around the potted palms, zig-zagging back and forth as they aimed for the staircase door.

Under her feet, Angel felt another tremor.

That one felt bigger.

She told herself she was imagining things, that it was just fear, that she wouldn't be able to feel the building shake while she was running.

Then the next one hit.

That one threw her to the ground.

She stumbled, slamming into a pool chair.

She managed to catch herself on the edge of a glass and metal table, but her knees hit painfully into the deck.

"Fuck!" Cowboy burst out.

He threw himself at Angel once he regained his own balance, helping her back to her feet. Then he was running with her, faster now, still holding onto her arm as they made their way towards the emergency door.

Michelle was holding it open, bracing it with her body.

Standing there, she waved people through and into the stairwell, her normally tan face pale as chalk.

"MOVE IT!" she shouted, her voice deeper than Mika's. Her arm waved sharply, as much of a command as that booming voice. "GET DOWN AS FAR AS YOU CAN! GO ALL THE WAY TO THE LOBBY! STAY BY THE WALLS!"

Panting, her knees and hands burning from where she fell, Angel glimpsed Mika and Ace as they disappeared through the door.

They were followed by Kiessa, Luce, Javier, Miguel, Alice, Johnson.

Then she and Cowboy reached it, and reached Michelle.

It occurred to Angel only then that they were dead last.

Cowboy pulled her through the doorway in front of him, following close behind as Angel started throwing herself down the stairs, gripping the handrail to keep from falling as she skipped steps, jumping over as many as she could in her haste to get her and Cowboy downstairs.

Just being in the stairwell felt safer.

She knew it was probably an illusion, but she could feel her mind starting to clear, even as she heard the metal door slam shut behind them. It didn't hurt that the square stairwell had a bunker-like feel, and was mostly cement.

She and Cowboy made it about three floors down, Michelle and Avery following close behind them... when the building shook for real.

Angel saw Mika stumble in front of her.

The Chinese-looking seer looked like she was going to fall, head-first down the stairs. Even as her feet left the ground, she was caught, midair, by Ace, who ran behind her. The lanky male wrapped a long arm around the seer's waist, yanking her up against him.

He didn't stop running down the stairs as he did, taking them three steps at a time.

Angel saw Luce and Johnson stop, hanging onto the bannister for dear life. She heard Devin let out a yell when he was thrown to his knees, which looked like it hurt like hell.

Then Angel looked up.

She heard when the roof above them went, even as a familiar roar shattered the air above the resort.

"Jesus," she muttered.

She wasn't particularly religious.

Even so, she had to fight not to cross herself.

Just below her on the staircase, Miguel did cross himself, staring up, his face going as white as Michelle's had been.

All of them briefly stopped trying to flee.

They crouched there, in the stairwell, gripping the bannisters, panting.

They didn't speak.

They stared up, frozen, like frightened animals.

Panting and staring up with the rest of them, Angel listening to the sounds overhead, the screams, crashes, thuds of cement and steel hitting the ground below the building. She heard glass shattering, the rain of broken shards pelting down from the building's height. She heard human screams, the terror in them so intense they made her heart stop.

There was another of those long, wailing, dinosaur-like shrieks.

It seemed to pierce the sky, bringing Angel's hands to her ears, making her wince.

When the scream came again, it shook the thick windows of the stairwell, echoing down the cement passageway. Hurricane-like winds shook the windows yet again, and more thuds hit the ground below the resort's main building.

Angel listened to all of it in awe, her feelings still verging on disbelief.

As she did, she realized whatever this standoff had been... it was over.

Black, in dragon form, had ended the debate about which side was stronger.

He'd ended it decisively.

❧ 31 ❧

NOT A VAMPIRE

I felt his fear.

Black's fear rippled through my light, bringing up my own fear, even as it brought a stronger, more urgent compulsion in my light to reassure him, to calm him down.

Honestly, I just wanted to hold him.

I wanted to hold him, to take him out of there.

But I needed to calm him down first.

I couldn't jump him like this.

Not when he was already half out of his head.

He stood there, naked, panting.

He'd only been himself again for a few seconds.

I'd helped him transform back to his "seer" form as soon as I possibly could.

I'd had to wait until Coreq finished making the resort safe for us.

I'd had to wait until after Peter was dead, only managing to discharge a single bullet in Black's direction before the half-transformed Black sent a claw through his old friend's middle, ripping the human more or less in half.

The six cyber-soldiers ran at Black as soon as Black attacked their maker... but by then, it was well past too late.

Black's full, transformed body crashed through the floor and ceiling—more or less at the same time. It knocked out walls, screaming upwards as it unfolded its wings. From what I could see, watching through Black and Coreq's eyes, debris from the roof, chunks of cement from the pool, not to mention being slammed into by Black's claws, feet and tail, more or less ripped those six cyborg soldiers apart.

I think the first two were killed as much by the effects of the transformation itself as they were by Black actively trying to kill them.

Either way, I didn't wait a second longer than I had to.

Given how little agency Black had over the whole "turning into a dragon" thing, how completely unenthused he'd been about the whole prospect, I didn't want him staying in that form any longer than absolutely necessary.

Luckily, the whole thing was over fast.

The entire incident didn't last very long.

Fifteen, maybe twenty minutes in total, from initial transformation to dragon back to Black being Black again.

Damn, though.

It *felt* long.

It felt interminably long while I watched Black in his dragon form rip through the bones of the resort building, clawing out and killing every one of the cyborg soldiers he could find with his eyes, resorting to sniffing out the rest with his dragon senses, once there weren't any more of them actively attacking him.

Luckily, those soldiers really were stupid.

From what I could tell, they never stopped actively attacking Black.

Even after he grew into a dragon, they single-mindedly tried to kill him. They didn't stop even after Peter was gone, even after I'd already disappeared.

I waited a few minutes after the last soldier attacked Black, just to be sure.

I wanted to be sure.

I waited until Black and Coreq's feet were solidly back on the ground.

I waited until Black finished sniffing through the remains of the building, and through the grounds down to the beach.

I waited until I was sure he was totally safe.

Parts of that were hard to watch.

I'd been forced to jump out of the suite's closet more or less the instant the transformation began.

I jumped, taking myself down to the driveway in front of the resort.

I reappeared, naked... just in time to see Black's dragon head burst through the top floor of the building, sending up a plume of fire, water, palm trees, splintered wood, and chunks of cement as he crashed through the rooftop pool and surrounding deck.

Stone and palm trees rained down, chunks littering the circular driveway in front of the resort. Luckily, most of the bigger pieces crashed down on the opposite side of the building. Even so, the sounds alone were alarming, and had me backing up the sloped driveway, even stark naked, until I was nearly all the way to the road.

Once I got there, I put up a seer's shield, trying to keep humans away.

The few humans near enough to the commotion that they heard it and approached, curious, I pushed to lose interest.

I had all of them wandering backwards, or simply speeding forward in their cars, their eyes trained straight ahead as they drove by.

Still, I worried.

I worried about satellites.

I worried about military planes.

I worried about drones, and other ways where footage of the event might surface.

But I'd known that was a risk, going into this.

I'd known this would be a PR disaster, likely reversing everything Black tried to do in coming here. I also knew we didn't have much choice.

If there had been another option, I'd been unable to think of it.

After throwing up a shield around the whole resort, I eventually ventured back down the driveway towards the main building.

By then, the worst of the damage had already been done.

I'd stood there, listening to Black's powerful jaws snap and crunch, making his way through the soldiers who'd been waiting for him on the ground floor.

Once he'd ripped apart Peter's remaining robo-whatevers in the lobby and by the pool, crunching through them methodically as they attacked him, both singly and in small groups, everything grew strangely quiet.

He made short work of them.

I watched him dispatch them more or less one by one, with teeth, with claws, with fire, even taking care of a few with precise, crushing blows of his tail and claws.

Then he finished, and it grew quiet. I saw Black, wings folded, drinking from one of the resort swimming pools, his large, clawed feet resting in the pool's bottom, cracking the previously pristine blue tile and white cement.

While I watched him drink, I'd checked in the with the drone operators.

It took me a few minutes to get answers out of anyone.

Eventually, Dexter, who was still out by the beach in the hide with several others from our team, answered me.

"Is it all clear?" I said, probably for the twentieth time in a lot fewer minutes. "Are you getting any more readings from those cyber things?"

"I don't..." Dex hesitated.

I heard him take a breath.

"Yes," he said, sounding more sure. "I don't see any more. That's all of them."

"Is your team okay?" I said.

"We're... yeah. We're okay, Miri."

"Are you coming back up here?" I'd asked.

"We will," Dex said, hesitating again. "We will, doc. As soon as..."

He trailed, never finishing that thought.

I knew what he meant.

He meant as soon as Black was no longer a dragon.

He meant as soon as Black was himself again.

"Black," I said to him now, watching him fight to control himself, to pull himself back into his body, back to me. "Black... it's going to be okay."

He was still staring at me when tears began running down his face.

"Miri," he said, his voice choking. "Miri, take me out of here. Please."

Walking up to him, studying his face, I saw the pleading in his eyes.

When I reached him, I didn't say a word.

I wrapped my arms around him, and ignited those structures above my head.

We vanished, before I could take another full breath.

❧

Honey, I sent, soft. *It's okay. It's going to be okay.*

Black's light emitted a strangled laugh.

Jesus, Miri.

His head was in my lap. I was stroking his hair.

We were on a different beach now, under trees that arched over us like a silent, vibrant green cathedral. In the water, I heard otters barking to one another, playing in the surf.

Well, I called them otters.

They weren't really otters, of course.

They looked a bit like them, only they were the size of German Shepherds, and about as smart. They were also really friendly, whenever we went out to swim with them.

Looking around at the perfect white sands of this otherworldly beach, I wondered if it was smart to take him here, to comfort him here, instead of letting him adjust to all of this at home, on our own world.

Peter already knew you weren't human, I reminded him. *I heard what he said. He said a lot of people knew. He may have gotten the race wrong, thinking you were a vampire, but the cat was already more or less out of the bag. Now that vamps have been outed, it's only a matter of time before humans know about seers.*

Miri, you don't understand. Black shook his head, tears coming to his eyes. *You don't understand what that kind of world was like. You don't know what I grew up in, what the humans were like, on my world. And not just the humans,* he added, looking up at me. *The seers, too. There's a reason Charles is the way he is.*

At my silence, Black swallowed, staring up at the bowl of blue sky.

I'm not trying to be a dick, he sent. *But humans? Not all humans, but your run-of-the-mill, ordinary human? They don't do difference well. They especially don't do difference well when those differences scare them.*

Swallowing, he gestured with a hand, a graceful, distinctly seer gesture.

Most humans on our Earth will be terrified of us. They won't give us a chance. They'll be one hundred percent certain we're controlling them from behind the scenes. They'll want us all to wear something so they know who we are. They'll want collars, and special tattoos. They'll want assurances we can't use our sight against them. That means implants, reg tags, a Seer Containment Bureau... all the same shit my birth planet had. They'll want to experiment on us. They'll try to enslave us, Miri—

I know. I sent more heat into his light, fighting to calm him down. *I know, honey. I really do. But I'm telling you... they're going to find out. So maybe it's time to think about how to deal with it, when they do. And maybe how to control how it happens.*

Pausing, I added,

If you don't control it, Black, someone else will. Someone like Charles.

Black grunted, shaking his head.

I knew he wasn't disagreeing with me.

He more wanted to deny it was true.

He didn't want to believe it.

This isn't the absolute worst timing in the world, Black, I sent then. *You just saved them. You saved them from Charles. If you can make them understand that—*

But he interrupted me, speaking aloud.

"*You* saved them, Miri," he said, his voice a warning. "I didn't do that. *You* did."

"Black," I said, exasperated. "I know what happened at the resort was bad, but the reality is... it wasn't *that* bad. We can do damage control on this. We emptied out the resort, including staff. As far as I could tell, no innocent people got hurt."

Pausing, I added,

"Our people are likely dealing with the surveillance feeds as we speak. They'll memory wipe guests if they have to, along with hotel staff and security. I doubt it will be necessary for you to 'out' yourself as a non-human... not for this. I'm just saying, maybe we need to *think* about doing that. At some point. Or at least having a plan for when it happens."

Pausing when I saw his lips curl into a frown, I added,

"I told you what that prescient seer told me, right? Terian?"

Black's frown deepened.

His eyes grew distant as he stared off.

I felt him remembering.

I felt him breathing harder as he remembered.

I found my own mind drifting back to the Blue Sail, back to how it all went down in that suite at Peter Yarrick's high-end resort.

I remembered being inside that dark closet.

I'd had my ear pressed to the crack between the two closet doors. I'd been straining to listen to the exchange between Yarrick and Black ever since Black shut the doors to the balcony, dulling the sounds from outside enough that I could make out individual words.

As I listened, I'd been getting increasingly worried.

Black was getting more and more sarcastic as the conversation wore on, which wasn't a good sign. He was antagonizing Peter deliberately, giving him fewer and fewer straight answers, cooperating with him less and less.

Worse, he was spending a lot more of his time mocking Yarrick outright.

While I couldn't exactly blame Black for any of that, I wished he would stop going out of his way to piss off the guy aiming a gun at his face.

When Coreq first spoke into my mind, I was still listening at those closet doors.

I'd already communicated important bits to Mika and Yarli, but mostly I was going back and forth with them about possible ways to extract Black without getting him killed.

I was so focused on that, when Coreq spoke, I almost shrieked.

What's wrong, Miriam? a soft voice asked.

I nearly jumped out of my skin.

Worse, I nearly crashed through the closet doors, spilling into the suite's lounge.

Luckily, I caught myself.

I didn't dare touch the doors, so I held my hands out, biting my lip so hard my teeth drew blood. Waiting a few beats, if only to make sure I could keep silent, I forced myself to breathe through the shock, to not move until I could control my body, and most of my mind.

Coreq? I sent back, tentative.

Yes.

The answer came through so clearly, I bit my tongue.

What's wrong? he asked again softly. *Are you okay, Miriam?*

There was a silence.

I could have sworn I saw the presence yawn, like I'd just woken him up.

...Why are you in a closet, Miriam? Coreq asked. *Where's Black?*

For a long-feeling few seconds I stared at the dark closet doors, at the thread-thin crack of light visible between them.

I took another breath.

Then I found myself explaining.

I explained all of it to Coreq, in detail... every word and step that got me and Black to this exact moment in time. I spoke to Black's alter-ego easily, casually, without holding anything back, like it wasn't the weirdest fucking thing in the world, talking to this presence in Black's light like we were old friends.

Coreq listened patiently.

He didn't interrupt.

He didn't ask me any questions.

When I finished, he also didn't hesitate.

I can take care of this, he sent. *Do you want me to take care of this, Miriam?*

I hesitated.

Then, before the answer fully solidified in my mind, I found myself nodding.

Yes, I sent. *Yes, Coreq. I want you to take care of this for me.*

Swallowing, trying to see through the closet doors at where someone was aiming a gun at my husband's face, I clenched my jaw.

Protect Black, Coreq. Protect Black for me.

Coreq hadn't hesitated.

Okay, the presence had said agreeably.

⚜

B lack fell asleep on the sand.

I sat there with him, his head pillowed in my lap.

I tried to decide whether I should call Revik and Allie in the space, let them know we were back in their dimension.

Something stopped me, though.

Something told me not to do it, at least not until Black woke up.

I sat there with him instead, watching the sun sink slowly in the sky, leaning on my hands and watching the surf, watching the otters, and eventually watching a pod of larger animals, what looked like a strange cross between dolphins and birds.

It was the first time we'd been to this part of this world.

Really, it was the first time we'd been to this world where we hadn't landed in this dimension's version of California—San Francisco, specifically.

Instead, I was looking out over the unique land formations and mountains of this dimension's Hawaii.

I thought about all the things we still had to deal with.

I thought about the things I'd been working on, the last time I'd been in this dimension. There was still the matter of all the fragments of the "dragon" presence, scattered around the various dimensions. I still wasn't sure what I was supposed to do about that, or if I was supposed to do anything about it at all.

I know Allie and I speculated I was supposed to unite those disparate pieces in some way.

Somehow, I was supposed to bring them all together.

To recreate them into a single being.

After everything that had happened over the past few months, I had my doubts that was such a great idea, though. Given the damage Black could do now, all on his own, I wasn't sure if making Black *more* powerful, uniting even *more* of that dragon energy into his immediate proximity, or even linking Black to it via my light, was really the best idea.

I also had no idea what it would do to Coreq.

Since "Coreq" might actually *be* that dragon energy, at least in terms of how Black and I experienced it, it was possible it would strengthen it to the point where neither Black nor I could control it at all.

"Coreq" could take over even more of Black's light.

That dragon energy could subsume Black himself entirely.

It wasn't something I particularly wanted to experiment with.

In the end, I pushed that from my mind, too.

Closing my eyes, I fell into the rolling waves, listening to Black sleep.

Listening to him dream.

Strangely, I felt more relieved to be with him... *alone* with him... finally... than I felt worried about anything we'd discussed, or even anything I'd been thinking about.

Maybe that's why, when he opened his eyes, an hour or two later, when the moon was rising up over the black and blue ocean, I didn't say anything to him at all.

Leaning down, I kissed him, sliding my fingers into his hair.

Half awake, he kissed me back.

I could tell he did so mostly in reflex at first.

Then he woke up for real.

His fingers tightened in my hair. He pulled me down to him, clenching his hand more, rising slightly in my lap to meet me. His mouth grew warmer, softer, even as the heat coming off his light ignited, spreading through my body like liquid.

Then that fire-like light was pulling on me, pulling on mine inexorably, with an urgency and insistence that caught in my chest, making it difficult to breathe.

It hit me again how little time we'd had together.

It hit me how much less time we'd had together alone.

I really wanted to marry you there, he sent, his thoughts a bare whisper. *In Hawaii. I really wanted to, doc... for us to be really married, in an actual damned ceremony. I didn't give a fuck about the publicity shit. I wanted to have a real ceremony and get drunk with our friends. Eat cake. Spend a few weeks fucking on the beach afterwards.*

I raised my head, gazing down at his faintly-glowing, tiger-like eyes.

Sliding my hand over his jaw, I kissed him again.

His tongue grew hotter in my mouth. His body melted in my lap.

I got lost there.

I don't know how long I got lost there.

At some point, he sat up, rolling over with me in the sand.

I'd almost forgotten we were both naked.

Can we still do it? he murmured in my mind. *Can we do it somewhere, at least? It doesn't have to be Hawaii. I'll get down on a knee. You can pick everything out. It can be as small or as big as you like, Miri. You can invite anyone you want.*

I kissed him again.

It sounds lovely, Black. Romantic. Really romantic.

Another hard flush of heat left his light.

He yanked me further under him, pulling my head back to kiss my throat, working his way down to my breasts. By the time he was inside me, the pain in my light was so bad I was whimpering, clutching at his back, biting my lips to keep from biting him.

You can bite me, doc, he sent in that lower, deeper murmur. *You can bite me whenever you want. You can do whatever you want.*

"I thought you didn't like that," I gasped, digging my nails into his back. "I thought you didn't like it when I did that... that it reminded you of vampires..."

He sank his teeth into my shoulder.

I let out a shocked gasp.

My body arched, sliding sinuously up against his, and he let out a low groan.

His voice went deeper again, heavier... I almost came right then, from that alone, but he stopped me, using his light.

He gripped my hips in his hands, stopping both of us then, stopping us physically, his skin flushing hot under my hands and against my skin as he closed his eyes. His voice shifted downwards, growing so deep, I felt every word down to my feet and the ends of my fingers.

I hadn't heard his voice like that in so long, it hurt.

"Would you have done it, doc?" he said, gruff. "On that beach tonight? If I'd ever fucking asked... if I'd ever gotten a *chance* to fucking ask you..."

When I fought to press up against him, he gripped my hips tighter, holding me down.

His voice remained that low, heavy growl.

"Gaos... untielleres..."

I shivered, closing my eyes.

That heavy tone his voice got, him speaking in seer, the emotion I heard behind his words, his heat flooding my light... all of it drove me out of my fucking mind.

I'd forgotten, somehow.

I'd forgotten what it was like, when it was just the two of us.

I'd forgotten what it was like, when things were right with us.

In thinking that, I realized it was gone.

That silent, closed strangeness... that gulf hanging between us after Nick, after what happened on that roof... it was gone.

It was finally gone.

The realization brought tears to my eyes.

Looking up at those glowing, cat-like irises, I gripped him tighter, blinking away the tears, fighting to catch my breath.

"Is that why?" I managed. "Is that why you wouldn't have sex with me?"

I felt an emotional reaction on him, intense enough that I gasped, gripping his arms. I felt him staring down at my tears. He kissed my face, kissing my closed eyes, and I kissed him back, reaching for his hair, tugging on him, wrapping my legs around his.

He arched into me, all the way, and my mind blanked.

He did it again, slower that time, deeper, and a harder shock of pain ran through me. I nearly came again. When he stopped me that time, I cried out in frustration.

I felt grief on him, but he didn't close.

Realizing I'd been feeling him closed since I got back to him in California, pretty much the whole time we were in Hawaii, even before someone started actively trying to kill both of us, tears came to my eyes all over again.

That time I couldn't stop them.

I remembered the fight we got into in the desert, right before the missile hit.

I remembered the emotion on him then, the near-loss of control over his light, even then.

He'd been accusing me of keeping him out, of closing my light to him, of lying to him about it. I don't think either of us mentioned Nick anywhere in that conversation... but Nick hung there, between us, like some kind of ghost.

I didn't feel him there now.

He was gone.

He was finally gone.

I love you, he sent.

I felt his words so intensely, I bit my lip, my fingers winding deeper into his hair.

I felt Black open more, and I lost control, to the point where I was half-fighting his light, fighting the part of him that was still trying to hold me off, to control things.

I had no idea what changed.

Maybe I should have let well enough alone. Maybe I should have, but somehow, not knowing why it was different, what changed, brought my fear up all over again.

"Do you trust me again?" I said.

I saw him flinch. I saw his eyes close, even as he stopped over me a second time, lowering his forehead to mine. I felt that heat on him intensify. I felt my fear affecting him, even as I felt him trying to calm my light, to wind it protectively into his.

"You want Nick alive," he said, instead of answering me.

I tensed.

Then, when he didn't go on, I fought to think.

I made myself really think about what he'd said.

I was afraid to tell him the truth.

"You don't have to tell me anything, doc," Black said, gruff. "It wasn't a question. I know you want him alive. I can feel it. You really believe he's back, that the Nick you met in Russia is your friend Nick from before. I can feel that. You think newborn Nick... Brick's 'Naoko'... is dead."

I nodded, strangely relieved by his words.

"Yes," I said.

"And you're absolutely certain you're right?" Black said, his voice still gruff. "It's not just wishful thinking? It's not just you *wanting* to believe it?"

I felt my jaw harden as I thought about that.

I made myself think about it, really think about it.

I remembered Nick in Russia.

I remembered him with Dalejem... with my dog.

I remembered his facial expressions, his mannerisms, the shame I'd felt off him, even as a vampire. I remembered his jealousy when he thought Dalejem was flirting with me.

I remembered the self-loathing I'd seen on him, when he looked at me.

I remembered how he could barely meet my eyes.

"I'm sure," I said.

My voice sounded sure.

It sounded one hundred percent positive.

Pausing as I pondered that, I added,

"It was weird, how clear it was when I was with him, Black. I was terrified when I first saw him... scared out of my fucking mind. But even with that, I swear to God, he was more terrified of me. He didn't want to get close to me. He definitely didn't want to touch me. After I talked to him, and I watched him with Jem, it was like that other Naoko was just... gone."

Stilling thinking about that, I frowned, remembering.

"By the time we left Russia," I went on. "I almost forgot that Nick and Naoko were the same person. He was just Nick again. I mean, he was a vampire, but the vampire stuff was more or less a detail. Honestly, I was more weirded out by him and Jem. And how different he looked, despite being *exactly the same* as the Nick I remembered, in pretty much every other respect."

Black didn't answer at first.

He hung there, unmoving.

Nodding then, he slowly exhaled.

"Then he's dead," Black said, his voice strangely matter-of-fact. "Brick's newborn is dead. If you can accept that... I can accept it. I have no right not to."

There was a silence.

I could feel he wasn't done.

I felt it tangibly, so I just watched him, holding my breath.

"Miri," Black said, his gold eyes refocusing on mine. "If he ever comes back... if I ever see that other Nick... that vampire, 'Naoko'... again, I'll kill him. I won't ask you first. I may not even tell you I intend to do it. I'll just kill him, Miri."

My throat closed as I looked at him.

I didn't have to ask him if he meant it.

Slowly, I turned over his words.

I found myself nodding then, almost before I knew I meant to.

"I understand."

"Do you?"

"I didn't say I like it," I said, a touch sharper. "But I understand. It's clear you mean it, and I understand why... to keep us both safe, not to mention your team."

Still thinking, I added,

"Dalejem is in love with him."

Feeling a reaction in Black's light, I looked up, studying his eyes.

"You would have to go through Jem, I suspect, to do it," I warned him. "You might have to kill Jem. He'd definitely be a threat to you, during and after."

When Black didn't answer, I went on in the same voice.

"I get the feeling this thing with them... with Nick and Jem... it's not going away, Black. I don't know how vampires mate, but it feels like that, like they're together now. It feels like how seers are, when they're together like that. It feels like you and me... how we are."

Black's expression didn't move.

I thought he was thinking about my words at first.

Then I realized he wasn't.

He wasn't thinking about them.

He'd heard me.

He understood me perfectly.

It just made zero difference to how he felt.

It made zero difference to what he'd said he'd do about Nick/Naoko.

Looking up at my husband's face, feeling that harder edge in his light, I couldn't help wondering if that was one hundred percent Black sending me that message, or if Coreq was weighing in on the Nick issue, as well.

Either way, I felt something in my chest relax.

Part of that was for Nick, sure.

Nick had a reprieve... at least for now.

It was more than that, though.

As selfish as it was, the Nick thing might not even have been the main cause for my feelings of relief.

Most of that relief came from how Black's light felt, with mine.

I could feel Black again, with me.

I could feel him really *with* me.

I still didn't fully understand it, but I understood enough for my fears to ease.

Something in this Nick thing brought an acceptance to Black's light.

A coming to peace, maybe.

In the same way I'd been able to "forgive" Nick by seeing him as "healed," as wholly separate from the newborn on Black's roof... Black could now do the same. He'd come to peace with Nick being Nick again.

Well, until he wasn't.

If Nick ever went back to being that thing on the roof, the one Black shot through the chest... Black would protect what was his.

While that probably should have made me nervous as hell, given what I knew Black was capable of, how unstable both of us could be, light-wise, jealousy-wise, bond-wise, not to mention how hair-trigger Black was likely to be on this particular issue, somehow it didn't.

It didn't make me nervous.

Really, it did the opposite.

For one thing, I was sure I was right about Nick.

For another, I really did accept Black's take on things, even if the more human part of my mind, the part that was still a psychologist, knew I probably shouldn't. That part of me could tell me how unhealthy it was, how possessive both of us were, how much we associated our bond with our own very survival... but the seer part of me didn't much care.

The seer part of me agreed with Black.

It saw his words as simply true.

It saw them as perhaps even *right* in some fundamental sense.

Maybe I was finally almost as seer as he was.

Maybe I'd finally shed the last of the misgivings I'd had as a human, when Black's light and life seemed almost to subsume my own... or the two of us together, our relationship, seemed to subsume us as individuals.

I found it strangely comforting now.

It felt like looking down, to find I'd regrown a limb.

"Do you trust me?" I asked him again.

He was watching me. When I glanced up, I realized he'd been watching me that whole time, nervous about how I might react to what he'd said. I felt through his light he hadn't meant his words as an ultimatum, more as a statement of the way things were.

He was worried I would take them as an ultimatum.

"Do you trust me?" I said, needing an answer.

Hesitating, he met my eyes.

After a beat where he just looked at me, I saw something in those gold irises relax.

"Yes," he said, sounding relieved.

Feeling his relief, the truth of his answer, my own relief hit me.

I let out a breath, sliding my hands around his face.

For a long-feeling moment, we just hung there like that, winding into each other's light, each of us pulling the other deeper into our *aleimi*. I felt my relief expand as he opened, letting me do that to him more... then letting me do it to him more still.

I knew we'd finish having sex after that.

I knew we'd do that a few more times before we headed back to our "real" world, back to the mess we'd left behind there.

I knew the others might wonder about us, depending on how the time thing went. I knew it might give us more to explain when we returned.

For some reason, I didn't mind.

With Black's light coiling into mine, pulling on me with increasing urgency, merging us together...

I didn't mind at all.

A NEW WAY FORWARD

"Miri and Black are back at the Raptor's Nest," Dalejem announced, walking into the living room from the kitchen and holding a plate with a roast beef sandwich on it.

Nick, who'd been sniffing the air, curious about his boyfriend's food, stiffened when Jem's words sank in.

He glanced up, craning his head and neck to watch Jem walk to the couch near where Nick sat, where he'd been watching television.

"I am told they arrived there yesterday afternoon," Dalejem added, folding himself into the couch above Nick, who sat on a round cushion he'd placed on the floor. "There appears to be some question about whether they are staying, or if they will be traveling again soon. I received somewhat mixed word as to this point from Yarli. She seems to think they might be leaving on some kind of belated 'honeymoon' within the week—"

"Yarli?" Nick frowned, staring up at the seer. "You're talking to Yarli now?"

Dalejem exhaled.

"Yes. She knows." Pausing, Dalejem added, "So does Black."

Nick tensed.

The dog, who'd been napping on his lap for the past thirty or so minutes, twitched violently, then jumped, lifting his head. Nick felt a twinge of guilt, realizing he'd probably alarmed the pup enough to wake him.

Looking up, Panther studied Nick's face, clearly feeling something was wrong.

When Nick looked back at the dog, frowning, Panther barked.

"What?" Nick growled. "What's your problem? Am I disturbing your beauty sleep?"

Panther barked again.

His voice was almost comically deep for such a young dog.

Nick knew Panther would grow into it. He already looked like he'd grown an inch in the week or so since they'd broken him out of that chateau in Moscow.

"Don't get snippy with me, little man," Nick groused. "You're not the one who's about to get his head cut off by Uncle Quentin—"

"Neither are you," Dalejem said, his voice a touch warning. "Stop joking about that, Nick. It's not amusing."

"It's a *little* amusing."

"No," Jem said, twisting his fingers into Nick's hair from behind and tugging on it, tightening his hand into a fist. "It's really not."

Nick glanced back, smiling at him.

Then his smile faded.

"Seriously," he said. "Should we be getting ready to leave town?"

Dalejem exhaled. Releasing Nick's hair, he leaned back into the couch, even as he wrapped his legs around Nick's back from either side.

"Yarli says no," he said, giving a seer's one-handed shrug. "She seems to think Miri's gotten him to back off for now. I couldn't get a strong sense of how long that might last, and I suspect Yarli herself didn't know either. Yarli *did* caution it wouldn't likely be a good idea for you to go anywhere near Black, though... in the flesh, that is... at least for a while."

Nick let out a disbelieving grunt.

"Yeah," he said. "No shit."

"Yarli also mentioned there was an... incident. In Hawaii."

Nick frowned, turning to look at Jem. "What kind of incident?"

"A dragon-y sort of incident."

Nick stared at him.

Then he scowled.

"I thought the whole point of them going there was to throw up some kind of smokescreen around all of that. To play weirdo rich Quentin again."

Jem held up a hand. "It was. I believe this was purely an emergency-type situation. I didn't get the full story, but he was forced to shift... in order to save his and Miri's lives. It was fairly short-lived, whatever it was. Maybe twenty minutes."

Jem made another of those graceful hand-waves.

"Then Miri aided him in transforming back... and jumped him out of there."

"Back here?" Nick said, still frowning. "Is that how they got to the California Street building?"

"I believe it was not a *direct* trip... but yes, it is how they got here eventually."

Pausing to take a bite of his sandwich, Jem went back to caressing Nick's hair and neck with his free hand.

After he'd swallowed, he motioned towards the television with the same hand.

"Yarli also informed me there was something we should probably see. She suggested one of the major cable news stations. They're about to have a press conference. She said all of the major media outlets are likely to be in attendance."

"Right now?" Nick checked his watch. It was three in the afternoon. "At the California Street building?"

"Apparently. Yes." Jem motioned towards the television again. "Do you mind finding it? I admit, I was... intrigued. By Yarli's tone around the whole thing."

Nick felt his own curiosity piqued.

Picking up the remote, he switched channels, finding the major news stations and clicking through until he found one with a live broadcast.

He recognized the art on the walls in the lobby of the California Street Building at once, as well as the black and white tiles. He also glimpsed the edge of the large, modern art fountain that took up a big segment of one wall.

A crowd of people filled the lobby, spilling out onto the street.

Through the glass walls, Nick saw people waiting, trying to get inside, while Black's security people monitored the doors, checking press badges and running metal detector wands over everyone they let in, stopping each one individually and searching their bags.

A podium stood on the far end of the lobby.

Seeing the line of people standing there, Nick blinked, realizing he recognized all of them.

Black was leaning against a metal divider between two glass panels, eating what looked like a green chili burrito. He swallowed, wiped his mouth, talking to a woman with long, straight black hair in a business suit and high heels.

Black was smiling, relaxed.

Nick saw him reach for the woman then, caressing her cheek with his fingers, his smile growing.

Nick realized only then that the woman in the business suit was Miri.

"What the hell is going on?" Nick muttered.

"No idea, brother," Dalejem said, sounding as puzzled as Nick felt.

Nick's eyes scanned through more faces, picking out Dex, Angel, Cowboy, Ace, Mika, Jax, Kiessa, Luce, Miguel, Javier, Alice, a few other seers he recognized from *Koh Mangaan* and from the San Francisco building before then. He didn't know the names of a lot of those, or couldn't remember them, maybe, since he'd only heard them as a human.

He saw Kiko then and winced.

Jem caressed his neck, his fingers warm.

It's okay, brother, he sent softly through the blood, along with a plume of denser heat and affection. *Baby steps.*

Both things, the seer talking to him through their connection, and Jem touching him like that, not to mention the love he felt from him, got Nick instantly hard.

He closed his eyes briefly, longer than a blink.

When he opened them, Black had finished the burrito.

Nick watched the seer ball up the wrapper, handing it to someone, Michelle maybe, before he turned to face the room, scanning the crowd with his gold, tiger-like eyes. Watching him assess the crowd, Nick felt a confused mix of emotions, in spite of himself.

He and Black never exactly had an *easy* relationship, but Jem had been right, all those months ago.

Black had been his friend.

He'd been one of his closer friends.

Thinking about that, clenching his jaw, Nick watched as the tall, gold-eyed seer moved so that he was standing directly behind the podium. Once there, Black reached out with muscular hands, gripping the podium's two sides as he continued to survey the room.

He looked unusually tall standing there, his light-filled irises soaking up the lobby, as if measuring his words before he spoke them.

"Black is giving a statement?" Nick frowned, trying to remember if he'd ever seen the seer do that before.

He'd seen him on talk shows, in New York, but that had been a few years ago now.

It felt more like a million years to Nick.

Not only had he been human then, that was before... well, everything.

It was years before Charles and his crazy attempt to take over the world.

It was strange to think, back then, Nick thought things couldn't get any weirder. That was when he'd first been introduced to the idea of vampires, not long after he'd first been introduced to the idea of seers, of psychic inter-dimensional travelers living among them.

Glancing up at Dalejem, he couldn't help smiling cynically at the irony.

"Watch," Jem urged, his eyes riveted to the television. "He's about to speak."

Nick turned back, focusing his vampire eyes on the television.

Black frowned, clearing his throat.

Leaning his weight forward on the podium, he tapped the microphone, leaning closer to speak into it directly.

"Hey," he said, his clear, deep voice resonating through the room.

At that one word, everyone seemed to fall silent.

The room went quiet so quickly, it was almost unnerving.

Nick almost wondered if Black pushed them to be quiet, but, looking at him, he found himself thinking he hadn't. Not unless he got his team to do it, meaning some number of the row of seers now standing behind him.

To his right, and only just behind him, Miri stood near him in that black, form-fitting suit, her hair hanging straight down her shoulders and back. She looked positively stunning, her light hazel eyes shining from her oval face, somehow exaggerating the slant of her high cheekbones, the curve of her full mouth.

From behind him, Jem smacked the back of Nick's head.

Nick laughed. "What?" he said turning.

"I can *feel* you, you know."

"I was *looking,* brother Jem... and not in the way you clearly think. She looks good, don't you think?"

"You clearly think so."

Nick let out an exasperated sigh. "I noticed. I fucking *noticed* she looks good. They both look good. They look happy. Black looks good to me, too. Do you expect me to not notice other people at all anymore?"

"Depends," the seer grumbled.

"I could gauge my eyes out, if you prefer?"

"I might," Jem grumbled back.

Smiling, Nick reached back, clasping the seer's ankles in his fingers and tugging his legs further around him. As he did, he felt another surge of heat, enough to thicken his tongue, as he remembered the night before.

It definitely wasn't aimed at the female seer in Angel's television set.

"Better not be," Jem muttered.

Nick growled, a low, deep sound, but it was more like a purr.

When he did, he felt Jem relax.

Just then, Black began to speak.

"I apologize for the drama," he said, his deep voice reverberating through the cavernous lobby. "...In asking you all down here. I thought I should clear a few things up. Given everything that's happened in the last few months, my *lawyers...*"

Black turned to his left that time, quirking an eyebrow at a man wearing a bad toupee above an ill-fitting suit. Poking out of the bottom of those wrinkled pant legs were white tennis shoes that looked like they'd come out of a discount warehouse bin.

"...thought it would be a good idea," Black finished, his voice holding a wry humor.

Nick happened to know the guy in the bad toupee was Lawrence "Larry" Farraday, one of the best lawyers on Wall Street. Black had Larry on the payroll even back when Nick first met him. In fact, Nick encountered Larry for the first time in the Northern Precinct on Fillmore Street, when Nick was still a homicide detective and had just picked Black up on suspicion of murder.

Frowning at the thought, he glanced at Farraday again, then back at Black.

So Farraday was behind this?

That must mean this was going to be a vague, cover-your-ass type of disclaimer, a pre-written public relations statement about how Black had been on that dream-walk, woo-woo vacation with Miri down in Patagonia for the last four months.

"My lawyers," Black went on, his voice booming louder. "Want me to reassure all of you that all the rumors and crazy stories you've been hearing about me over these last few months aren't true. That they're balderdash. Nothing but poppycock."

Pausing, Black glanced around the room, raising his eyebrow again.

"...My lawyers," he added. "Aren't going to be happy with what I've decided to say instead."

Behind Black, Nick saw Larry jump, real alarm coming to his face.

From what Nick knew of Larry, that wasn't a feigned response.

Black's words had just set off a four-alarm fire in Farraday's head.

Even as Nick thought it, Larry stepped forward.

Black covered the podium's microphone with a hand as he listened intently to Farraday speak. When the human lawyer finished, Black broke into one of those smiles of his, the ones that made him look like he was up to no good, but were disturbingly charming at the same time.

Nick knew Miri called them Black's "killer" smiles, and joked the damned things were deadly... especially on women, apparently.

Aiming that smile at Larry and winking, Black turned back to the podium, upping the wattage of his smile for the crowd.

"See?" Black said, humor in his voice. "I'm going to get an earful after this. I guarantee it."

The crowd of journalists, which had been raptly silent up until then, laughed and chuckled, the sound echoing up the glass walls.

"So, here's what I'm going to tell you instead," Black said, resting his arms on the podium, so that he looked even more relaxed. "While there's a lot of bullshit buzzing around right now... there's some truth mixed in with that bullshit."

Black's expression, and his voice, grew serious.

"There are things going on in the world that people have a right to know. You're no longer alone on this planet. You never were, really. You need to know that, too."

Nick felt his chest clench.

"Christ," he muttered. "He's going public. He's going to out the fucking races."

He heard Jem swear from the couch in seer.

He could hear the seer's heartbeat speed up from where he sat on the couch.

"He's suicidal—" Jem began.

But Nick shushed him, holding up a hand when Black went on.

"All of this is a much longer discussion, of course," Black said. "But I don't want to do what my predecessors did. Any of my predecessors. I don't want to lie to the human race... not anymore. The only way we're going to make this thing work is if we build a multi-racial society together. That means being upfront about the fact that one already exists."

Leaning harder on the podium, Black looked around the room.

"You've been hearing a lot about vampires these past few months," he said. "These have mostly been postulated in the form of rumors, with dubious film footage... with more rumors about how the government faked that footage... with conspiracy news and conspiracy websites screaming hysteria and fear to high heaven. Spouting all kinds of asinine theories."

Pausing, Black gazed around the room again, his mouth hard.

"Vampires exist," he said, blunt. "Another species exists here alongside humans now, too. In my world, my *real* world... where I was born... we were called seers."

There was a silence.

Nick didn't have to breathe.

Even so, he could swear every human and seer in that room was holding their breath.

From the looks on most of the seers' faces in the line behind Black, none of them had known what this speech was going to be about, either.

Only Miri looked totally calm, her expression serene.

Into that silence, a hand shot up from the crowd.

Black paused, staring at the hand, his mouth pursing, as if its presence there, waving at him, surprised him.

Then he surprised Nick, motioning expansively to the hand and its owner.

"What is it, David?" he said.

"Can you turn into..." The human stopped, a half-smile on his lips.

Journalists around him tittered, grinning as they realized what he was about to ask.

"...a dragon?" the journalist named David finished.

Scattered laughter broke out across the floor of the lobby.

Something about the journalist's question broke that palpable tension, giving everyone an excuse to release it, to laugh.

Black smiled from the podium.

He waited for the laughter to die down, for all eyes to be back on him again.

Then he smiled wider, letting it turn into another of Miri's killer smiles.

The gold-eyed seer tilted his head, making a graceful, distinctly-seer gesture with one hand.

"Yes," he said simply.

There was a silence after he spoke.

Then the whole room erupted.

Nick felt his chest constrict painfully.

He stared in shock, watching flashes spark and fade on Black where he stood at that old-fashioned-looking podium, hearing the shouted tangle of questions from all sides as the journalists pushed forward, their hands in the air.

Black just stood at the podium for those few seconds, watching the chaos he'd unleashed, a bemused smile on his face.

Behind him, Sphinx-like, Miri gazed out over the same crowd, her pale green and gold eyes glowing as she watched the room erupt.

Fuck, was all Nick could think.

Just... fuck.

WANT TO READ MORE?
Check out the next book in the series!

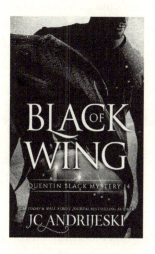

BLACK OF WING
(Quentin Black Mystery #14)

Link: http://bit.ly/QB-14

Brand new installment in the Quentin Black Mystery series by USA Today & Wall Street Journal Bestselling Author, JC Andrijeski!

"There is always a bigger dragon," my mind whispered.

Black's secret identity is out... as in WAY out... as in, he more or less announced who and what he was to every media outlet in the world.

But not everyone in the human world is thrilled at the prospect of losing their status as "dominant planetary species." Some will do just about anything to prevent that from happening... including risk wiping out every living being on Earth.

The real problem of course, is fear. Miri and Black walk a tightrope around the growing fear of their kind, with Black hitting the talk-show circuit while Miri sits at the table with world leaders, trying to come up with solutions that won't lead to inter-species war.

Oh, and Black's trying to plan a wedding.

Not to mention the fact that Nick is back, and his presence, after everything he did as a baby vampire, can't help but split their team apart.

But an even bigger danger looms from the shadows of another world.

Miriam's Uncle Charles, after banishment to a distant dimension, has grown to hate his niece, along with everything Miri and Black stand for. When he gets an opportunity to fight back, he grabs it with both hands... and brings a new kind of monster with him to Earth.

NOW ON SALE!

WANT TO READ MORE?
Or check out another epic series about seers!

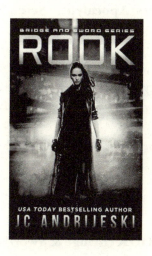

ROOK (Bridge & Sword #1)

Link: http://bit.ly/RookBS01

In a world populated by a second race, having the wrong blood can be deadly.

Raised human, Allie lives in a version of Earth populated by seers.

Psychics enslaved by governments, corporations and wealthy humans, seers are an exotic fascination, one Allie knows she'll likely never encounter in person, given how rich you have to be to get near one.

Then members of rival seer factions show up at her work.

Soon Allie finds herself on the run from the law, labeled a terrorist and in the middle of a race war she didn't even know existed.

From USA TODAY and WALL STREET JOURNAL bestselling author, a psychic warfare adventure set in a gritty alternate version of Earth. Contains strong romantic elements. Apocalyptic SciFi. Psychic Romance.

The world is dying.
Everyone feels it, and yet... no one knows.
They said that when the end was near,
a Bridge would come, and lead them out of the darkness of that dying world.
My name is Allie Taylor, and I am that Bridge.

❧

BUY NOW!
ROOK (Bridge & Sword #1)

Link: http://bit.ly/RookBS01

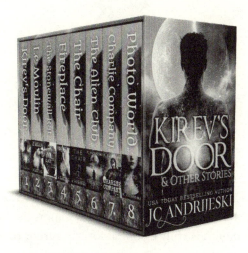

REVIEWS ARE AUTHOR HUGS

Now that you've finished reading my book,
PLEASE CONSIDER LEAVING A REVIEW!
A short review is fine and so very appreciated.
Word of mouth is truly essential for any author to succeed!

Leave a Review Here:
http://bit.ly/Black-Hawaii

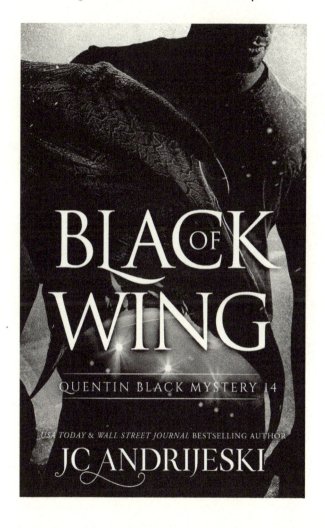

PROLOGUE / PARADISE LOST

Love's breath ignites in pools of gold, but it is not the first...
...Nor the last, nor even the beginning.
A people swim the surface of Muuld, in a world marked garden for the
chosen.
~ The Myth of Three

It is said The Demon would live in paradise for a month and a day...
...And they would writhe in pain
As though a thousand knives punctured every inch of their skin.
So much would the One Light wound them.
~ Anonymous

CHARLES... FAUSTUS... raised his head from a soft surface, squinting into the sharp sunlight shining through a tall doorway made of thick, green and black trunks.

He remembered.

He remembered where he was.

He remembered who put him here.

That she would leave him here, of all places. That she would dump him *here,* knowing he would hate it here with every fiber of his being. There was no possible way she wouldn't *know* how much he would detest the base existence such a world offered.

All of it was so primitive.

It reeked of early life, of the vapid idiocy and superstition of primitive minds. The hut was like something his one and only human wife's people would have made, beginning a thousand years earlier, back on the version of Earth he'd left behind.

Of course, that had been a different history.

It had been a different people... a different Earth.

Sadly, this new version of Earth had apparently never evolved past that stage of existence at all. They'd never climbed out of the mud and base simplicity of a subsistence culture, or learned to command the vagaries of their environment.

They remained at the mercy of the elements.

They remained at the mercy of the indigenous animals and plants.

Hell, they remained at the mercy of the *weather*.

From what Faustus could tell from the months and months he'd spent here... easily over a year by now, and likely more than one, although he loathed to think about it... no one had advanced any form of *real* civilization at all.

Nor would they, likely until long after he was dead.

She'd done it to him on purpose.

She'd sent him here, a final stab of the knife into his heart.

Faustus stared at the carvings in the dark wood, and fought to make them mean something to him. He fought to make sense of where he was, in a way that didn't anger him beyond reason.

He couldn't do it.

His mind simply returned to the same thing, the same face.

Miriam.

His own goddamned niece.

Little Miri.

That race-traitor *cunt* had destroyed everything.

Literally *everything* he had worked for, she'd blown to ash and dust.

Remembering her, remembering how she'd looked at him, in the seconds after they landed here, those few seconds she bothered to regard him at all before she jumped away, his rage turned to something blinding, something murderous. She'd looked at him pityingly, maybe even with some maudlin sense of nostalgia.

Then she'd simply vanished... leaving the air to rush back into the space she'd occupied with a shocking *POP*.

Remembering that look on her face, the bullshit, performative *regret* in her eyes, he felt a cold hatred that made it difficult not to scream into the rising sun.

She had betrayed him.

Not just him... she had betrayed her entire race.

She had betrayed all of them.

Like every morning here, the thought got him out of bed.

Anger powered most of what he'd done here, in the years since he'd arrived.

He knew that wouldn't sustain him forever, but for now, he wouldn't think about that.

The locals were easy to push into feeding him, and into giving him the largest of their primitive shelters. He'd slept with a different female every night, more out of rage and feelings of impotence over his situation than out of any true desire.

He'd become their king in less than a day, and it meant nothing to him.

He punished the primitives because he had no one else.

He had nothing else.

Walking out of the fifteen-foot tall, narrow doorway, he gazed down a grass-covered hill towards a swampy lake. He'd more or less pinpointed where he was on the planet that roughly approximated the other Earths he'd known, in geography at least.

This version was relatively unspoiled, for all the same reasons he despised it.

The waters teemed with fish.

The trees they cultivated were mostly the same as those he'd known before, with versions of fruits and nuts he'd known from those other Earths. Between them, the venison, the fish, even the occasional bear, the land provided more food than he would ever need, in a temperate climate with few meaningful predators.

An idiot would love it here.

Someone who required no real intellectual stimulation, who could sit around eating berries and nuts, watching the sunrise and going for a naked swim before spending their day doing needle-point and rug-weaving, sewing their own clothing, making pots from mud and clay, whatever... they would probably find this wooded existence some sort of spiritual paradise.

Kneelers would love it, too.

They could pray and chant and commune with the Ancestors.

They could spend all of their days congratulating themselves for their incorruptible magnificence... build constructs full of fluffy animals and rainbows and perfect peoples living together in harmony without any sense of reality or self-preservation.

If an alien race ever landed here, this settlement would be wiped out in nanoseconds.

More to the point, as far as Faustus was concerned... this type of living was what ruined the seer race on Old Earth.

It practically ensured their enslavement, when humans finally stumbled upon them. The ancients sat in their sanctimonious caves, chanting their sanctimonious, superstitious nonsense, and allowed themselves to culturally atrophy to the point of learned helplessness.

They'd destroyed themselves.

Seers on Old Earth conquered themselves.

They made themselves into sheep.

They created slaves out of warriors, through sheer force of will.

Faustus raised a hand against the bright sunlight, squinting over what had been called the Potomac River in the two worlds he'd occupied before this one. Old Earth, he now realized, had been far more similar to the version he'd just left than he'd ever known.

The location also told him just how much thought and care

Miri put into bringing him here. She'd left him on this version of Earth more or less in the *exact same* geographical location from which she'd taken him.

Clearly, she hadn't much cared... as long as he was out of the way.

His stomach growled.

Realizing he was famished, remembering he'd barely eaten the night before, he turned away from the view of the river and the verdant valley below.

He was about to walk to the center of the village, get one of the squaws there to cook him some breakfast, then maybe suck his cock while he ate it—

When something trembled his seer's light.

Power.

So much power, he came to a dead stop.

It brushed him again, and he sucked in a breath.

It barely touched him, both times, but every hair on his arms and the back of his neck rose. He felt it in his gut, his groin, his tongue, the ends of his fingers, his lips.

He stood there, feeling the vibration and reverberations for seconds after the presence had left his light. Holding his breath, he remained totally still.

He waited to see if it would return.

Then he was breathing hard, his heart pounding in his chest.

Gaos.

Holy fucking gaos, gaos, gaos...

He hadn't felt anything remotely like that since—

His head and eyes jerked around, looking behind him, then up the hill.

His body followed, a half-second later.

He walked in the direction of his best guess, then stopped again.

He never stopped looking around.

He scanned his environment frantically, with his eyes and light, searching for the source of that intense flood of presence that scarcely passed through his *aleimi,* or living light. He searched the hill above him, the trees, the grass, the bushes, the various wooden houses and tents that dotted the settlement of humans.

He felt a yearning so intense, he cried out in frustration.

Then... out of nowhere.

"Do I know you?"

Faustus turned, so violently, he hurt his neck.

A male seer stood in front of him, stark naked.

Seer in cock, in height, in the eyes, the strange symmetry of his body.

The male stood there, eyes glowing the palest of golds, nearly white with a faint reflection of gold sunlight. The being's expression remained blank as he stared, utterly lacking in emotion. Despite his words, the question they formed, he didn't even sound curious.

He didn't sound anything.

He sounded blank.

Faustus turned around, looking for where he might have come from.

There was nothing nearby.

Not a tree close enough to have hidden behind, not a bush.

The doorway to the house where Charles had slept stood maybe twelve feet away. It was the closest thing, but surely, Charles would have seen him? He had been staring up the hill, right in the direction of that door. The door stood just to the right of his focus, the carved wooden trunks of the doorway directly within the main arc of his view.

Behind the man himself, Faustus saw only the sloping field of grass.

"I felt you," the male said. "I felt you come."

There was another silence.

In it, Faustus only stared at the other seer.

"It took some time. I was... away. I was in another world."

Faustus blinked.

The strange, blank seer now stood so close, Faustus felt his heart pounding in his chest. His skin flushed from the contact with this brother's *aleimi*. He had never felt so much power in a single being before. The closest he had ever felt, was—

"You were not alone," the being said. "You did not come here alone."

Faustus stared up at him.

He fought to think, to make sense of this new development before he spoke.

If there were other seers here, if he wasn't alone, as he'd believed—

"I have been looking for her," the being said. "I cannot find her now."

Faustus stared at those pale, glowing eyes.

He remembered the old stories... the ones from the First Earth.

He remembered what they said about beings whose eyes glowed.

First Race.

Intermediary.

The Old Gods.

"Where is she?" The gold-eyed seer took a step closer. "Where did she go?"

Faustus blinked.

"Can you take me to her?" he said.

For the first time, Faustus truly noticed the being was naked.

He'd *noticed* of course, almost in rote. He'd noticed well enough to identify him as a seer, without thinking about the nakedness itself.

But now, that information penetrated his forward mind.

It impacted him in a way that was meaningful.

The male seer's skin steamed in the morning sun.

He emitted so much *aleimic* light, it blended with that steam, making the creature's skin appear to be smoke and shadows. The combination gave his whole outline a strangely blurry quality, like he only half-existed here, like he only had one foot in this world, and the rest of him remained elsewhere.

Staring at that nakedness, at the glowing eyes, the steaming skin, Faustus found he understood.

He understood how the being had come to be here.

He understood how he, Faustus, hadn't seen or felt him approach.

He understood how he'd felt the being's presence, a bare second before he appeared.

He understood.

When Charles' vision clicked back into focus, he found the naked seer looking at him, head cocked, that inhumanly calm expression on his face.

Faustus remembered Black inside that bunker under the Pentagon.

He remembered talking to the thing inside Black, right before his nephew-in-law ripped his entire research facility apart.

Looking at the naked being in front of him, Faustus felt the first faint flicker of hope.

Redemption.

Resurrection.

Revenge.

The being in front of him seemed to understand.

Relief flickered across that empty face, even as those pale eyes glowed brighter.

"Can you take me to her?" the being asked. His voice remained calm, polite, but now the faintest edge of eagerness tinged his words. "Can you show me where she is?"

Faustus stood there, paralyzed.

Then, slowly, as the being's words sank in...

He smiled.

1 / THE BIGGER DRAGON

My love, my brother, my God...
It is time to come home.
We whisper together.
Love together.
Always one, always bound...
I drown with you in the ether.
Leathery wings beat clouds in night skies.
Stars rotate in the darkness.
Into the blackest night...
Our love will never die.

My dreams had been waking me for weeks... two, three, four, five in the morning.

The voice.

That heartbreaking, love-filled voice.

There didn't seem to be any pattern, any rhyme or reason to when it came.

It started seemingly that first morning back on this version of Earth, back in our bed at the building on California Street, inside the penthouse that finally felt like home again, even after all the horrible things that happened there.

Black and I hadn't really talked about Nick yet.

To be fair, we hadn't really had time, and other things took precedence.

After Black gave that press conference, after his announcement about vampires being real... that yes, he could transform into an enormous dragon... and yes, he'd been fighting the United States military at the border wall with Mexico... and yes, he'd been involved in the disappearance of dozens of people who'd worked inside the U.S. government... and yes, he'd been behind that crazy thing in Hawaii... and yes, he was one of those so-called "seers" from another dimension... oh, and he'd been fighting with *other, anti-human* seers who'd been in the process of overthrowing the human governments across the globe...

After all *that,* we'd been a little busy.

A lot of decisions had to be made, and damned fast.

Some of those decisions, Black and I already discussed, even before he gave that crazy speech to the press. We'd discussed a lot of the "what next" while on that other version of Earth, in that other-dimensional version of Hawaii.

A lot of things we'd discussed sounded crazy now.

Things that struck us as clear and self-evident in that other place—that place without humans, or vampires, or messy governments, or hundreds possibly thousands of traumatized, angry seers who hated human beings—now sounded a little naïve and a lot nuts.

At best, they sounded pretty damned reckless.

At worst, they sounded like the "I have this cool idea" phase that occurs right before an apocalypse where millions of people die.

Of course, that hadn't stopped us from starting to implement some of those ideas.

Like me going to London.

Like Black approaching the military leaders here in the United States.

Like me trying to find us a potential Plan B via another dimension, in the event we needed to move all seers off this version of Earth, to somewhere we wouldn't be risking a massive race-war, whether with humans or vampires or both.

Like us talking about forming some kind of non-human bureau that dealt with seer and vampire affairs.

Most of it, maybe all of it, sounded a bit nuts to us now.

Not only because Brick the Vampire King was a malignant narcissist.

Not only because Brick seemed to thrive in chaos.

Not even because Brick remained completely untrustworthy, open to massive corruption if we gave him any kind of *real* power, and fundamentally wired to hunt, eat, and mentally enslave seers and human beings.

Even apart from all the vampire complications, the idea that these institutions and "world rules" could be created or implemented cleanly, that they wouldn't evolve in directions Black already experienced on the human and seer world he'd left behind... a world that didn't have the added complication of vampires, or vampire venom, or the problems both things presented for humans and seers...

Well. It all just struck us as a pipe dream.

We were building a new world.

It was impossible not to fear we might be putting the building blocks in place for a new world order that resulted in suffering on a scale I couldn't really imagine.

So maybe that's all the dreams were.

Maybe it was all of that rolling around in my head.

Maybe the pressure was getting to me.

Maybe those thoughts, those worries, those impossibilities are what brought them on, creating vague anxieties that overcame my mental space.

That's what I told myself.

That's what I told Black, when I inadvertently woke him up.

I didn't tell Black about the dreams themselves.

I told myself he didn't need to know the content of my stress-induced anxiety dreams, much less the details of how my mind translated my worries into images.

I didn't really believe it, though.

I didn't really believe any of it.

Truthfully, I wasn't entirely sure those places and beings I saw were "dreams" at all, or even that they originated from something inside my own mind.

I heard them calling for me through the ether.

I heard them calling for both of us.

I even recognized a few of them.

I remembered them from trips I'd taken, back in the early days of my other-dimensional traveling. I remembered seeing them in those worlds... feeling their resonance with Black... knowing what they were, even before I'd admitted to myself that Black was the same.

Massive, leathery wings beat hard against solar winds.

They were free now, untethered from their worlds.

Not just one, but many came to me.

Many, but they morphed into one at the end of every dream.

That, or the largest of them—the most powerful, the most demanding—pushed its way to the forefront, past the rest, looming in the darkness of my mind.

It stared at me with brightly-colored, fire-filled eyes.

Pale, gold eyes, like a burning sunset.

Like a burning world.

There is always a bigger dragon, my mind whispered.

As big as Black was, as seemingly invincible in that form...

...he wasn't alone in that interconnected labyrinth of threads connecting all of our worlds.

He wasn't alone, and I could feel them now, vibrating those strings that tied them to us, resonating at a frequency that shocked my heart, making it beat painfully hard inside my chest. That solid, stone-filled heartbeat vibrated my body at a molecular level, turning my bones to liquid, my skin to air, my limbs to fire.

It burned me alive, from the inside out.

The changes woke me up.

The changes terrified me, right before they reached their culmination.

I never got to see how things came out.

I could feel them coming though.

I felt *it* coming.

The bigger dragon.

I was certain he was out there. I was certain he'd been waiting.

Now, that time was slowly ticking down to its end.

Because, as my mind whispered.

...There is always a bigger dragon.

2 / REAL TALK

I frowned, coming back from wherever my mind had gone.

Luckily, my mental wandering had been short.

A silence fell after I finished speaking.

Somehow, I managed to bring my mind back before it ended.

The one guy at the table I hadn't yet been able to identify, at least not to my satisfaction, gave me serious side-eye through most of my longest speech yet.

I felt his cold stare, the entire time I was talking, but I didn't react.

Well... I *mostly* didn't react.

Hopefully, I didn't react where the humans could see it.

I was exhausted though, and still not sleeping well, so I couldn't be sure.

Even in my half-delirious state, I had theories about who the mystery guy was, sitting at the table full of world leaders, giving me a forty-year-old's version of stink eye.

I strongly suspected he came from the same world I had, back before I knew what I was. I strongly suspected he was military intelligence. Possibly military intelligence with a strong psychology background, from the little bit I'd picked up off his heavily-shielded mind.

Given where we were, I assumed he worked for the United Kingdom.

That meant probably Mi6.

Well... it meant that for now, anyway.

Black already warned me it was a damned good bet the human governments would band together and quickly start to build branches of government—not to mention courts, law enforcement, military and intelligence services—solely dedicated to dealing with races other than the human one.

In that sense, Mi6 constituted more of a temporary relic of a past world... a world that still mostly existed a few months ago, until Black blew it up.

For now, however, the humans were stuck with the institutions they had.

I knew the UK's Prime Minister wanted him here, and the other leaders must have okay'd it, as well. We'd already positively ID'd at least one member of the French security services. That one sat at the table even now, masquerading as an advisor to the German Chancellor, likely to throw us off.

I suspected we hadn't found even half of them yet.

Most probably didn't sit at the table for meetings like this, but I had zero doubt other intelligence agents worked here in the building, likely at least one from every world power.

To say the humans were nervous was a laughable understatement at this point.

I knew behind the scenes they had to be losing their collective minds.

We're only in the early stages of this, I reminded myself. *Breathe, Miri. Don't freak out. Don't give up on them when we've barely started. Don't let Black and Charles psyche you out. Most of all, don't let their paranoia about humans from Old Earth get to you... or influence how cynical you let yourself become...*

I knew it wasn't all Black and Charles.

Every single one of the seers I'd met from that version of Earth maintained a deep paranoia and suspicion around human beings.

Understandable really, since seers had been slaves there.

But that was then.

This was now.

Circumstances were so different in that other world, in terms of how First Contact occurred, the two worlds were unable to be compared at this point. As Black told me, time and again, this current generation of seers, the generation that came to this world, weren't a bunch of monks singing *kumbaya* in the mountains, the way their forebears had been.

Most were vets of multiple wars, and had a significantly less mystical view of their role in the multiverse, particularly *vis a vis* the human race.

Still, things were tense.

Things were tense on both sides right now.

For the same reason, we'd only pulled in a relatively small group for this.

We weren't ready to start giving speeches in front of the United Nations.

We weren't even close to that.

These early discussions were supposed to lay the groundwork for something more official, but even at this stage, we had leaders refuse our invitation.

China wouldn't respond to our attempts to contact them.

The Russian president gave us a hard no at first, then attempted to negotiate a private meeting that all the seers vetoed on our end.

The United States refused as well, and denounced the meetings aggressively, claimed we were terrorists, and *blah-blah-blah*... which made sense, whether or not we'd managed to root all of the seers out of the current administration. Of course, after it came out that the U.K., Canada, Mexico, India, Japan, and the European Union were sending people, President Bradford "Buck" Regent changed his mind and wanted to come after all.

We told him no.

It was a LONG discussion, but in the end, we all agreed. From his speeches and rhetoric, it was pretty clear Regent only wanted to go so he could derail the talks.

In some ways, I wished we'd just told him yes.

I mean, I knew we needed him.

We needed the United States.

We talked about letting him come and maybe pushing him... psychically, that is... to keep him from blowing up the talks.

We decided against that, too.

For one thing, it would have been a hell of a way to start negotiations. For another, there was a chance other countries would have noticed. It definitely would've raised eyebrows if Regent suddenly started acting calm and reasonable.

Or remotely intelligent.

Sadly, Uncle Charles, despite being wrong about humans in so many respects, was a thousand percent right about our country's current Commander in Chief.

Regent was an absolute moron.

Unlike the leaders of the E.U. and the United Kingdom, he also didn't seem to have even a basic understanding of what was currently at stake.

I knew a handful of the human governments already had preliminary cooperation agreements in place, specifically to deal with the threat of "intelligent non-human species," which is how they termed seers and vampires in most of their official documents. Those same human governments had already begun the process of joining forces to deal with the non-human threat.

I mean, come on.

They were still in full-blown panic mode.

They were sitting here, looking grim and serious and official, but I knew they were mostly shitting their pants.

Which is why I got paranoid whenever I saw new faces at the table.

We're working on it, Mika murmured in my mind. *That guy, doc. We're working on identifying who he is. Don't sweat the small stuff, okay? We're on it. Whoever he is, there's nothing there you need to worry about.*

We need that big doc brain of yours focused on the bigwigs, okay? On the geo-political threat. We need you to figure out how to reassure them we aren't about to enslave them all with our psychic powers... or eat them...

Quirking an eyebrow over her faint smile, Mika added more seriously,

Let us handle security, doc. We won't let anyone fuck with you. Promise.

I knew she was right.

I knew she was right that I was distracting myself.

I also knew what she was telling me about that man at the table.

She was telling me he wasn't a seer.

He wasn't one of Charles' plants.

Still, there was *something* there.

He might not be a seer, but his living light didn't feel quite right.

His mind was too silent.

We don't think he's a vampire, either, doc, Mika sent, sighing a little at me. *Really, you don't need to worry about this. We're going over his living light with a fine-toothed—*

Is he wearing something? I sent. *Some kind of blocking mechanism?*

There was a slight pause.

It was small, but I heard it.

Then Mika sighed, at least on the inside.

Yes, the infiltrator said, clearly reluctant to answer me, but likely thinking it would be faster if she did. *We think a number of people in here are using various forms of sight-blocking tech. Apparently Charles had a few things at the prototype stage. We're not pushing back on those devices too hard just yet, in part because we want to see if we can get around them on our own. They aren't overly sophisticated at this point...*

She must have felt me about to say something.

She quickly cut me off.

...I've already sent a number of things back to the labs, doc. Implants, a few organic wristbands that emit fields, even a type of human "collar" meant to block seer sight. But we need to trace them back to the source.

That's the bigger issue right now. We need to figure out who's creating all of these things...

I nodded to myself, thinking about this, even as I refocused on the Prime Minister sitting in front of me. Next to him, the side-eye guy from Mi6 watched me a little too closely, a faint frown hardening his mouth.

He was handsome.

Maybe forty-five years old.

Brown hair, green eyes, a ruggedly handsome face, one that looked like its wearer had spent a lot of time outdoors, in pretty heavy sun.

The Middle East? Somewhere in Asia?

Doc... Mika warned.

Refocusing on the actual words the Prime Minister was saying, I found myself shaking my head, interrupting him without thought.

"No," I said. "We can't do that. Not yet."

Pausing at his silence, I glanced around the table a second time, modifying my voice to make it more polite, if not exactly full-blown friendly.

"I'm sorry," I said, letting my eyes return to Prime Minister Garrity. "But we're going to have to insist on being treated more or less as a sovereign nation. Or at the very least... as a private company with proprietary information we are legally entitled to protect. That includes what relates to whatever security measures we might have in place... to maintain safety and privacy for ourselves and our employees."

There was a silence.

I let my eyes flicker around the long table, taking in faces.

"Black Securities and Investigations is the primary employer of most of the seers we have pulled into our orbit," I added. "Through that organization, we have strong contractual alliances with the largest organized segment of the vampire population as well."

I gestured vaguely with a hand, not fully realizing it was a seer gesture until I'd done it.

"...But really it's Black Industries as a whole that's providing the organizational focal point for the seer race at this time. Even in terms of housing, which we are currently supplying out of our own resources."

Prime Minister Garrity frowned.

"But that's only the seers who've joined *your* side, correct?" he said, his voice sharper. "It doesn't include the *other* side... the ones you claim pose the far greater risk to humans."

I leaned back in my seat, keeping my posture and facial expression calm.

"That is correct," I said, holding his gaze. "We are willing, however, to claim responsibility for the maintenance of peaceful relations with the seer race as a whole. We are attempting to 'police' our own people, as it were... at least within our somewhat limited means."

I was understating that.

By a fair amount, really.

Our means were pretty significant, even for a lot of mid-sized countries.

But I was there to downplay the scary factor with us, not give them more reasons to be paranoid. Black and I talked about how truthful I would be, and decided it would fall into the range of "mostly truthful"—meaning firmly in the "hoping to be allies" camp, while recognizing they had very different goals and concerns in some areas.

And also recognizing that yes... they were likely to be pretty twitchy when it came to us.

Right now, the older man sitting across from me, his previously black hair now mostly gone to gray, watched me warily, obviously suspecting me of withholding information.

Of course, we knew they weren't telling us everything, either.

"Look." I changed tacks slightly, leaning over the table, resting my arms on the polished wood. "I get that you have no reason to trust us right now. I really do. We're more than willing to do our best to reassure you on that front... including entertaining any good-faith gestures you'd like to see from our camp. The truth is, our people are just as afraid of you as you are of them. We'd like to keep things calm... and non-reactionary... on both sides."

I saw Garrity flinch perceptibly, as if my words surprised him.

He didn't change expression apart from that.

I had to give him credit.

Guy was pretty danged cool, even for someone in his position.

I shuddered to think what President Regent would be doing, if he were here.

There was a reason the other human leaders chose Garrity to lead the initial discussions.

As I watched, he glanced at his colleagues on both sides of the table, most of whom represented countries in the E.U., along with the Indian Prime Minister, and the leader of Japan. From his unspoken question to them, I definitely got the sense he'd expected me to say something like this, that the human leaders discussed it.

Even as I thought it, Garrity looked back at me.

"But you're reading our minds right now," he said. "Aren't you, Dr. Fox?"

Pausing meaningfully, he added in a harder voice.

"Not only that, you've told us that your kind can... what is the word you used? *Push* human minds to do your bidding? Manipulate our thoughts, our belief systems, our loyalties... our entire view of the world?"

He paused again.

I watched him gauge my eyes openly.

"How can we possibly trust you," he said. "If what you say is true? Do you expect us to just take your word that you won't enslave us, when clearly, that would be the easiest path forward for you and your kind?"

I held his gaze.

When he finished speaking, I held up my hands in a shrug, letting them fall back to the table.

"I'm sorry to say this to you, sir..." I kept my eyes on his, my voice firmly polite. "...but I'm not sure you have much choice."

Pausing, I added,

"My people were enslaved in their previous world... by human beings. They won't allow that again. They just won't. The reality is, the seer race has learned a lot since that time. Moreover, their culture has evolved as a result of that experience. It's a longer story, in terms of seer history, but suffice it to say, these seers are not the same as those who allowed that enslavement to happen. That means, in part, that they won't do the things you would likely ask for, in order to feel totally 'out of danger' from any rogue seers who might abuse their powers..."

Seeing the alarm verging on anger in Garrity's eyes, I held up a hand.

"Nor would you, if you were them," I added, warning. "Both races have to compromise. It's not fair in any way to put the entire burden of this on the seer race. You can't expect them to willingly succumb to restraints on their powers, their freedom of move-ment, their free will... any more than you would agree to this for humans."

Pausing to let my words sink in, I leaned back in my chair.

I dialed back some of the warning in my voice.

"That being said, most seers have absolutely no desire to impinge on the freedom or free will of human beings either, Prime Minister... in part for those same reasons. My people love freedom as much as yours do. Are there seers who lust for power over others? Yes. Of course. Just as there are humans who do the same."

I let that sink in, too.

I added, "We've already told you about one of our kind with that kind of... instability. My uncle, Charles Vasiliev, was damaged from his time on that previous world. His fear of humans got the better of him, and he decided the best way to deal with it was to do to them what was done to him."

My voice shifted back to a near warning.

"He won't be the last to try this. But the truth is, that's the very reason you *need* us. You *need* seers of integrity, and you need strong allies among my people. You *need* a functioning government of seers with which to negotiate, one that desires the same kind of world that you do... one you can build strong alliances, treaties, and peace agreements with. You need us to police those seers who are more dangerous... like my uncle."

"And where is he now?"

My head turned.

I found myself looking at the man from Mi6, who was now staring me straight in the face. His voice was deep, and surprised me by sounding American.

"This uncle of yours," he said, gesturing to the side, his eyes remaining coldly on mine. "No one seems to know where he is. No one seems to know where a good *number* of people are... including appointees to the United States' presidential cabinet... and a number of high-ranking officials in other parts of your government..."

His eyes grew a few shades colder.

"...notably, quite a number of people who used to work in your Pentagon. And in the C.I.A. Not to mention the F.B.I."

I held his gaze, feeling his attempt to intimidate me.

Truthfully, humans couldn't really get away with that, not when it came to seers.

They just didn't have the mental *oomph* to push us around.

Which, of course, tended to really piss them off, if they were used to being able to do this with other humans.

I didn't shove that aggression back at him, I only nodded, my voice calm.

"Yes," I said. "Quite a few people were removed. Charles' people. We were transparent about this."

I felt humans stiffen around me, and I folded my arms, staring around at them pointedly.

"What race do you suppose they were?" I said then, gesturing expansively. "Why do you suppose we felt the need to remove them, when... like you said... if they were human, we could have merely taken over their minds? Pushed them to do our bidding?"

The silence after that felt more weighted.

I saw them exchanging looks.

I knew I was taking a risk, saying such a thing.

There was a lot we couldn't tell them, at least not yet.

Black and I both agreed we'd need to ease people into certain facts, as we began to educate them more about seers... while still telling them the important things they needed to know.

One of the big things we needed them to understand... hopefully without scaring the *bejesus* out of them... was the severity of the dangers and security risks posed by Charles' seers, and how they needed us to lead the teams addressing that.

"So this... 'policing' of your people you mentioned," Garrity said, exchanging looks with the President of France, and the representative from Germany. "That would include these so-called 'disappearances'? Is that what you are telling us?"

He glanced sideways, that time looking at the man I'd pegged as Mi6.

I now questioned whether he was C.I.A., thinking maybe the other leaders allowed the United States into the meeting, after all, if indirectly.

Bingo, doc, Mika murmured grimly in my mind. *Which explains where he got the sight-blocking tech. We're working on getting more out of him now—*

I absorbed her words, still focused on Garrity in front of me.

"...all of those government appointees and career officials, not to mention military leaders, scientists, members of the Defense Department and the military contractors. You want us to believe that all of those individuals within your own country..."

The Prime Minister paused, as if second-guessing that, given what I'd just said about Black running a quasi-sovereign, independent nation-state of seers.

"...err, I mean the *United States* government... they were, literally *dozens* of them, extra-judicially *removed* by your people as part of this 'self-policing' of seers?"

When I glanced across the table, I saw the C.I.A. agent glaring at me.

I saw him about to open his mouth.

I turned to Garrity before he could.

"Yes," I said, blunt. "That's exactly what I'm telling you."

WANT TO READ MORE?
Continue the rest of the novel here:
BLACK OF WING
(Quentin Black Mystery #14)

Link: https://bit.ly/QB-14

❦

BOOKS IN THE VAMPIRE DETECTIVE MIDNIGHT SERIES (RECOMMENDED READING ORDER)

VAMPIRE DETECTIVE MIDNIGHT (Book #1)
EYES OF ICE (Book #2)
THE PRESCIENT (Book #3)
FANG & METAL (Book #4)
THE WHITE DEATH (Book #5)

❦

BOOKS IN THE BRIDGE & SWORD SERIES (RECOMMENDED READING ORDER)

New York (Bridge & Sword Prequel Novel #0.5)
ROOK (Bridge & Sword #1)
SHIELD (Bridge & Sword #2)
SWORD (Bridge & Sword #3)
Revik (Bridge & Sword Prequel Novel #0.1)
SHADOW (Bridge & Sword #4)
KNIGHT (Bridge & Sword #5)
WAR (Bridge & Sword #6)
BRIDGE (Bridge & Sword #7)
Trickster (Bridge & Sword Prequel Novel #0.2)
The Defector (Bridge & Sword Prequel Novel #0.3)
PROPHET (Bridge & Sword #8)
A Glint of Light (Bridge & Sword #8.5)
DRAGON (Bridge & Sword #9)
The Guardian (Bridge & Sword #0.4)
SUN (Bridge & Sword #10)

❦

Books in the Gods on Earth Series
(Recommended Reading Order)

THOR (Book #1)
LOKI (Book #2)
TYR (Book #3)

Books in the Alien Apocalypse Series
(Recommended Reading Order)

THE CULLING (Part I)
THE ROYALS (Part II)
THE NEW ORDER (Part III)
THE REBELLION (Part IV)
THE RINGS FIGHTER

Books in the Light & Shadow Series
(Recommended Reading Order)

LIGHTBRINGER
WHITE DRAGON
DARK GODS
LORD OF LIGHT

LIGHT AND DARK
LOVE AND MAGIC

JC Andrijeski is a *USA Today* and *Wall Street Journal* bestselling author of urban fantasy, paranormal romance, mysteries, and apocalyptic science fiction, often with a sexy and metaphysical bent.

JC has a background in journalism, history and politics, and has a tendency to traipse around the globe, eat odd foods, and read whatever she can get her hands on. She grew up in the Bay Area of California, but has lived abroad in Europe, Australia and Asia, and from coast to coast in the continental United States.

She currently lives and writes full time in Los Angeles.

For more information, go to: https://jcandrijeski.com

         facebook.com/JCAndrijeski
         twitter.com/jcandrijeski
         instagram.com/jcandrijeski
         bookbub.com/authors/jc-andrijeski
         amazon.com/JC-Andrijeski/e/B004MFTAP0

Made in the USA
Monee, IL
01 September 2021